SINS

JILLIAN GREY

ZEBRA BOOKS
KENSINGTON PUBLISHING CORP.

ZEBRA BOOKS are published by

Kensington Publishing Corp.
850 Third Avenue
New York, NY 10022

Copyright © 1994 by Jillian Grey

All rights reserved. No part of this book may be reproduced
in any form or by any means without the prior written con-
sent of the Publisher, excepting brief quotes used in reviews.

If you purchased this book without a cover you should be
aware that this book is stolen property. It was reported as
"unsold and destroyed" to the Publisher and neither the Author nor the Publisher has received any payment for this
"stripped book."

Zebra and the Z logo Reg. U.S. Pat. & TM Off.

First Printing: December, 1994

Printed in the United States of America

*This is for the three playmates
closest to my heart:
Michael, Janna, and Christianne,
each so unique and all so beautiful.
I love you.*

January 15, 1995

Prologue

Carrie Roberts Pearson was caught unaware by the innocent looking package. Slitting the oversized manila envelope's flap with the letter opener, she pulled the magazine from inside, her smooth, flawless brow furrowing with puzzlement. But dawning horror cleared away the lines of confusion as she met the stare of the woman on the cover of *Playmate Magazine*. "Oh, my God," she gasped, grabbing hold of the corner of her desk as she sank into her chair.

It had been ten years and the face on the magazine cover had changed, matured, become that of a woman rather than a girl but she would have recognized it anywhere. The hair—that glorious mane she'd always envied. Those eyes.

Her hands quaking now almost uncontrollably, she flipped through the pages **until** she arrived at the centerfold and another picture **of** her childhood friend. The picture was voluptuous as the photographer had intended, but it was the look in those eyes which captured her attention. They were taunting, defiant even, and for an unrealistic moment Carrie imagined that the challenge was being issued to her.

Envy that she'd almost forgotten welled up in her as she took in the details of the provocative photograph. She hadn't quite remembered the impossibly long legs, the ivory hue of flesh, the amazing proportions of slender hips to full breasts. But the rest—the full, pouting lips, the eyes the color of a summer azure sky, the slender perfection of her nose, and that blazing riot of thick red hair—she remembered every detail of the last time she'd stared into her best friend's face. It had been as beautiful ten years before, only not challenging, contemptuous, or sultry and sassy. No, then it had been tamed by misery, washed with tears and tempered by terror, though none of it had detracted from the girl's beauty. In fact, if anything, the vulnerability had softened the extraordinary beauty, lending her an air of ethereal fragility that had enhanced her loveliness. Carrie remembered well that last meeting for it was the first time she'd ever experienced the alien emotion of hatred for her friend.

Turning the page, she barely scanned the pictures that followed, looking instead for the article that accompanied the suggestive photo layout. There!

Rikki Blue. She'd changed her name. Well, that certainly wasn't a surprise. Who could blame her after what had happened?

Carrie read on, her eyes flying across the lines until she stopped at the sentence that confirmed her fears. Ericka Blue Cassidy, *nee* Rikki Blue was coming home to St. Joan.

The magazine slid from her lap as she rocked in her chair, keening the same refrain over and over. "Oh, my God. Oh, my God. Oh, my God."

He'd just entered his office when his secretary buzzed him. "Got a special delivery for you, Mr. Bohannon. Marked personal and confidential. Want me to bring it in?"

Of course he wanted her to bring it in. Might be the information he'd requested from the FBI.

It wasn't.

Keen Bohannon dropped the magazine onto the desk only then realizing that he hadn't drawn a breath since he'd pulled the copy of *Playmate Magazine* from the manila envelope. He exhaled slowly as he stared at the face from his past, the face of the first girl he'd loved. Hell, the *only* girl he'd loved. God, she was more beautiful than she'd been as a girl. Changed, matured, and yet still so much as he remembered.

The full lips, those sapphire blue eyes shaped like marquis cut jewels, that tumble of dark red hair. He felt the first stirring of longing, of desire that he'd allowed himself in years . . . and regret for what they'd lost. No, damn it, for what had been *stolen* from them.

His eyes scanned the article stopping halfway through. "Why, Blue?" he asked. "Why are you coming back now?"

"It's blasphemy!" Reverend Brett Pearson raged as soon as he stepped into his house. He dropped a copy of the magazine onto the coffee table, his green eyes blazing with fury as he faced his wife. "That whore sent this filth to the church, Carrie! To *my* church! Two of the ladies who were there helping out in the office saw this . . . this garbage. Can you imagine what they must have thought?"

"I know, Brett. I'm sorry. She sent a copy to me, too."

"Why? What is she up to?"

"Did you read the article?" Carrie asked, nervously wringing her hands.

"Of course not! I just told you, two of our sisters were in the office with me. Why? What did it say?"

"She's coming back, Brett. She's bought the radio station. She'll be here next month."

"Good God!"

* * *

Aaron Grant was in his office when his wife came in, dropping the magazine in front of him on his desk. "Well, doctor, do you remember her?"

Aaron let loose a low whistle. "Holy cow, that's our Ericka? Damn, babe, she doesn't look too bad."

Pam swatted her husband's shoulder. "Seems to me I remember you thought she was pretty good looking even then."

"I think your memory serves you well, hon." He picked up a copy of the magazine, flipping through it until he arrived at the centerfold. "Holy shit! Look at the bazookas on that baby!"

Pam scooped the magazine from his hands, pretending anger but laughing. Her husband had an eye for the ladies, but she was dead certain he was faithful to her. Like she'd always told him, she'd castrate him if he ever did more than look.

He pulled her onto his lap, circling her expanding middle with his arms as he wrestled her for the issue of *Playmate*.

"Stop, Aaron. You'll hurt the baby."

"Are you kidding? This kid's bigger than me already. Now let me see—" He successfully grabbed it from her hands. "I just want to look," he said in a cajoling tone that made her giggle.

"You're a dirty old man."

"Me? I'm not the one that just bought this magazine."

"I didn't buy it either. It was delivered express just ten minutes ago."

"It took you ten minutes to bring it in here to me?"

Pam blushed. "I was looking at the pictures, too. So sue me."

Aaron was looking at the pictures now as well. Again the wolf whistle. "You gotta admit, she ain't hard on the eyes. But I thought she was in radio now or something.

Some big star in New York, is it? What's she doing in a girlie magazine?"

Pam scooted gracefully from her husband's lap, no easy feat considering she was in the eighth month of her pregnancy. "She is in radio. Boston, not New York. I'm not sure I understand what this magazine layout is all about either except that it's pretty obvious she wanted to serve notice that she's coming back to St. Joan."

Aaron Grant swiveled his chair around to look at his wife. "Why?"

"She's bought the radio station, but I guess we both know that's not the only reason."

"Hey, Junior, your dad said to tell you to get your butt into his office as soon as you came in," the pretty blonde dispatcher told Deputy Allan Witcomb as soon as he stepped into the sheriff's office.

"What's got his shorts all in a bunch?" Allan asked.

"Could be a certain magazine that was delivered here to you by express mail this morning."

"Yeah? Where is it?"

"Your father's got it."

"How come if it was addressed to me?" he asked.

Tanya Sweeny shrugged. "You know how it is. The mail comes addressed to A. Witcomb I just automatically assume it's to the sheriff. Didn't notice the Jr. until he already had it."

"So give me a clue."

"Well, it's one of them porn magazines, you know? *Playmate,* I think. Anyway, an old playmate of yours is on the cover." Tanya laughed. "Get it? *Playmate Magazine,* your old playmate?"

Allan scratched the back of his neck, exasperation sparking in his eyes. "I get it, Tanya. But I don't know what you're talking about."

"Well, her name used to be Ericka Cassidy, but she's

changed it to Rikki Blue. Don't ask me why. Anyway, the pictures are hot, *very* hot." She shook her hands as if she'd been burned by the sizzling pictures. "But the article's what's got your dad all excited."

"Spit it out, Tanya."

Tanya pouted for one split second until the look in his eyes warned her she'd better do just as he'd asked. "She's coming back to St. Joan. That's all."

"That's *all?* Damn, girl, trust me, that ain't all. That's trouble with a capital T."

Sally Jane Matthers had read the article as well. Now she sat staring out the picture window that overlooked the lake. Today in the bright spring sunlight it sparkled like a sheet of blue glass dotted with diamonds. It was beautiful, this Ozark paradise. But it hadn't always been so.

There'd been a time when the entire area had been tainted by violence and fear. But, Jesus, that was ten years ago.

She glanced down at the enthralling face of her childhood friend. "So, Ericka, what the hell are you up to?"

BOOK I

Playmates, come out and play with me
And bring your dollies three
Climb up my apple tree
Hollar down my rain barrel
Slide down my cellar door
And we'll be jolly friends
For ever more.

—Saxie Dowell

Chapter One

They were the beautiful ones. It wasn't something they thought about. It really wasn't that big of a deal. Not in the small lake resort town of St. Joan, Missouri, population 8,335 . . . that is if Mrs. Bennett hadn't delivered her twins yet . . . or if there hadn't been another murder.

But today Ericka Cassidy and Carrie Roberts were not concerned with unborn babies or murder. They were looking toward the most important week of their young lives to date. They were on the verge of that giant leap into adulthood—graduation.

They crossed the commons in the center of town, approaching the exclusive boutique which pandered to the lake area resort's rich residents and the affluent visitors who descended on their community every spring and summer.

Heads turned, but neither girl noticed. Rather they would have been more likely to notice if people *didn't* look. They were both uncommonly beautiful though their good looks were radically different. As radically different as their histories and the futures they'd mapped out for themselves. Perhaps it was the mere fact that they were so different that had drawn them to each other in the first place. But for all the curiousness that is indigenous to youth, they'd never probed the disparities that were probably responsible for the depth of their friendship. And they *were* close.

"So tell me the truth," Ericka prodded as they waited for the light to change. "Is it everything that *Cosmopolitan* says it should be?" She was referring to sex, of course, and though her tone was serious, she was teasing her friend and not expecting an honest answer.

"Oh, Lord, Ericka, give it up!" Carrie groaned, not looking up at her friend as she would have had to do if she'd looked at the other girl at all considering Ericka's height of almost five feet ten inches and her own short five feet three inches. "Brett and I have *not* done it!"

"Yeah, right, and the Pope's not Catholic. Give me a break, Carrie, I know the difference between goo-goo eyes and lustful, hungry 'I want you' looks like you and Brett give each other when you think no one else is noticing. You're my best friend. You should tell me the truth."

"You're a royal pain in the ass, you know it?"

With the change of the light both girls had stepped from the curb, but now, midway across, Ericka stopped, slapping her chest with a dramatic protest. "I can't believe that the future wife of the future Reverend Brett Pearson would talk that way."

Carrie giggled as she looked at the drivers seated in their cars at the light and tossed her long blond hair over her shoulder. Tugging on Ericka's arm, she said, "Would you come on! People are staring at us."

"People always stare at us," Ericka said immodestly.

"Ericka!"

"I'm not taking another step until you tell me if sex is as fantastic as they say it is. It's important to me."

Carrie's face flamed, but she didn't stop laughing. "Then find out for yourself next week when Bo comes home from school."

"I just might," Ericka said, giving up her protest to hurry on after her friend when the light changed and one driver honked his horn and yelled, "Crazy kids!"

"Where to now?" Carrie asked ten minutes later when they emerged from the boutique, plastic-bagged dresses over their arms.

Ericka shrugged. "Doesn't matter to me. We can go to your house and model the dresses for your parents first or to mine. Your choice."

"Let's go to mine. It's lunchtime and your mother doesn't cook."

"God, what logic! Does Brett realize what a help you're going to be to him?"

"Does Bo realize what a bitch you are?" Carrie countered smartly.

"Of course not. We've only been out three times and that was almost two months ago. But now that he's coming home from college, I've got all summer to slowly indoctrinate him to all my charms."

As they reached the compact red convertible that had been an eighteenth birthday gift to Ericka from her parents the week before, Carrie waited for her friend to unlock the car. Leaning against the right front fender, she shook her head. "I don't get it."

"Get what?" Ericka asked, tossing her bag into the small back seat, then climbing in behind the wheel.

A few seconds later, seated beside Ericka, Carrie answered. "You've always been so straight arrow. A perfect 4.0 average, dating only dweebs, reading books in your room when you could have been watching MTV. Then wham, suddenly you're going out with the hottest guy in St. Joan, buying slinky dresses, and asking questions about sex. What's with you?"

"Nothing's *with* me," Ericka replied good-naturedly as she started the car and backed out into traffic. "I've always prioritized. I'm a Taurus. What can I say? We're orderly."

"Yeah, so you're saying your newest priority is sex."

"Maybe. I don't know yet. But my priorities are changing and well they should. Think about it. Order is the first law. Change is the second. Besides, I like to read. And as for guys, who else was there for me to date but dweebs? Our graduating class is only 121 and even though Brett graduated last year, he and Danny Lightner were the only two good-looking guys in the school since we were in ninth grade."

"And Danny's gay and you don't even like Brett."

Ericka laughed but rolled her eyes. "Danny is not gay! God, what a provincial you are, Carrie. Where do you get these ideas?"

"You *ever* seen him with a girl?" Carrie challenged.

"You know I haven't, but that doesn't prove he's gay. He's going to be a priest. A *Catholic* priest."

"Which just lends credence to my theory that he's gay. Celibacy is an unnatural state. Jeez, just look at all the stories we hear about priests messing with little boys."

Ericka shook her head no longer amused or laughing. Carrie's narrow-minded attitudes toward anyone who disagreed with her philosophies annoyed her greatly. "You are a bigot, Carrie Roberts, and a self-righteous bigot at that. God, I'm amazed that we became friends. I'm Episcopalian, don't forget."

Carrie wasn't offended. She rarely was. Too thick-skinned and sure of herself, Ericka thought.

"Well, sugar, you're still Protestant. Of course, Brett would probably be more accepting of our friendship if you were Southern Baptist like us, but even he admits that without the misguided and the sinners of this world there'd be little use for his services as a minister." Her dark eyes were twinkling with mischief and Ericka chuckled in spite of her irritation.

"Up yours, Roberts," she said.

"Now is that nice?"

"No, but don't push for more. I wouldn't be so forgiving of your arrogant self-righteousness if I didn't understand that between your parents and Brett you didn't stand a chance. I knew when you two started going out in eighth grade he was going to complete the ruin your parents had started."

"You love me and you know it."

"Yep. It's the one flaw in my otherwise perfect existence."

"Ha ha ha," Carrie said.

"So speaking of your man, when's he coming home from Springfield?"

"Tomorrow. Said he'll come by the house tomorrow night after he visits with his folks."

"Ah, well that explains the color in your cheeks. Getting all heated up over thoughts of your reunion."

"Would you stop? What's with all this sex talk anyway? Are you really that interested in Keen Bohannon?"

Ericka shrugged. "I don't know. I mean he's gorgeous and fun, but we don't know each other very well yet. But he does kiss like a man born to the job." She glanced Carrie's way as they sped down the highway toward the Bar-Ber-Keen Estates. "Why don't you and Brett meet us on the strip tomorrow night? You can tell Brett to watch the way Bo does it. Maybe he'll learn something."

Carrie laughed, but when she looked at her friend, her eyes reflected a serious question.

"What?" Ericka said in response to the question her friend seemed reluctant to ask.

"Nothing. I just wish you liked Brett better."

"It isn't that I *dis*like him, Carrie. He's just not my type." She bit her lip to prevent a smile as she added. " 'Course I still think his pious, preppy attitude is all a sham. He probably is really kinky when the lights are off."

Carrie didn't answer but huffed indignantly as she folded her arms over her small breasts and turned her head to look out the window.

Ericka couldn't prevent a teasing chuckle. "Sorry. I won't rib you anymore. I do sound preoccupied with sex today, don't I?"

Unable to resist, Carrie gave up her sulk to look at her friend. "I'd say! I swear I'm not sure I think it's safe for you to spend the summer with Bo. Does your mama know what's on your mind?"

"No, but she wouldn't hit the roof like your mother would. My parents are very liberal."

"Ha! That's probably the grossest understatement of the decade. My mama practically has heart palpitations every morning when your mother jogs by in that tight little exercise getup of hers."

Ericka laughed. She shook her head as she slowed the car and eased it to the curb in front of Carrie's house, but her tone sobered when she spoke again. "It's not just sex that's on my mind. It's everything in life I haven't done yet. I guess Cindy Richvalski's death started me thinking. There's so much we haven't experienced. What if something happened to us like that? Can you imagine being dead just two years from now?"

At the mention of the murder of the young woman neither girl had known well, Carrie ran her hands through her long hair, her brow furrowed and her mouth puckered with distaste. "I can't help but think she was asking for it."

"You're kidding! That's terrible! Why would you even say such a thing? I don't care who she was or what her lifestyle was, no woman deserves to have her head bashed in with a baseball bat."

"Oh, I know it was awful, but she did hang out with some nasty people. Why, do you know my daddy said she was friends with that Bunny Apperson woman who got her throat cut just a week before Cindy got killed, which means she probably knew that pawn shop owner, too, since he was murdered the same way as Bunny."

"And I suppose you think they all deserved what they got?"

"Well, no, of course not. Nobody deserves that. But let's face it, Ericka, the world's an evil place. If you let yourself become a part of evil, you have to worry about consequences."

"Oh, Lord, is that what your mother says or is that doctrine preached by the future Reverend Brett Pearson?"

"Neither!" Carrie said, reaching behind her for her dress and opening the car door. "I just know what's right and what's wrong, that's all. And you know it, too. Look at us. We don't go out to parties that last all night and nobody's tried to kill us."

"Straight from the mouth of Mrs. Roberts," Ericka muttered as soon as Carrie stepped from the car.

"What?" Carrie asked.

"Nothing," Ericka said.

"Well, you coming or not?"

Ericka shrugged off her irritation. Today was no time to be worrying about her friend's ever increasing sanctimonious views. Grabbing her dress and tossing her keys into her purse, she hurried across the lawn after Carrie. "Wait up! You sure your mom isn't busy today? I can go on home."

"Don't be silly. She has her hair done in the morning on Fridays while our girl cleans the house. She's more than likely gabbing on the phone with one of her friends."

When they entered the house, Carrie yelled for her mother. "I'm home, Mama. Gonna try on my dress for you."

"I'm in the kitchen on the phone, Carrie Ann. Come in when you've got it on."

Carrie gave her friend an "I told you so" look, then

gestured with a nod of her head toward the hallway. "You change in the guest room. I'll go on upstairs, but don't you dare show Mama yours 'til I get back down here."

"Then don't go fixing your makeup and bothering with panty hose. I'm starving."

Ericka went to the downstairs bedroom as instructed, laying the dress bag on the bed. She started to pull her shirt over her head but decided instead to go to the kitchen and tell Marylou Roberts that she was there as well in case the woman decided to go into the guest room for any reason. She didn't want to startle her.

She paused in the entryway waiting for a break in conversation when she could announce herself.

"Didn't I tell you when they moved here that they didn't belong? Damned Yankees! He's all right I suppose except for his airs of superiority. Poet laureate indeed! But her. Who does she think she is writing a book about us? Why, Wanda Mae says she's going to make St. Joan sound like a regular den of iniquity. Another Peyton Place. I'm telling you, Phoebe, we need to get together and find a way to stop—"

"Mrs. Roberts!" Ericka interrupted when she couldn't stand to hear another word. Those were her parents she and Brett's mother were talking about! She was shaking from head to toe, struggling with her desire to slap the woman. She wanted to defend her parents, point out to the ignorant hillbilly that her parents probably had more decency in their little fingers than she and all of her hypocritical friends put together. She wanted to ask what the *hell* they were talking about. Her parents, who were a successful writing team of pop fiction, would never write a biography of the people who were their neighbors and friends. Scratch that. These women were not her mother's friends. But the shocked expression on Marylou Robert's face was almost as satisfying as the diatribe she'd been about to deliver.

"Why, Ericka, dear, I didn't know you were here."

"Obviously. I'm sorry to interrupt, but would you please tell Carrie that I had to leave. I just remembered that I promised my parents to join them for lunch."

Without waiting for Carrie's mother to regain her composure, she spun on her heel, almost running to the front door. When she was outside she did run . . . and she cried. How dare they? How?

Carrie came downstairs only minutes after her friend's abrupt departure. "Ericka, I'm ready if you are!" she called from the living room.

Her mother came into the room then, her perfectly made up face splotched with circles of red. "My don't you look lovely, hon."

Carrie quickly forgot the telltale blotches on her mother's cheeks and turned in a perfect pirouette. "Do you think Brett will approve?"

Marylou Roberts chuckled. "Brett Pearson would think you looked divine no matter what you wore, but that dress is certainly becoming. White has always been a good color for you. Shows off your perfect honey complexion."

"Wait 'til you see Ericka. Hers is mint green. Mint parfait, Mary Kate called it. With all that red hair, she looks like a dream. Hers has a full skirt that makes her long legs look even longer." She turned back toward the guest room in back. "I can't imagine what's taking her so long."

"Um, I'm afraid she's gone, Carrie Ann."

"Gone? Where?"

"Home, I think."

"But why? Did her mother call?"

"No, I'm, uh, afraid that she overheard me talking on the phone to Brett's mother, and she got upset. I would have apologized but she didn't give me a chance.

Maybe when you talk to her, you can tell her I'm sorry for embarrassing her. Even though I don't approve of Linda or Lawrence Cassidy, I wouldn't hurt Ericka for the world. She's probably the one thing they've done right."

"Mama, what are you talking about? What were you saying on the phone to Phoebe that could have hurt Ericka enough to make her leave?"

"I wasn't going to say anything to you about it, Carrie Ann. I know how close you and Ericka are. But it seems that her parents have turned their professional attention on us, their neighbors, and I'm not going to just sit idly by while they expose our secrets to the world and turn us into laughing stocks."

Carrie inhaled deeply, revealing her impatience. "I don't know what you're talking about. What do you mean they've turned their professional attention on us?"

"A book, Carrie Ann. They're writing a book about us."

"Oh, that's ridiculous. They wouldn't do that. Besides, they write fiction." Carrie smiled, her gold-flecked, brown eyes teasing. "Anyway, what secrets do any of you or your friends have that would be so interesting to write about?"

"Don't be fresh. They *are* writing a book. Wanda Mae actually copied several chapters of it at the print shop for Linda. She said she was only able to get a peak or two, but she says it's sexually explicit and vulgar in tone."

Carrie frowned. "And it actually named you and your friends?"

"No, of course not. The names have been changed to protect the innocent as they say on those television shows, but everyone will know it's us. Anyway, Howard Barnes over at the grocery confirmed that Linda has been asking questions for months. Research, she calls it."

Carrie shook her head. "I still don't get it. If the names aren't the same, it must be fiction. So what are you so worried about? Authors use real life towns and situations and even people all the time. That doesn't mean the story is true."

"Oh, what do you know?" Marylou said with a flip of her hand. "You're only a child."

"I know enough to know that you're being silly. It's not like anyone we know has any deep, dark secrets to hide. Who cares if they write a book about a town like St. Joan? And I know enough to realize that you've always been jealous of Dr. and Mrs. Cassidy."

"That's nonsense and you're being a very rude young lady! Why would I be jealous of them? They're Yankees, for heaven sake."

"Yeah, and they both have degrees up the kazoo. And don't tell me it doesn't rankle that all the men in Bar-Ber-Keen Estates get up early every morning just to watch Mrs. Cassidy jog. She's a hot mama to quote Daddy."

"That's enough, Carrie Ann! I'm not going to stand here and be made to feel like an uneducated frump by my own daughter."

Carrie took a couple of steps toward her mother then kissed her cheek. "Don't be silly, Mama. You're still a pretty hot-looking little number yourself, and just because you never finished college doesn't mean that I think you're stupid. I just wish you'd lighten up on Ericka's parents. She's my best friend and her parents are pretty cool. You've never given them a chance."

"I've had them to dinner on several occasions, young lady. We all belong to the country club, and I've even played tennis with Linda."

"Yes, and the second you're away from them, you're on the phone gossiping with Phoebe or Wanda Mae or Sissy." Without waiting for her mother to argue further, Carrie pecked her cheek again and turned toward the stairs. "I'm going to go change before I mess up my dress." Halfway up, she paused and looked down at her mother once again. "Then I'm going to call Ericka and apologize."

"You'll do no such thing! She shouldn't have been eavesdropping to begin with."

Carrie laughed under her breath. Sometimes her mother was simply impossible. "I doubt she was eavesdropping, Mama. She probably just wanted to tell you hello. But whatever, I'm still going to tell her I'm sorry and explain that you've just been given some misinformation. She's my *best* friend, Mama, and this is graduation week. I don't want anything to ruin it for us. *Please . . .*"

"Oh, very well. Tell her whatever you like. I'm going to fix a fruit salad for lunch. Do you want one?"

Carrie's smile of approval was wide and warm. "Fruit salad sounds great. See you in a few minutes." She practically skipped up the steps, but slowed when her mother called after her to remind her that ladies didn't run.

She called Ericka even before getting out of her dress, but Dr. Cassidy told her that his daughter hadn't gotten home yet.

"Well, would you ask her to call me? It's very important."

Lawrence Cassidy chuckled. "Have you ever called here when it wasn't?" He teased in his well-modulated, calm voice that drew a smile from Carrie.

"Maybe once or twice," she laughed. "But this time it really is important." She hesitated just a minute, feeling a little disloyal to her mother, but going ahead anyway. "I'm afraid Mama hurt her feelings. She—Mama, that is—was talking to Brett's mother on the phone. They were talking about you and Mrs. Cassidy, sir."

"Oh?" he said, waiting.

"About your book. Someone told my mother that you're writing about St. Joan." She laughed again, this time nervously. "Everyone's afraid you're going to make it sound like a real-life Peyton Place."

"Is that so? Well, they're half right. Our latest book is about a lake resort town, and Linda has been gathering research while I pen the body of the book, but I promise that we're not writing an expose on our neighbors and friends."

"I told Mama that I was sure you weren't, but for some reason everyone seems to be in a tizzy."

"Perhaps Linda and I will call a few people and reassure them."

"That would be great," Carrie agreed.

"Or even better. Dr. Grant has helped Linda with her research. Perhaps it would be better if he talked to everyone." His deep baritone voice erupted into gentle laughter once again. "After all, he may be a sneaky, conniving Yankee, but he's been here longer and people have forgotten his roots."

Carrie was embarrassed that Ericka's father knew what people said about them, but she couldn't resist the pull of his charm. "You're probably right," she said, giggling with him.

"In the meantime, I'll ask Ericka to return your call, my dear."

"Thank you," she said, hanging up the receiver and already unzipping her new dress. It was a tight, fitted dress but she slid it over her hips rather than pulling it over her head. As she put it back on the hanger, then covered it with the plastic bag once again, she caught her reflection in the mirror. Clad only in panties now, for she rarely wore a bra—her small breasts made it unnecessary—she was reminded of her conversation with Ericka on the way to the dress shop. She saw her face redden with memory of her friend's teasing questions about sex with Brett. She'd lied when she'd insisted that they'd never done it. They'd been doing it since tenth grade, but Brett had made her swear never to tell. It was the only thing she'd ever kept from her best friend—well, except for the way her mother and several of the other women in St. Joan felt about the Cassidys—and she felt guilty for lying. But, darn it all, Brett was going to be an ordained minister. It was important that he keep his image untarnished.

Hanging the dress in the closet, she frowned. Besides, she didn't want to admit that as much as she loved him, she'd never enjoyed their sexual encounters. She read the same articles in *Cosmopolitan* that Ericka did and couldn't help but wonder why she always felt so dirty and cheap after they did it. Was something wrong with her? Or was it Brett? Normally warm and caring, he was different when they were having sex. Almost mean and definitely selfish. Did other guys really make love to their girlfriends and wives, romancing them with sweet talk like all the articles claimed or were they like Brett, just interested in getting it off?

Well, no matter, she couldn't tell Ericka about it, and besides what good would it do? Ericka was still a virgin. They couldn't even compare notes.

Carrie sighed as she sat down on the edge of the bed to pull her jeans back on. Maybe when they were married, when they could do it in bed instead of the cramped back seat of a car or the hard ground or on the counter in his father's workshop, it would be different. She hoped so. She loved him so much. That was the only problem they had and he didn't even know it *was* a problem. She'd never tell him. Brett didn't like criticism. Besides, in every other way he was perfect.

Ericka drove around for a good thirty minutes before going home. She'd forgotten her dress at the Roberts' house but she wasn't going back for it now. She was still too angry to talk even to Carrie right now.

She should have said more, defended her parents, but

how could she? She didn't even know what they'd been talking about. But she was sure her parents weren't writing a book about the townsfolk of St. Joan. They just wouldn't do that. She laughed bitterly. Damned Yankees! What a joke. For all that Mrs. Roberts claimed to be a genteel Southerner, her mother and father had more aristocratic qualities in their little fingers than she had in her whole body. For one thing, they *never* gossiped. Marylou Roberts could take a lesson from their book on warmth and compassion and charity!

In spite of her indignation, Ericka was as easy going by nature as her parents, and the fuse that had been burning so hot and fast inside her began to lose its spark and eventually snuffed itself out. She turned for home.

Her father was seated at his desk in his office when she came in. He called out to her as soon as she shut the door behind her.

"Yes, it's me!" she called in return, heading upstairs toward her room.

"Come in here, would you, Rikki?"

"Hi, Dad," she said, leaning against the door jamb.

"Carrie called. Asked me to apologize for her mother's rudeness. Seemed quite embarrassed."

Without commenting, Ericka entered the room, lowering herself onto his ottoman a few feet away from where he sat. "I was so mad I could have screamed at Mrs. Roberts. How dare she talk about you and Mom like that!"

Lawrence Cassidy's blue eyes sparkled with amusement above his salt and pepper beard. "It does make one wonder if there aren't some wonderfully spicy secrets everyone's worried we'll uncover, doesn't it?"

Ericka couldn't resist a giggle, but she shook her head. "I'd like to think so, but you've said yourself that except for those murders a few weeks ago, this is the most prosaic, uninspired town in the world. I can't imagine why they're in such a snit. Probably wish they did have some exciting, dirty secrets for you to uncover."

"Ah, I think you've hit the nail on the head. But I suppose Linda and I are partially to blame here, sweetheart. We should have told everyone what we're doing. We are writing a book about a community very much like St. Joan, and your mother has been gathering information that will give us the proper tone, but I assure you it will be a fictional piece just like all our other books."

"I know that. I didn't even intend to mention it to you." She stood up and took a few steps to plant a kiss on her father's wrinkled brow. "Don't worry about me. I could care less what you write as long as it's hot and steamy."

"Well, I can assure you it will be that." He laughed softly as if to himself. "And you can tell your friends' parents that Linda and I don't need to look elsewhere for our research on that end."

"God, don't I know it! I have to sleep with the television on most nights just not to hear what's going on in your bedroom."

Her father tried for a properly contrite expression though he didn't quite manage to rid his eyes of their laughter. "And I thought we were so discreet."

"Ha!" she said, walking toward the door. "That's probably the one word I'd never use to describe you and Mother." She paused, hand on the door to look over her shoulder at him. "I only hope I'm as lucky as the two of you when I get married."

"Not too soon, I hope. I'm not old enough to have a son-in-law."

Ericka laughed as he'd meant for her to do. Lawrence Cassidy was sixty-two years old, twenty years older than her mother. But in spite of his advanced age, he was younger at heart than most of her contemporaries. "You'll never be old," she told him.

"Good God, I hope not! That's why we moved to this haven of fresh air, so that we could stay perpetually young."

She smiled tenderly. "I love you, Daddy."

"Of course you do. What's not to love? I'm wonderful."

"And modest."

"I don't believe modesty is a genuine virtue. People are either very aware of how good they are or insecure. If they're certain of their worth and deny it that's false humility. If they're insecure they don't believe they've value at anything."

Ericka rolled her eyes, then waggled her fingers in a farewell gesture. "See you later. I'm going to go start writing my valedictorian address."

"Call Carrie," her father reminded her.

"I will."

She was already out the door when her father stopped her once again. "Oh, Ericka, a young man called here for you."

She hurried back into the room. "Who?"

"Keen Bohannon."

"Bo! He called me? When? Is he home? Was it long distance or local?" But before her father could answer her string of queries the telephone rang. "I'll get it in my room," Ericka yelled as she dashed for the stairs taking them two at a time.

"Hello?" she said breathlessly a few seconds later.

"Hi, sweet stuff," Keen Bohannon drawled.

"Bo! Hi!" Then lowering herself to the bed, she tried for a more casual tone. "It's good to hear from you. Are you home?"

"Just two miles away from you, babe."

"When did you get in?"

"About an hour ago. I called as soon as I unloaded my car, but your dad said you were out."

Ericka was grinning from ear to ear as she toyed with

the telephone cord. "I would have been home if I'd known you were getting in so early."

"Can I see you tonight?"

"Sure. Where do you want to go?"

"Some of the kids at school said they were meeting on the strip tonight. Thought we could start there then see what's happening."

"Sounds good. What time?"

"Eight o'clock okay for you?"

"Perfect."

"So what's happening in good old St. Joan?" he asked.

"Nothing. You know how it is here. Never any excitement."

He laughed. "Seems to me there were a couple of things to get excited about last time I was home for spring break. Kinda remember the windows of my car getting steamed up a couple of times."

She giggled.

"And weren't there a couple of murders?"

"Don't remind me," she said. "That's all anyone's talked about at school."

"Bummer. Okay, then we'll just talk about us. Are you still the most gorgeous girl on the lake?"

Remembering her father's observation on modesty, she laughed. "Of course."

Chapter Two

The "strip" was a mile-long ribbon of novelty and souvenir shops, fast food joints, carnival concessions, and game rooms. In addition, there were bumper cars, boat rentals, one nice restaurant, and three bars. For the kids who lived on the lake, the gathering place was a hamburger place called simply "Buns" with an outside patio that overlooked the horseshoe-shaped lake. It was there that Bo and Ericka met several of their friends that night.

"Whoa, getta load of that baby," Aaron Grant said as soon as Ericka stepped from Bo's Corvette. "Old Judge Ramsey should outlaw anything that good looking and Scooter ought to be out here arresting her."

Ericka laughed, pleased with the offhanded compliment yet not taking the guy seriously. Not that she wasn't confident that she looked good. On the contrary, she'd worked more than two hours on her hair and makeup that afternoon and then spent another hour putting together the casual but perfect outfit.

But Aaron Grant was an outrageous flirt. At twenty-three, he already had a reputation as a womanizer. In fact the joke was that no woman would be safe once he received his medical license and hung up his shingle beside his father's. Shorter than average, not quite five feet six, he was nevertheless a good-looking guy with sandy hair and deep-set hazel eyes and a ready grin. In honesty, folks thought he would make a fine addition to his father's long established practice. Ole Doc Grant, as his father was called, had a very relaxed, pleasant bedside manner, and Aaron promised the same easy way that was so comforting.

Bo looped Ericka's neck with his arm. "Just keep in mind that this is mine, man," he told Aaron, sticking his hand out for a modified handshake of several quickly articulated movements including gripped fingertips and a high five. "How you doin', buddy? Getting to cut on anyone yet?"

"Ooh, that's gross," Pamela Sue Brown, Aaron's date, said.

"Hi, Pam," Ericka said to the young woman she knew only because she lived in the same subdivision. Pamela Sue was the same age as Bo, but age wasn't an issue in the small community as it would have been in a big city. The "haves," as the twenty or so affluent families who owned most of St. Joan were called, congregated together. The "have nots" did the same, but farther up the strip at another burger joint called "Big Jim's."

Junior Witcomb, the sheriff's son and his date, Sally Jane Matthers, exited Buns with a bag of burgers and fries, and greetings were exchanged once again. "Come on, guys, dig in," Junior invited. "Bought a ton of burgers. Help yourselves."

Sally Jane, a homely girl of nineteen with red hair—though not the dark, vibrant red of Ericka's but rather carrot colored—pale, mostly lashless eyes, and skin that God had unkindly blotched with a sea of freckles, was nonetheless one of the most popular girls in St. Joan by merit of her personality and having the richest father not only in the lake area but in the entire state of Missouri. Like Bo's father, Clemens Matthers was into real estate. Unlike Bert Bohannon, his success as a land tycoon was not by luck or accident, but the reward of a shrewd, innate talent and ruthlessness. Many unfortunates had fallen victim to the recession in the past ten years, and Clemens, with the nose of a ferret, was always there to take advantage of their ill luck. An outgoing man with a ready smile, Clemens often bragged that he could outtalk, outsmart, outmaneuver the best of 'em. Fortunately, Sally Jane was blessed with her father's gift of gab though not his merciless streak. A perfect matching of character producing genes had graced her with her mother's sensibilities while the same genes had proven a disastrous match in the looks department. She smiled, her long gum and horsey teeth intensifying her plainness.

"Hi, Ericka. Jeez, you look great!"

"Great doesn't even begin to describe it," Bo said, letting his arm which had remained possessively around Ericka's neck slide down to rest around her waist.

"Yeah, there's no justice in the world. Some just get more than their fair share."

"You do all right for yourself," Bo said.

Sally Jane wrinkled her pert little nose—her best feature—as she smiled at Junior. "Yeah, well, God did give me a rich daddy and a natural instinct for what to do when we get in the back seat. Can't complain."

Everyone laughed, though Ericka felt her cheeks heat when she felt rather than saw Bo looking at her. Did he know that she'd been thinking about him that way since their dates six weeks before?

"Hey, where's your sidekick, Ericka?" Sally Jane asked. "I thought the two of you were joined at the hip."

"She's getting ready for Brett's homecoming tomorrow night."

A pair of Harley riders slowed in front of Buns to rev their engines, then sped on by when the group congregated on the patio looked their way.

"God, they're already descending," Pam groaned. "I think Scooter should put up 'No Trespassing' signs until next month. Let us enjoy our own territory before all the low lifes hit town."

"I won't tell my dad you said that. He'd have a stroke," Bo said. The others all commented or nodded their agreement. If not for the "lakers" as the tourists were called by the residents, St. Joan would become a ghost town. Businesses depended on the tourist trade, and nobody more so than Bert Bohannon who owned Bar-Ber-Keen, the most lavish resort in the mainland states.

"Even your dad wouldn't object to those losers being kept out for a few more weeks," Junior said. "They're nothing but trouble."

Bo shook his head. "Naw. They're just loud."

"Yeah, but they're tight, too. Don't spend any money except for beer," Junior said. Then with a shrug. "But who cares, right? Live and let live. That's my motto."

"Yeah, 'til you go to work for your dad. Then you'll be singing a different tune. Then you'll be the one out there giving tickets instead of sitting here with us," Sally Jane said, sliding her arm through his.

"So, when does that happen?" Ericka asked, sitting down at the table with Junior and Sally Jane.

Junior handed her a sandwich and a bag of fries as he answered. "Becoming a deputy? Monday. Just keep your fingers crossed that there aren't any more murders. I don't want to be broken in like that."

"Oh, great. Not home an hour, and already I'm hearing about murder again," Brett Pearson said, rounding the corner, his hand linked with Carrie's.

Hamburgers were forgotten for a few minutes by everyone but Sally Jane who groaned in sync with her growling stomach as everyone greeted the newcomers and expressed surprise at their appearance.

"He wanted to surprise me," Carrie said, rolling her eyes. "That's why I look like such a grub."

"Oh, right," two or three of them chorused. Carrie Ann Roberts never looked anything but perfect.

"Sit down," Bo said, then slid onto the concrete bench beside Ericka. "We've got enough burgers to feed an army."

As Carrie reached for a fry, Brett looked around at their friends. "So what were you saying about murder?"

"Nothing," Pamela Sue said. "Junior's going to work for his dad Monday. He's just hoping he won't have to investigate one too soon."

"Why would you worry about that? St. Joan's one of the most crime-free communities in the country," Brett said.

"*Was.* Past tense," Junior pointed out. "Those three in April didn't help the stats. And don't forget little Dottie Hooper last summer."

"That's different. Her father killed her," Sally Jane pointed out around a mouthful of juicy burger.

"Poor little thing," Carrie said. "Only six years old. It's ironic, isn't it? If her father's dogs hadn't dug up her grave, no one would ever have known what happened to her. She'd just be another unsolved mystery like the three in April."

"Well, we might not know who killed Cindy and those other two, but my dad thinks they must have been running drugs or something. They were all friends. Hung out together."

"I don't know," Aaron said, shaking his head and raising a foot to rest it on one of the concrete benches that encircled the table as he joined in the conversation. "They might have been *running* drugs, but Cindy at least wasn't using. My dad said he thought most people who sell use as well."

Ericka shuddered. "I'd forgotten that your dad is the

coroner as well as the G.P. Will you do that, too, Aaron?"

Aaron shrugged. "I guess. When and if he ever retires."

"What about Bunny and that Roper fella? They use?" Ericka asked.

"According to my dad, it didn't look like it. I overheard him talking to Junior's old man after he performed the autopsies. Said there weren't any signs of drugs in their blood, but that doesn't mean they never did them. But Cindy was a patient. He knew she was clean."

"Then what would the connection be?" Carrie asked.

Aaron shrugged. "Who knows? My dad said Cindy came to see him the day after Bunny was murdered. Said she was real upset."

"Well, that's understandable," Brett put in. "She was Bunny's friend. If they were involved in something illegal, she probably suspected she was in danger, too. Did she tell Dr. Grant anything?"

All eyes turned expectantly toward Aaron.

"I don't know. He didn't confide in me. I just overheard the tail end of what he was telling Scooter. But I guess not if Scooter's telling the truth about not having any leads."

Now the group turned their attention to Junior who was busy gobbling a sandwich. He shrugged. "Don't look at me," he said, capturing a dangling piece of lettuce and stuffing it into his mouth. A few seconds later, his bite swallowed and chased with soda, he added. "All I know is what I read in the papers, but I think every trail has led to a dead end. Did hear Dad tell my mom that unless Dr. Grant remembers a name Cindy mentioned, we might never know what happened."

"What name?" Carrie and Pamela Sue asked at the same time, their eyes bright with morbid fascination.

"I don't know. What is this? Mystery Pursuit? That's all I heard," Scooter protested.

"So let's talk about something else," Ericka suggested. "My parents were talking about this just before Bo arrived. That's all anyone's thought about for the past six weeks. It gives me the creeps."

"Your parents putting the murders in their book?" Sally Jane asked.

"Uh-uh," Carrie warned. "Her parents' book is taboo."

"Oh, it is not," Ericka said with undisguised exasperation. "I just don't like people accusing them of writing what they're not."

"Have we missed something?" Sally Jane asked.

Ericka sighed, wishing the subject had never been brought up. She glanced sidelong at Carrie. "Her mother and some of the other women in the area think my parents were writing a tell-all about St. Joan, when in fact, they're not doing that at all."

"Well, they are, sort of," Carrie said, defending her mother's assumption. "The book *is* based on St. Joan."

"No it's not," Ericka bit out slowly, her annoyance sparking in her blue eyes now. "I told you on the phone, it's about a fictional town that's similar to St. Joan, but it has nothing to do with any of you or your families."

"Then how come your mother has been running around the lake interviewing everyone and spending hours on the microfiche at the library reading old issues of the *St. Joan Banner?*"

"God!" Ericka groaned, running her hands through her long, thick mane of fiery hair. "You're really starting to make me mad, Carrie. I told you on the phone this afternoon that my mother is just being thorough. She's picking up the flavor of small town America. That's all."

Carrie's feelings were hurt by her friend's tone. Her dark eyes flashing with a mean glint, she said, "Does your dad know how much time your mother has been spending out at the Circle G with Aaron's dad?"

"Ooh, meeeow," Sally Jane said.

"Hey, it gets lonely out there for a divorced man living all alone on twenty-six hundred acres. Since he and my mom divorced ten years ago, he's missed having a woman around," Aaron offered, trying to diffuse the argument that the two girls seemed about to get into.

Ericka was really angry now, but she laughed at Aaron then turned her attention to her best friend. "Why, I swanee, Carrie Ann, I do believe I hear the genteel, well-bred voice of Marylou Roberts coming out of your mouth, sugar."

Carrie's face blazed red even beneath her natural olive complexion, but before she could answer, Bo stood up, pulling Ericka to her feet beside him. "Come on. I think I want to stroll the strip with you. Show you off. See those pissers on the motor bikes turn green with envy."

Ericka smiled her gratitude at him for delivering her from the tense situation. She was immediately sorry for making fun of Carrie's mother by mimicking her exaggerated southern drawl, but it had come out before she'd realized what she was saying. "See you later, guys," she said, careful not to look at her best friend, but before she could make her escape, Brett was standing face to face with her.

"I think you should pray about the anger that's in your heart, Ericka. Carrie is your best friend."

"Sit on it, Pearson," Bo said, taking Ericka's hand and leading her away from the group.

But they'd walked only a few feet when Ericka heard Carrie defending herself. "I don't know why she's so mad at my mother. It's *her* mother that's putting herself in a position to be talked about."

She stopped, putting on her brakes, but Bo tugged at her hand. "Come on. Don't let her get to you. She's just parroting what Marylou has been saying and the only reason she's talking about your mother is because she's jealous." He glanced down at her, his lips parted in a sexy half grin. "You gotta admit your mom is pretty special to look at. If she was single I'd have a pretty tough time deciding which one of you I want to date."

Ericka smiled her gratitude. "Thanks."

"Come on, let's skip the strip."

"What you got in mind?"

"Being alone with you. Six weeks has whetted my appetite." At her nervous side glance, he laughed. "I want to get to know more about you. I didn't learn much on our dates over spring break. I want you to tell me everything."

"What's to tell?" she asked with a self-conscious giggle. "I've lived just down the street from you for ten years. Our parents have been friends since then."

They'd arrived back at his car. Bo opened the door for her, waiting to answer her until he was behind the wheel and headed down the highway. Then he glanced her way, grabbed her hand, drawing it to rest on his jeans as he picked up where they'd left off. "Anyone ever call you Ricky?" he asked.

"My dad. Why?"

"I don't know. Just wondered. I think of you as a Ricky. Mind if I call you that?"

"No. I'd like it, but only if you spell it right. It's R-i-k-k-i."

"Ah, the lady has exotic tastes. See, I've already found out something about you. Maybe I'll give you a boa constrictor for your birthday."

Ericka laughed. "No way. Besides, my birthday was two weeks ago."

"Yeah, seems to me I remember that," he said, letting go of her hand to open the console compartment between them. He handed her a small, foil-wrapped box. "Happy birthday, Rikki."

Ericka was surprised that her hand was shaking when she accepted the gift. "You shouldn't have."

"Ah, she's coy, too."

She laughed as she slapped his leg. "I am not. I mean it. You shouldn't have. But I'm glad you did."

"How do you know? You haven't opened it yet."

"I don't want to open it yet."

"Why not?" he asked, his tone changing suddenly to that of little boy disappointment.

"It's a thing of mine. I like to savor things. Make them last. My dad's the same way. My mom is the impulsive, 'don't make me wait one' in our family."

"Okay. I can buy that. So tell me something else about you. What's your whole name, for example."

"Don't laugh," she said.

"Why would I laugh?"

"Because my middle name's Blue."

He'd turned onto a side road that wound to the top of one of the Ozark mountains. He stopped midway up the hillside, putting the car in park and turning in the seat to look at her. "Nothing funny about that," he said quietly. "You got the damnedest blue eyes I've ever seen. In fact, I don't think I'll call you Rikki. I think I'll call you Blue."

Ericka smiled but lowered her eyes to the package in her lap. He was embarrassing her looking at her like that, his long lashed black eyes roving so slowly over her face, yet she liked it, too. "What about your name?" she asked, toying with the ribbon that he'd obviously tied himself judging from the poorly fashioned bow. "Why did your parents name you Keen?"

She had looked up at him again with the question and was surprised by the flush that rose to his face. He was so handsome, so confident, so . . . so . . . perfect. Did men like him really get embarrassed? "You don't have to tell me if you don't want to," she said.

He shrugged and the grin that was so easy for him,

slid into place. "Naw, it's no big secret. Hell, you know my old man. Land, boisterous, rough-edged—"

"I like your dad," she defended.

The frown that appeared was gone so quickly, Ericka wondered if she'd imagined it. He shrugged. "So do I. In fact, all of the above are why I like him. He's rich— stinking rich to hear him tell it—but he wasn't born to it like the Pearson and Roberts and Matthers folks. He didn't even earn it. Just stepped in, literally. But the point is wealth didn't change him. I guess that's cool."

"It is," she agreed. "But back to how you got your name."

"But back to that. My dad just thought it was pretty keen to have a son. He told my mom that and one of them decided on naming me that."

"So why do you go by Bo?"

"Are you kidding? Can you imagine explaining to everyone who meets me how I got the unusual handle?"

Ericka chuckled. "I see your point. At least having my middle name be Blue doesn't require constant explanation."

Bo didn't answer but reached for her face with his pinky finger. "Do you know that the entire tip of my finger fits inside your dimple?" he asked.

"Stop," she said, pushing his hand away. "You're embarrassing me."

"Now that I can't believe. I know guys have been sweet talking you since the first time you ever smiled."

She shook her head.

"Aw, come on. Who do you think you're kidding? Looking like you do?"

"No, really. I've never dated much."

"Why not?"

"You forget how small St. Joan is. The pickings are pretty slim, and I guess I'm pretty particular."

"Well, after this summer, your world will open up when you go back East to Harvard."

She nodded her agreement. "Funny how our dreams change. At Christmas I thought I couldn't stand it until I went. Now I wish I could go somewhere else."

"Like where?"

"Like Northwestern," she said after only the briefest hesitation.

His grin flashed across his face and his dark eyes glittered with obvious pleasure. "So why don't you?"

"I can't. Harvard's my parents' alma mater . . ."

"And they'd shit if you didn't go," he finished for her.

"Oh, they'd probably say I had to do what I want, but I know they'd be disappointed."

"And Ericka Blue Cassidy never disappoints her folks."

"No, not if I can help it."

He leaned across the console to capture her face between his hands and kiss her mouth. "God, you're sweet, Blue," he said when he let her go a long moment later. "The first time I saw you, you couldn't have been more than eight or nine—"

"Ten," she said, honestly not caring that she was giving away her secret of having watched him for eight years.

One of his dark eyebrows raised slightly with that, but he didn't miss a beat. "Ten. I thought 'that is the most beautiful girl I've ever seen.' " He laughed then, turning in his seat so that he was staring up at the bright summer sky. " 'Course, even though I was almost fourteen, I was only a little over five feet. You were already almost that tall yourself. Told myself I'd better wait and see if you became a giant."

"Oh, stop," she laughed. "I wasn't that tall."

"Huh, but that wasn't the worst part. The next summer when I saw you again, you were already two inches taller than me. I vowed then and there to give up my fantasies about you. My macho pride couldn't risk falling for a girl who was destined to tower over me."

"But you're a good four or five inches taller than me now."

"Sure, now. But not back then. I didn't start shooting up until I was almost sixteen. By then I was avoiding you, afraid you were still growing faster than me. I don't think I saw you once for three or four summers. Not until you were sixteen."

"My parents and I went to Europe, then Asia, then Australia. A different place each summer. They talked about doing Africa and South America, but my dad had a heart scare that spring."

"Yeah, I remember my mom talking about it. Had to have one of those tests. He looked great tonight. Must be doing better."

"He's perfect, but Mom fusses at him constantly. Wants him to quit smoking and drinking."

"No go, huh?"

Ericka was laughing as she shook her head. "No. He says smoking might give him cancer, the drinking might drive him mad, and my mother's libido may well give him a heart attack. On the other hand, smoking mellows him, drinking makes him lighthearted, and my mother sates him. He said he can't think of a better way to die than being mellow, lighthearted, and sated."

"Couldn't ask for more than that. Smart man, your dad."

"The smartest."

"Hey!"

"Present company excluded," she laughed.

"So, want to get out and stare at the lake from a couple hundred feet above?"

"Sure, but I want to open my present first." She slipped the ribbon then the paper off with haste, handing the discarded wrappings to him while she lifted the lid. Reaching into the box, she breathed, "Oh, Bo . . ."

"My fraternity pin," he explained unnecessarily. "I

couldn't decide what to get you. Then I thought about you going all the way to Harvard in the fall, and I thought about the one gift that would keep the wolves at bay and keep you thinking about me. Will you wear it, Blue? Go steady with me while you're at school? I know it's asking a lot when you haven't even had much chance to date, but I care about you . . . in a big way."

She studied his face, fighting the lump in her throat. God, he was handsome. Even more than he'd been the first time she'd seen him two years after moving to St. Joan. She'd watched him every chance she got, often sneaking over to the hotel resort with the faint hope of getting a glimpse of him on the tennis court or running room service for his dad. She'd thought him the most perfect-looking person she'd ever seen. Now he was a man. His lean body had filled out, muscles creating bulges where they hadn't been before. His face which had been softer and rounder had narrowed, his cheekbones becoming angular, his jawline firmer and more sharp edged. His aquiline nose which had once appeared just a touch too long for his face was now in perfect proportion to his full lips. Only his pitch-black hair and deep-set, long-lashed eyes had remained unchanged by maturity and time. And he was asking her to go with him, to promise not to see anyone else while she wore his pin. It was all she could do not to kick her feet and scream her delight. All these years, she'd kept her crush a secret, not even telling Carrie or her parents. Now she wanted to jump from the car and scream it for the whole lake area to hear.

"Uh oh," he said when she didn't answer. Without giving her a chance to say the words that would crush the hopes he'd been building for the past six weeks, he opened his car door and stepped out.

Ericka climbed out of her side quickly after him.

He turned at the sound of the opening car door, forcing himself to listen to her explanation, but rather than walk toward him where he stood by the hood of his car, she walked to the edge of the hillside. "Blue, it's okay, you don't have——"

"Hey, down there!" she yelled, her hands cupped around her mouth. *"You listening, St. Joan? I'm going steady with the hottest guy in the United States!"*

He captured her from behind, lifting her off her feet and carrying her away from the edge. He set her down at the base of a giant oak, turning her with his hands at her waist so that she faced him, then pinned her with his hands on either side of her shoulders as he kissed her long and hard. "You're crazy," he said a few seconds later, his voice a husky whisper. "And you're mine."

"Put this on me," Ericka said in a breathless voice as she held up his frat pin. "Then kiss me again like that."

This time, he circled her with his arms, pressing the length of himself against her. His tongue brushed the tips of her teeth for several teasing seconds before entering her mouth and meeting hers. She wore a loose-fitting half shirt and with her arms raised around his neck, his hands touched the flesh of her middle, but after only a few minutes of control, his fingers began to move up her back, then around the front, and finally to the bottom of her bra. He groaned a query: Could he touch her there? Her answer was to tighten her grip around his neck, and then his fingers were working their way beneath the elastic, touching the soft flesh of her full breasts. "Oh, Blue, you're soft," he groaned into her mouth. The he pushed her bra up over her breasts and captured them fully with his hands, his palms kneading her swollen nipples as he sucked on her tongue and nipped her lips.

Ericka felt as though she'd been shocked with a cattle prod. Only surely that pain wasn't delicious like this was. She moaned as he caught one of her nipples between his thumb and forefinger, and realized that she was moving her hips against his. A few seconds later, she felt his hand pressed between them against the crotch of her jeans and for just an instant she froze.

"Oh, don't stop now, Blue. You feel too good. Keep moving. Move like you were before against my hand. Oh, God, Blue, don't stop now."

But she did stop. She pushed him away. "I can't," she whispered before slipping past him and running the short distance to the car where she leaned against the hood, half hoping he would stay by the tree until she could regain her composure, half hoping he would come to her, hold her while he told her it was all right; that he understood.

He did neither. Instead he walked to the mountain ledge where she'd gone only ten minutes before. He was still breathing hard, unable to speak, so he bent over, placing his hands on his thighs as he drew in great gulps of steadying air. Once he'd regained his equilibrium, he straightened to cup his mouth with one of his hands. *"Hey, St. Joan, Blue Cassidy is my woman! Eat your heart out!"*

Chapter Three

Ericka leaned against the door after Bo dropped her off from their date. She listened to the sound of his car disappearing in the night toward the resort hotel where he lived with his parents. A slow smile spread across her face as her hand touched the small pin on her blouse. She was going steady! She was going steady with Keen Bohannon, the handsomest man she'd ever seen!

As she went upstairs to her bedroom, she glanced toward the third floor where her parents had converted the attic into a spacious bedroom suite. Light spilled down the stairs toward her, so she called out a greeting. "I'm home!"

"Come up, darling," her mother invited.

She sighed. She loved her parents ... inordinately, judging by the way most of their friends complained about their parents. She had no complaints, no reason to ever groan about restrictions or punishments. The trio of father, mother, and daughter shared a unique relationship in that arguments almost never occurred, voices were almost never raised, and openness was encouraged. But for now, she wanted to hold the memories of her special night inside, to herself, just for a while.

Dutifully, she went upstairs, leaning against the door jamb as she greeted her parents who were lying in bed, both reading, both peering at her over the tops of their glasses.

"I think it must have been a successful date," Lawrence said to his wife.

As he'd known she would, Ericka smiled. "Very successful."

"So the young man is not just another pretty face?" Linda asked.

"No," Ericka agreed.

"But you don't want to talk about it yet," her mother said.

Ericka sighed again. The last thing she wanted to do was hurt her parents' feelings. "It's just that this is so new to me, so different. I kind of want to savor it."

Linda and Lawrence exchanged smiles. "We know how that feels don't we, darling?" Lawrence asked his wife. "We still have moments even after twenty years that we enjoy savoring."

Ericka smiled as she crossed the room to go first to the left side of the bed to hug her father, then to the other side for an embrace with her mother. "You two are so neat. I bet any other parent in the world would have insisted on hearing every detail."

Lawrence frowned with exaggerated seriousness. "Ah, then perhaps if *every* other parent in the *world* would insist, we're not doing this parent thing right after all. What do you think, Lin?"

"I think we should change the subject," his wife said, at the same time, reaching beneath the covers to rub her hand along her husband's thigh. Then back to Ericka, "Did you see any of your other friends?"

Relieved, Ericka plopped down at the foot of their king-sized bed, folding one of her long legs beneath her. "Everyone. They all got home from their various schools either yesterday or today. Even Brett Pearson, who wasn't supposed to be in until tomorrow." She hadn't realized she'd frowned with the last statement until her mother asked what was wrong. "Oh, nothing. Really. Just Carrie. We kind of had an argument."

"You and Carrie? I can hardly believe that," Linda Cassidy said.

"About the book again, I suppose," Lawrence said.

"Yeah, kind of. No big deal. She just listens too much to what her mother says, and everyone knows Marylou Roberts is a champion gossip."

"Well, the book is finished. Mailed off this afternoon as a matter of fact. The talk and speculation will die down in a few weeks, and if it doesn't, we'll deliver a copy of the bound galleys to Marylou to disprove her theory that we set out to embarrass her."

"I'm not worried about any of that," Ericka said with a dismissing shrug. "It's more the way Carrie's changed lately that's been bothering me . . . that and all the talk about the murders whenever any of us get together."

Ericka noticed another quick exchange between her parents, but this time there was no accompanying smile. Instead, she thought the glance had held a measure of fear. But that was silly. She let it go as she stood up.

"Anyway, once Bo and I left the strip, the date was perfect." She pointed to the pin on her shirt. "We're going steady."

"So I noticed," Linda said. "But since you didn't want to talk about it, I decided not to say anything."

"Tomorrow. I'll tell you everything then. Right now I want to go to sleep and dream about him."

"Ah, young love," Linda said, not mocking but serious.

"But, my darling, don't you still dream about me?" Lawrence asked, his tone decidedly teasing.

"Of course, but not about tender looks and discovery. Mine are definitely lascivious."

"Oh, you two," Ericka said, rolling her eyes, and scooting from the bed. "Night. I love you both." At the door, she glanced over her shoulder. "Could you keep it down tonight? I intend to make my own dreams without interference from the two of you."

Her parents laughed though they made no promises Ericka noticed as she went back to her own room.

As she readied herself for bed, memories of her date mingled with fresher images of her parents. She recalled the rich deep timbre of Bo's voice, the feel of his hands on her skin, then thought about her parents above her in their bed. Her mother still so young and fit, looking almost like a teenager herself in her sheer pink nightgown, her brown hair piled on top of her head with a matching pink ribbon tied around it, her blue eyes still sparkling with love for the man she'd married two decades before.

Her father slept nude, always had, and though his body bore more signs of the ravages of time, he, too, was still amazingly fit. Perhaps it was love that kept them so young and vital. As she pulled her shirt over her head, laying it on the bed to unclasp the pin, she wondered if she and Bo would be together as long as her parents, and if they would be as content, as compatible? But, she thought, as she wiggled from her jeans and panties, that was silly. They'd just met, were still in the discovery stage that her mother had mentioned. They were a long way from love.

Well, maybe not that far away.

Fifteen minutes later, she crawled beneath the covers and as always turned onto her stomach. A few seconds later, she flopped onto her back instead. She'd read once that people dreamed more on their backs than in any other position, and tonight she looked forward to the happy memories that she would relive through her dreams. Besides, this way, she could drift off to sleep with her hand on the pin she'd hooked to her night shirt.

But she didn't dream, at least not of Bo. She didn't dream at all until daybreak when the sound of sirens in the distance conjured a nightmare so vivid, she awakened screaming. She sat up in bed with a start, memories of the horribly visual dream making her shake. She hugged her knees, and in the distance she heard more sirens on the highway. Must have been a terrible accident.

Scampering from the bed, she ran to the window to look out, but the morning was foggy and she couldn't make out the highway as she could on most days.

She went into the bathroom to splash cold water on her face. She wondered why her screams hadn't brought either of her parents running to comfort her as they had when she was a young child troubled by frequent nightmares. But a glance into her room at the clock on her night stand answered the query for her. Five-fifty. Her mother was already running, and her father was taking his morning walk.

Ericka was tired. She'd only slept five hours. Well, maybe she'd adopt her parents' routine by taking an early afternoon nap. For now she was too charged up to even try to go back to sleep.

She thought about the dream and shuddered. Forcing her thoughts away, she conjured Bo's image in her mind. A smile came easily into place. He was picking her up at five o'clock for the Memorial Day barbecue at the country club. She'd looked forward to the event all month, but now she wasn't so sure. Carrie would be there as well as her parents, and Brett, and his folks. All the people who'd been gossiping about her mom and dad. Well, at least, there wouldn't be any such talk tonight. Not with her parents there, too.

She dressed in shorts and an oversized T-shirt, then knotted her thick hair on top of her head, securing it in place as she skipped down the stairs.

She had coffee brewing by the time her parents returned thirty minutes later.

At the sight of their daughter standing in the kitchen, both Linda and Lawrence froze in the entranceway.

"My God, all that running to keep my heart strong, and you almost give me a heart attack the second I come home," Linda said.

"You? You're still young, darling. My poor ticker is too old for shocks of this magnitude."

"Ha ha ha," Ericka said. "You're both just too funny."

"Well, you have to admit, this is a first. I can't remember a Saturday when you've ever been up before ten," her mother said.

"Oh, but I can," Lawrence said. "Remember, Lin, when you were trying to study for your finals? Seems to me a certain young lady not only was awake every morning before daybreak, she didn't sleep all night."

"Oh, yes, how could I have forgotten," Linda said with a giggle and a hug for her husband. "Well, I guess every seventeen or eighteen years isn't bad." She wagged a finger in her daughter's face. "But don't make a habit of it, sweetheart. Your father and I are very mired in this rut and quite comfortable with the status quo. We don't handle new adjustments well."

"You two are just a laugh a minute."

"Ah, at least she's still grumpy in the early morning. I was afraid she might actually be cheery," Lawrence said. Then swatting his wife's bottom, he told her, "You go on up and get your shower. I'll heat the bagels."

A few minutes later, Lawrence joined his daughter at the kitchen table. "Why are you up so early, Rikki? Not because of your young man, I suppose?"

"No. I had a nightmare. I think it was the sound of all the sirens that brought it on. Anyway, once I woke up I didn't want to go back to sleep. It was awful." She shuddered as if for emphasis.

"Want to tell me about it?"

"I don't remember all of it. Just one of those crazy

dreams that doesn't make much sense. All my friends and I were standing on the edge of the road and someone was hitting Cindy Richvalski with a baseball bat. Some of the kids were cheering. Saying things like 'hit her harder.' I was sobbing. Then the sirens started and she was dead. We were all just standing around her while the police and ambulance came. Scooter arrived and he asked everyone who did it, and everyone pointed to someone else and said 'she did,' or 'he did.' " Ericka shrugged. "I told you it was silly, but it scared me."

"I suppose you dreamed about her death because of your friends talking about it last night. I know it was terrible for you, but remember that dreams, even nightmares, are often cathartic. Now that you've dreamed about it, you can probably stop worrying. Murder is always terrifying, but particularly when it happens to someone we know. I suppose your mother and I should have talked to you about all the murders, instead of trying to ignore them."

"No. I don't really like to think about them. Death frightens me."

"Death shouldn't frighten you, Rikki. It's merely the final phase of life. It's the one inevitability we must all face. I know it isn't pleasant to contemplate, but it's rumored to be quite something, though, of course, none of us wishes to put in for a rush order."

Ericka stood up and circled the table to hug her father's neck and kiss the top of his head. "I love you, Daddy. You always make me feel better."

"What about me?" Linda asked as she came into the room.

Ericka looked over her shoulder at her mother. Clad now in cutoff jeans and a halter top, Linda Cassidy looked like a woman half her age. Her legs, which were almost as long and slender as Ericka's, gleamed golden under the sky lights. "Unh uh. You, I'm jealous of. You look too darned good for someone your age. Besides, you have that same perfect coloring that Carrie has. Even without a tan, you look great. Me, I had the misfortune of inheriting Daddy's pale skin."

Linda busied herself getting jam and butter and cream cheese from the refrigerator, talking as she went. "You'll be glad for your fair skin when you're my age. It wears better."

Ericka laughed. "God, then I ought to still look eighteen, because you still look twenty-five."

"I do think you're a mite prejudiced, darling girl, but thank you."

"I'm serious, and it's not just me. Everyone thinks you're a real babe. Bo even said last night that if you weren't married he wouldn't have known which one of us he wanted to date the most. And the women in the subdivision are so jealous they can't stand themselves."

Linda put the warmed bagels on a plate then carried them to the table. "I'm flattered, Ericka, really, but I don't want people to be jealous of me for the way I look. Not that I'm not glad I'm still in good shape. I work hard at it, but only because I adore your father and want him to always be as hot for me as he was the day we married. From everyone else, I want to be admired. Remember you can get all the attention you want by being beautiful, but you won't keep it unless you've got something more than beauty."

"Really?"

That came from Lawrence who was rewarded with a bagel tossed very accurately toward his head. Ericka was still laughing when her mother turned on the radio to catch the six o'clock news. God, she loved her parents. If every parent was like hers, there wouldn't be—

"The body of Dr. Jason Grant was found early this morning at his home on the Circle G Ranch by his son who had agreed to meet his father at five a.m. to go fishing. Police have not commented on the cause of death, but Aaron Grant spoke to a reporter just minutes ago. He said that his father was the apparent victim

of a shooting by a person or persons who had broken into the house. He speculated that it was a burglar who had been surprised by Dr. Grant. We will bring you more details as they are forthcoming.

"In other news—"

"Oh, Lord, Lawrence. Jason's dead." Linda clasped a hand over her mouth as her eyes filled with tears. "You don't think—"

Lawrence was out of his chair and standing behind his wife before she could complete the question. His hands gripping her shoulders, he bent low to talk into her ear, his voice soft and calming. "I don't think anything yet, Lin. We don't know more than what we just heard."

"But what if . . . ?"

But what if what? Ericka wanted to know. "What's going on?" she asked, directing her question to both parents.

"Nothing, Rikki. Nothing's going on. We've just had a terrible shock. That's all."

Ericka was hurt. It was obvious her parents were keeping something from her, and that was a first as far as she knew. "You've never lied to me before," she said, her tone reflecting her disappointment.

"Oh, darling, we aren't lying to you," her mother said, seemingly somewhat recovered.

"Then tell me what you meant," Ericka demanded, feeling tears needle her eyelids and panic well within her. Aaron Grant's dad was dead! Murdered in his own home! Aaron had found him! How terrible! How sickening!

"Calm down, Rikki," her father said in a gruffer tone than usual. Giving his wife's shoulders one last squeeze, he reclaimed his seat. "Your mother is worried that there may be some connection between Jason's . . ." his voice broke, but he cleared his throat, fighting for composure, then began again. "Your mother is afraid that

Jason's death might be somehow connected to the three murders last month."

"But they said it was a burglary."

"And that's probably all there is to it."

Ericka shook her head at her father's simplistic explanation. "But you don't think so. Why? *Why?* Answer me! You're scaring me to death."

It was Linda who answered her daughter's panic this time, apparently having conquered her own. "Your father's absolutely right, Ericka. It was probably a hysterical reaction on my part."

Ericka slammed her hand on the table. "Damn it! Quit treating me like a child. Why did you even think there was a connection?" As she waited for an answer, she witnessed the same enigmatic exchange between her parents as the night before when the subject of the murders had been brought up. "Please, just tell me."

Lawrence shook his head. "There isn't that much to tell. As you know, Jason and your mother spent a great deal of time together during the research of the book we just completed. It was centered around the life of a small town doctor, after all, and Dr. Grant was very helpful. But during their times together, Jason mentioned the murders very much the same way as your friends have been doing. Speculation. Little more than that really, though he did share some concerns with your mother that she in turn passed on to me."

"Like what."

"Nothing that we're going to discuss, Rikki," Lawrence said, his voice no longer gentle and patient, but stern and august, very much the professor of the past. "He ran some theories past Linda that may or may not have held merit as to the identity of the killer, but after we discussed it, I spoke with Jason and he agreed that we had very little to go on. He had promised to talk it all over with Scooter. I don't know if he did or not. But, Rikki, it's important that you not discuss this. Lives could be ruined by conjecture that is based largely on coincidence."

"Your father's right, Ericka."

"I won't say anything," Ericka huffed indignantly. "I'm not a child and I'm not stupid."

"Of course you're not. We weren't inferring any such thing. It's just that Jason's theories made sense on one hand, but on the other, he could very well have been totally off the wall on this."

"I *know*. Jeez, you two act like I haven't got a lick of sense."

"We don't act that way at all, but if you want us to believe you're a mature adult, don't overreact to our counsel. We're your parents and we have a right to worry about you."

Ericka's blue eyes widened. "Then you do think there's something to Dr. Grant's theory."

"We think there's a possibility, but again, we could be wrong. Either way it's important that no one know that Jason spoke with me about this. Either way it could prove disastrous."

"I won't say anything to anyone. It's bad enough that Carrie's mom has been talking about your frequent visits to his house, Mom. I certainly don't want to fuel her fire."

"Ah," Lawrence said, "so that's what got you so mad at Carrie last night."

"I'm not mad anymore, but she is beginning to sound more and more like her mother. Jeez, can you imagine how bad she'll be after she marries Brett. Just think of all the gossip she'll be privy to as the wife of the reverend of the largest congregation in St. Joan."

"Now that's a thought to make one shudder," Lawrence agreed with a deep rumbling laugh.

But the moment of levity was quickly gone, replaced at once with memory of the announcement of Jason Grant's death. "Poor Aaron," Ericka said softly.

"Poor Rhonda. Even though they were divorced, Jason said they'd had dinner a couple of times recently. He said Rhonda was pushing for a reconciliation."

Ericka shrugged away her mother's comment. "I don't know." Then with a wry grin. "I think I would have heard if that were true from Carrie. Mrs. Roberts is pretty good friends with Rhonda Grant."

"Ericka!" her mother said, clapping a hand over her mouth to stifle her laughter. "That's terrible."

"No it's not. It's true."

"She's right, Lin," Lawrence said with a soft chuckle as he pushed his chair back. "Well, I suppose I should call Rhonda and Aaron. Ask if there's anything we can do."

Linda put a hand on her husband's arm. "Wait a bit, darling. Let them have some time together. It's only six-thirty. I think eight o'clock will be early enough."

Ericka stood up. "Well, I'm going to go shower. Then I think I'll lie back down for awhile." She paused at the kitchen door. "Wake me up if Bo calls. I don't guess they'll be having the barbecue now."

"Oh, I imagine it will still go on," Lawrence said. "If for no other reason than to give everyone a chance to discuss all the gory details."

This time none of them laughed. Gossip in St. Joan could be fun or ugly.

Chapter Four

"Gawddamnit!" Scooter Witcomb said, tossing his hat down onto his desk. "Gawddamnit! What's happening to our town?"

It was a rhetorical question if for no other reason than he was alone in his office. He'd just returned from the murder scene of Dr. Jason Grant. The fourth such scene in the past seven weeks. He didn't like it one little bit. Not just the murders. It was more than that. It was all the gawddamned blood. Scooter hated blood. Always had. Made him queasy; sick to the bottom of his stomach. 'Course this one hadn't been as bad as the others. Lawd, but those had been awful. He still gagged when he thought about them. Two with their heads cut almost off; and the other one, why, she hadn't even looked human after her assailant was done bashing her head in with a baseball bat.

But the other part, the worst part really once his stomach stopped its roller coaster ride at the sight of the blood, was talking to the family members. Especially when the victim was a friend. And Jason Grant had been a friend to the whole town. Oh, not at first. At first he'd just been another gawddamned Yankee. But old Jason—young Jason then—had worked hard to earn the respect and friendship of his neighbors. He'd won the battle, too. Ignored all the naysayers, their skepticism and wagging tongues. He was a good doctor and an even better friend.

Scooter wiped a tear from the corner of his eye as he lowered his tubby butt into his chair which creaked with protest. He rubbed briskly at his face and a low growl of grief died against the buffer of beefy palms. "Gawd-damn it," he muttered once again before straightening at the sound of the knock on his office door. "Come in!"

Waylin Parks, his chief deputy for more than fifteen years, stuck his head around the corner of the door, proffering a manila file folder. "Here ya go, Sheriff," he said. "Doc Ohtau said he'd get over here this evening or tomorrow mornin' at the latest to perform the autopsy."

"Yeah, well, that'll be good enough. Ain't like we don't know what killed him."

"Yeah, guess that's right," Parks said, dropping the folder that was still empty except for the label that had been applied to the tab with Dr. Jason Grant's name typed on it. "Well, I'll leave you to write your report. I'll have my own typed up in an hour or two. Thought I'd grab some lunch. Want me to bring you anything?"

"Nope, just tell Martha not to put any calls through 'til I tell her otherwise. Wanna get on this while the details are still fresh in my mind."

"Yeah, okay." Waylin opened the door, then changing his mind, closed it again softly. "You got any thoughts about this, Sheriff? I mean, you think it really was a burglar?"

"I got some thoughts."

Waylin waited but when his boss didn't elaborate, he merely shrugged and left the office.

Scooter scratched the base of his head, then reached for a pencil, but a stack of thick folders on the lefthand corner of his desk caught his attention. With a ragged sigh and another curse, he tossed the pencil across the room, experiencing a faint twinge of satisfaction as it hit the wall, the sharp point snapping off with a loud click. Seven unsolved murders in the past year. Thank God the public wasn't aware that there had been that many, knew only about four . . . five now with Jason's death.

He pulled the stack of folders toward him, letting his hands glide over the dusty surface of the one on top. Then with another loud sigh, he picked them up, one at a time. Why he did this, he didn't know. Perhaps, he thought as he had at least a dozen times before in the past month, he might hit on something, an idea or a clue that would provide an answer. If he could just solve one of them . . .

Katy Bryant. Nine years old. Body discovered in the lake June 14, 1984. Drowning victim. At least that's what they'd thought until Dr. Grant performed the autopsy and discovered that she'd strangled on her own panties. Found a couple fibers lodged in the little girl's throat. Pretty good sleuthing that. Raped, too, and sodomized. 'Course the family had been notified as well as investigated. Just lucky that they were from Virginia. Only in St. Joan for a month's vacation. They'd left right after the child's body was found, so the first, unofficial verdict that had been given to the press wasn't changed. No sense spooking the residents. Even Jase had agreed that it wouldn't do any good. The perp was probably a transient who was long gone by the time the corpse was found after floating for three days.

Jimmy Baer. Six years old. Found in a shallow grave some sixty miles outside of town in the hills by some campers July 3, 1984. Not his jurisdiction so officially not considered a St. Joan casualty, though old Jase had performed the autopsy and the sheriff from over Black Mountain, Missouri, had xeroxed the entire file for Scooter in case he ran across anything that sparked an idea. The kid had been sodomized just like the Bryant girl. Tortured, too. Could have been the same perp. Who knew?

Scooter's hand shook when he came to the next file. This had been the toughest. Not only because of the violence—victim's throat had been cut so severely it had almost been severed completely. The sheriff shuddered. All that blood. He'd never forget it as long as he lived.

Bunny Apperson. Twenty-six years old. Body found by landlady in her apartment April 4, 1985.

Scooter could barely stand to remember this one. He'd known Bunny . . . intimately. That was the thing that was causing his hell.

Arvis Ray Witcomb, Scooter to his friends and neighbors, had been married since he was seventeen years old, almost half his life. He was only thirty-nine years old.

Son of one of the biggest cattle ranchers in Missouri, he'd been headed for college, going on a football scholarship. He had plans for a big future until homecoming night when he had coaxed pretty little Althea Macomber into the back seat of his dad's Cadillac Seville. They'd been married in the St. Joan First Baptist Church nine weeks later, and Allan Ray had been born six months and one week after that.

Althea had been a good wife and an even better mother. She doted on both her men as she called him and young Allan. Hell, she'd even wanted to name the kid Arvis Ray Witcomb Jr. Scooter had put his foot down to that. He wouldn't have stuck a dog with a moniker like that. He smiled now with the memory. It hadn't mattered. They'd named him Allan instead, but everyone including Althea still called him Junior.

He'd never regretted the detour his life had taken, not even having to sacrifice his dreams of pro ball. He'd finished high school while working two part-time jobs to support his new family, refusing help from his old man because the strings that were attached to financial help were just too gawddamned tight. He'd never wanted to farm cattle. Instead, as soon as he graduated high school, he'd applied for the position of deputy in the sheriff's office. He'd had no regrets about any of it excepting his relationship with Bunny Apperson. Not that he'd planned it. It had been an accident pure and simple. She'd just walked into his office one day and the next thing he knew . . .

"Hi, sugar, you the big man around here?"

Scooter looked up from his desk, annoyed by the interruption and wondering vaguely how in Sam Hill this young woman had gotten past Martha in the front office. "Excuse me, ma'am, but what are you doing in here?"

She smiled, not flirty like, just a friendly open grin and said, "Why, I'm looking for the man who's in charge." She slung her purse over her shoulder just missing his face by inches as she pointed toward his door. "The sign says that's you. No one was outside there in the other office to tell me different, so here I am."

In spite of his initial irritation, Scooter smiled. She was pretty—brassy and saucy looking with her hair dyed that kinda way that only came out of a bottle, and her clothes hugging her curves the way they did, but pretty nonetheless. Might have been her eyes that he liked. They were round and big as nickels and sparkling like new copper pennies. "What's your name, honey?"

"Name's Bunny. Bunny Apperson."

"Okay, Bunny, what can I do for you?" he asked.

"What you can do is find the asshole who stole my car."

Scooter stood up at this point, circling his desk and resting his hip on the corner as he answered. "When was it stolen?"

"Not ten minutes ago and not two hundred yards from your office. I'll tell you what, if that don't scare a person having their property swiped right under the law's nose, nothing will."

"Where exactly were you parked?" Scooter asked, though he should have escorted her back out to the front office and asked Martha to take the report. The fact was he enjoyed talking to Miss Bunny Apperson (he assumed she was a "miss" rather than a "missus" because she wasn't wearing a wedding ring).

"I just told you. Just down the street. On the far side of the court house."

Scooter grinned. "You from around here, Bunny? I don't remember seeing you before."

"Just moved to St. Joan about a month ago," she said, then with a smile that was teasing. "Why? Folks around here only steal cars from strangers?"

"Nope, leastwise not in broad daylight. We're more clever than that," Scooter said, teasing back and enjoying himself. "But I'm afraid we do have a nasty habit of towing cars that are parked in No Parking zones."

"Oh, hell, you're not going to tell me you towed my car. I didn't see a sign." The grin came back into place again. "Well, maybe I did see one itsy bitsy little sign, but I was only in the courthouse for ten minutes, Surely you wouldn't have towed my car *that* fast."

"Not me personally, no, but my deputy probably did. Tell you what though, since you're new to St. Joan and not familiar with how well we enforce our laws, I'll give you a break this time. Give me a minute and I'll get on the radio and call my deputy and tell him to bring it over here to my office."

"Oh, you mean it? That's super! I've just got a job as a waitress over by the dam at the Purple Hooter—you know it?—and anyway, I don't know how I would have paid to get it out." Without waiting for him to comment, she reached up on tippy toes and kissed his cheek. "Make you a deal though, you ever come in for a drink, I'll give it to you free."

"You've got it," Scooter laughed.

He hadn't intended on ever collecting on the drink. He wasn't a heavy drinker, and the two or three beers he did drink in a week he enjoyed at home or at the cafe with some of the boys around town. But the next night he found himself walking into the Purple Hooter.

Bunny seemed real glad to see him, and true to her word the drinks had been on the house. He'd drank two beers before slipping off the stool and heading for the door. Bunny rushed after him to thank him for coming by. That had touched him, the way she made it sound like he'd just stopped by her house for a cup of tea instead of a honky tonk for a brew.

Three nights later, he'd gone to the Purple Hooter again. Bunny wasn't there when he arrived. Disappointed, he'd decided to drink a beer then skedaddle on home, but before he'd emptied his glass he saw her come in the door. She'd smiled right at him, then after a few words with Red Duncan, the owner, had come over and slid onto the barstool beside him.

"Hi," she said. "How's the world's sweetest lawman?"

"Gawd, don't rightly know who that'd be," he said, scratching the back of his neck. "But I ever meet him, I'll ask."

It wasn't that funny, but she'd laughed like he'd just told the greatest joke in the world. He'd ordered another round, one for her this time, too.

He'd stayed 'til closing then walked her home when she told him she just lived up the street in the apartment building behind the strip.

She'd invited him up, but he'd refused, telling her he'd take a raincheck, and he'd discovered that he liked the way her look of disappointment made him feel. Like he was special or something. Gawddamn, he couldn't remember the last time Althea had looked at him that way.

A week later, he'd gone by her place on a Sunday.

Just one of those spur of the moment things. He hadn't planned on it. No one ever planned things like that, did they? Not when they were happily married. Besides, though the badge he wore made him a servant to everyone, there were social lines in the community of St. Joan that neither side crossed except in official capacities like law enforcement. And even though he hadn't spoken to his father in more than fifteen years, he was still a Witcomb.

But here he was ringing Bunny Apperson's doorbell on a Sunday afternoon when he was off duty and should have been home with his wife and kid.

She looked embarrassed when she opened the door, but she seemed pleased as well. The embarrassment was quickly explained by the mess inside. "Sorry," she said with a slight shrug. "Wasn't expecting company." She gathered up discarded clothing and newspapers, food wrappers and some glasses and managed to carry it all in one load. She was back a few seconds later, wiping her hands on her jeans. "Guess I'm not much of a housekeeper. But have a seat."

"Hey, it's my fault for just dropping in like this. Shoulda let you know or something."

"Oh, that's all right. I love it here, but I haven't made too many friends. Gets sort of lonely sometimes, you know?"

"Yeah, I can imagine. Me, I've been here since I was born. Where you from anyway?"

She put her hand on his knee for a second, then surprised him by stepping over him to sit down between his legs on the coffee table. "Now don't laugh," she said. "Promise."

"Swear to Gawd," he said.

"Okay. I'm from a little town in Arkansas called Hog Holler Gully. There's only six hundred people in the whole town. I left there when I was nineteen. Moved to Little Rock. Damn! I couldn't believe there were so many people in one place!" She wrinkled her nose as she laughed at herself and the next thing Scooter knew, he was leaning forward and kissing the freckle on the end of it.

"You're sweet," she said. "Most men would have laughed at that. I mean, it's not like I went to New York or something. Anyway, I saw an advertisement for St. Joan, Missouri, called it 'a little bit of paradise.' I said to myself, 'Bunny Apperson, that's the place for you.' So here I am." She glanced around them at the dingy walls of her apartment. "Doesn't hardly look like paradise, does it?"

"You ever been out on the lake?" he asked impetuously.

She shook her head.

"Well, that's why you haven't found paradise yet. It's out there." He grabbed her hands, pulling her to her feet as he stood. "Come on. I'll take you out."

"You've got a boat?" she asked.

"Yep, and she's a beaut!"

They'd gone swimming in a cove. Skinny dipping actually, and somehow Scooter had ended up making love to her in the water. It was the sweetest experience of his life, but Lawd, the guilt had been something fierce.

He'd stayed away from Bunny for several weeks after that, avoiding the damn area entirely. But then one night there he was at her door again.

He'd seen the hurt in her eyes when she opened the door, saw who was standing there, but she hadn't railed at him like Althea did. Just taken him by the hand with a soft smile that held just a hint of reproach and led him inside. This time they'd made love in her bed.

Bunny was a woman who expressed her satisfaction without inhibition, and Scooter had felt about ten feet tall when he'd walked out the door two hours later.

He'd returned the next night and the night after that, always thirty minutes after she got off work at the

Hooter. He didn't know why he'd fallen into the relationship with the young barmaid. Hell, he loved his wife. But Bunny made him feel like a man. Besides, she didn't question him . . . about anything. Not about his wife or his work or his past. She didn't ask where he was when he wasn't with her. When he stayed away for two or three days, there were no questions. With Althea there were questions about *everything*. Shitfire, the woman even grilled Martha and Waylin about him.

He and Bunny went on that way for almost a year. As far as he was concerned they could have gone on that way forever, but then he supposed that wasn't fair to Bunny. She was only twenty-five years old. And him, why he was married with a kid, at least forty pounds overweight, and well on his way toward middle age. Still it hurt when Bunny told him that maybe they shouldn't see each other anymore.

"I've made some friends, Scooter," she said. "My life's changing. You'll always be my first friend here in St. Joan, but I think you should go back to your wife and forget what we had going. It's a nowhere street for both of us."

He was standing at the door. She hadn't even let him come inside for her farewell speech. And she was whispering and glancing nervously over her shoulder. Gawd, but he felt like a fool when he realized she had someone else there, someone she didn't want to find out about him. "Yeah, sure, Bun. See ya," he said. He smiled, winked even and told her he was going to miss her, but he cried all the way home.

He stayed away like she asked, but he didn't stop thinking about her. He was miserable during Christmas. He'd bought Bunny a present back in October. He lost count of the times he took it out of his desk drawer and looked at it, wishing he'd had the chance to give it to her. Then in February he decided to do just that.

It was a Saturday night. He'd gone by the office to

pick up a file that he wanted to review over the week-end. It was a case he was scheduled to testify on in Jefferson City on Monday. He'd seen the box and thought, what the heck? Why not just drive over to the dam on patrol then stop by the Hooter and give her the present?

But Bunny wasn't at work. He asked one of the other girls about her and one of them told him she'd quit. "Got some big paying job, she told us. Don't know doing what. But says it won't be long 'til she'll have enough money to move down the lake to the high rent district."

Scooter had been surprised by the news. Bunny had no education. Couldn't even type or work a calculator, she'd told him once when he asked why she didn't get a job in an office instead of working in a bar. What kind of job had she landed that promised the kind of money she was bragging about?

He went by her apartment intending to ask her exactly that.

He could hear the music blasting from the street as he parked his car and felt the sense of loss again as he realized she had indeed made friends, enough to support a loud party. He almost changed his mind about giving her the present, but what the heck? He wanted to see her. He'd just give it to her, make sure she was okay, then leave.

He heard her laugh even before she opened the door, and he saw the surprise and dismay in her eyes when she discovered who was there. "Got a minute?" he asked.

She glanced over her shoulder, hesitating, but then with a shrug, she'd started to close the door but not before Scooter had made out the face of Cindy Richvalski and heard her say, "Turn down the music. It's the law."

"Didn't know you and Cindy were friends," he said once Bunny had stepped out into the hall with him.

"We're not. We just work together."

"Yeah, I heard you changed jobs. What you doing now?"

"Not tonight, huh, Scooter? I've got company."

"Oh, yeah, sure. Well, I won't keep you. Just wanted to give you this." He held out the small box. "It's not much. Just a little something I picked up for you at Christmas. Started not to give it to you, but then I figured what the heck? I bought it for you. You might as well have it."

She didn't look at him for a long moment. Just stood staring at the box. Then with a small, quivering smile, she'd opened it, handing him the green and red paper and ribbon as she opened the lid. There were tears in her eyes when she slipped the ring onto her finger, and Scooter felt a knot form in his own throat.

"Hey," he said gruffly, "don't cry. It's not that big of a deal. Just something I saw that reminded me of you. They call it Dakota gold."

"It's beautiful," she said, then dashing away a tear, she asked, "why did it remind you of me?"

He was uncomfortable with the music blasting away behind her in her apartment. It wasn't the right time to be telling her the way he felt about her, but there might not be another time. Shifting his weight, he said, "I don't know. I always thought of you as two sided. Smart and gutsy, yet kind of naive and innocent on the other side. The ring's like that. Different colors but all gold just the same. You're pure gold in my book, too, Bun."

She started crying then. Put her arms around his neck and pressed her face against his shirt. He started to say something then, tell her it was all right, that he'd come back the next day when they could talk, but car lights flashed on them as someone pulled into the parking lot, and Bunny pulled away with a jerk, quickly swiping at her eyes, and looking around with a scared animal look on her face. "You'd better go, Scooter." She kissed him on the cheek then turned away without another word.

"Can I come by some other time to talk to you? Maybe hear about your new job?"

"No! Go away, Scooter! Stay away! I've got new friends now."

Before he could say another word, she slipped back inside her apartment. He stood there feeling like someone had just sucker punched him, and he heard someone inside ask if the sheriff was going to shut down the party. Then Bunny's voice, laughing. "No, he just asked us to keep it down. No big deal."

As Scooter turned away and started down the stairs, he almost ran into the man coming up. He knew him. Lonny Roper. He owned the pawn shop on the strip.

"Got a problem, Sheriff?" Lonny asked.

"No," Scooter said. "No problem. Just asked the lady to keep the noise down. Neighbors complaining."

"I'll make sure she does it, Sheriff. Thanks for stopping by."

"Yeah, you all take care."

"Oh, you can bet on it, Sheriff. I'm the most careful person around."

Scooter shook his head now as he read the names again on the last two file folders. Cindy Richvalski and Lonny Roper. What in the hell had they had in common with Bunny that had cost them all their lives?

If only he'd gone back to talk to Bunny one more time. Found out what she was doing, who she was hanging out with besides the other two murder victims. Well, no use beating that horse. It was long dead.

With a ragged sigh, he opened his bottom drawer and extracted a report form. He had to get busy filling out the report on Jason's murder. He took another pencil from his top drawer but sat thumping it on the desk top as he recalled Deputy Parks's question earlier. Did he think it was really only a simple burglary gone bad?

Chewing on his bottom lip, he remembered the message Althea had given him when he'd returned home the night before from a three-day fishing trip.

"Jason called, A.R. He said he needed to talk to you," Althea said as he stripped off his dirty waders and boots in the basement of their home.

"Yeah? When'd he call?"

"Yesterday. Seemed real disappointed that you were down at Branson." She laughed. "Said to tell you it doesn't help the tourist trade for you to go off fishing in lakes other than our own, but before he hung up he said to tell you to call a.s.a.p."

"Wonder what's so important?" Scooter said, looking at his watch. "Guess I'll try him in the morning. It's too late tonight."

"I don't know, A.R. Maybe you should call him now. He said he'd been talking to someone, and he thought he might have an idea about those murders in April." Althea huffed indignantly. "Told me not to mention this to anyone else. Acts like I don't have a lick of sense. As if I'd discuss police business with my friends."

Scooter ignored her pique. "Gawddamn, Althea, this could be the break we've been looking for. He say anything else?"

"No, not a word. Guess he thought I couldn't be trusted."

Scooter sighed. His wife was a sweet woman, yet a touch sensitive. He gathered her into his arms, kissing the top of her head. "Now, sweetheart, I'm sure Jason didn't mean anything like that at all. He's a doctor. Used to keeping secrets. Patient–doctor confidentiality, and all that. Besides, since he and Rhonda divorced, he hasn't even had his wife to talk to. Now, come on. Stop looking like a kicked pup. Let's go to bed. I haven't held you in three nights."

"I don't want to do it, A.R."

Scooter sighed. So what else was new? When was the last time she had wanted to? "I can still hold you, can't I?" he asked.

"As long as . . ."

"I won't touch you, damn it!"

"Why don't you just sleep on the couch if you're going to yell at me?"

"Shitfire, why don't I just not sleep at all? Maybe I'll just go out on patrol. Drive around the rest of the night. That way we won't even be in the same house and you won't have to worry about me touching you!"

"Well, at least I won't have to worry that you're going to be with that Apperson woman," she said cruelly.

Scooter sank down onto the basement steps putting his face in his hands. "You're never going to let me forget, are you?"

"Your own son saw you, A.R. He saw you fornicating with that woman in the lake in broad daylight. How can any of us forget that?"

"Junior doesn't seem to be holding it against me. After she was killed and he came to me and told me what he'd seen last summer, I talked to him. He understands that it was a mistake. Why can't you understand that too?"

"Because it wasn't just a mistake, A.R. It wasn't a thing that just happened in the heat of the moment like when we did it as kids. You had an *affair* with her. You fell in love with her."

"I should never have told you. I thought I was being fair with you. Doing as the church recommends. Unburdening my guilt and confessing my sin. But no one told me I was going to have to pay for it for the rest of my life."

"Bullshit! You only told me because Junior caught you. You were afraid I'd find out. But remember one thing, A.R. I won't be humiliated. I won't have my friends knowing that you were sleeping with that ... that whore. You go digging into her murder, you just make sure no one learns about you."

"I've got a job to do, Althea. I can't be worried about what people find out," Scooter said, suddenly more weary than he'd been in years. "Go to bed. I'll sleep on the couch."

Althea didn't move except to fold her arms over her flat chest. "Aren't you going to call Jason?"

"No, I'll call him tomorrow. I'm suddenly too tired to think."

Why hadn't he returned Jason's call? With a long sigh, he printed the deceased name on the top of the form. "Gawddamn, Jase, I'm sorry," he said. Then, "What did you mean you'd talked to someone? Did someone confess something to you? Did someone else witness the murders? Who did you talk to, old man?"

Pinching the bridge of his nose with his forefinger and thumb, he cursed his luck, then his wife, then Bunny. Poor, dead, Bunny. Then he started the report on the murder of Dr. Jason Grant.

The doctor was apparently awakened by a person or persons who had broken into his residence between midnight and five a.m. Aaron Grant, the son of the deceased, said he had spoken to his father just before midnight. They agreed to go fishing for a couple of hours prior to Dr. Grant opening his office at nine a.m. Aaron arrived at the house at five-ten. He said the back door was open. He found his father lying on the kitchen floor, dead from two gunshot wounds to the chest. Although it appeared that nothing was missing from the house, it appears that Dr. Grant surprised the person or persons in the process of burglarizing his property.

"Gawddamnit!" Scooter cursed, throwing the pencil against the wall again. He'd taken an oath to protect the citizens of St. Joan. Instead, the only person he was protecting was himself. Five people were dead and he was worried about his reputation. He buried his head in his arm and wept as he hadn't done since the day he'd promised to marry Althea.

Chapter Five

The barbecue at the St. Joan Country Club was an annual affair. Attendance always bordered on three hundred. It was one of the few events that were centered around the family rather than merely the members. Though it was the custom for families to arrive together, then split up—children to the pools or game room, parents to the lounge for drinks or to the golf course for a round—this year families stayed together, hovering in private clusters or grouped with another family as everyone discussed the latest tragedy, the murder of Doctor Jason Grant.

As the Cassidys entered the room, they picked up pockets of conversation about the physician's death.

"Said he was shot three times."

"Oh, really? I heard only twice. But either way it makes one wonder. Why would a burglar invest so much time? I mean, why not just shoot and run? He had the element of surprise on his side."

"I'm telling you it's time Scooter cracked down on crime. God knows we allow any Tom, Dick, or Harry to come into the area. Ought to be some way to screen the tourists."

"We don't even know it was an outsider."

"Surely you don't think it could be one of us?"

"Not *us*, dear. But it could well be someone from St.

Joan. We do have more than our share of the indigent. Why, have you forgotten that just four weeks ago some guy was arrested for trespassing on Jason's property? Could even be the same fellow."

Ericka shuddered. "It's scary, isn't it?" she asked her parents.

"Yes it is," Lawrence agreed. "But we have to keep it in perspective. One burglary doesn't mean we're all in jeopardy."

"No, that's true," Linda agreed. "Jason did live by himself on all that property." She rubbed her arms briskly as she looked around. "It feels wrong today, doesn't it? I wish they'd cancelled this. No one could feel like partying."

"No, but the rationale was good. It is a Memorial Day weekend, and I think Rhonda was right when she insisted we not cancel. Jase would want us to come together as friends to remember him."

Ericka was hardly paying attention now. She'd spotted Bo with his sister and parents. When he turned her way, she smiled, wiggling her fingers slightly in greeting and felt a thrill when he winked, then after a few words to his family, started toward her.

He greeted her parents politely, then as soon as he could, pulled her away to tell her how pretty she looked. "You look prettier every time I see you, Blue."

She blushed as much over the use of her middle name which felt somehow intimate as the compliment. "Thanks," she said, smiling into his dark eyes. She nodded in his family's direction. "Petite looks real pretty, too. I like the way she's wearing her hair now."

Bo followed her gaze but shook his head. His sister was as little as he was large. Aptly named, all of her features were in miniature except her eyes which were oversized buttons that looked even bigger with the severity of her ebony hair which had been cut short to frame her tiny face. Today she was dressed in coordinated apricot and lime shorts and shirt which set off her perfect olive complexion and suited her age of sixteen. Obviously a selection made for her by her mother, for she was rarely dressed in anything but ragged jeans and tattered sweatshirt or severe black biker's shorts and tank top. Ericka smiled as she noticed the earrings. Petite's rebellion was captured in the oversized earrings which dangled from her lobes reflecting her penchant for the bizarre: a two inch skeleton hung from her left ear, while the right ear boasted a miniature coffin.

Bo shook his head. "My mom picked out the outfit. Guess you figured that out yourself. When we got here, Petite went into the ladies' room and came out wearing those things on her ears. My mother almost passed out, but she's trying to avoid a scene. The thing is with Petite there's no leverage they can use. If they ground her, she's perfectly content to stay in her room listening to those hard rock tapes with the volume turned way up. If they take the stereo away, she makes up her own lyrics and sings them at the top of her lungs until the entire hotel shakes."

Ericka laughed. "She's different, all right. But I like her. She's individualism at its best."

"Or worst," Bo said, but not with much conviction. It was evident that he was crazy about his strange little sister, and Ericka felt a burst of love for him as she saw the pride shining in his eyes.

Bo glanced around the room. "Kind of weird in here, isn't it? Feels more like a wake than a party. Think your parents would spaz out if we went for a walk?"

Ericka laughed. "My parents rarely spaz out about anything. Let me just tell them where we're going."

"I'll wait for you at the door."

He watched her as she crossed the room and felt pride stir in his chest. She was his. Wearing his pin. He'd seen that right off. And damn if she wasn't the prettiest thing he'd ever looked at. That tumble of red hair shining like a halo of fire, and those long, gorgeous legs. He saw her laugh at something her father said, then glance over her shoulder at him, laughing again. What the hell were they saying? He shrugged mentally. It didn't matter. She looked happy. The only person in the room with the courage to laugh in the face of fear and gloom. Bo glanced around them at the others. Hypocrites most of them. Especially Marylou Roberts and Phoebe Pearson. Hell, they hadn't even liked ol' Doc Grant. Talked about him like he was some sort of spy sent down by the north to infest the enemy with some deadly disease. Why, he knew for a fact that the Pearsons didn't even take their kids to Doc Grant. Went all the way to Jeff City to some fancy pediatrician. And the only reason Marylou Roberts didn't do the same was the gossip she would have missed out on if she didn't pretend ailment after ailment just to snoop. Look at them both dabbing at their eyes with their dainty lace hankies. Bo shook his head. Thank God his mother wasn't so affected.

His gaze went automatically to where his mother stood talking with Althea Witcomb, and his smile softened to tenderness. So maybe she did wear her skirts too tight and a few inches shorter than decorum dictated. And maybe her hairstyle was a bit overdone, but at least what you saw was what you got. No phony crap there. She had the biggest heart in town, big enough to excuse the faults of her neighbors even when their vicious tongues were wagging about her. "You got to feel sorry for them, Bo. If they weren't so miserable, they wouldn't have to talk bad about others." That was just the way she was. Even on Sunday when the "good" citizens of St. Joan shunned her in church, she pretended not to notice. Only true Christian in the building, he'd often thought.

Bo's gaze went to his sister, saw the familiar pout as she stood off by herself in the corner. He watched as she pulled a cigarette and lighter from her purse. Frowning, he shook his head with disgust. Damn it, Petite. Why couldn't his sister understand that she was the only person in the world who could hurt their mother? If she excused the entire world's faults including those of her children, theirs still wounded her. Even his father couldn't hurt Bobbi Bohannon anymore . . . at least not in her soul where it counted. Oh, he could still inflict bruises, but the funny thing was, once she'd stopped caring what he did, he'd seemed to back off with the beatings. But Petite could hurt her mother to the core, and too often did. It was almost as if she took pleasure in doing it. Just like now, he thought, when he saw her gaze lock with his mother's, saw her lift her chin and let loose a long stream of smoke.

He didn't realize that Ericka had joined him again until she touched his arm and said, "What's the matter?"

He only half looked her way. "Would you wait for me a minute, Blue? I've got a certain sister who needs her neck wrung."

"Don't be too hard on her, Bo," Ericka told him, looking at Petite across the room. "She's at a tough age."

"Yeah, well it's about to get tougher," he said, striding off, his hands balled into fists at his sides.

Ericka watched as he grabbed his sister by the arm, then jerked the cigarette which dangled from her lips, but suddenly Carrie and Brett were standing in front of her, and the rest of the scene was obscured from her view.

"Hi!" Carrie said as if they hadn't had an argument just the night before.

Ericka decided to let it go as well. She'd been dreading seeing her friend. She smiled in genuine relief. "Hi, guys. You just getting here?"

"No, we were walking around the grounds for an

hour or so. Looks like rain though, so we decided to come in and join the mourners."

She'd wrinkled her pert little nose in the way that was both comical and cute, and though Ericka felt the subject of Dr. Grant's tragic death too serious to laugh about, she giggled nonetheless. "It is pretty sober in here. Guess everyone's still in shock. It just doesn't seem possible that he's dead. My mom was just over there talking to him yesterday."

"Still writing that book?" Carrie asked with an impatient roll of her eyes that was meant to tease.

Ericka didn't laugh this time, but neither did she spark as she had the night before. "No. The book's finished, I'm told. Mailed off to the publisher."

"Then why was she seeing Dr. Grant? Is she sick?" Brett asked, his tone solicitous.

Ericka searched his expression for sarcasm, but finding none and feeling guilty for her suspicions, she granted a rare smile his way. "No, she just promised him one of her pineapple passion cakes in exchange for all the help he gave her with her research." Then pointedly to Carrie. "The book's a medical thriller. About a physician like Dr. Grant from Smalltown, America, who is killing his patients." She laughed. "She said he had quite a clever, diabolical mind. Gave her several great twists. Mom said she told him she was glad he was so intrinsically good or he would have been positively evil. Kind of ironic, isn't it? Him helping writing a murder mystery about a doctor and then getting killed himself. I just can't believe he's dead."

"Really going to put a damper on next week's celebration," Carrie said.

"Carrie!" Brett said in a reproachful tone that sounded amazingly like his father.

"I know. That sounds mean, but it's true. Look at everyone today. Your mother and mine haven't stopped crying since they got here."

No one does grief better than them, Ericka thought but smiled blandly as she defended her best friend's position. "It does sound mean, Brett, but I know how Carrie feels. My parents even told me to add something in honor of Dr. Grant in my address at the graduation ceremonies. Talk about depressing."

"Jeez, I'm glad it's you and not me," Carrie said. "I liked Doc Grant, but I wouldn't be able to think of one thing that would fit in with the theme 'Tomorrow's Horizons.'" She paused to look around. "I thought my mother said Rhonda and Aaron were going to come by today. I haven't seen them yet, have you?"

"They'll probably come by later for a few minutes," Brett said.

"Yeah, well I just hope Scooter doesn't come. Mama said Martha called this morning and told her Scooter's real upset about the murder. Going to ask everyone he can where they were this morning between three and four. That's when they figure Doc Grant was killed."

Bo joined them then, his dark features even darker for his apparent anger. "Hi, Pearson, Carrie." Grabbing Ericka's hand, he said, "Let's go."

Ericka shrugged a quick apology as she skipped after him. Outside, he stopped abruptly, gathering her into his arms and kissing her. When he let her go a long moment later, Ericka inhaled deeply. "Wow, if anger makes you kiss like that, I'll have to think of ways to make you mad."

He didn't laugh as she had expected, but she thought him even handsomer with a brooding scowl on his face. Still, she missed his crooked smile. She tried again. "You're sexy when you're so intense."

The smile appeared and along with it, a gaze that could only be described as hot and hungry. "Then let's go find a place by ourselves so we can see how sexy I am."

Ericka giggled as they hurried down the steps, but

their walk slowed as they passed the balloons and lanterns in red, white, and blue that had been hung along the walkway in honor of the patriotic holiday.

They didn't speak, but their fingers brushed from time to time as did their hips. Ericka sighed with satisfaction, realizing how right she felt walking at his side, the need for conversation not there, the company being enough for them both. As they left the formal walkway, stepping onto a dirt path, Bo draped an arm around her neck and a few minutes later, Ericka hooked her fingers in the corner of his back jeans pocket. The path they were on wound through the hills and woods for miles, and Ericka wished they could follow it to the end. Not likely, she thought with a surreptitious glance toward the darkening sky. Though only a little past three, there was no sunshine to light the way, and she knew that the storm the weatherman had promised couldn't be far off.

"Want to go back?" Bo asked.

She looked up at him in surprise. "No, why?"

"Saw you looking up at the sky. It is going to rain. If you're worried about it, we can go back."

She shook her head. "No, I'm right where I want to be."

He let his arm slide from her neck to the small of her back, guiding her from the path to a small clearing in the woods. He glanced around for a place to sit, then folded himself Indian style on the ground, pulling her onto his lap. "How's this?"

"Perfect," she said with another small sigh. "Really perfect."

Again they lapsed into silence, but a few minutes later a deer bounded into the clearing startling them as well as itself when it spotted them not ten feet away. Its dark eyes reflecting its panic, it turned in a graceful half leap in the air and disappeared into the thick foliage of the deep woods. "Wasn't it beautiful?" Ericka asked.

"Umm, long legged, graceful, wild, and free. Reminds me of you."

"Oh, I'm not wild. I'm about the tamest creature in St. Joan. Sometimes I wish I were . . . wilder I mean, freer, but I like harmony too much to ever test the boundaries."

"That why you've never had a serious boyfriend before?"

Ericka looked away, following the path the deer had taken as she answered. "No. I was waiting for you," she said honestly. She heard his sharp intake at her confession and wondered if she'd been too frank. Was he laughing at her?

"I'm going to fall in love with you, Blue. I've never felt the way I do about anyone else." There was a deep chuckle, then his command. "Don't be embarrassed. Look at me." When she did, he kissed her, softly, tenderly. "I've had a lot of girlfriends, Blue, but none of them was like you. I'm glad you waited for me. I wouldn't want to think about anyone else holding you, kissing you, making love with you."

She felt the fire his words had sparked in her face and in the pit of her stomach.

"Don't look like that. I'm not going to rush you, but I gotta tell you, I want you. I want you real bad."

"I can't. Not yet."

"But you want to."

She nodded. "Yes, but I can't yet."

"Okay," he said, but she heard the disappointment in his voice. Wiggling around so that she was turned fully toward him, she captured his face in her hands, her long fingers splayed into his black hair. "Don't sound like that. I've never done it, Bo. When I do, I want it to be with you, but I want it to be right. I want it to be one of the final discoveries we make about each other."

"We have to know each other better, is that it?"

She shrugged her shoulders but answered, "Yes. I guess that's what I mean."

Wrapping his arm around her back, he turned them so that she was lying on the grass and he was positioned above her. She squealed in surprise, but laughed once she was settled. "Okay," he said. "Tell me all about you and don't leave anything out."

"You're crazy, you know it?"

"Crazy in love."

She frowned with the statement. "Don't, Bo. Don't say that to me until you mean it. I told you I'm not wild and free. I'm serious about my feelings. They're the only thing that's completely mine, and I want you to be serious about this, too."

"Oh, baby, I'm as serious as it gets." He searched her face with his eyes, letting them roam over the perfect features languorously, and she felt the magnetism of his eyes pulling a part of her inside him. "Tell me," he said in a hoarse whisper.

A nervous laugh bubbled from her lips. "Like what?"

"Like what your favorite color is. What you like to eat. What you want to be when you're finished with school. Do you want to live in St. Joan forever or are you planning on leaving and moving to a big city like Boston where your parents are from? Who's your favorite music group? Are you happier in the morning or at night? Are you good at math or do you prefer English subjects?" He paused for a moment, then rushed on. "Do you have allergies? Do you like cats or dogs? What's your favorite sport? What kind of movies do you like? Do you—"

"Whoa! I'm already lost," she complained, but she was laughing hard now. "You're crazy," she said again.

His eyes were laughing as they stared into hers. "I guess so, 'cause I coulda sworn we already did the 'crazy' routine a few minutes ago."

She hit his arm with a balled hand. "Be serious."

"Didn't we do that one too?"

"Bo!"

"Okay," he said, pretending defeat. "You don't want to tell me all about yourself, we'll just have to pass the time some other way." He captured her hands in his, pinning them to the sides of her head as he kissed her. This time his mouth wasn't soft or tender, but demanding and hungry, and Ericka responded with only the slightest hesitation.

After a few minutes, Bo stretched out fully on top of her, and his kisses intensified. His lips sucked at her tongue, then nipped at her bottom lip. She could feel the stubble of his beard scratching the tender skin on her chin and cheeks and then her neck when he kissed her there, but she hardly registered it. Instead she was concentrating on the fire he'd started inside her and the way her body was responding. As he let go of her hands, his own slipping under her shirt to knead the tender flesh of her belly, her own rifled through his thick hair at the base of his head, and under his shirt in the back to rub the brawn of his shoulder muscles. When his pelvis began a slow circular grind against hers, she arched up to meet him, and felt a thrill run the length of her at the telltale bulge that was suddenly pressed against her thigh. She heard him groan and answered with a muffled moan of her own. Then he'd pushed her bra above her breasts and his mouth was suckling on her nipple. She gripped the flesh of his back with her nails. And then his other hand, the one not kneading her breast was inside her shorts and panties, plucking at the nest of curls between her legs. She raised her hips to his seeking fingers, intuition guiding her, and her protests about waiting lost in the onslaught of unfamiliar passion. When his fingers touched her between her legs, then after a moment of teasing, slipped inside her, she pressed her face against his neck and bent her knees as she lifted her hips to him. "Oh, God, Bo . . ." she groaned.

"Don't make me stop, Blue. Please."

She grabbed his head between her hands, drawing his lips to hers every bit as needy as he, her promise to herself to wait forgotten.

He pulled away from her devouring kiss long enough to unzip her shorts. Once that was accomplished, he met her gaze, the crystalline blue changed with the heat of her desire to a stormy gray blue. "Tell me, Blue," he said in a husky soft tone that was all he could manage in his own need. But before she could answer, the first drop of rain splattered against her chest, followed quickly by the next and the next. With a growled curse, Bo laid on top of her for one long last second before giving in to defeat. Then he moved off her, reaching for her hand to draw her to her feet. "Come on," he said. "We're going to be soaked in another five minutes."

Ericka hesitated, brushing her hair back from her face which was already damp, though with passion rather than rain water. "We'll never make it back to the club in time to miss it," she said.

"I know," he said taking her hand and pulling her in the opposite direction. "But we can get to the fire station if we run like hell."

"Wait," Ericka said, stopping and turning away from him. "I have to zip my shorts."

He heard the embarrassment in her voice and muttered another curse word beneath his breath.

"What did you say?" she asked with a glance over her shoulder.

"I said I'm sorry."

Now she turned around to look at him. She searched his face slowly even as the rain began to pelt them in earnest. "Don't be," she said. "I should have been the one to stop it."

He started to argue with her, but now wasn't the time. Later, when they were out of the rain. Taking her hand once again, he pulled her after him.

The run changed quickly to a race, and by the time they were safely inside the ranger's cabin, they were both breathless and laughing.

Her hands braced on her knees, Ericka inhaled deep breaths before asking. "You sure we're allowed in here?"

"Don't know, but I think it's better than getting struck by lightning."

"How long's it supposed to last?"

Bo glanced out the window at the angry sky. "Could pass over in a few minutes or last the rest of the day and night." Catching the worried look in her eyes, he asked, "Your parents going to be real worried?"

"They're pretty cool," she said, "but then I'm usually pretty predictable. Come home on time. Come out of the rain." She shrugged. "With the party and all, they might not even notice I'm gone."

"Baby, somehow I don't think anyone could not miss you for long."

She smiled shyly, his tone suddenly reminding her of how far out of hand things had quickly gotten back in the glade before the rain had started.

As if reading her thoughts, Bo turned away to look out the window again. "I'm sorry, Blue. You said no and I pushed for more. If it hadn't started——"

She walked up behind him, encircling his waist with her arms and pressed her cheek against his shirt which was wet and clinging to his sinewy shoulders. "I didn't stop it either," she said in a soft whisper.

With a ragged breath, he turned, drawing her into his arms. "We'll take it slower from here on out."

"Guess you must think I'm pretty uncool, huh?"

"No, Blue, I think you're just about perfect. I don't want to mess things up between us by moving too fast. I wasn't lying when I said I was falling in love with you. I know that sounds like a line, something I lay on all the babes, but I swear to God, I've never said that before. I want it to be right between us when we make love."

"I want that, too," she said, pushing herself up on to her toes to kiss him. "And I don't want to wait forever, I just want the first time to be special, okay?"

He grinned slowly, that crooked, cocky smile that had made her heart jump the first time she'd seen him when she was just a child. "Yeah, Blue, it's okay, but damn it, with you looking at me like that, we'd better stick to group outings or public places, or I'm not sure I'll be able to control myself."

"Me either."

He groaned, making her laugh again at his comical expression of exaggerated pain. "You do make it tough on a guy."

"Good, I've been reading *Cosmopolitan*. Their advice is to make 'em wait before you make it worth their while."

He shook his head and rolled his eyes. "God, as if you women need anyone tutoring you on how to make it harder on us."

"Well," Ericka said, stepping to the door and pulling it open, "I hear cold showers and exercise will cure what ails you."

"Smartass," he said, stopping long enough to pull her to him for one last quick kiss. "If I get struck by lightning, remember that I could have died a happy man."

"Don't even joke about that," she said seriously.

"Yeah, guess that was in poor taste considering that Aaron's dad just . . . well, you know."

Ericka rubbed her arms with her hands as a shiver raced down her spine. "Just hurry back."

She watched him from the window until the rain and foliage swallowed him, then went to the chair in the corner to sit down and wait for him to return. It was eerie sitting alone in the small, poorly lit cabin, and memories of all the talk about the recent murders began to flood her thoughts.

Jumping to her feet, Ericka resolutely pushed them away, calling up the image of the man she was falling in love with. She was on the threshold of discovering all the wonders of womanhood, and the most handsome man in the world was going to be her teacher. She wasn't going to let anything ruin that for her. Going to the window, she drew a heart with her finger in the fog on the glass pane. Then, "E.C. loves K.B."

Ericka's wait in the ranger's cabin wasn't a long one. Bo arrived to pick her up in his father's Cherokee Jeep as promised just thirty minutes later. But he was subdued, sullen even and though she tried to tease him out of his mood which was as dark as the weather, he'd remained uncommunicative and withdrawn for the rest of the evening. Even when they'd left the barbecue and gone to the movies, he'd been quiet.

"Did something happen that I don't know about or are you angry with me about . . . well, you know," she asked on the way home from seeing *Fatal Attraction*.

He smiled at the question, even reaching across the console to take her hand. "Naw, I'm not sore at you, Blue. How could I be? I think you're just about the only perfect thing in my life right now."

"Then what's wrong? You've been quiet since you came back to rescue me from the storm."

"Nothing." Again that dazzling smile. "Really."

"Okay," she finally conceded though she was hurt by his reticence to confide in her.

At the door, he kissed her once, just a peck. "I'll call you tomorrow. Maybe we can go up to Stone Fall, have a picnic."

Ericka shrugged her acquiescence. Actually she was thrilled with the prospect of eating on the romantic site that legend claimed had once been a castle built by a young French aristocrat, Jean Paul Deveaux, in the early 1900's. It was said that he had discovered the Ozark mountain site while on a land acquisition trip in the United States. The Frenchman had fallen in love with the spectacular view—the three hundred foot cliff that overlooked the lake on one side, the meadows and springs that wound their way down the other side. He'd spent five years hauling boulders up to the top of the mountain where he'd built a castle fit for a queen. But his "queen" had been a highstrung young woman from genteel Boston who had hated the wilderness setting. She'd deserted him and the two babies who were born during her brief stay at Stone Fall. Less than three weeks later, the bereft father had died along with his children in what some called a tragic accident while trying to escape the fire which had swept through the house when lightning hit it. Others said that he'd torched the house, then jumped with his babies clutched in his arms from the highest point of the mountain. Regardless whether fact or fiction, young lovers had sought out the ruins of Stone Fall for decades. Ericka had been to Stone Fall many times with her parents or with classmates but this would be the first time she would enjoy the romantic ambience she'd scarcely noticed before.

As Bo walked away, Ericka nibbled on her bottom lip. "Bo."

He stopped, half turning and this time his smile was teasing, and even from the distance of more than a dozen feet she could see the lights in his eyes again. "Thought for a minute you were going to let me get away with that puny kiss." In a few long strides he was back, gathering her into his arms and kissing her the way he had earlier. She felt her insides tingle, experienced the same rush of pleasure.

When he pulled away a long, heated moment later, her lips pulsed and her breathing came in quick rasps. Giggling, she put her fingers to her mouth and said, "You certainly know how to get my blood stirring."

He winked. "You ain't seen nothin' yet, baby."

She laughed as much from relief as amusement. Bo was back and whatever it was that had been bothering him was apparently forgotten.

As if in tune with her thoughts, he sobered. Putting a hand on the wall near her head, he leaned against the house. "Sorry about the rotten mood earlier. Guess I haven't been fair to you by not explaining. No big deal. Just my dad. Lambasted me pretty good for getting you stuck out in the storm."

"But that's not fair. Didn't you explain what happened?"

The crooked grin slid into place. "Couldn't very well tell him about that, now could I?"

Ericka laughed as she swatted his hand. "I didn't mean *that.*"

With a short laugh, he pushed away from the house, pecking her lips once again. "I'll call you early, Blue. Get some sleep and dream about me."

As always after ten o'clock, her parents were holed up in their suite on the third floor. The light burned from beneath their door, but it was closed, signalling their desire for privacy. Ericka called out a greeting, then stepped into her own room, but less than a minute later, her mother knocked on her door.

"Ericka? May I come in, honey?"

"Of course." She smiled as she pulled her top over her head. "I would have come up, but your door was closed."

Linda ignored that as she sat down on the bed. "Have a good time?"

"All right."

"Just all right?" Linda pressed.

Ericka stripped from her shirt and shorts, then shoved both in the hamper and crossed the room to the closet to pull out her terry robe before answering. As she knotted the sash around her waist, she smiled. "Well, it ended better than it started. Bo is a fantastic kisser."

Though her mother had been watching her with her brows knitted, she smiled at that. "Well, that's very important. One of the things I quickly liked best about your father. But you haven't said why the rest of the date wasn't terrific."

Folding her long legs like a pretzel, Ericka settled on the bed beside her mother. "It was okay. Bo was just kind of quiet. Said his dad gave him trouble about leaving me in the woods."

"More than that, from what your father and I saw," Linda said as she rubbed her arm absently.

"What do you mean?"

"I'm afraid I'm responsible. I was kind of antsy today what with Jason's murder last night. When it started storming and you didn't come back, I got anxious. Your father told me I was being foolish, but I kept pacing in front of the window. I guess people noticed, Bert Bohannon included. He was just asking me what was wrong when we saw Keen running across the lawns. Before I could even answer, he went outside. Barbara went rushing out after him. I saw Keen talking to them, laughing, so I knew everything was all right. I started to turn away, but I noticed that Bert was waving his arms, looking real agitated. Barbara put her hand on his arm, but he knocked it away. She said something else, and the next thing I knew, he backhanded her. That's when Keen stepped between them, and Bert punched him in the stomach."

"Oh, my God. Just because we got caught in the rain? That's terrible. Bo couldn't have acted more responsibly. He got me to the ranger's cabin before I was hardly even wet."

"I know. I was livid. I told your father what I'd just seen, and we went outside to calm Bert down."

"What did he say?"

"That's the oddest part. All of them acted like everything was just fine. Bert said something about you both being 'dern fool kids who didn't even have enough sense to come in out of the rain,' and Bobbi laughed and added something about young love making a person even forget about the weather."

"What about Bo? What did he say?"

Linda shook her head. "Not much. He wasn't as quick to recuperate as his mother. Just explained what had happened and told us he was going to take his father's Jeep and go get you. Bert tossed him the keys like nothing had happened."

"Well, at least that explains why he was so quiet most of the night." She drew her knees up, hugging them and resting her chin on the plateau they created. "Ooh, I'd like to punch Mr. Bohannon in the stomach. What a creep! No wonder Bo only talks about his mother and sister. He hardly ever mentions his dad."

"You like him a lot, don't you?"

Ericka nodded, smiling slightly with the admission. "I think I might even be falling in love." Tilting her head to the side, she looked at her mother. "Sound silly?"

"Not at all. I was only three years older than you when I met your father and fell in love. But go slowly. Kids who come from abusive households sometimes have a lot of anger stored up. If they don't have an outlet, they sometimes blow up and take it out on innocent victims."

"Mom, this is Bo we're talking about."

"I know, and I've always liked him, but, well, just don't go too fast. Make sure you really know him before you give him your heart."

Ericka stared at her mother for a long moment. "Gosh, you're actually worried about him, aren't you?"

Linda leaned forward to kiss her daughter's forehead before scooting from the bed and crossing to the door. "No, actually I trust your handsome young man, but I don't want you hurt."

"Trust me, Mom. I *know* him. He wouldn't hurt me."

"Okay," Linda said simply, but Ericka noticed that her eyes still held a glimmer of concern.

"Mom?" she prodded.

"It's probably nothing, but when Jason and I were talking about the book, we kind of segued to the murders last spring. Got to discussing profiles—you know, the kind of person who would kill with such violence."

"Oh, Mom, you don't think Bo could do something like that," Ericka said in a voice barely raised above a whisper.

"No, I don't," Linda said with conviction. "But one of the profiles that Jason detailed was the victim of abuse."

Ericka felt a rare flash of anger directed toward her mother. "That's sick! I can't believe you would even think something like that about Bo. Gosh, we've known him since he was a kid."

Linda ran her hand through her hair, then sighed. "I don't, Ericka. I really like him." At the doubting expression on her daughter's face, she added, "I swear. But I'm a mother and I worry."

"Well, don't worry about Bo."

Linda sighed as she opened the door. "Actually, honey I can't help worrying about all of you kids until whoever murdered Jason and the others is caught."

"But Dr. Grant was killed by a burglar, Mom. And whoever killed Cindy and the others is probably long gone by now. Junior says his dad is convinced of it."

Linda Cassidy rubbed the back of her neck. "I guess I've been listening too much to those tapes Jason and I made. With his death this morning, my imagination is in overdrive."

"Well, chill out, okay? Jeez, you'll give me nightmares."

Now Linda laughed. "Then think about how good Bo's kisses are and I'm sure you'll take care of that."

Ericka smiled. "You should practice what you preach. Stop thinking about murder and go kiss Daddy."

"Best idea I've heard in a while. Good night."

"One question, Mom?"

Linda looked back expectantly.

"Dr. Grant was killed by a burglar, wasn't he?"

"Of course," Linda said, but Ericka overheard the added postscript after the door closed behind her mother. "God, I hope so."

Chapter Six

"*Tomorrows. That is what each of us must set our sights on now, plan for, dream of, work toward. Today we have a commonality, our commencement exercise, the walk down the red carpeted aisle, the presentation of our diplomas. But our tomorrows will be as diverse as each day's sunrise. For some, they will be days of amazing achievement, reward, discovery, and promise. For others they will be times of struggle, frustration, dejection, and even depression, but for each of us they are our future. How we have prepared these past four years will largely affect the tomorrows that loom before us now.*

"*One man, a friend to many of us, a caregiver to most of us, believed in our tomorrows and worked toward making them easier for us all. Dr. Jason Grant was the physician who gave us our vaccinations, our physicals, and our balloons if we were very good during the examinations, but he gave us something most of us didn't even think about. He gave us hope of better tomorrows. Dr. Grant won't be here to share those tomorrows. A senseless act of violence prevented that from happening, but I know . . .*"

Keen looked around him at the faces of the other friends and parents who had come to the St. Joan High School commencement exercises. There was hardly a dry eye. Most were weeping tears of genuine regret with the reminder of Dr. Grant's murder, but others, his father included, were nothing but a bunch of hypocrites.

Keen twisted the program in his hands. He was angry.

Glancing back toward the podium where Ericka was continuing her valedictory address, he thought about the yesterdays of the past week rather than the tomorrows she spoke of. He'd looked forward to this week, hell to the whole summer, for weeks . . . ever since his first date with Ericka. But already everything had been changed. Well, not everything. There was still Blue. God, she was something. Beautiful—beautiful enough to take his breath every time he looked at her—smart, fun, and warm. Everything a guy could want. And he did want her. Like a sonofabitch.

But the rest of the homecoming had gone to hell in a hand basket.

Petite, for one, was worrying him. He'd been home only one week and already she'd sneaked out twice. His mom had covered for her both times, successfully avoiding a row with Bert. (Bert, God how Keen hated him. And he wasn't *Dad*. He was just the jack-off his mother had married.) But worse than the sneaking out with Christ only knew who, was the fact that Keen had caught Petite smoking pot, and he suspected that she was using the hard stuff as well. Hell, most of the times he could have used her eyes as a mirror to comb his hair by, they were so glassy. And her moods were erratic as all get out.

Keen grimaced with his next thought. At least if Bert found out, she wouldn't have to worry about a beating. No, that would be saved for his mother . . . or him. Well, better him than his mom. He glanced to his right, saw his mother watching him, and rewarded her with a grin. She reached for his hand, giving it a tight squeeze.

"She's really something, your girl, Keen," she said.

"Yes, ma'am, she is."

"I wish your father could have gotten away from the hotel. He would have been impressed."

Like hell. The only thing Bert is impressed with is himself.

The crowd was suddenly applauding, and Keen realized ruefully that Ericka had finished her address. He caught her gaze and standing, put two fingers in his mouth and let go with an appreciative whistle. She rewarded him with a brilliant smile and a tiny wave, a wiggle of her fingertips.

Now the principal had a few things to say. Keen tuned him out at once, letting his mind drift back to his father, to Bert, the man he hated.

It was at the funeral, Dr. Grant's that is, on Monday, that Keen had first put a label on his feelings for his father. Not that he had ever liked him. Shit, no one liked Bert Bohannon. Some admired him though Keen couldn't quite figure that one out. Sure, the little toad had money. Hell, he was rolling in it, but it wasn't as if he'd earned it by the sweat of his brow. He was too ignorant to have done that—a simple Cajun with the ambitions of the amphibian he resembled. He would have been content to sit out in the swamps for the rest of his life, poaching gator hides from his neighbors, swilling whiskey in a dive, and screwing broads he picked up. If it hadn't been for his brother, Roy, Bert Bohannon would have never amounted to the cost of one of his bottles of cheap booze.

Roy Bohannon had been the hustler. He'd left the swamps when he was only fourteen and gone to Oklahoma and gotten hired on by some big oil company. Just six years later, he'd bought himself a small piece of land—bought it cheap at some government auction according to Keen's mother. He'd parked an old rattletrap trailer on the property which consisted of thirty-three acres of prairie and two good-sized ponds. Three years later he'd built a house. Nothing fancy. Nothing like Bar-Ber-Keen.

Bobbi still liked to look around her at the fancy resort

and shake her head. "Roy sure would have been amazed that his money could have built a place like that. Don't think he ever stayed in a motel fancier than one of those strip places down the road. Even after he had all that money, he wasn't a man who dreamed big. Said if a man had a good sturdy roof over his head and a good woman at his side, he had heaven on earth."

Keen had often resented his mother's assessment of what Roy Bohannon would or wouldn't have wanted had he had the chance to spend some of his money. Money changed people, changed their dreams. Hell, just look at the toad. Who would have thought he'd ever wear silk designer suits or sportswear that cost more than the average man earned in a week? Shit, when Roy had struck oil on his land, Bert hadn't owned more than two pairs of jeans according to Bobbi. She ought to know, too. Hadn't she grown up in the same Louisiana swamps just a mile or two down the road from the Bohannons? She'd been Roy's girl from the time they were both hardly old enough to distinguish between male and female.

Roy promised to come back for her as soon as he was established, and he was as good as his word. They were married only two weeks after the roof was on his house. The happiest day of her life, Bobbi still said, and then with her gentle smile that lit up her dark eyes, she always added, "Or maybe the second happiest. Could be the day our son was born was the happiest. Hard to decide." Then she always laughed. Roy liked to tease her . . . later, after they struck oil on the property, say that was the *happiest* day.

This was the point of the telling that Keen always dreaded, because it was here that his mother's eyes always filled up, the point when reality smacked her up side the head, reminding her that just six months later, Roy had been dead.

He'd been killed in a hunting accident in the Bayous when the family had gone back to Louisiana for a visit. Four months after that, she'd married Bert.

Keen shook his head now in the school auditorium as he watched the graduating class file up the aisles to receive their diplomas.

He'd never get it, why she'd married him. Oh, he knew the reasons she gave. Bert was good to her. There for her when she was alone with a baby and not sure what to do with her life or all that money. And it hadn't been all bad. Look what he'd done with the money Roy's oil wells had brought in. Roy would be proud.

Keen doubted that. He didn't think his dad would have been proud of the way Bert treated the bride he'd loved from childhood or the boy they'd had together. He doubted he'd even be proud of Bar-Ber-Keen. Oh, sure, it was fancy, offering all the amenities and diversions that the richest tourists expected, but Keen didn't doubt that it had been built with his father's blood rather than his money.

He'd never thought that before, never doubted the story his mother told about the tragic accident that had killed Roy. Until Dr. Jason Grant's funeral.

He didn't know if it was looking at the doctor's body that had first put the thought in his head or if it had been the expression on his mother's face when he'd seen her looking at Bert, then heard him say under his breath to her, "Pull yourself together. Holy Christ, you act like that's Roy lying there. You want people thinking you don't love me, that you're still pining after *him.*"

"I do still love him," Bobbi had said in a trembling whisper, but not so low that Keen hadn't heard. Then with her eyes shining brightly behind the film of tears, she'd raised her chin in a rare act of defiance and met her husband's gaze steadily. "You should be thinking of him, too. It's his money you've lived off of all these years."

Keen had expected a reaction, but not the one she got. Bert had merely hung his head and chuckled under his breath, and then he'd put his arm around his wife's shoulder, looking every bit her comforting hero to the rest of the mourners gathered in the funeral parlor. "Roy didn't build Bar-Ber-Keen, Bobbi. *I* did. He just got lucky."

"He worked hard," Bobbi hissed. "He was ambitious and smart and it paid off."

"*Smart?*" Bert asked in a voice that was too loud and caused several people around them to look their way. In a softer tone, he bit out. "Yeah, Bobbi, he was real smart. So smart he didn't have the sense to get out of the way of a gun that was lined up on him." Again that low rumbling, self-satisfied chuckle under his breath. " 'Bout as smart as snake piss."

Bobbi hadn't answered, had just sat there weeping and shaking.

But as soon as they arrived home from the funeral, Keen had confronted his mother about the conversation. Had Bert meant he'd shot his father on purpose?

Bobbi had acted shocked that he would even pose such a question. "Of course not, Bo! That's not what he meant at all. Why, Bert was crazy about Roy. Roy was only eleven months older than Bert, but Bert idolized him. He was devastated by the accident."

"Then why did he say what he did today at Doc Grant's funeral? Sounded like he was bragging about killing him."

"No, honey," Bobbi had said, sinking down onto the sofa with a weary sigh. "He didn't mean that at all." Then she'd looked up at him, smiling thinly. "Trust me, Bo. Bert's not always easy, but you got to understand how it's been for him. I married him when he asked, but there were no lies. I told him right off that the only man I'd ever love was buried right there in those swamps. It's not easy for a man like Bert to know his wife doesn't love him the way he wants. And he knows you've never loved him either." She laid her head back on the cushion, letting loose another long, soul-weary sigh. "I've always blamed myself for that. You were too young to know your father. Maybe I should have just let you grow up believing Bert was your natural father instead of your uncle and the man who adopted you."

"You think that would have made him love *me?*" Keen asked before stalking out of his mother's suite.

He'd run headlong into Bert on the staircase. "Your Mama still crying about her lost love?" he'd asked.

Keen had glared at him. Bobby was wrong, he thought. It wouldn't have mattered if he'd known Bert wasn't his biological father or not. He would always have hated him. Staring into Bert's black eyes, he'd smiled slowly, letting all the insolence that he felt come out with his grin. "No, I think she's mourning for poor Doc Grant. Me, I was thinking, maybe someone ought to tell Scooter Witcomb how accident prone you are with a gun. Were you home last Saturday morning when Doc Grant was killed?"

Bert had raised his arm to strike Keen as he had too many times before to count, but this time, Keen caught his wrist in his hand. "Not anymore, you bastard. I've taken the last punch from you. You're a bully, but I've let you get away with it because I knew you'd turn her into your punching bag, but I'm warning you, leave her alone or you might find out that I'm as accident prone as you."

"Don't you threaten me, boy," Bert had sputtered.

Keen had let go of his wrist, continuing on down the stairs to his own room without another glance in Bert's direction. It had felt good. Damned good, but now he wondered if he hadn't made things worse for his mother. She'd looked so drawn and pinched in the past four days. He was almost certain that Bert hadn't hit her since then, but he knew bullies. They didn't always use their fists. And what about in August when he left again?

Keen looked over at Linda and Lawrence Cassidy. They were so different from his parents. The other night Blue had talked about them, called them her best friends, and he'd actually felt jealousy stir inside him, and then something else, something that worried him more. Was it fair to introduce her to a family like his? Dysfunctional. That's what the psychologists called them these days. Pretty apt. Maybe he'd be doing Blue a favor if he just stepped out of her life now.

As everyone gathered in the gymnasium twenty minutes later for punch and cookies, Ericka looked around for Carrie.

"Looking for Bo?" her mother asked.

"No, he had to run his mother home. He said he'd be back in thirty minutes. I was looking for Carrie."

"I think she's outside getting her picture taken," her father supplied.

"Oh."

Linda laughed. "Go ahead. Go find her. We'll wait here."

"You don't mind?"

"Of course not," her mother said, then her father reinforced their position. "Actually, we'd like a few minutes to ourselves. We're plotting a new book that's set at a university. We'll just use our over-fertile imaginations to pretend this is a college campus rather than a high school."

"Not another murder mystery, I hope," Ericka said, only half-teasing. "You've both been acting like amateur detectives for so long, I've almost forgotten that you're writers."

Both Linda and Lawrence laughed, but declined to

answer. "Read the book and find out." Lawrence told her.

Ericka rolled her eyes comically as she walked toward the exit, but once outside, her light expression faded as she remembered the somber mood in her home this past week. Her parents had taken Dr. Grant's death hard as well they should, but it was more than that. They were secretive for the first time that she could remember, and she was worried. She promised herself to talk to them about it that evening before Bo picked her up for their date. Something was going on. Something that scared her.

Someone tapped her on the shoulder, making her jump. "Oh, Petite, hi," she said, her hand on her chest reflecting the start the pert little brunette had given her.

"Sorry, didn't mean to surprise you. I just wanted to tell you how much I enjoyed your talk. Usually those kind of things bore me to death, put me right to sleep, but yours, well, it really made me think. It was heavy. Good, you know? All that stuff about shaping our own tomorrows like molding clay. You really think that's possible . . . I mean, even if a person's not real smart like you are?"

Ericka smiled, then laughed softly under her breath. "That's the whole point, Petite. Everyone's smart in his or her own way. All you have to do is be smart about choosing the direction you go in."

"Sounds easy," Petite said yet wrinkling her nose as if negating it. "I want to be a hairdresser. Not impossible, right, and I guess not even very exciting. But I, like, really dig messing with hair and make up and stuff. It's creative like art and that's what I really love." She shrugged. "I mean, it's not like I want to be a rocket scientist or anything."

"It doesn't matter what your goal is, Petite, as long as it's in proportion to your talent. Anyone can see you've got a flair for style. The main thing you have to do is keep your eye firmly fixed on your target." She looked past the smaller girl to where a guy stood leaning against a motorcycle. His hair which might have been blond was so dirty the color was almost impossible to discern. He looked to be as old as Bo, maybe older, but Ericka was sure he was a stranger, and just as certain neither Bo nor his mother knew Petite was hanging out with the likes of him. "You can't let anyone or anything sidetrack you, Petite," she added pointedly.

Petite glanced over her shoulder then laughed shortly. "By anyone or anything you mean guys like Mike. Hey, he's cool. Besides he doesn't exactly figure into my tomorrows. Just a guy who's down here for the week with a bunch of buddies. Gonna party with them, listen to some music, you know."

"Doesn't look like your type," Ericka offered tentatively, concerned yet not wanting to hurt the younger girl's feelings.

"No, you mean doesn't look like *your* type or Bo's type," Petite said. "He's exactly my type."

"Why? Because he's someone your parents wouldn't approve of?"

"Exactly. He's so radically different from my old man, it's hard to figure they're from the same planet. Mike might not look like your image of the knight on the white charger or like my brother, but he's not a creep like my old man either."

Ericka knew she'd hurt Petite's feelings. Reaching for her hand, she tried to give it a squeeze, but Petite pulled it away. "Hey, it's okay. You don't have to feel sorry for me. Like I said, I've got my dreams same as you and I'm going to remember what you said about keeping myself focused." She smiled then, brightly as if the tense moment had never occurred. "By the way, I think it's awesome that you and Bo are tight. He's so cool I get shivers. He deserves someone like you."

"Thanks," Ericka said, taken aback by the swift

change in mood. Was Petite as easygoing as she seemed or merely a chameleon capable of changing colors in a flash to protect her vulnerability?

She watched the young woman walk away then climb on the back of the Harley, hooking her arms around the biker's waist. As the bike pulled away from the street with a loud roar, Petite lifted her hand, offering the peace signal in farewell. Ericka shook her head as she turned away. Bo's family was certainly complicated, she thought. Each of them was so different. Ericka had never known a family like that. Most shared traits, desires, dreams, but the Bohannons reminded her of the different species of animals she'd seen in the zoo in St. Louis once. They were a family only because circumstance had brought them together.

Petite Bohannon was like one of those spider monkeys. Tiny, yet clever, and bright, and rambunctious. Bobbi was more like a seal. Shiny and elegant but accommodating—performing tricks at the master's command—and friendly. Bert was obviously the snake even though he reminded her more of a weasel. What about Bo? She smiled. That was easy. He was a panther. Dark, sleek, muscled, and intelligent, and so, so handsome.

The Bohannons were as disparate as the animals in the zoo, and they shared another common bond—hatred for the snake.

Chapter Seven

"You're going out with your friends tonight?" Rhonda Grant asked.

Aaron turned toward the sound of her voice as he pulled a T-shirt over his head. He hadn't known she was standing there. "Yeah," he said.

"I don't think I'm ready to be alone, Aaron. You have all summer. Can't you see them another time?"

Aaron braced his hands on his dresser, inhaling slowly. "It's been a week, Mother. I haven't been out of your sight—"

"That's not true. You went to the graduation ceremonies this afternoon."

"I wasn't finished," he said slowly, reaching inside himself for patience. "I was going to say except for an hour this afternoon. I need some space, Mother. I think you would want some time to yourself, too."

"I would want time to myself? I've had nearly a year alone. Ever since your father left me."

Aaron straightened, looking at his mother standing in the doorway of his room. She was still a beautiful woman at forty-seven years old, or could have been if she didn't have such a perpetual bitter expression on her face. "Well, that's the point, isn't it? You and Dad were separated for almost a year. Now you're acting like you've lost the man you couldn't live without. Well, seems to me you lived without him quite well when he was alive. I don't think he'd want you mourning something that died long before he did."

"How like him you're becoming," she said, biting the words out between clenched teeth.

"Oh, Christ, Mother, give it a rest, will you? One minute you're sobbing your heart out because the man you loved above all else is dead. The next you're insulting him. Which is it?"

She folded her arms over her thin, nearly flat chest, which heaved with indignation. "And you're going to tell me you loved him? Seems to me I remember that the two of you argued almost incessantly when you were home on spring break last month."

"We had resolved our differences," Aaron said quietly.

"Had you? Or were you going fishing with him that morning because you wanted one last chance to plead your case?"

"Let it go, Mother. He's dead. Let him rest in peace." He grabbed his nylon jacket from the back of the chair and stepped past her into the hall. "And let me live in peace. Please."

But Rhonda was apparently not inclined to do that. She followed him down the hall to the front door. "What did that Cassidy woman want when she called?"

Aaron stopped, but didn't turn to face her as he answered. "I'd called them. I wanted to thank Ericka for the kind things she said about Dad at the commencement exercises this afternoon. Mrs. Cassidy merely wanted to add a few thoughts of her own. Very considerate lady."

"After my husband," Rhonda muttered. "Everyone was talking about them."

"He was helping her with her research, Mother." He'd been holding onto the doorknob, but now he let go to slam the door with the flat of his hand. "Christ! He's dead! Leave him alone!"

He'd turned with the last of his tirade and saw her eyes, those incredible pale gray eyes that could embrace with a glance or censor as fast, swimming with new tears. "He was loving and considerate of everyone in the world but me, Aaron, but I still loved him."

With a sigh, Aaron capitulated. Taking his mother in his arms, he rested his chin on top of her head. "He loved you, but your jealousy drove him nuts. His nature was implacable, he couldn't change the way he was to accommodate your needs, to disprove your suspicions."

She was sobbing now, her tiny frame rocking in his arms with the force of her grief. "I can't forgive him for leaving me, but I don't want him to be dead."

"I know, Mother. I know."

Suddenly angry, Rhonda stiffened in her son's arms, then jerked free of them. "How could you know? You're just like him. The only thing he ever asked of you, you refused to give him."

"Well, he's won after all, hasn't he? I'm going to practice here in St. Joan like he always wanted."

Rhonda laughed, surprising him. "And here you thought you'd be free to do as you wanted if he weren't around." At her son's shocked expression, she shook her head. "Oh, don't look at me like that. I'm your mother. Did you think I didn't know what you were thinking that morning when you came to tell me you'd found him?"

"You're sick," he ground out.

"Am I? Or is honesty just too tough to take? I understand, Aaron. I thought I'd be free of him now, too. But it turns out Jason is more powerful as a ghost."

"You look like a picture," Marylou Roberts told Carrie as her daughter came into the dining room. "Of course, you always do."

"Gotta look pretty so Brett will want to kiss her," Carrie's eleven-year-old sister teased, pursing her lips in imitation of her sister puckering for a kiss.

"Sit on it, Megan."

"Where are you kids off to tonight?" her father asked.

"We're meeting everyone at Buns, then going to the Alley to dance. Probably won't be home until one or so."

"Be sure and tell Ericka again how well we think she did today," Marylou said, at the same time slapping Megan's hand as the child reached across the table for a biscuit. "Remember your manners. Ask if you want something."

"You told Ericka three times this afternoon, Mama," Carrie said. "I think she knows."

"It doesn't hurt to tell someone more than once when you think they've done a good job," Marylou said, just a hint of hurt in her tone. But then she brightened. "Look how often I tell you how pretty you look. You don't seem to mind hearing that over and over."

Carrie laughed. "True, but that's because I don't have anything else going for me like Ericka does. I'm not brilliant like she is."

"You don't have to be brilliant, Carrie Ann. You're sweet, and decent, and the most beautiful girl in Missouri. And you've captured the most handsome young man."

"I think the Cassidys would argue with you there. They looked pretty proud of how Ericka looked standing beside Keen today."

"I thought it was pretty disgusting myself, watching him draped all over her like that. I'm glad Brett is such a proper young man. At least I don't lie awake at night like the Cassidys must do wondering whether or not you'll end up pregnant or something."

"Mother!" Carrie protested. Her hand went unconsciously to her throat where she'd spent the last half hour covering a hickey with makeup. "Ericka has never even had a steady boyfriend before."

Brian Roberts frowned at his wife. "That was unkind, Marylou. Ericka's a nice girl. I don't think it's fair of you to make judgments just because the Bohannon boy had his arm around her."

Marylou had been buttering the biscuit her youngest had been reaching for. She slapped it on Megan's plate then answered the charges against her. "I'm not saying Ericka isn't a nice girl. You know I adore her. But that's how things get started. Why, I remember Cindy Richvalski when she was just a tiny thing. Couldn't ask for a sweeter child. Then she got to going around with the wrong crowd, and . . ." she paused for a long second as she glanced at Megan. "Well, you know. And Dr. Grant, too."

"Dr. Grant?" Both Carrie and her father asked in amazement together.

"Come on, Marylou," Brian continued. "Jason was killed by a burglar. Saying that his lifestyle got him murdered is a stretch, even for you."

"Maybe it is and maybe it isn't. If he hadn't moved out of his home with Rhonda and started seeing other women, he might very well still be alive today. We don't *know* that he was killed by someone who was breaking into his house with the intention of stealing from him." She shook her head, sending her blond curls into a dance, then added with conviction, "In fact, the more I think about it, the more I'm convinced, the scriptures are right. You reap what you sow. Just ask our future pastor if he doesn't agree with me, Carrie Ann."

The future pastor was washing his face in the upstairs bathroom when his father entered, shutting the door behind him. "How's my number one guy?" Jimmy Wayne Pearson asked.

Brett jumped at the unexpected voice, then howled with pain, hopping on one foot while he quickly rinsed his face trying to wash the soap from his eyes.

Jimmy Wayne's deep baritone voice boomed with amusement. "Always were a pussy."

Brett reached for a towel, patted his face then glared at his parent with one eye as the other one was still on fire and squeezed shut. "Where's Mom and the kids?"

Jimmy Wayne's grin was slow spreading, taunting. He scratched the back of his beefy neck pretending to try and recall his wife's whereabouts as well as that of his younger children. "Don't rightly recall where your ma is. The kids are all out back playing. Thought I'd take advantage of the rare quiet and come up here and talk with you for a few minutes before you head out of here tonight." He lowered the toilet lid and sat down. "Got a date with your sweetie tonight, huh? How many nights does that make this week? Four? Five?"

Brett turned away from him, grabbed his shirt, and quickly pulled it on. He didn't want to talk about Carrie with his father. Didn't want to talk to him at all. But to refuse to answer would only postpone the confrontation, and that's what it was. That's what it always was.

Jimmy Wayne Pearson was a bully. He'd been born mean and would no doubt die even meaner. In fact the only thing he did better than mean was talk. That's how he'd gotten to be mayor. Brett's mother had once jokingly said "Jimmy Wayne could talk himself out of having to attend his own funeral." As a child, Brett had been terrified by the statement and had prayed fervently that his mother was wrong. Everyone knew how well he could talk. Problem was his meanness was a secret. Oh, folks thought him a shrewd businessman. Called him ruthless. Even called him cutthroat, but they didn't suspect that he was rotten through and through as Brett knew he was. And he knew something else about Jimmy

Wayne Pearson that would have shocked the good citizens of St. Joan to their core.

His fingers trembled as he hurriedly buttoned his shirt and answered his father's query. "I've been out with her five times since I got home." Swallowing quickly, he turned to face his father and pulled a smile into place. "We're in love, Dad. Can't see enough of each other."

"Can't see enough of each other or *get* enough?" the bully asked with a leering grin that made Brett shudder.

"I'm going to be a minister of the church in a year's time, Dad."

"Yeah, that's a good one, huh? My boy becoming the Reverend Pearson."

Brett struggled to find a reply, but was saved by his mother's voice on the landing. "Jimmy Wayne? Brett? Where are you boys? Dinner's served. Ya'll hear me?"

"Be right down, Mom!" Brett yelled, relief coursing through him. To his father, "Well, I guess we'd better not keep her waiting. The little guys will be banging the table for their dinner."

"Yep, suppose you're right there," Jimmy Wayne said, pushing his heavy form to his feet.

Brett pulled open the door, fighting the urge to dash ahead of his father instead of keeping his pace moderate.

"I was thinking maybe you and I could go fishing tomorrow. You know, just the two of us, like old times."

"Sorry, can't tomorrow. I've got to help Reverend Rose get the chapel ready for Sunday services. I gave my word already."

Jimmy Wayne shook his head. "I'm real disappointed, boy." He shrugged. "Ah, well, another time maybe." They were halfway down the stairs when he paused as if struck by an idea. "Guess I could wait up for you tonight. We could have us one of our private get togethers just like we used to before you went away to school. A man gets lonesome for his firstborn's company. What do you say?"

"I might be out late, Dad. In fact, this being Carrie's graduation night, I'm sure we will be."

"Oh, yeah, forgot about this being a special night." He smiled at his son and patted his shoulder. "Well, another time. But you kids take care, ya hear? These aren't safe times. Why, people have been getting killed right and left around here lately."

Too bad one of them hasn't been you, Brett thought. His hands began to tremble once again, this time with excitement over the notion. He shoved them into his pockets and squeezed his eyes tightly shut.

"That soap still burning your eyes, boy?"

Brett opened them, shaking his head and smiling. "No, just thinking about the murders you mentioned. Terrible. Makes me hurt for them."

Jimmy Wayne's laughter echoed around them. "Like I said, Brett, you always were a pussy."

Honor thy father, Brett reminded himself silently. He repeated the litany throughout dinner and all the way to Carrie's house.

"Here, Junior," Scooter said as he exited the garage with a sleeping bag slung over his back. "You can take my car. I won't be needing it."

Junior caught the keys his father tossed him, mumbling a grudging "thanks."

"You taking Sally Jane out again tonight?"

"Yeah," Junior answered, not offering more as he handed his father the last of the fishing gear.

"Well, hope you have a good time. She's a real sharp gal and got a helluva shape on her. Even if things aren't lively, at least you can sit there and stare at her curves all night."

"Not everyone thinks about sex all the time, Dad. Sally Jane and I are more buddies than anything else."

Scooter paused in his task of arranging the back of the Blazer. He'd heard the accusation in his son's tone that was even clearer than his words, but he let it go. What could he say, anyway? "Whatever. You have fun, but don't keep that girl out too late. Things being the way they are these days, nobody's safe late at night anymore. You'll be finding that out for yourself now that you're a bona fide police officer yourself."

"Yeah, I guess. 'Course I imagine it'll be awhile before you let me work on anything more important than writing traffic tickets or directing parade traffic."

Scooter slammed the tailgate then rounded the side of the vehicle. "Gotta learn the ropes. That takes time."

"And then I can solve real police riddles, huh, Pop?"

Their gazes met and locked. "It ain't easy, son," Scooter said, feeling the accusation all the way to the pit of his stomach. "There's a lot of steps to solving murders, Junior. Pieces of evidence have to be gathered. If there's not enough there to work with, it's harder."

"Sounds like you've got yourself a real clever killer."

"What you trying to say?" Scooter said, giving up the charade of pretending things were right between his son and himself. They hadn't been since Junior had seen him with Bunny.

"Nothing. Just what I said. You haven't solved even one of the murders. Must be a real smart guy. Maybe more than one. 'Cause I know how smart you are. Have to get up pretty early in the morning to get anything past you. Maybe even know how to think like a cop, huh?"

Scooter recognized the challenge which was offered in his son's eyes as well as his tone. He ignored it. "See ya, boy. Take it easy tonight. Don't drive too fast. The tourists are out in force. You run into any trouble, call

Waylin." Then he laughed. "Or break out your own badge. You're one of us now."

"Well, look what the cat drug in," Sally Jane said when she opened the front door. "Thought you were Junior," she told her father who was just returning home from a three day business trip to Little Rock.

Clemens Matthers frowned. "You going out with him again?"

"Don't start, Daddy. Junior's a nice guy. We have fun together."

"He's a yokel. A bumpkin. Why can't you find someone with at least as much up here," he said, tapping his temple with his index finger, "as you've got. You're too smart for the likes of Junior Witcomb. Hell, he's just like his father."

Sally Jane turned away from the door with a frustrated sigh. "Glad to see you too, Dad. Yes, I've been fine since you've been gone. Business has been brisk. The weather? Oh, it's been glorious. No, I didn't have any trouble taking care of that fax you sent me. Let me see. What else did you want to know? Oh, yes, Dr. Grant's funeral was beautiful. Tragic but beautiful all the same. I offered your apologies to the widow and her son."

"Smartass," Clemens said with an appreciative laugh. "Sorry about lambasting you the second I walked in the door. I guess I just worry about you." He wrapped an arm around her waist, leading her to his den. "In fact, I've been thinking, we've about tapped out all the good investments here in the Ozarks. Maybe we should move our headquarters to a bigger city where you could meet the right people."

"I like it here. Besides, we've talked about this before. You'd never be able to outwit city folk like you do these bumpkins." That wasn't the way Sally Jane felt at all, but it was a parody offered to shame her father. She did it a lot, though it never worked. She sighed. Ah, well, a sow's ear was still a sow's ear no matter how much silk one wrapped it in, she thought as she ran a hand over the sleeve of his Armani suit.

"Guess you're right," Clemens said, leaving her side to drop into one of the twin burgundy leather chairs. "I'm beat. Fix me a Manhattan, would you, sweetheart?"

As Sally Jane stepped behind the bar, she asked, "You going to be home for awhile this time?"

"Couple of weeks. Then I've got to go to Nashville. Want to come along?"

"What? And miss all the fun I'm going to have with my friends this summer?"

"Friends! Ha! You run with a different group every year. Last year it was—"

"You don't have to remind me," Sally Jane said, feeling her neck heat. Her emotions still ran high when she thought about Cindy and Bunny, the girls she'd taken up with the summer before. She still missed them, still hungered for the things they'd taught her, the forbidden pleasures they'd introduced her to. But . . . she shuddered. No, she couldn't think about them any more. She'd taken care of everything. Removed all the evidence of her friendship with them. With luck, no one would ever remember that she'd been friends with them. Her father brought her back to the present. "I'm sorry. What did you say?"

"I was asking who else you're going out with."

"Oh, Pam and Aaron, Carrie and Brett, and Ericka and Bo. Going dancing."

"Ah, well, that's better. That's a good safe crowd for you to be with."

Maybe not, Sally Jane thought as she plopped a cherry into her father's drink. One of them just might be my undoing.

* * *

"Where you going all spiffed up?" Bert called out to his son.

Keen stopped, his back stiffening with the too-loud voice. His father had to make sure everyone in the hotel lobby knew he was talking to his son. He had to show off his authority, his power. Asshole.

"I asked you a question, Keen. Where you headed?"

"Out with friends."

Bert had crossed the expansive lobby, and was standing directly in front of his son, blocking his exit to the door as he stuck his hands in his pleated trousers and rocked on his heels.

The nattiest hotel baron west of the Mississippi. Asshole.

"Gonna take out Miss Fancy Pants again?"

Keen clinched his jaw but managed, barely, to keep his tone civil. The last thing he wanted tonight was a run in with the prick his mother had married. "If you mean Ericka, yes, we're meeting friends."

Bert reached up to tug at one of Keen's sports jacket lapels. "So where you going so dressed up?"

"To the Alley. Ericka's not twenty-one. None of the girls are. It's the only underage club in town."

"Oh, that's right, Mizz Valedictorian graduated today, didn't she?"

"Yeah, gave a hell of a speech, too. Should have been there."

"Ha! I don't need any hoity-toity Yankee talking down to me." Bert laughed. "Ain't gonna take her long to realize you're just a Cajun pissant who isn't worthy of her. When she gives you the old heave ho, you come talk to your old man. I'll fix you up with the right kind of woman. Woman like your mother."

"Someone I can slap around? Control? No thanks."

"Why you little punk. I ought to take your keys away

from you. Ground your ass. Just 'cause you're grown
don't mean I can't still tell you a thing or—"

"Oh, yeah, it means exactly that. You don't control
me or my money. My *dad* left me my own money that
you can't touch. The only reason I even live here is because of Mom and Petite." He took a step nearer, tow-
ering over his stepfather and enjoying the intimidation.
"And you better hope they never get tired of putting up
with you, 'cause then I won't have any reason to keep
quiet about how you got hold of all your money."

Bert chuckled as he ran a hand over his greasy black
hair. The Rolex on his wrist flashed in the bright light
of the setting sun with the movement as did the heavy
gold chain around his neck. "Well, that wouldn't work
so good, Keen, 'cause then I'd just have to counter with
a few accusations of my own." He poked the younger
man's chest with the tip of one of his manicured nails.
"Hasn't occurred to Scooter Witcomb yet that all three
of them murders happened during spring break when
you college kids was home. Nope. All he's thinking
about is the tourists. 'Course he could be right, but then
Jase was killed the same night most of you pulled back
into town. I don't know where your buddies were, boy,
but I know where you weren't. You weren't home one
of those nights."

"You're nuts. What reason would I have to kill any of
them? I didn't even know any of them except Dr.
Grant."

"Says you."

"Prove otherwise."

Bert chuckled again, this time louder. "You're right. I
can't prove anything just as you can't, but I can hurt the
reputation of a future young lawyer pretty bad if I start
mouthing off." He slapped his son's arm. "Well, guess
we've come to a sort of impasse here. What would you
call that in fancy lawyer talk?"

"Asshole," Keen muttered under his breath.

This time, Bert's laughter was loud causing heads to turn their way. "You're a very funny boy, Keen. And you know what, that's what I used to call your pa."

Keen's hands balled into tight fists at his side.

"Watch it, boy. These are touchy times. Don't need to go showin' what a bad temper you have. People might start thinking about how violently those three people died the last time you were home."

Ericka stood in the doorway of her parents' office. She smiled. She loved to watch them together. So comfortable. So uninhibited and at ease with each other.

Their chairs pulled close, her mother had her feet tucked under her father's cushion. She wore only a long T-shirt and with her knees bent like that, and her legs slightly open, she imagined that her father was privy to quite a view.

"Better get some pants on, Mom. Bo will be here in a few minutes."

"Hand them to me, sweetheart," Linda said, pointing over her head toward the sofa where she'd dropped them a couple of hours before.

Ericka tossed them into her lap, then leaned on the back of her mother's chair. "What are you two working on? Your new book?"

"In a manner of speaking," Lawrence said, peering at her over his bifocals. "We just finished listening to some tapes Jason Grant and your mother made while researching the last ones. We were just making some notes."

"Ugh, you're writing another murder mystery. Why don't you write a romance? I hate all the blood and gore in your books."

"Unfortunately, romance rarely emulates real life and I'm afraid we're just too well grounded in reality."

"Then write an autobiography," Ericka teased. " 'Course that might be more porn than romance."

Her parents rewarded her with a shared laugh.

"Well, I'm going to go up and brush my hair. Listen for the doorbell."

She returned downstairs ten minutes later. She could hear her parents' voices raised slightly in lively conversation and decided not to interrupt their plotting session. Instead, she claimed a seat outside their office in the entry way as she waited for Bo.

"I know Jason wasn't sure about his suspicions, Lawrence," Ericka heard her mother say. "But what if he was on the right track? What if he told someone other than me and that person killed him?"

"Then I'm sure Scooter will find out."

"How? You know Jason told me he wouldn't go to the sheriff until he had more to go on. I think we owe it to him to at least ask Scooter if one of Jason's shoes was missing like with the others. I mean, that would prove or disprove my theory. You heard the tape, Lawrence. Jason may have claimed not to be sure, but he sounded damned convinced to me."

"He had a list of possible suspects, Linda, and all of them based on conjecture, nothing more. We can't just go giving the sheriff names that might well disrupt innocent lives. This is serious business, darling."

"I know how serious it is, Lawrence. And I know that our daughter is out there running around—"

"Ericka, we didn't hear you come downstairs," Lawrence said, effectively cutting off what his wife had been about to say.

"Obviously," she said, stepping around the back of her mother's chair to stare at them both. They both looked so guilty, she almost laughed, and would have if not for the seriousness of what she'd overheard. "You think you know who killed Cindy and the others, maybe even Dr. Grant, and you didn't tell me?"

"No! We don't think we know *who*," her father said. "We only have suspicions and *not* enough to take to the sheriff." The last was added for his wife's benefit. "But, Ericka, you have to promise not to mention any of this to anyone. This isn't one of our book plots. This is the real McCoy."

"What were you saying about shoes? I never read anything about the killer taking their shoes."

"Not shoes, sweetie. Shoe. The killer took one shoe from each of his victims after killing them. Dr. Grant was privy to that information as the coroner who performed the autopsies. In fact it was he who noticed that one of Bunny Apperson's was missing after she was killed."

"But he probably shouldn't have shared that even with your mother," Lawrence interjected.

"Maybe not, but knowing that, we might want to remind Scooter. See if one of Jason's shoes was missing. At least then we'd know whether or not it was the same person or a burglary as they're telling everyone."

Ericka lowered herself onto her father's ottoman which had been pushed to the side when they'd drawn her mother's chair up to his. "Well, you can't talk to Scooter tonight. He's gone fishing. He won't be back until Sunday unless something really terrible happens."

"So the question of whether or not we should call him is moot, at least for the moment," Lawrence said smugly.

Linda stuck her tongue out at her husband, then to her daughter, "We would have told you, darling, but we're not sure of anything ourselves. All we have are some profiles that Jason and I put together, and the shoe thing."

"You mentioned names."

"Jason mentioned two or three who fit the profiles, sweetheart, but your father and I don't intend to point a finger at anyone. We mainly want to share some of the information that he discussed with us and remind Scooter about the missing shoe in each instance."

"Is Bo's name on your list?" Ericka asked quietly.

"Bo's? Good heavens, no!" Lawrence said, questioning his wife with his eyes.

Linda reddened slightly. "It's my fault, Lawrence. I mentioned the scene between Bo and his father last weekend at the country club. But, Ericka, I don't consider Bo as even a remotely possible suspect. Okay?"

Ericka breathed a slow, relieved sigh. "Good."

The doorbell chimed. "Speaking of the devil," Lawrence said with a soft chortle.

"He's not the devil," Ericka said, springing to her feet at the same time.

"Oh, I don't know, you certainly act like someone who's been bedeviled. Walk around here with your head in the clouds most of the time."

"That's called love, Daddy. Remind him, Mother."

"My pleasure."

Ericka was still laughing when she opened the door.

"What's so funny?" Bo asked as he stepped into the foyer.

"Nothing, just my parents acting like kids again. I think they're in there making out."

"Ah, no wonder you're such a quick study. You have such good examples here at home."

Ericka laughed again, but she was looking into his eyes and wondering why his mood didn't seem to be reflected in them. "Something wrong?"

"What could be wrong when I'm going out with the prettiest girl in St. Joan?"

She smiled at the compliment, taking a step closer as she wrapped an arm around his neck and kissed him. "Guess you're right."

"Ready to go?"

"Just let me say goodbye to the two juveniles in the other room."

"Guess maybe I ought to say hello at the same time, huh?"

Linda was sitting on Lawrence's lap when they entered the office.

"Didn't I tell you?" Ericka asked with a laugh.

"Aha, she's been talking about us again," Lawrence said.

"Hello, Bo," Linda said, starting to slip off her husband's lap.

"Don't get up, Mom. We're leaving. Just wanted to tell you good night. Probably won't be home early."

"Well, have fun," her mother said. Then to Bo, "But drive safely."

"Ugh, has any kid ever escaped that lecture since chariots were invented?" Ericka asked, rolling her eyes.

"So parents worry. It's one of our main duties," Linda said.

"You two worry inordinately. If you two'd get your minds off of murder and back to romance, you might ease up."

"You do the same. Forget what we were talking about and only think about this handsome young man," Lawrence said with a teasing tone, but with a serious undercurrent that Ericka didn't miss.

"Am I missing something here?" Bo asked.

"Not a thing, trust me. It's just the kind of doom and gloom talk that goes with people who have overactive imaginations. You can't imagine the nights I've actually conjured blood and gore after reading one of their books."

"Sounds too heavy to me," Bo said, putting his hand on the small of Ericka's back as he steered her out of the room. With his other hand, he waved in farewell. "Keep the doors locked, folks, so none of your goblins sneaks in here to get you."

Chapter Eight

"Hail, hail, the gang's all here," Junior said as the last of their octet stepped out of Bo's Corvette. "Where the hell you guys been? We're all ready to start dancing." He did a comical imitation of one of the latest dances, twisting and gyrating on the fast food patio. "Get down! Can ya dig it?"

Both Bo and Ericka laughed.

"You want a burger or something before we go?" Bo asked Ericka.

"No, I'm not hungry."

"Then let's hit it," Pam said, springing up from the concrete bench and hesitating only long enough for Aaron to join her.

"Shall we leave the cars here or drive the three blocks?" Aaron asked.

"Leave them!" Junior and Sally Jane voted simultaneously.

Ten minutes later they were all seated around a table at the Alley, the teen spot in St. Joan.

"I thought things would be hoppin' by now," Junior complained, slapping the table top with his fingernails to music only he could hear.

"The band starts up in thirty minutes. Everyone will start drifting in then," Bo said. "In the meantime, why don't we order? Beer for the guys? Soda for the ladies?"

"Ooh, he called us ladies," Pam said, patting her heart to still the imaginary flutter. "Well, as they say, you can fool some of the people some of the time, but you can fool a post-adolescent all the time."

"Cute," Bo said, hooking Ericka's neck with his arm at the same time and drawing her closer. "What about it, Blue? You my lady?"

"Yes, sir!" she said enthusiastically, granting him a quick kiss for emphasis. She was relieved that he finally seemed to be getting into a party mood. He'd been so quiet when they'd first started out, noncommittal and taciturn. She'd even queried him about what was bothering him, but he'd shrugged the question away, saying only that he didn't feel much like partying with the rest of their friends. She'd offered to change their plans, take in a movie or something, but he'd insisted that it was her night. Apparently, he was enjoying himself now. She was relieved.

"So, Carrie, tell Ericka and Bo what we were discussing before they arrived," Sally Jane said.

"My dad got some tickets to the Royal's game in Kansas City for Sunday. I thought we could all go up for it. Everyone else has already agreed. You two want to come?"

"Sounds okay to me. What about you, Blue?"

"I don't know. Sounds like fun, but I'd have to check with my parents."

Carrie rolled her eyes. "As if your parents wouldn't say yes without even batting an eye. Have they ever denied you anything? Give me a break, Ericka. You're the must indulged, spoiled girl I know."

"True," Ericka agreed good-naturedly, "but they're kind of uptight right now. I'd better check with them before committing myself."

"Something wrong?" Aaron asked.

"Don't tell me," Carrie said. "Their publisher turned down the St. Joan look-alike book?"

Ericka felt a twinge of hurt at her friend's insistence on ribbing her about her parents' latest novel but pushed it away. "No, it has nothing to do with the book."

"Then what could they possibly have to be uptight about?" Pam asked. "They're stinking rich, so enamored of each other even after twenty years it's nauseating, and their daughter is the most beautiful valedictorian St. Joan ever had."

Ericka laughed even as she bit her bottom lip. She'd promised them that she wouldn't say anything. "Nothing really."

"Nothing? I don't believe your folks would get upset about nothing, Ericka," Brett prodded not so gently.

Carrie chimed in again. "I agree. Your parents are too cool. The things my parents have an absolute stroke about yours don't even spring a gray hair over."

"You're right, but the murders in the past couple of months have stirred them up," she admitted, then meeting Aaron's gaze, she blushed. "Oh, I'm sorry, Aaron. That was insensitive of me."

"No, it's okay. My dad was upset about them, too. Guess he didn't know he'd be next."

"Jeez," Carrie said. "You sound like he was one of the stalker's victims. He wasn't, was he?" She addressed the last to Junior.

"I don't know. My dad hasn't said anything like that to me. Far as I know, though, he thinks just what the radio and TV have been reporting. Burglary gone sour."

"Anyway, we're *leaving* St. Joan," Sally Jane, the most pragmatic of them pointed out. "We're getting away from the big bad murderer."

"I'll ask," Ericka said, looking away from her friends with the hope that they'd let the subject drop.

"Your parents know something the rest of us don't, Ericka?" Aaron persisted.

"No," she said quickly, too quickly. No one said anything. They just kept waiting, staring at her, not believing her. "They don't, okay? They're just like everyone else. Looking for answers and coming up with theories."

"What kind of theories?" Aaron pushed, his green eyes bright with intensity. "Come on, Ericka, he was my dad. If your folks think they might know something, you owe it to me to share it."

Unreasonably, Ericka felt like crying. She'd given her parents her word that she wouldn't talk about what she'd overheard them discussing. But these were her friends. More importantly, except for Carrie, these were her *new* friends who had just accepted her in recent weeks because she was on the arm of the most popular guy in St. Joan. She liked them. She trusted them. She shrugged in capitulation, then said, "They don't *know* anything for sure. Only that Dr. Grant had put together some kind of profile that he thought fit the killer. They're worried that if he told them about it, he might have told someone else. The *wrong* someone else."

"Like the killer," Carrie said, sitting forward eager for more.

"Yes, exactly. They're worried that whoever killed Cindy, and Bunny, and that guy, might have found out that Dr. Grant was on to him and killed him, too."

"Jesus," Aaron said, running a hand over his sandy hair.

"But they don't know if Dr. Grant suspected anyone in particular?" Junior asked.

"They have a list," Ericka admitted reluctantly. Then she remembered the part about the shoe. "But, hey, they might be all wet. They're going to talk to Scooter when he gets back from his trip, see if one of your dad's shoes was missing."

"Shoes?" Brett asked.

"Why would one of his shoes be missing?" Pam seconded.

"You've got to swear you won't tell anyone," Ericka said.

"I swear!"

"Me, too."

"Scouts honor."

"Come on, Ericka, spit it out. You've got us on the edges of our chairs," Sally Jane said.

"Tell them so we can dance," Bo said with a disgusted shake of his head.

"The man the media has dubbed 'The Stalker' took one of each of his victim's shoes."

"From everyone?" Pam asked.

"That's what they said."

"That's sick!" Carrie said.

"*He's* sick!" Sally Jane corrected.

"Shit, can we talk about something else?" Bo groaned. "We came to party, didn't we?"

Everyone seemed as relieved as Ericka to let the subject drop. Aaron signaled for a waiter as Pam and Sally Jane excused themselves to go to the powder room. Carrie and Brett turned to each other and began "sucking face" as Junior put it.

"Come on," Bo said, taking Ericka's hand and pulling her after him as soon as the music started.

The band kicked in with an uptempo current favorite, but quickly slowed the pace down with the next number and Ericka went happily into Bo's arms.

They didn't **talk.**

They hardly **moved,** just swayed more or less in time with the music, and as soon as it ended, Bo bracketed her face with his hands, pinning her there on the dance floor. "I want you," he said. "I can't keep holding you, touching you like this. Either we stop dancing except the fast tunes or I take you home. You're driving me crazy, baby."

"Take me somewhere else," Ericka said, hearing the breathless tone in her voice that was inspired by the hungry look in his black eyes and wishing he could touch her the way she wanted him to right then.

Bo didn't need further encouragement. Her hand in his, he led the way to the table where their friends were sipping drinks and playfully tossing popcorn to one another. "We're outta here," Bo said succinctly, grabbing her purse and giving an aborted wave. "Have fun."

"Woo, from the look in his eyes, someone's about to get laid," Pam said.

"Yeah, but the question is, is he the layee or the layer? Ericka looked like she wanted to eat him alive."

"Stop!" Pam said, pressing her hands to her face. "I'm getting hot."

Aaron cooled her down by fishing an ice cube from her cola and dropping it down the bodice of her shirt.

"You are just too cool," she said, laughing as she wiggled. "Sorry, bucko, I'm just too much woman for one teensy little ice cube. It melted on the spot."

Aaron was instantly on his feet. "See ya, guys."

Pam squealed with delight as she followed after him.

"The party's over," Junior sang off key.

"Not if I have anything to say about it," Sally Jane quipped. "Come on, let's dance."

"Isn't this just my luck?" he complained as he stood up. "Bo and Aaron get girls who want to make like the birdies and bees. I get one who wants to do the electric slide. Where is the justice, God?"

"What about you?" Brett asked Carrie as soon as they were alone.

Carrie didn't meet his gaze. "I'd like to dance for awhile."

Brett's handsome face split with his wide grin. "Spoken like the true fiancee of a future pastor."

"You don't mean that," she said, looking his way at last. "You'd rather be out there doing what the others are."

"Hey, I'm a man first, seminary student second. But

I promised we'd spend the evening like you want. This is your night." He put a finger beneath her chin, tilting her head up a few inches. "I love you, Carrie Ann."

"I love you, too," she said. And she did. He was so handsome. Her blond Adonis. She'd been in love with him since sixth grade though he hadn't looked her way for two or three years after that. Only she wished she liked the sex part better. As he offered her his hand to lead her to the dance floor, she remembered how nervous she'd felt when they'd talked about the stalker. Maybe that was a good excuse to stay inside dancing. As she stepped into Brett's arms, she gave a fleeting thought to Ericka out there in the night.

The night was starlit, magical. A gentle breeze stirred the trees as Bo and Ericka wound their way around the lake. Music drifted to them from a party on one of the yachts anchored in a cove. At Bo's side, Ericka sighed. He glanced her way and she smiled dreamily.

"Penny for your thoughts," she said.

It was his turn to grin. "They're worth more than that. I was thinking about you, which makes them worth a fortune." He winked and they lapsed into silence once again, but after a few more minutes, he pulled the car over to the shoulder of the road. Turning to her, he put his hand on the seat behind her head. He didn't speak for a few minutes, and she didn't press him. When he did, his voice was soft, his tone tentative. "I want you, Blue. I want you so bad I hurt. But you gotta be sure. This isn't just about tonight. This is about us being together for a long time."

"I know. If it was just about tonight I wouldn't have agreed."

"You want to get a room somewhere?"

She shook her head. "No, I don't want to share this with anyone. I just want it to be between us. I don't want some motel manager making what we're doing something ugly or tawdry."

He cupped her chin then, leaning across the console to kiss her. "I love you, Blue."

"I love you, too," she whispered and he heard the truth in the way she said the words, softly yet with certainty.

You were wrong, you bastard, he thought. She loves me and nothing you can do will change that. A moment later he pulled away from her to ease the car back onto the highway.

"You're frowning again," she said.

"Sorry, I was thinking about my dad."

"Then don't think about him. I don't like to see you look so angry."

He reached for her hand, squeezing it tightly. "You're right. This is our night. I'm not going to let him ruin it for us."

Ten minutes later he pulled the car off the road once again, this time onto a grassy patch of land that was mostly hidden by shrubbery and trees. A few seconds later he was helping her from the car. He led her through the foliage to a small clearing a few yards from the water's edge, encircling her waist with his hands as he drew her against him. "You sure?" he asked one last time.

She answered him with a kiss.

His breath already becoming ragged five minutes later, he captured her thick hair in his hand lifting it from her back as he kissed the slope of her neck. Free wisps of hair feathered his face, and he drank in the scent of her. He pushed them both to their knees. Then with his free hand, he slid her skirt up and kneaded the soft flesh of her thighs and buttocks. "Your dress is going to get wrinkled," he said in a hoarse whisper.

"Then take it off," she said, her own voice breathless.

He worked the zipper down her back, then slid the

bodice down her arms. Stopping there, he bent his face to kiss the flesh above her french cut bra. With his tongue, he traced tiny circles and felt her answering shiver.

When he'd worked the dress down her hips, he sat back on his haunches to look at her. It was dark in the circle of trees and brush, but the moonlight reflected against the water created a backdrop of light that bathed her in a subtle glow. "God, you're beautiful."

She didn't answer, only smiled, creating deep dimples in her cheeks as she reached for his shirt and began to unbutton it, slowly, artfully, with instinct guiding her. It was her turn to push it off his shoulders, and shyly at first, she lowered her mouth to one of his nipples, kissing him timidly in the beginning, then drawing it into her mouth with more certainty. Her hands worked the buckle of his pants free at the same time, then shimmied them down his hips.

"Stand up," he said, almost growling as he struggled for control, fought the urge to hurry the sweetest moment of his life.

She lifted her feet allowing him to remove the dress that had puddled to the ground, then stepped from her shoes and stood waiting for him to pull off his jeans and shoes.

She was perfect. Long and lean, her skin shining like alabaster in the dusky light.

His hands slid over her hips, coming back up to her shoulders and beginning their descent anew to pause at her back and free the clasp of her bra. He cupped her breasts in his hands, his thumbs flicking over her swollen nipples. "Oh, God, Blue, you are the most perfect woman I've ever seen."

"Then make love to me," she said, stepping closer so that her pelvis was pressed against the swell between his legs.

He spread her dress out on the ground, apologizing, "I didn't bring a blanket."

"We don't need anything," she said as she allowed him to lay her down.

Though she was lying on her dress, his hip and thigh were pressed to the cool earth which tempered the fire which was already burning inside him.

The water lapped at the shore, and the leaves rustled with the breeze, but neither of them noticed.

His lips suckled on one of her breasts, as he kneaded the slight swell of her belly with the heel of his hand.

Her hands massaged the sinewy muscles of his shoulders, then slid over his back to his hips. She kissed the hollow between his shoulder and neck, moaning softly as his mouth and teeth created waves of passion within her.

When his hand slid into the waistband of her panties, she raised her hips to him, urging his fingers lower, and when he complied, dipping lower to part the lips of her sex and slip inside her, she stiffened with the incredible thrill that made her tighten her pubic muscles and spread her legs wider. Instinct was her only guide, but she didn't worry about her inexperience. She only welcomed him as her hands pressed his face against her breasts. "Oh, God, Bo," she cried out.

He pulled away from her, getting up onto his knees and for just a moment she was afraid he'd changed his mind, but then his gaze met hers, his black eyes narrowed almost to slits. He offered a smile, but it was more the primitive grimace of a wild, untamed beast, and she felt another rush of prurient need.

Placing her hands on his powerful biceps, she urged him down to her with her fingertips.

"Wait, baby," he said between clenched teeth as he coaxed her hips up and slid her panties down to her ankles. He stood then, quickly stepping out of his own shorts, then fell back to his knees between her legs.

His penis stood erect and proud and Ericka followed the innate instinct to take it in her hand. It pulsed between her fingers, and she drew it down to her, raising her hips and sliding the tip along her own sex.

"Not yet," he groaned, raising his head as he struggled against the need to give in, plunge into her. He took a couple of long stabilizing breaths, then looked into her eyes again. "I want you ready for me, Blue."

"I'm ready now."

"Not yet. Not yet."

He forced her knees up, then spread her legs further and lowered his face to the opening she provided.

As he touched her there with the tip of his tongue barely brushing the moist flesh, she writhed beneath him. "Oh, God, Bo, no. I don't know what I'm supposed to do!"

He didn't answer, only introduced her to more exquisite torture. He felt her orgasm as her body shook, and when she started to cry out, he raised himself up to lie atop her, burying her mouth with his. "Now," he said, raising her hips slightly with a hand slipped beneath her.

He'd never felt so powerful, so in control, but it nearly escaped him as he entered her, felt the resistance of her tight muscles, then the evidence of her virginity.

He raised his hips slowly, straining against his need. He didn't want to hurt her.

His lips pulled back, he held her pinned tightly against him as he lifted his hips again, this time pushing harder and breaking the barrier that had separated them.

She stiffened with the searing pain, pulling back though there was no place to escape to, but she felt him push again, slipping deeper and the pain was gone leaving only a faint burning in its place, and then the rush of such incredible pleasure, she cried out with it.

"Oh, God, baby, I'm sorry," he groaned.

She smiled against his throat and signalled her forgiveness with her hips raised to meet him, her legs locking around his thighs.

It was a hard ride that left them both trembling and weak, and clinging to one another. "I love you, Bo," she whispered into his ear after he collapsed on top of her.

"I love you, too," he said, and then, "you're mine, now, Blue."

"I was already yours," she whispered.

"No, not like now." He buried his face in the crook of her neck, tasting their mingling perspiration against his lips. "Not like this. He was wrong."

Ericka frowned. Who was wrong? What was he talking about? She asked him, then wished she hadn't when he pulled away from her, sitting up, and pressing his eyes to his drawn up knees.

"Forget it," he muttered.

She sat up, too, putting an arm around his shoulder and kissing the space between his shoulder blades. "Tell me," she urged.

"My dad. Bert. Forget it."

"Your dad? What does he have to do with us? With this?"

"Nothing!"

"Then what did you mean?" she asked, letting her arm fall away from him.

"It's nothing, damn it. Just something he said before I left to pick you up tonight."

"What?"

Bo shifted his position, turning so that he was facing her. He placed a hand on her calf, rubbing the shin bone with his thumb nail. "He said I wasn't good enough for you, that you'd never belong to me. But he was wrong. You do belong to me, now. That's all."

"That's all?" Ericka cried, scampering to her feet. "That's *all?* Pretty damned much, if you ask me. You bring me out here, make love to me, make me believe this is the most significant event of our lives, and all because your father made some kind of dare?" She reached for her dress, whipping it into her hands and stalking away from him toward the lake. It was then that she saw the blood. It was then that she started to cry.

"I didn't mean it like that, Blue," Bo said, only inches behind her.

Ericka didn't hear him. She was staring at the front of her dress, at the blood that had saturated the fabric, spread in a circle then smeared by their movements.

She felt Bo's hands on her shoulders, but jerked away from him. "Don't touch me."

"Blue, listen to me. I didn't mean it like it sounded. I love you. Bert doesn't have anything to do with that."

She spun around on her heel, her face contorted with hurt. "I trusted you!" she cried. "I was giving myself to you because I love you, and all it was to you was some macho game; a way of proving yourself to your father."

"Fuck that. That's not what I'm saying. That's not even close to the way it is."

"Oh, you're right there. It's me you fucked." Holding the dress against her as if to prevent him from seeing how much of herself she'd actually given, she stepped past him, stopping only long enough to gather up her underwear and sandals. She walked into dense foliage where not even a single beam permeated and began to dress.

She heard Bo curse but kept her back turned as she struggled with trembling hands to cover herself. She felt dirty and used and for the first time in her life, ashamed.

Bo was waiting for her by the car when she stepped out. He opened his mouth to say something then noticed the blood stains on her dress. "Oh, Blue, I'm sorry. Please, don't mess up what this means to both of us. I love you." He reached for her hand, but she sidestepped his grasp.

"Just take me home, Bo," she said, her back to him.

But when he opened the door, she turned to meet his gaze. "It's still early. If you hurry, maybe your dad will still be up when you get there. You can brag about your conquest. Set him straight."

"Jesus Christ! You don't understand. He didn't have anything to do with this. Only with what was going on up here." He slapped the side of his head with the heal of his hand. "It didn't have anything to do with us. Just with me."

She slid into the car seat, pulling the door closed behind her with a loud bang.

Bo hesitated only a few seconds before going around to the other side of the car and climbing in behind the wheel. "We're not going anywhere until you listen to me. I shouldn't have said anything. Didn't mean to."

"But you did, and somehow I think you said exactly what was uppermost on your mind. You made love to Ericka Cassidy, proving him wrong. You can have anyone you want. You're a stud. Now take me home."

"Blue—"

"Take me home!"

"Fuck it," he muttered, but he felt tears needle his eyelids.

"No, Bo. Fuck you and your father."

They rode in silence until he turned into her driveway ten minutes later. Then he made one more try. "Please, Blue, hear me out. Let me tell you about my relationship with Bert. There are things you don't know."

"I know that you used me. You made me think you loved me just so you could prove something to yourself . . . and to your dad. Well, you've made your point." She was crying now, and her humiliation was intensified by tears she hadn't meant to shed in front of him. He laid a hand on her arm, tried to pull her toward him, but she jerked free and opened the car door. She ran toward the front door, not even stopping when she heard him open his door and call out to her again.

She was halfway up the stairs when she heard him back out of the driveway and roar away down the street.

"Ericka, honey, is that you?" her mother asked from upstairs in her room.

Ericka froze on the stairs. Oh, God, she thought, please don't let them see me like this. She dashed tears from her eyes as if that would clear them from her voice as well. "Yes, Mom, it's me."

"Is everything all right?"

"Umm, sure. Everything's fine. I'm just going to change my clothes, then we're going out again."

"Didn't I just hear Bo leave, honey?"

"Uh, yes, but he's just going down to the Stop 'N Shop for some soda and chips to take with us to a party we're going to hit. He'll be back in ten minutes or so."

"Well, be careful."

Ericka heard her father's voice, his words indiscernible, then her mother's laughter. "Your father says not to do anything he wouldn't do."

"Which means I have *carte blanche,* right?" Ericka said with a laugh herself. She hoped her mother didn't notice the way it ended on a sob.

"Exactly," Linda Cassidy agreed. "Good night, darling. We love you."

"I . . . love . . . you, too," Ericka managed.

Her mother's footsteps which had been headed back toward her bed immediately reversed. Ericka pressed a fist to her mouth, choking back the sound of her sobs.

"Are you crying, sweetie?"

She closed her eyes, swallowing hard. "No, Mom. Just laughing at Dad."

Her mother's tinkling laughter floated down the stairs to meet her. "Ah, well, don't share your father's counsel with Bo. We wouldn't want him to know how liberal he is."

"I won't," she said, but this to herself as she climbed the last three stairs to the landing, and let herself into her room. She flung herself onto her bed, burying her face in her pillow. She probably wouldn't be telling Bo anything at all ever again.

Chapter Nine

Ericka leaned against the door, shutting out the sound of her parents' voices above, but failing to shut out the memories and the pain of Bo's confession. He'd made love to her because he was proving something to his father. He didn't love her. She'd simply been a trophy to hold up to Bert. She stood with her eyes squeezed shut, the tears escaping to river down her cheeks. She wept silently until she opened her eyes again to meet her reflection in the mirror. Then she sobbed aloud as she faced her image. Saw the ruined dress.

The sickening, sweet smell of her blood nauseated her as she pulled the dress over her head. Yet it wasn't as terrible as the bitter taste in her mouth that Bo's betrayal had left in its wake.

She shoved the stained dress into the back of her closet, thinking to discard it later when opportunity presented itself. Then knotting her hair on top of her head, Ericka stepped into the shower. Perhaps the hot sluicing water would rid her of both. She scrubbed her skin, flinching only when her hands touched her sore nipples and the tender place between her legs. She still felt unclean when she stepped from the shower ten minutes later, but at least her tears had stopped.

She pulled on a pair of shorts and matching top, then slid her feet into a pair of sandals. She left her hair

in the careless knot on top of her head, merely brushing
the damp tendrils that clung to her face and neck away,
then grabbed her purse and keys from the dresser.

"I'm outta here!" she called to her parents as she exited her room. "See you tomorrow!"

"Have fun!" her parents returned in unison.

She drove aimlessly around the lake for the next two
hours, and little by little the soothing ambience of rural
night sounds began to do their trick. By the time she
turned into her drive again at a little past two, she felt
partially restored and with the resilience of youth, even
relenting in her anger toward Bo. Perhaps she'd been
unfair to him. Perhaps she'd overreacted.

As she inserted the key in the front door, she thought
maybe she would call him in the morning. Maybe. After
she'd let him worry for awhile.

She was surprised to see the light still spilling down
the stairs from her parents' room. They almost always
shut their door before going to sleep for the night. She
paused at her door, listening for evidence that they were
awake, but the house was quiet. And then she smelled
the blood. Gagging with the reminder of her dress hidden on the floor of her closet, she hurried upstairs, then
scrambled to her knees to find it. She had to get it out
of her room, out of the house.

A few minutes later she dropped it into the trash bin
in the garage, carefully rearranging the plastic bags to
cover it.

Though she knew her parents would understand, she
wasn't ready to tell them about what she and Bo had
done in the woods. Not until she sorted out her feelings,
found out what he felt. She'd been quick to believe that
he'd used her to get back at his father, but in the past
two hours, she'd had time to reconsider, to remember
the other times she'd spent with him. He'd given her his
pin. Told her he loved her. Shown her in many thought-
ful, romantic ways.

Like the gift he'd given her for graduation. A picture of the two of them taken the Saturday before by his mother. Just a candid snapshot, but he'd had it blown up and framed for her. And like the way he'd treated her when they'd gone to Stone Fall for the picnic the next day. He'd been so careful with her, acted like she was something fragile and delicate that needed careful tending. Even her parents had never treated her with such gentle care.

She remembered his kisses—the fun ones which were given in a moment of teasing as well as the sweet, loving ones and the passionate ones. He'd promised not to push her into something she wasn't ready for, and though they'd spent several hours together every day since his homecoming, he hadn't. Not until she'd given him the okay.

Their lovemaking had meant more to him than just a victory over his father. It had to.

She felt better when she climbed the stairs a few minutes later. Almost lighthearted. And guilty for the quick verdict she'd passed on Bo. She'd call him in the morning.

At her door she paused again. It was still there, the sweet, coppery scent of blood. As she reached for the doorknob her fingers trembled slightly and she felt fear trickling in her arms and knotting in her stomach. Her heart began a frantic beating in her chest. All this before her brain even registered the terror.

As if of their own volition, her feet turned toward the stairs leading to her parents' suite above. But this was silly. This was just a nasty trick her guilty mind was playing on her.

Still she went up, continued the climb to the attic apartment. She was two steps from the top when she saw it. Blood smeared on the wall by her head. A sob caught in her throat, and she hesitated, hardly noticing that her entire body shook with dread now.

Forcing herself to take another step, and another, she groaned. The smell of blood was so strong now, she bent over at the waist, retching.

It was everywhere. Splattered, smeared, sprayed, and pooled.

They were there as well. Her parents. Dead. Lying in their blood.

Her mother was lying near the foot of the bed, her blood pooling beneath her face and chest. Her father was just a few feet away. One arm outstretched as if even in death, he'd been trying to reach his wife. And then Ericka saw further evidence that he had, in his dying moments, done exactly that.

A long trail of blood, smeared pink in the white carpet showed the effort he'd made to reach her, perhaps to protect her.

Ericka didn't cry out. She didn't cry at all. This discovery was too shocking for that and the pain went past tears.

She merely stood there staring, rocking, her arms wrapped around herself in an unconscious gesture of self-protection.

Her gaze drifted back and forth between her slain parents. Her father was nude but blood covered nearly every inch of his body. His blue eyes were open, staring at nothing yet directed at his dead wife. Blood trickled from his nostril and mouth.

Her mother was dressed in her blue satin nightshirt, which had ridden up on her buttocks with her fall, and ridiculously Ericka thought how beautiful her long shapely legs looked. Oddly, there was little blood on her mother. It merely pooled beneath her. One of her hands rested in its puddle. Her red hair was fanned out as if arranged as a dramatic backdrop to the grisly scene. Her eyes were closed. Her lips parted in a grimace of agony. And her head rested at an awkward angle.

Her throat had been slit.

The quaking which had wracked Ericka a few seconds earlier ceased. Her breathing slowed. Even her nausea passed. But she couldn't move, couldn't think.

Then it came to her. She had to tell someone. But who? Scooter was out of town. Carrie? No, Carrie hadn't liked her parents. She'd been mean to them, talking about them. Bo?

With thought of his name, the catatonia that had frozen her began to abate.

She started down the steps, walking slowly, watching her feet as if unsure what they were about. Over and over she repeated Bo's name in her mind as if afraid if she stopped she'd forget where she was going.

The grandfather clock chimed two-thirty as she stepped out the front door. She didn't bother to shut it behind her. What was the point? Her parents were dead. They didn't need protection from intruders any longer.

She crossed the yard, stumbling when she tripped on a tree root but not stopping nor hardly even registering the pain which shot up her foot from her stubbed toe.

She walked slowly toward the Bar-Ber-Keen resort hotel. She was in the middle of the road though she didn't realize this until a car horn blared at her. Turning toward the headlights, she squinted against the bright beams, but she didn't move out of the way. The driver was forced to detour around her onto the far shoulder of the road. He shouted something to her as he passed but she didn't register his words. Only after his tail lights had disappeared in the distance did it occur to her that she should have asked him for a ride.

She walked on.

Bo was headed for St. Louis. The clock in his car registered two forty-five. He was tired but too wired to pull over. Anger fueled him, driving him on.

He'd been hurt when Blue had refused to listen to him, let him explain. But no longer. Now he was just good and pissed. Who the hell did she think she was anyway? He laughed then. Oh, he knew just who she thought she was. The pampered daughter of the famous Cassidys. He hated to admit it, but maybe Bert was right. Maybe he wasn't good enough for her.

Fuck that. He remembered what he'd written in the note to his parents and laughed but there was no humor in the sound.

He'd changed his plans for the entire summer after he'd started going out with Blue over spring break. He'd been planning to go to Jamaica for six weeks with his buddies from school. After just two dates with her, he'd cancelled out. He hadn't wanted to miss a single day with her. Well, now he was going to rectify that mistake. Let her wonder where he was.

But she wouldn't wonder. Hell, she probably wouldn't even care. She'd made it clear that she didn't want to hear from him again.

He rubbed at his eyes with the heel of his hand, stretched to shake off some of his weariness. Maybe he should make a pit stop. No, screw that. He still had nearly three hours of driving ahead of him. The airline reservationist he'd spoken to on the phone had told him that the earliest flight departed at seven ten. He needed to be there a good hour before then. Should get to the airport around five forty-five. Plenty of time to doze then while he waited for the flight to be called. And he could sleep on the plane.

He wondered if Blue was asleep. Probably sleeping like a baby. Well, screw her. A spoiled little girl. That's what she was.

But God, she'd felt sweet in his arms and sex with her had been so good. Better than anything he'd ever known.

Slapping the steering wheel with his hand, he cursed

again. "Forget it, man," he said aloud to the night. "She blew you off."

But he couldn't forget. He loved her. He knew that now more than ever. If he didn't love her, it wouldn't hurt so damned bad.

He felt the first tears fall in almost perfect synchronization with the first droplets of rain that pelted his windshield. He flipped on the windshield wipers then dashed the tears from his face. He wasn't going to cry for her! He just wasn't. He was a man and men didn't cry . . . no matter how badly it hurt. Hell, he hadn't cried since he was five years old. Not even when Bert had taken the belt to him or later, used his fists instead. He wasn't going to cry over a woman . . . even if he did love her.

He forced his thoughts away from her, concentrating on the rain and all the women he'd have once he got to the Caribbean.

Ericka was soaked by the time she arrived at the lobby doors of Bar-Ber-Keen. It had started to rain some thirty minutes before. She had hardly noticed.

But as she stepped into the lobby, her sandals squeaked and the rain dribbled down her face from her hair.

Bandy Marshall, the night clerk as well as one of Ericka's classmates for the past four years, chuckled. "Well, look what the cat dragged in. Hi ya, Ericka. Get caught in the storm, did ya?"

"Could you call the apartment? Tell Bo to let me in?"

"Don't think he's there," the young man said.

Ericka didn't move. Just kept standing there. Waiting.

"Well, why don't I call up and see." He picked up the phone, punched in a couple of numbers, staring at the bedraggled young woman standing in front of him. She was obviously upset about something. She was acting weird.

When the phone was picked up on the other end, he turned his back to Ericka. "Uh, sorry to bother you, Ms.

Bohannon. This is Bandy down in the lobby. Ericka Cassidy is here. Wants to see Keen." He glanced over his shoulder to cast a smile Ericka's way, then lowered his voice. "I told her I didn't think he was in. I saw him leave about an hour ago. But she's just standing here like she doesn't believe me. Acting kinda funny. You want I should have security help her back out to her car? Or call her folks?"

He listened a moment, then hung up. "You wanna have a seat, Ericka, they're coming down."

"Bo?"

"Uh, maybe," he said nervously. "Just go on over there and wait."

Bobbi Bohannon stepped out of the elevator five minutes later. She wore a brightly patterned dressing gown and fuzzy mules. Her face was devoid of makeup and her hair wound up in curlers, but she didn't pause as she strode toward the young girl sitting quietly across the lobby.

Bandy Marshall, the desk clerk, liked that about his employer's wife. No phoney baloney there. Oh, sure, she liked to dress up in fancy clothes and maybe she wore a tad too much makeup most of the time, but she was genuine. Not like the butthole she was married to.

"Oh, honey, what's wrong?" Bobbi asked, taking Ericka's hands in hers. "Why, you're as cold as ice. Come on upstairs. We'll get you dried off before you catch pneumonia."

Ericka stood obediently and let Bobbi guide her toward the elevator.

Bandy shook his head. Jeez, Ericka was messed up tonight. He'd never seen her like that before. Could be drugs, he thought. But he'd never thought Ericka would get into that stuff. Ah, well, Ms. Bohannon would get her straight before letting her go home.

Upstairs, Bobbi escorted Ericka into her parlor. "Sit down, sugar. I'll get a towel. Be right back."

"Is Bo here?" Ericka asked as she sat on the edge of the sofa.

"You just wait here. We'll talk as soon as I get you warm."

Less than two minutes later, Bobbi was back, a towel and terry robe draped over her arm. She handed Ericka the towel. "Dry yourself off, then you can take off those clothes and put this on. I'll go get you something to drink that'll warm your insides."

Ericka did as she was told, slipping out of her soaked clothing, pulling on the warm robe, then toweling her hair. Her teeth were chattering now and her skin had puckered to goose flesh. Only her mind remained numb. She clung tenaciously to thoughts of Bo even though she no longer remembered why she'd wanted to see him. But it was important. She knew that.

She circled the room, letting her fingers brush the surface of a table, then the back of the sofa. When she arrived at the mantlepiece she stopped. A sheet of paper was propped up against the rock wall, held in place by a tiny crystal bird. She recognized Bo's bold scrawl. It was a note left for his mother, but she took it down, read it anyway.

Mom—
   Change of plans. Gone to Jamaica to join my buddies. I'll call in a few days. Don't worry about me. Just needed to get away.
                                   Love,
                                   Bo

   P.S. Tell Bert he was wrong. Ericka Cassidy isn't good enough for me.

Ericka hadn't heard Bobbi come into the room, but she saw her now standing beside her. Their gazes met and locked and Ericka's eyes filled with tears inspired by the pity she found in the older woman's eyes.

"He didn't mean it, sugar," Bobbi said.

Ericka didn't answer, just kept staring at the note still held in her hand.

"Come on over here and have some hot chocolate. Then we'll call your mother, have her come get you."

Ericka sat down on the sofa and accepted the cup that Bobbi held out to her, but she didn't drink. Instead she shook her head. "We can't call her. She's dead."

The cup Bobbi had been holding clattered to the floor. "Oh, my Lord, what did you say?"

"My . . . my mother's dead. My father, too. I just remembered. That's why I wanted to see Bo."

"Oh, honey," Bobbi began, then stopped as she circled the coffee table to sit at Ericka's side, gather her into her arms. "What are you talking about? What do you mean, they're dead?"

"There's blood everywhere," Ericka said in a voice so flat, so devoid of emotion, Bobbi trembled. The hot cocoa drink was sloshing over the rim of the cup now onto Ericka's hands, but the girl didn't even seem to notice. Bobbi took the cup from her, setting it down with a loud clatter, then reaching for a napkin to wipe the chocolate from the girl's hands.

"Oh, sugar, your hands are burned." Bobbi clasped them tenderly between her own for just a moment before abruptly jumping to her feet. "I've got to get Bert. He'll know what to do." She paused at the door to look at the beautiful young woman who sat staring straight ahead at nothing. "Oh, Lord, honey, I don't know what's happened, but I hope it's only your mind you've lost."

* * *

"Lawd have mercy," Scooter Witcomb muttered as he pulled off his fishing cap and scratched the back of his head. He'd gotten the emergency page on his beeper at five a.m. It was now seven fifteen. He'd driven straight to the Cassidy home. Waylin and Junior were waiting for him in the living room. "That's the grizzliest scene I've ever come onto." He wiped at his mouth with the back of his arm, then looked around at the others sitting in various places in the slain couple's living room. "Where's the girl?"

"In the kitchen. Bobbi's with her," Bert Bohannon volunteered. He cast an accusing gaze toward Waylin, then said, "The wife wanted to take her straight to St. Joan General, but your deputy here wouldn't let her. Says she's a suspect. Biggest bunch of nonsense I've ever heard. The girl's in shock, Scooter. She's bad. Hasn't cried. Hasn't talked. Come around looking for my boy. Walked the two miles from here to the hotel."

"That true? The girl being in shock, I mean?" Scooter asked his deputy.

Waylin didn't like the way the sheriff's eyes had brightened with the question. He'd been a deputy for more than ten years, and had only seen that look a couple of times, but he recognized it for what it was. Anger. Pure and simple. He lifted his chin in a gesture of mild defiance. "Yeah, she's acting real strange—"

"*Strange?* Mother Mary, that girl's eyes are flat as washboards and her skin is downright clammy," Bert said, jumping to his feet.

"Go tell your wife to take her on over to General. I'll talk to her later on after she's calmed down." To the others in the room, he said, "I'm going to the dining room table. I want you all to come in there one at a time, give me a statement, tell me what you saw."

"We didn't see anything, Scooter," Brian Roberts said. "We just came over when we heard the sirens stop up the street."

"You're their neighbors. You must've seen something. Cars coming into the subdivision. Cars leaving."

"Didn't see anything," Brian insisted.

"The killer could have come by boat," Marylou pointed out.

"Yeah, I've thought of that," Scooter said. Then focusing his gaze over their heads out the window, he added, "Or it could have been someone who lives in Bar-Ber-Keen Estates. I want to talk to each one of you. Later on," he said, directing his gaze to the Pearsons and Roberts, "I want to talk to your kids."

"Why?" Jimmy Wayne Pearson asked. "What they gonna be able to tell you if we can't tell you anything?"

"Seems to me I recall it was graduation night. Your kids were more'n likely out late. They might have noticed something, a car that didn't belong in these parts, someone on foot." He looked at Bert who was just coming back into the room. "I want to talk to your kids, too, Bohannon."

"Keen's out of town, but I'll bring Petite over to your office when you're ready."

Scooter stared at him hard for a few minutes. He'd never known Bert Bohannon to be so agreeable about anything. Usually a royal pain in the ass, likin' to throw his weight around. Maybe the gruesome murder of two of St. Joan's leading citizens had gotten to him as well.

Scooter looked for his son, found him standing in the corner. "What about you, Junior? You were out tonight. You see anything that struck you as odd?"

Junior hunched his shoulders. "Nope. I was with Sally Jane until about midnight. We were dancing over at the Alley. I took her home, then went on home myself."

Scooter started to say something else, but Ben Ohtau, the coroner from Camdenton, Missouri, came down the stairs. "All finished, Sheriff. You can have your boys take the bodies on over to the hospital now. I'll do the autopsies this morning."

"Get anything?"

"Not much. Looks like the killer surprised the woman who was apparently lying in bed. I'd guess she jumped up when she saw him. Tried to run past him. He cut her throat."

"What about Lawrence?" Scooter asked, feeling bile rise in his throat with the question. Gawddamn, he'd never seen so much blood in one room before. Looked like a gawddamned slaughter house.

"He was in the bathroom. Must have heard his wife scream or something but didn't even get out the door before the assailant nailed him. There's blood smeared on the jamb there and splattered on the door. Looks like he put up quite a struggle. There's a deep gouge in his throat kind of makes me think whoever did this was determined to slice it open, too, as he did the woman's, but either the victim was too tall or too strong so the killer stabbed him repeatedly 'til he brought him down. Cassidy didn't die quick like his wife, though. Managed to drag himself halfway across the room before he ran out of strength. I won't know for sure 'til I start cutting, but I'd guess he bled to death."

"Got the time of death pinned, Doc?"

Ben scratched at his unshaven jaw. "Just a guess?"

"Close as you can call it at this point," Scooter said.

"Well, judging from the degree of rigor mortis and body temps, I'd say they've been dead four or five hours."

"So that'd put it between midnight and one, huh?"

"Closer to one'd be my guess, but I'll know more in a few hours. I'll stop by your office when I've finished."

"Okay, boys, you heard the doc. You can bag the bodies. But I still want to have another look at the room when you're done, so try not to trample all over the evidence," Scooter told Waylin and his son and felt a twinge of compassion when he saw Junior swallow hard before starting reluctantly up the stairs.

"Well, folks, you can go on home, but I want to talk to you and your kids at my office later on."

As soon as the last of them had left, he sat down on the edge of the sofa and put his head in his hands. Lawd Gawd what was happening to his town?

Chapter Ten

Ericka had been hospitalized and sedated, but as the effects of the drug began to wear off, the realization of what had happened slammed into her like hammer blows.

Hugging the pillow beneath her head she thought about her parents and tears spilled from her eyes. Never again would she share the quiet times with her father, listening to his soft, soothing voice expound on the problems of the world, the solutions politicians seemed set against finding or pointing out the simple joys of life that most were too busy to notice. She'd never feel her mother's energy, hear her gay laughter, see her pert nose wrinkling comically or feel her hands on her face, her arms around her back.

Someone had taken them from her in an act so violent she still could not fully comprehend it. So she didn't try. She didn't look for the why, only faced the consequence. She was alone and already she missed them so terribly she didn't know how she'd face the tomorrows she'd only the day before spoken of with such hope in her address to her graduating class.

Bobbi Bohannon entered the room, her step tentative.

Ericka had forgotten the woman, forgotten her kindness during the early morning hours. But remembering only brought a new rush of tears.

"Oh, sugar," Bobbi said, sitting on the edge of the bed and gathering Ericka into her arms. "I know how terrible this is for you. I wish to the good Lord I could take away your pain. You just go ahead and cry. Let it all out."

After a time, Ericka raised her tear-stained face to say, "I don't want them to be dead."

"I know, sugar."

Ericka sat up in the bed, drawing her knees up and hugging them tightly. "Have you talked to Bo?" she asked quietly, her face averted as if she couldn't quite face the answer.

Bobbi stroked the back of her head. "No, honey, I tried, but none of the major hotels in Kingston have him registered. But don't worry, I'll find him, and he'll come when I do. You can count on that."

A nurse came into the room, her expression as chipper as her gait. "Well, I thought it was about time for you to be waking up. I just need to get your vitals, Ericka, then the doctor has said it's all right for you to check on outta here."

Ericka felt panic at the pronouncement. Where would she go? She couldn't go home. She shuddered.

Bobbi seemed to understand her fear and patted her leg. "Don't you worry, honey. You're coming to the hotel to stay until your grandmother arrives from Boston."

"My grandmother's coming?" Ericka asked. She hadn't even thought of her, but of course she would come. "When will she be here?"

"Tonight. Bert drove to St. Louis to meet her plane. Insisted on going there personally. They should be arriving in St. Joan in about two hours."

"She knows?"

"Yes, sugar. Scooter spoke with her early this morning."

Ericka wondered how her maternal grandmother had taken the news of her daughter and son-in-law's deaths.

Probably the same way she accepted everything. Stoically, calmly. Unlike her feisty, dynamic daughter, Julia Hanover rarely demonstrated emotion. They were as different as two women could be and somehow that thought brought on another bout of grief and loneliness. Ericka buried her face in the ample bosom of Bobbi Bohannon as the nurse continued to take her blood pressure, clucking her tongue in sympathy.

Thirty minutes later, Ericka stepped into Bobbi's car. "Are we going to the hotel now?" she asked.

"No, sugar, we have to go by the sheriff's office first. Scooter needs to take a statement from you."

"But I don't know anything," she said in a small voice.

"Then that's all you need to tell him, isn't it?"

Ericka glanced at the woman behind the wheel. As always Bobbi'd applied her makeup with a heavy hand, and her dress was a concoction of frills and ruffles. Folks considered her shallow and frivolous. Ericka had always thought of her as cute in an oddball sorta way, but that was before. . . . Now, she was a wonderfully caring woman who had been there for her when no one else was. No wonder Bo loved her as he did. "Thank you," she said softly.

Scooter Witcomb had just concluded another interview with the residents of Bar-Ber-Keen Estates. The result had been the same. No one knew anything. He was reminded of the three monkeys. See no evil, hear no evil, speak no evil. Only the last wasn't true. Two of the women he'd spoken with had been only too happy to talk about their slain neighbors and it appeared that Marylou Roberts wasn't finished yet as she paused on her way to the door.

"Scooter?"

He sighed, waited.

"You know, it has occurred to some of us that all of these murders have been of outsiders. Think about it. None of them were from here. You might consider that their deaths were all connected."

"Thank you, Marylou. I have considered that very thing."

"Well, I'm not trying to tell you how to do your job, you understand, but I wouldn't be a bit surprised to learn that even Jason's death was connected. And I think you should be looking for one of them as the killer."

"By one of them you mean one of the outsiders," Scooter said.

"Well, yes, exactly. We've never had murders in St. Joan before we started letting them buy land from us and move on in. I think it's perfectly obvious that they brought all this . . . this carnage with them."

"On the other hand, maybe it's one of the narrow-minded citizens from St. Joan who has a prejudice against outsiders. Have you considered that, Marylou?"

Scooter had the pleasure of seeing her face turn almost purple with her indignation, but his amusement was short-lived as he spotted Ericka Cassidy standing in the doorway. He wondered how much she'd overheard. It was a question that was answered at once by Ericka herself.

"You're a mean, spiteful woman, Mrs. Roberts. My parents never did anything but treat you with graciousness even though you gossiped behind their backs every chance you got. Don't they teach you charity in your church?"

Marylou was speechless for the first time since Scooter had known her. He almost applauded the girl's accomplishment.

Carrie Roberts stepped up to defend her mother. "Don't talk to Mama like that. She's cried all day for your parents. For you, too. She even wanted to offer for you to come stay with us. She's just saying what everyone else is thinking, Ericka. It is weird that all of them were people who moved to St. Joan in the past ten years. Not one of *us* has been killed."

"I trusted you, but you're not my friend," Ericka said in a whisper. "You never were. None of you."

"Come on, Carrie Ann," Marylou said, grabbing her daughter's hand and almost running from the room. At the door she hesitated long enough to add, "We've been more than charitable to you and your kind, Ericka Cassidy. We welcomed you into our homes, and all we got for our kindness was dragged into the middle of a horrible mess. Well, you can bet we'll be more careful about including strangers into our circle again."

Scooter had heard enough. He pushed heavily to his feet and lumbered across the office in a surprisingly quick few steps. "Thank you for coming in, Marylou, Carrie." He almost shoved them out the door. To Bobbi, he said, "You want to stay while I talk to Ericka?"

"Of course."

He closed the door behind them, motioned to chairs in front of his desk, then reclaimed his own seat. His voice when he spoke again was almost gentle. "You feeling better, kiddo?"

Ericka only nodded, but tears she couldn't seem to control filled her eyes with the kind question.

"Well, don't you go paying any attention to what Marylou said. She's just scared. People get scared they tend to say things they don't mean."

Ericka didn't answer as she accepted a tissue from Bobbi and dabbed at the corners of her eyes.

"You want to tell me about last night," he prodded in

the same quiet tone. His voice was deep and gravelly, but he was doing his best to temper its roughness.

"About when I found my parents?"

"Well, let's start before then. You were out with Keen Bohannon, Bert tells me. What time did he drop you off?"

Ericka opened her mouth to answer the question, tell him about coming home, then leaving again, when his deputy knocked on the door, then opened it without waiting for a summons.

"Sorry to bother you, Sheriff, but we just got finished at the Cassidy place. Found something in the trash can thought you might be interested in seeing."

"What is it, Waylin?" Scooter asked with exasperation that was brought on more by the sight of Marylou and Carrie Roberts still standing outside the door.

"Found this dress. Mrs. Roberts here says it belongs to Ericka. It's got blood all over the front of it, Sheriff."

Scooter looked at Ericka, saw her face blanch, saw her shoulders hunch forward. He'd never witnessed anything more pitiful. His voice was even gruffer than usual when he barked an order for Waylin to bring the dress in. He snatched it from the man's hands. "Now clear that office outside, and tell Marylou that if I hear one word of this from anyone I'll charge her with obstruction of justice." But even Marylou's indignant huff didn't offer much satisfaction as he looked at the ruined dress in his hands.

"You wanna tell me about this, Ericka?"

She was trembling now. Bobbi reached for her hand, drew it into her lap and gave it a fierce squeeze. "I . . . I didn't kill my parents, Sheriff Witcomb. You have to believe that. I loved them more than anything in the world."

He smiled, hoping to lend some reassurance. "Now, I didn't think any such thing. But you have to explain how the blood got on this dress and why it was in the trash bin."

"It . . . it was my graduation dress," Ericka began. "I went dancing last night with Bo and some of the other kids. Bo and I left kind of early." She stopped. She couldn't tell them. It was too personal.

"Go on, honey," Bobbi prodded.

"I can't."

"Ericka, would it be easier to talk if it was just the two of us?" the sheriff asked.

"No!"

"Okay, then, honey, go on. I give you my word, whatever you say in here will stay inside these four walls."

Ericka was quiet for a long time. But suddenly, she said the words. "Bo and I made love. It . . . it was the first time I'd . . . I'd ever done anything, gone all the way. I was lying on my dress."

Gawddamnit. No wonder people call us pigs.

"We had a fight afterwards. He dropped me off at home. I showered and hid the dress in my closet." She'd been staring at a spot on the floor, but she raised her eyes to meet Scooter's. The worst had been told. She could face him now. "It wasn't that my parents would have been angry. They would have understood. That's just the way they were. But I was hurt by something Bo had said. I didn't want to talk about it with them yet."

"What time did Bohannon drop you off?"

"I don't know. Not exactly. I think it was around eleven-thirty. Maybe twelve."

"Did you talk to your parents at all?"

The tears had started again. They spilled over her eyelids and choked in her throat. "Yes, I lied to them. I told them Bo and I were going out again to a party. I just wanted to be alone for awhile to think about the fight we'd had—"

"Mind telling me what your fight was about?"

"I don't think that's really any of our business, Sheriff," Bobbi interjected.

"Maybe not, but we don't know that, do we?" He directed his gaze to Ericka. "I'm sorry to have to get so personal, hon."

Ericka hardly heard the apology. She answered his question. "He—Bo—said something about his dad being wrong. I guess Mr. Bohannon had argued with him before he left to pick me up. He told him I was too good for him. Bo said something about proving his dad wrong. I was hurt. I thought that was the only reason he'd pushed me into . . . doing it, having sex with him."

"Oh, sugar, he didn't mean that," Bobbi said, putting an arm around the young woman's shoulder and wiping tears from her own eyes now.

"I know. I left the house and drove around the lake for a couple of hours. By the time I went home I wasn't mad at him anymore. I was going to call him today and tell him."

"What time was that? That you got home, I mean?"

"Just after two."

"And that's when you found them?"

Ericka shook her head. "I didn't find them for another ten minutes or so. I noticed that their bedroom door was still open—the light was shining down the stairs—and I thought that was weird. But I smelled the blood. Only . . . only I thought it was from my dress. I got it out of the closet and took it to the garage. I hid it under some bags so my mother wouldn't find it." She paused, swallowing convulsively a few times as she fought the wave of nausea that came with remembering the smell of all that blood. "When I went back upstairs I could still smell it. I don't know why, but I think I knew right then. I went upstairs and they . . . they were there."

"Then you went to the Bohannons'. Why was that?" Scooter coaxed.

"I knew you were fishing. So I thought I'd go find Bo."

"But why didn't you take your car?"

"Oh, for Christ's sake, Sheriff. She was in shock. She wasn't thinking straight."

A knock sounded on the office door again. Scooter muttered a curse under his breath. "Come in!" he barked.

Opening the door only far enough to stick her head through, Martha announced Julia Hanover's arrival.

"We're about finished here. Tell her we'll be out directly." Scooter turned his attention to Ericka. "You didn't see anything else? Hear anything when you got home?"

"No."

"Well, then I think that about does it for now." He glanced down at the dress in front of him, gathered it up and dropped it to the floor underneath the desk. "I'm sorry you had to tell me something you should have been able to keep private, Ericka. I'm gonna forget I ever heard it, and I want you to forget it, too. All I want you to do is take care of yourself. Get some rest."

"Thank you," she responded properly, politely.

"Don't you be going and worrying about what Marylou Roberts said either, you hear me?"

"Yes, sir."

"I don't know why anyone would want to hurt your parents. They were good, decent people. I was very fond of them both."

"Thank you," Ericka replied dutifully again. She stood up, started for the door, then stopped. "Sheriff, may I ask you something?"

"Anything at all."

"Did . . . did he take one of their shoes?"

"Who we talkin' about?" Scooter asked, but Ericka wasn't fooled.

"Please, Sheriff Witcomb. It's important that I know."

Scooter sighed heavily, ran a hand over his hair, then scratched at the back of his neck in an effort to avoid an answer. Finally, he shook his head. "Can I ask you something first?"

"I suppose."

"How did you know about the missing shoes?"

"My parents. They told me yesterday just before I went out."

"Do you happen to know how they found out about the shoes, Ericka? We were kind of careful about keeping that to ourselves."

"Dr. Grant told them. They planned to talk to you tomorrow when you got back from your fishing trip."

Lawd have mercy.

Ericka waited, then pressed for an answer to her original question. "Did the killer take one of my parents' shoes, Sheriff?"

"Yes, hon, he did. But I don't want you worrying about that. We'll find him. You hang onto that notion, girl."

This time Ericka didn't speak. She couldn't. She didn't believe him.

The following evening Ericka accompanied her grandmother to the Bohannons' private apartments for an informal dinner that Bobbi had organized.

In the first few hours, Ericka hadn't talked much with her grandmother. Words hadn't been adequate to the devastation of their loss. But on Sunday as they'd shared their lunch in the privacy of the hotel suite the Bohannons had so graciously put them up in, her grandmother had surprised her by reaching across the table to take her hand in hers. "You're all I have left,

Ericka. I'm going to do the best I can to help you recover from this tragedy. I wasn't always there for your mother, child. I let my career as a lawyer then later as a judge get in the way. She turned out so beautifully all on her own. Married that marvelous, brilliant man and found a career of her own. None of it any thanks to me. I was proud of her, Ericka. I didn't tell her enough how very proud I was. But I can tell you, and I will. Unfortunately I didn't make enough memories with either your mother or your father after they were married but I promise you I'll share them all with you. And I'll be there for you as I wasn't for my Linda."

"She was proud of you, too, Grandmother. The day you became a judge, she told me it was one of her proudest moments."

"Bless you, child."

After that, they had both gone to their separate bedrooms to lie down. When they awakened, a young man was at the door with suitcases filled with Ericka's clothing and personal effects. "Ms. Bohannon said to tell you she got as much as she could from your house," he told Ericka.

Now, in the Bohannons' dining room, Ericka thanked Bobbi. "I'll never be able to repay your kindness to me. You didn't have to go to the house. I know it had to be difficult."

"Nonsense. It was no trouble at all. Petite went with me."

"Thanks," Ericka told Petite.

"No big deal."

But it was a big deal. Ericka had known the Bohannons for more than ten years, but only as the people who owned the resort hotel. Then there'd been Bo but he'd left her. Disappeared when she needed him most. But not his family. They'd been there for her and even in her grief she felt something new begin to grow within her. Tears that wouldn't stay pushed away needled at her eyelids again. "I love you all," she said.

Her parents were laid to rest Tuesday afternoon.

As Ericka stood beside their caskets at the grave site, she thought that all of St. Joan must have come out. All except Bo. No one had been able to find him. Well, that was okay. She didn't need him now. She'd survived the worst without him.

She slipped her hand into her grandmother's. She was leaving St. Joan in less than two hours, going to Boston. The thought of leaving the lake town that had been her home for more than a decade was the only thing that had sustained her through the past three days. Her parents had been murdered, but that wasn't the only thing that had been taken from her. She'd lost the boy she'd thought she was falling in love with. He'd deserted her. She'd lost her best friend. Carrie hadn't called once since their meeting at the sheriff's office. But she'd lost even more than that. She lost her belief in everything that was good and decent. Only her grandmother and Bobbi Bohannon had been there for her during these devastating days. They'd been kind and compassionate, loving and supportive. But it wasn't enough.

She looked around at the crowd which was gathered to pay tribute to her parents.

Hypocrites.

Her friends stood on the far side of the burial bier, all five of them, knotted together. Pam and Sally Jane weeping quietly. Carrie leaning on Brett. Aaron and Junior sober and ramrod straight.

Marylou Roberts held her husband's hand as she whispered quietly with Phoebe Pearson who clung to her husband's arm.

Rhonda Grant stood alone near the foot of Lawrence

Cassidy's casket. She looked lost and unapproachable. Every now and then she reached forward to brush her fingers over the gleaming mahogany as if she had confused his casket with that of her husband's who had been buried only eight days before.

Althea and Scooter Witcomb stood by the minister's side, the sheriff's face raised heavenward as if the answers he sought might suddenly come from that direction; hers contorted with grief that seemed somehow overdone.

Bobbi, Bert, and Petite Bohannon were gathered on Ericka's left. The only "outsiders" besides her grandmother and herself.

A sea of others stood behind the initial circle as far as Ericka could see.

The reverend asked the mourners to join him in the Lord's Prayer. Obediently every mouth began to form the words. All except Ericka's.

When the prayer was concluded, the reverend smiled benevolently her way. "On behalf of Lawrence and Linda Cassidy's daughter, I thank you all for this show of love. In the difficult days to come, I'm sure it will help her to know how well thought of her parents were. Please travel back to your homes in peace and safety."

Ericka hadn't planned on speaking. The words seemed to come of their own volition. "I want to say something!"

Everyone paused, stared at her, waited.

"My parents loved it here. They were happy. They loved you. They trusted you." She offered a small apologetic smile to Bobbi Bohannon, excluding her. "It was misplaced. One of you killed them." She heard the collective gasp, revelled in it. They were shocked. Good. "Sheriff Witcomb has vowed to find out which one of you it is. If he doesn't, I'll be back. You won't get away with it." She paused to meet the eyes of those nearest her, stopping on her playmates.

The five of them looked surprised, then uncomfortable, even afraid though they did their best to disguise it. Ericka's answering smile was confident. "I promise."

BOOK II

I don't want to play in your yard
I don't like you anymore.
You'll be sorry when you see me
Sliding down my cellar door.
You can't hollar down my rain barrel.
You can't climb my apple tree.
I don't want to play in your yard
If you can't be nice to me.

—Unknown

April 22, 1995–
April 29, 1995

Chapter Eleven

She was back. No longer a girl. No longer a victim. She'd shed the idealism of her youth, conquered the demons which had haunted her dreams after her parents' murder, squelched the hurt and heartache of her friends' betrayal. But victory had been costly. Now, someone was going to foot the bill.

He watched her carrying boxes from her car into the house she'd rented. It wasn't voyeurism, just an accidental sighting. But once he'd seen her, he hadn't been able to turn away. She was beautiful. More beautiful than she'd been ten years before. More beautiful even than her photo layout in *Playmates* had promised.

She wore little makeup. Her hair—still long—was pulled back from her face in an artless ponytail. She was dressed in a flannel shirt, loose-fitting jeans, and tennis shoes. Hardly the attire one expected to see on a celebrity.

Leaning against the door jamb, Keen swigged from his can of beer as if the thirst he was suddenly experiencing could be quenched by the foamy brew. He'd loved her the way lyricists described it in songs and poets in poetry. The memory of their brief time together had been seared into his soul, but then so had his guilt. And there was no separating one from the other.

Ericka paused to balance a box on her hip while wrestling with the front door of the house she was moving into. Pinning the box between her hip and the jamb, she wiped at perspiration which trickled from her hairline, then shoved the door open. The box tipped with the thrust of her body and she muttered a frustrated curse when she fell through the door and heard the telltale clink of glass as the box crashed to the floor beneath her. "Damn and double damn."

She scrambled quickly to her feet looking around with embarrassment though that was silly. She was isolated here. That was what had attracted her to the property in the first place. She'd wanted privacy and the "house on the hill" as the real estate agent had described it afforded her exactly that.

Located atop a timber-rich knoll and surrounded by eighteen acres of wilderness, it was the perfect hideaway. From the living room in the rear to the master bedroom it overlooked the lake several feet below. The only other building was below as well. A fisherman's cottage that was owned by the same people, but rented separately. It was toward that cottage that Rikki directed her bemused gaze once she'd picked herself up from her ungraceful entrance into her new home. But the place looked little better than a dilapidated storage shed. No one would be living there.

She squinted against the bright afternoon sun. She could have sworn she saw someone move behind the screen door. But that was ridiculous, wasn't it? Damn it, she wished she'd asked the realtor if someone was currently living there. Not only for the sake of her eccentric penchant for privacy that came with the territory of celebrity but for safety's sake. Besides, what if someone was using the house without the owner's knowledge? He'd want to know, wouldn't he? She made a mental note to call the agency as soon as she had the last of her boxes and luggage out of the car.

However, a glance at her watch forty-five minutes later told her that the call would have to wait until the next day. The young man who had arranged the lease on the house had told her the office would be closed at two on Saturday in deference to the annual Spring Festival. Did she know about it? he'd asked. Then without waiting for her answer, had gone into lengthy detail about the event which included a parade, carnival, and street dance. Rikki could have saved him the trouble. She remembered every detail of the festival. How could she ever forget? She'd attended every year, then gone on her first date with Keen Bohannon almost exactly ten years before.

Thoughts of the first man she'd ever loved created an uneasy sensation in the pit of her stomach. Rikki found it both pleasant and disagreeable. It wasn't that she harbored bitter feelings for him anymore. On the contrary, she could smile over the sweetness of their brief relationship. It hadn't always been so. For a long time after moving to Boston with her grandmother, she'd thought she hated him for abandoning her in her time of greatest need, had even wondered if he were the monster who had butchered her parents. But the last was absurd. She couldn't have loved the madman who had done that. And she had loved him. As for the first, she was over that resentment as well. They'd both been young, impetuous, easily moved to romance, and as easily hurt. Kids. Still, she wasn't sure how he'd react to her coming back . . . and in such a dramatic reappearance. Notice of her homecoming had been blatant and audacious. And her reincarnation into St. Joan society was going to be just as bold. She couldn't help but dread her first meeting with him. If she knew him at all, he wasn't going to be pleased. None of them were.

Dr. Aaron Grant slowed his car as he passed the house on the hill. He'd seen movement up there in the trees near the driveway. Could be a deer, but it had looked like. . . . Grabbing his binoculars from the seat beside him, he raised them to his eyes and aimed them toward the spot where he'd seen the flash of red.

"Son of a bitch," he muttered as he stepped on the accelerator and automatically flicked on the turn signal. Two minutes later he was climbing from his Jeep. "Hey, girl!" he called to Rikki.

Rikki spun on her heel, surprise on her face for only a second before the radiant smile he remembered from their youth flashed into place. "Aaron, hi." She tucked her hands into her jeans pockets as she walked toward him. "How did you know I was up here?"

"Didn't. Not 'till about five minutes ago when I saw something moving in the trees. Knew no one lived here, so I stopped to check it out. Looked through my binoculars and saw this strange redheaded creature. . . ."

Rikki laughed but sobered quickly. "Mind not spreading it around? About where I'm living, I mean. I've kind of gotten used to my privacy."

Aaron scratched the back of his neck. "Well, I won't say anything, but I don't think you'll be keeping your secret for long. You forgotten how nosy folks are around here?"

He was surprised by the way her blue eyes darkened. He hadn't meant to stir up painful memories. He'd actually expected her quick laughter again. Still, he supposed he should have known. She hadn't come back because her memories were happy ones. "Sorry, Ericka, guess that wasn't very tactful."

She smiled now. "No, you're right. I suppose I had

forgotten how fast word travels. But if you don't mind, let's let them find out on their own."

"Sure thing. Won't even mention it to Pamela Sue."

"How is she?"

"Good. Real good. Just had another baby two weeks ago."

"So, let me see, that must make four. The others are a boy and two girls, right? What was this one?"

"Boy," he said, grinning and rocking on his heels. "You've been keeping tabs on us, huh?"

"Read the papers."

"They sell the St. Joan Banner all the way up in Boston?"

"No," she laughed, blushing as if caught in a guilty secret. "I have a clipping service that sends it to me."

"Well, now anything you missed, you can catch up on in person."

"Yes, I plan to do exactly that."

Aaron studied her, noticing the way her expression had hardened with the last statement before settling back into a relaxed look of reserved friendliness. "Well, guess I'd better be getting on home. I promised Pam I'd give the baths before we go into town for the festival tonight."

"Tell her I said hello."

"Will do," he said, climbing back in behind the wheel. "Maybe you'd like to come out to the house for dinner one night." When she hesitated, he grinned. "I guess you didn't come back for socializing, huh?"

"Actually, I'm planning a dinner party of my own. As a matter of fact, the invitation should have arrived today."

Aaron didn't answer at once. When he did, his tone had lost much of its friendliness. "Gettin' right to it, huh?"

"Yes, Aaron, that's exactly what I'm doing."

"I hope you don't regret it."

"Is that a threat?" she asked, inadvertently backing up a step or two.

"From me? Lordy, no, Ericka. I'm in the business of saving lives, not taking them." He started to shut his door, but she signalled him to wait.

"One more thing, Aaron."

"Shoot."

"It's not Ericka anymore. It's Rikki."

"She's back!" Carrie said as soon as Sally Jane came onto the line.

"We must be talking about the infamous Rikki Blue," Sally Jane said, shaking her head at her friend's excited intro into their conversation.

"She'll always be Ericka to me, and of course that's who I'm talking about. We just got an invitation to a dinner party, and Aaron called. Said he'd seen her. She has a bright red Cherokee and it was loaded to the brim. Not exactly slinking into town."

"Oh, for God's sake, Carrie. She bought the radio station. She plans to do her own show starting Monday morning. They've been running promo pieces for a month. Why would she bother to 'slink' at this point?"

"I don't know. It's just all so bizarre. First that tasteless magazine with her nude pictures plastered all over, including the cover, now the radio show. I would never have thought Ericka would be so brazen."

"That's the key right there. She's not Ericka Cassidy anymore. She's a radio superstar, Rikki Blue, who took the airwaves by storm five years ago. I don't suppose coming to Small Town, America to do the same thing seems like such a big deal to her."

"You can't really be so blasé about this, Sally Jane. I mean it isn't as if we don't know why she's really here."

"Of course we do, but there's nothing we can do about it but sit back and enjoy the show."

"*I'm* not going to even listen."

"Bull shit!"

Carrie giggled. "Well, not if Brett has anything to say about it. He's forbidden me to turn the radio station on. He even spoke about it from the pulpit last Sunday. Cautioned his parishioners about being swayed by this disciple of Satan's. And he's been holed up in the rectory all day writing tomorrow's sermon. I imagine we're going to be treated to some real hell fire and brimstone preaching tomorrow."

"Give me a fucking break. No offense, Carrie, but sometimes that husband of yours gives me a royal pain in the back side."

This time there was no answering titters, but Sally Jane suspected only because Carrie was struggling against them. The Reverend's wife had never spoken a word against her husband—at least not to her—but Sally Jane wasn't deaf, dumb, and blind . . . or an idiot. And a person would have to be all four not to notice that for all his preaching about paradise, their marriage was far from perfect. Besides there'd been rumors about another man.

"Hey," Carrie said suddenly, "you must have seen her arrive, too. That's why you didn't sound surprised when I called."

"Nope. Just got back from Camdenton five minutes ago, but I knew she was arriving. Bobby Hayden, one of my agents, handled the lease on a house for her."

"And you never said a word." Carrie's tone was accusing.

"Sorry, honey, but that goes with the territory. Unwritten law of every successful real estate broker. We don't discuss our clientele."

"But you just did."

"You're right. I've said too much," Sally Jane said agreeably. "And lest I say more than I should, I'd better hang up now. But, hey, you need a safe place to listen to the broadcast Monday, come on over to the office. You can tell Brett that you're going shopping."

"Lie?" Carrie said with mock seriousness.

"Why not? It wouldn't be the first time."

"Sometimes you're an absolute bitch, Sally Jane Matthers."

"Most of the time, honey."

Carrie laughed. "Okay, I'll let you go, but first, aren't you a little excited to see her?"

"We're talking about Rikki again? Sure, why not? I liked her. I'm real interested to see what she's like after all these years."

"Me, too," Carrie admitted. Then, "Besides, I've missed her. I hope she doesn't still hate me."

"Honey, there's one thing you might as well admit. She hates us all, and who can blame her? She told us a secret the night her parents were killed. She made it pretty obvious that she believes one of us is responsible for what happened to them. I've got a feeling we're all guilty until proven innocent in this case."

"Then you think Brett's right when he says she's going to rattle our lives as surely as Joshua rocked the walls of Jericho?"

"Honey, I think your husband is a class A asshole, but yes, in this case I think his metaphor is apt. You know it too. All of us that were there that night know it. She promised."

Sheriff A. R. Witcomb stood in the doorway of the St. Joan jailhouse. The four cell building was packed full. Mostly drunks picked up for their own good. A couple of young men caught robbing Sam Peters's Bait and Tackle shop. One serious offender. A repeater. Already done two stints in Fulton Penitentiary. Last night he'd shot a clerk in a gas station down the highway. It wasn't in Scooter's jurisdiction, but an all points had been put out on the fellow and this morning, just before seven a.m., Junior had spotted him and brought him in.

But Scooter wasn't thinking about any of his "visitors." He was thinking of the arrival of Ericka Cassidy. Oh, he knew that she didn't go by that name anymore, but that was just too gawdamned bad. In his mind, she'd always be the Cassidy girl. And thinking about the homecoming of Ericka Cassidy reminded him of the murder spree of '85 that he'd failed to solve. It was a painful memory, that terrible six week period. Hated to think about it even now. He'd failed to do his duty as sheriff. Now, she'd kept her vow to come back and do it for him. Couldn't have that.

Scooter was a simple man. Not stupid but simple, and that meant there was a lot he didn't know about. But he knew lawkeepin'. He knew that sometimes criminals got away. But he knew, too, that just because they *got* away didn't mean they necessarily *went* away. In this case, he was pretty near certain the person who had killed Bunny, Doc Grant, the Cassidys, and the others had never gone anywhere. He'd known back then that the killer was a resident of St. Joan. He hadn't had proof, but he'd known it in his gut just as he knew that the murderer was still living in St. Joan. What he didn't know was who'd done 'em.

Those killings had haunted him for a good number of years. He'd always felt the failure personally, taken the blame squarely on his own shoulders. But he'd come to terms with it. For whatever reason that someone had killed six times, the murderer had stopped with Linda and Lawrence Cassidy. And Scooter was convinced that Ericka Cassidy's return could only force the bastard to kill again. Scooter had been fond of the girl. Didn't doubt he would be again if given half a chance. He didn't want the creep to make her the seventh victim. Her or anybody else. Besides, he was afraid. He'd never allowed the thought much prominence before, but what if the killer was someone he loved? What if it was his own son?

Deputy Allan Witcomb sat in his cruiser watching his father across the commons. The old man was stewing about Ericka Cassidy, no doubt about it. Probably afraid she was going to find out about him and Bunny. Junior couldn't blame him. He wasn't too thrilled with the prospect of that happening himself. But if she did, so what? What did that prove? Not a thing. Still, maybe he should keep an extra close eye on her.

He glanced down the street toward the bank parking lot where the floats were getting last minute repairs and touches. He was supposed to be keeping the main drag clear of vehicles. But, hell, it wasn't scheduled to begin for another hour. He could drive out to the place she'd rented, just have a look see and be back in thirty minutes.

He pulled off his Rayban sunglasses, gave the lenses each a shot of spittle and a quick rub with his shirt sleeve, then put them back on as he pulled away from the curb. He glanced into his rearview mirror and spotted his old man still standing out back of the jail. He grinned. It was a good bet that even Scooter didn't know where she'd moved. Hell, Junior had known before the ink was even dry on the lease contract. His dad didn't give him much credit as a deputy, but then that was fine. It proved beneficial being underestimated. And it suited his lifestyle just fine.

Brett took his wire-frame glasses off, hunched his shoulders, and rested his elbows on his desk in the rectory. He pinched the bridge of his nose with his thumb and forefinger. Lord, he was tired. He'd spent almost eight hours getting tomorrow's sermon just right. But the message he wanted to impart was vitally important. Especially now that Ericka Cassidy was coming back. Probably was back by now. Her radio show was scheduled to air on Monday. Then there was the dinner party she'd planned for Tuesday night.

He rubbed his hand over his face as if he could erase his weariness. But the kind of tired he was emanated from the soul. It wasn't easy being the shepherd of more than a thousand sheep. His responsibilities were heavy. Especially when he had a wife who was always testing him, thwarting his authority.

He glanced at the clock on the rectory office wall. It was time to meet Carrie now. He'd promised to have his sermon completed by five so they could get to town for the barbecue and street dance. His parishioners would be expecting them. But he had no desire to mingle with them tonight, putting on an act, pretending to relax and enjoy himself when he had other things on his mind.

Like Ericka Cassidy.

Like the invitation he'd received in the mail today.

Opening his top drawer, he pulled out the foil-lined envelope and read the powder-blue card again.

Rikki Blue requests the honor of your company
at a private dinner party Tuesday, April 18, 1995
8:00 P.M.
Bar-Ber-Keen Resort Hotel—Queen Ann Suite
Black Tie required
R.S.V.P. 555-9898, Mr. Hollins Parker, Hotel Manager

He'd ordered Carrie to ignore the woman's return to St. Joan. Pretend they'd never heard of her. Apparently that wasn't going to be possible. She'd returned to wreak havoc on their lives. He couldn't allow her to get away with it.

Picking up the phone, he telephoned his wife. "Call the resort, Carrie," he said without preamble when she answered. "Tell Mr. Parker that we'll be attending the dinner party Ericka is giving Tuesday night."

"But I thought you wanted me to ignore her."

"I've changed my mind. I'm the pastor, Carrie Ann. It's my duty to face the devil head on."

Carrie giggled.

"What's so funny?"

"You," she said laughing again. "You're so . . . so melodramatic. Ericka's not the devil. She's just a woman who's become powerful enough to throw her weight around. I can't imagine that you're letting her upset you."

"She's not upsetting me, dear. But I think it's a mistake to underestimate her. We've lived in peace for ten years. Now she wants to stir it all up again. As pastor of the largest congregation in St. Joan, I think it's obvious that I have a vested interest in seeing that she not be allowed to do that."

"Oh, for heaven's sake, Brett. You're not exactly Billy Graham." She laughed again, derision evident in the sound. "Are we still going to town for the festival?"

"Perhaps you'd rather go with someone else," he said softly.

"Of course not. Who would I rather go with than my own husband?" she asked.

Brett smiled into the receiver. He'd heard the nervousness in her voice. "Never mind calling Bar-Ber-Keen, I'll take care of it myself. I'll be home in five minutes. Be ready to go." He hung up the phone, then stared at the embossed invitation in his hand once again. Picking up the receiver, he called the hotel and accepted on behalf of his wife and himself.

That done, he grinned. He was going to enjoy this, he decided. He'd gotten real good at watching Carrie. Rikki Blue, as she was calling herself these days, should prove an interesting challenge.

* * *

"God should strike her down for coming back and making me relive the pain all over again," Rhonda Grant told her daughter-in-law as she peeled potatoes at the sink.

"Oh, come on, Rhonda, you haven't even seen her yet. How could her homecoming make you relive Dr. Jase's death?" Pamela Sue asked.

"You heard what Aaron said. She's going on the radio Monday morning. She's really going to do it, and we know what she's going to say. She's going to talk about the murders." She dropped the knife into the colander to wring her hands. "I just can't stand it."

"Then don't listen."

"You think it's as easy as that? If I don't listen, I won't know? Don't you think Marylou and Phoebe and Wanda May over at the library will be only too anxious to call me and tell me every single detail?"

"Then stay out here with the children and me. You could help with the baby and avoid their phone calls at the same time."

"That might be all well and good for me, but what about you and Aaron?"

Pamela Sue sighed with exasperation. "What about us, Rhonda?"

"You read that invitation and you heard Aaron say he intends to go. You don't suppose she merely wants to talk about the good old days, do you?"

"I don't know what she wants."

"Yes you do. I heard you talking about it with Aaron in your bedroom."

Pam started to jump her for eavesdropping but thought better of it. What good would it do? Rhonda had always minded their business. Especially in the past three years since she'd taken to spending more nights in their home than in her own. Probably even knew when the last two kids had been conceived. "Okay," she said, struggling to keep her tone civil, "so we don't believe it's to rekindle old friendships. You know that she apparently thinks one of us who was out with her the night her parents were killed did it since she's convinced no one else knew that they were even remotely involved with the investigation of the other deaths. But you also know that that's ridiculous."

"You're wrong, Pamela Sue. I don't know any such thing."

"*What?* What are you saying?" Pam demanded.

"What if I told you that Aaron dated that Apperson woman and Cindy Richvalski, too?"

"Oh, my God, you're sick," Pam said, pushing herself away from the table and hurrying from the room.

"I may be sick, but I'm not the one who hated his father!"

"Hello, Blue," Keen said.

Rikki spun around. She'd come to town to buy some groceries. She hadn't intended to join the festivities, but she'd gotten caught up in the traffic. She'd had to park her car a good half mile from the grocery store and walk. She was still wending her way through the throng of parade watchers when she heard her name. Unconsciously she ran a hand over her hair, then made a weak effort to smooth the wrinkles in her flannel shirt. "Bo, I didn't see you."

The same lazy grin she'd thought she'd forgotten slid across his face. "Obviously, though if you'd taken one more step backwards you would have knocked me down and landed in my lap."

"Oh, sorry," she said, feeling herself blush and hating herself for letting him fluster her. She shifted her weight from one foot to the other wishing she could just say "been good seeing you" and get on about her business, but she couldn't. She just couldn't. "How . . . how are you?"

"Can't complain. You?"

"Me? I'm fine. Good. Real good."

Again that slow spreading grin. "Yeah, I kinda saw that from the photo layout in that magazine."

"Leave it to you to miss the point," she said, starting to turn away.

"Oh, you're wrong there, baby. I guarantee I didn't miss a thing."

She stopped, clinched her fists, then slowly turned back to face him. "Then you know I mean business. I'm going to find out who killed my parents." She paused a beat, then added pointedly, "No matter who it is."

His casual attitude disappeared, and he visibly straightened. "You're asking to get hurt, Blue. I don't want to see that happen."

"I'm not a naive little girl anymore, Bo. I've learned to take care of myself. I learned the hard way."

Electricity charged the air between them.

"Well, then," he said, leaning against the wall of the building. "I won't worry about you."

"You never did."

He watched her walk away. He had no defense. She was right. He hadn't been there for her. He didn't want to be there for her now. He'd devoted a lot of time and energy to learning not to care, not to feel. Especially about her.

Chapter Twelve

The next morning Rikki was disoriented when she awakened. For ten years she'd woken up to bustling Boston traffic noises. The lake's quiet country sounds were alien and confusing. She turned on her side and stared out the window at the lake, focusing her attention on the voices that the water carried up to her, then on the birds that chirped and cried and screeched. The sky was as blue as she'd ever seen it, promising a glorious spring day. An early morning breeze whipped the tree branches, rustling the oaks that hadn't quite shaken off the dead leaves of the year before. It all brought back memories of her childhood when she'd thought life perfect, had considered herself part of an existence that was flawless and invincible.

Loneliness began to envelop her. Loneliness and renewed grief that she thought she'd worked through with the therapist she'd seen every week for more than five years. It was as if it had been captured here waiting for her return. Now it seemed to seep into her pores, enveloping her, and threatening to drown her.

"No," she said, resolutely flinging back the light covers which she'd drawn up over her during the night.

In spite of the spring day, the morning air carried a decided chill. Rikki thought about closing the window she'd left open during the night but decided against it.

She needed the cool to invigorate her. She smiled as she stretched, thinking of her grandmother. She could almost hear Julia's voice, softly modulated but chastising all the same. "You should be kicked for leaving the window open, Ericka. It's bad enough that you persist in this foolhardy quest of yours. Must you *invite* the killer into your home by giving him easy access." Rikki's grin, which had appeared with thought of Julia, disappeared. He wouldn't come yet, she thought. He'd wait. Watch. Find out what she knew. Then he'd strike.

She sat down on the edge of her bed, reached beneath her pillow, and pulled out the gun. She'd be ready.

Keen was ready. As ready as he'd ever be for the visit to the cemetery that he made every Sunday. His weekly pilgrimage. His penance.

He opened the door, started to step out, hesitated as he saw the red Cherokee come to life in the drive on the hill. He wondered where she was going so early on a morning when most lazed around. He wondered more than that about her. In fact the list of questions he would ask her if things were different, was endless. But things weren't different. They never would be. He'd fixed that the night he'd left for the Caribbean.

He ran a hand over his face. So many mistakes. How in the hell could one human being become such a fuck up?

Her hands shook as she placed the flowers in the vase in front of the marble marker, and tears burned in her eyes and throat. She arranged the bright bouquet with the same care one would a centerpiece for a dinner party. Stupid. They weren't here to see her artful arrangement. With the reminder, the tears she hadn't shed for more than five years pushed to the surface and overflowed. She slipped onto her backside and hugged her knees. "Oh, God, I still miss you both so much."

She buried her face against her knees and let the anguish drain out of her. She heard others drive into the cemetery, heard their footsteps, then their voices, but she paid them no heed. She didn't even look up until the last of her tears were spilled. Then she wiped at her face with her shirttail, laughing at herself. "Can you believe I didn't even bring any tissues?" The question was addressed to her parents. Ridiculous, but comforting all the same. She'd talked to them often during the years, but this was the first time she'd really felt close to them, felt like they could hear her. Not just ridiculous. Asinine. But she felt better.

Propping her chin on her knees now, she spoke to them again. "Everyone thinks I'm crazy for coming back here. I mean *everyone.* You should have heard my boss at WBOS. He ranted for two weeks after I told him I was leaving the show. He gave in finally, but he really lost it when he found out I'd bought the radio station here. I tried to explain to him, make him understand that I need autonomy, that owning the station was the only way to insure that, but he just shook his head and looked at me like I was one of those freak show attractions."

She laughed again, a sharp "ha" of a remembered hilarity. "Oh, but Kit was the worst. He threatened to have me locked up if I followed through with my plan to smoke out. . . . Anyway, he drove me to the airport, but he wasn't happy. You remember me telling you about him, don't you? He was the first friend I made at school. He's kind of stodgy for someone who's not even quite thirty yet, but he's a good friend.

"Well, anyway, I hope you both understand why I've come back. I just couldn't let it go. You deserve better. You were the best people I ever knew. Not just because you were my parents, though I expect people would accuse me of a certain amount of prejudice. You really were special. I knew it then. But I realize it even more today. The world's really gotten crazy. No one takes the time to sit back and just look at its beauty like you both did. Even me. But I will . . . once this is all behind me."

Another tear trickled along the bridge of her nose, fell to her hand. She smiled through trembling lips. "I don't want you to worry about me. I didn't come back without being prepared. I know it's dangerous and sometimes I even get scared, but I just have to do it. Besides, I know you'll look after me."

She pushed herself to her feet, dusted off her backside, then said, "Well, guess I'd better be going. I'll be back next week. Maybe I'll have something to tell you by then." She turned away, then hesitated and looked back. "I really love you guys . . . and I still miss you like crazy."

Jamming her hands into her jeans pockets, she turned on the ball of her foot and hurried away. She got only ten feet when she saw him. *Damn it!* She took a long, calming breath, then marched over to him.

"Is this going to become a habit?" she demanded. "I mean, I know St. Joan is small, but hell, I think I should be able to leave my house every now and then without running into you."

He was crouched down, resting on his haunches, so he had to crane his neck to stare up at her. He grinned. "You gonna be coming here very often?"

"I'd planned to," she admitted uncertainly. What did that have to do with anything? "Every Sunday . . . for as long as I'm here."

"Then I expect we'll be seeing each other at least every week unless you want to work out a schedule. You know, you come at nine or ten. I wait until one or two."

That's when she noticed the headstone.

Berton A. Bohannon & Barbara J. Bohannon
Aug 12, 1941–Jan 1, 1987 Mar 9, 1943–Aug 28, 1986

"Oh, Bo, I'm sorry. I'd forgotten that your parents are here." She stamped her foot. "I feel like an idiot."

Bo stood up to face her, and his grin was friendly, easy. "Hey, no big deal, okay?"

"You come here *every* Sunday?" she asked.

He laughed at the incredulity in her voice. "Hey, I was a shit, but not that big of a shit. I loved my mom, and Bert . . . well, he deserved better than he got from me. I just stop by and make sure their graves are being tended. No big deal. Just something I need to do."

"It is a big deal," she said softly. "It's one of the nicest things I've ever heard."

"You saying hello to your parents, too, huh?"

She was embarrassed by the tears which unexpectedly swam in her eyes. She looked away. "I didn't know how much I still missed them until today."

"They wouldn't want you to do this, Blue," he said so quietly she almost didn't catch it.

"Visit them?"

He frowned. "You know what I mean. They wouldn't want you putting yourself in jeopardy."

She bristled. She'd laughed about all the naysayers when she'd talked to her parents, but this was different. This was Bo. He had less right than anyone to tell her what to do. "I was sorry about your parents," she said stiffly. "They were very kind to me when. . . . Well, anyway, I'll let you get on with your visit."

"All done," he said with a nonchalant shrug. "I'll walk back to the cars with you."

They didn't speak again until they reached her Cherokee. Then they both paused, the moment awkward, neither of them seeming to know how to extract themselves from the awkward and uneasy meeting. "Well, I guess I'll be seeing you," she said at last.

"No doubt about it. Like you said, St. Joan's small."

She managed a smile as she toyed with the keys she'd fished out of her pants pocket.

He gave her a sort of salute and started to walk away. She stopped him. "I was sorry to learn that your marriage didn't work out, too."

He came back. "You been keeping pretty good tabs on us down here, haven't you?"

"I've subscribed to the paper. I read the announcement about your marriage, then your divorce. I was sorry. I wanted you to be happy." The last was said softly, an admission she hadn't known she was going to make.

He shrugged. "It wasn't meant to be. We got married for the wrong reasons. She didn't like living in Podunk. Wanted me to go into some big city law firm."

She laughed. "Yeah, that reminds me, you're the big man around town now, huh? Prosecuting attorney. Guess I'd better watch my p's and q's."

"I'm pretty easy."

"So if I get arrested for jaywalking, you won't throw the book at me?"

"I don't know about that. I might come down pretty hard on you if you're putting your life at risk." It was said as a joke, but the innuendo was clear.

"I can take care of myself like I told you last night. I'm real proficient at looking out for number one."

"I hope so, Blue, 'cause I got this nagging feeling you're about to stir up a hornet's nest, and the only way I know of to protect yourself from mad hornets is to run."

Instead of getting angry, she smiled. "You're pretty clever, Keen Bohannon. I bet you're one hell of a lawyer."

He looked away. He could have been. He wasn't. He shrugged it away, met her brilliant blue eyes again, grinned. "I'm real good at a lot of things, honey. Maybe

you'll be around long enough for me to remind you."
He watched the blue in her eyes turn to stormy gray.
Laughed.

"There isn't enough time left on earth, Bohannon."

He was still laughing when she drove away, but only
until she was out of sight and couldn't see him anymore.

Keen went home ... if one could call it that. The
two-room fishing cottage wasn't just small. It was run-
down and in need of some major repairs. Keen wasn't
a handyman. Besides, it didn't matter to him what it
looked like as long as the roof didn't cave in. It served
his needs.

It kept him dry.

It kept him warm.

No one bothered him here.

He could keep an eye on Blue.

Not that the last had been the reason for moving to
the tiny house. He'd just wanted escape after the sale of
Bar-Ber-Keen had been completed. He'd wanted time
to himself. A place to rail in private against a world that
had gotten too painful to face. His world.

But the amazing coincidence of Blue leasing the
house on the hill suited him just fine, he thought as he
poured himself a shot of Jack and popped the lid off a
bottle of Coors. That was another bonus of living in the
dilapidated house. He could drink whenever he felt the
need ... which was almost always these days.

He pulled a straight-back wood chair over to the window. He set the glass of whiskey and beer bottle on the
ledge, then propped his feet up there as well. Now that
he thought about it, maybe it wasn't such an accident
that Blue had leased the house. As a matter of fact, he
thought with a spreading grin, he'd bet a month's pay
that Sally Jane had steered her there on purpose. After
all, she was one of the few people in St. Joan who knew

where he hung his hat these days. He chuckled as he reached for his Coors, then raised the bottle in salute. "Way to go, S.J."

He sat at his watch post for more than two hours, two more bottles of beer, and three shots of whiskey, but gave it up when it became apparent that Blue wasn't coming back to the house. Probably gone to the radio station, he mused. Well, maybe she'd accommodate him long enough for a catnap. That was the only drawback of 'round the clock drinking. It dulled the painful memories—most of the time—but it made him sleepy.

He stretched out on the bed in the corner of the room. Folded his arms beneath his head and closed his eyes. He'd thought sleep would overcome him within minutes, but they ticked by without the usual result. His mind was unusually sharp this morning. He was tuned into every sound. The buzz of the refrigerator. The clicking of the big hand on the old clock. One of the few things he'd taken from the hotel. Belonged to his granddaddy, a man he'd never met, but a connection nonetheless. He heard children squealing and giggling on the pier around the bend, heard a dog barking in the farther distance. Heard tires crunch on the drive to the house on the hill. He didn't get up. Instead he conjured Blue's image in his mind. Saw her as she'd looked at the cemetery. Her face had been shiny with tears not quite dried. Her nose slightly swollen and red. Her hair, that flaming red mass of curls, had been tied back in a pony tail as it had been the day before, and she'd looked impossibly sexy in the ragged T-shirt and cutoff overalls. One of her tennis shoes had a hole in the toe. But she'd looked more beautiful than ever. He grinned, keeping his eyes closed. Guess it wasn't possible for her to look otherwise. When you've got it, you've got it.

He'd never deluded himself into thinking he'd ever gotten her out from under his skin. He'd been in love with her for a decade. But he'd thought he'd gone far enough in the healing process that seeing her again wouldn't twist his gut, cause his heart to jump, and his pecker to get involved. He was wrong. Some things just didn't go away or get any better.

With a growl of frustration, he turned onto his side, punched his pillow, and forced his thoughts away from her. Or tried. Problem was, sound carried in the country. He could hear the door slam on the house above him.

Then he heard the loud roar of a motor bike. *Sonofabitch.*

He scrambled from the bed to look out the window. *"Sonofabitch,"* he repeated aloud.

Rikki recognized her immediately, but it was no small wonder that she did.

Petite's black hair was cut in a radical hairstyle that Rikki had seen before in Boston and New York but hadn't expected to see in Middle America. Of course, even in 1985 Petite hadn't been Middle America. She'd always been different. Still . . .

"How are ya?" Petite asked with a wide smile that looked even bigger because of the bright red lipstick. Her dark oversized eyes, on the other hand, looked smaller because of the heavy black liner that rimmed them. "Hope you don't mind me stopping by. Had some extra keys I thought you might be able to use."

"Keys?"

"For the house."

Rikki was confused.

"I'm one of the owners." It contained the question "you didn't know."

"Oh, sorry, guess no one mentioned the owner's name to me."

Petite smiled, and ran her hand through her spiked coiffure. "Well, may I come in?"

"Oh, I'm sorry." Rikki moved out of the way, motioning with her hand for the other woman to enter. "I guess I must seem rude. I'm just so surprised to see you. I wasn't expecting . . ." She reached out, pulled the smaller woman into a tight embrace.

"Hey, it's cool. You didn't know. But I'm glad you're here."

"Thanks. It's good to see you again too. Here, sit down, tell me all about yourself," Rikki said, trying not to stare at the three inch tatoo that started at the other girl's shoulder and continued down her left arm.

Petite caught the look and grinned. This time the crooked grin reminded Rikki very much of another Bohannon.

"You like my snake? My old man did it for me. Got three more—tatoos, that is, not snakes. Got a rose on my tush. A butterfly on my ankle." She turned her leg to show it off. "And 'Mom and Dad' on my boob. Over my heart, you know? That was my first one. Had it done right after they croaked."

"I was sorry to hear about their deaths," Ericka said just as she had a few hours earlier to Bo.

"Yeah, it was pretty unreal. I mean we knew Mom was going. Doctors were real straight. As soon as they found the cancer, they told us she wouldn't last. But Dad's . . . well, his was a kick in the ass 'cause it came out of the blue." She met her hostess's gaze, adding, "Bo had a real hard time."

"He loved your mother a lot," Rikki said.

"That's the thing. It was Dad's death that shook him up the most."

Rikki didn't answer. The two men had not gotten along. Bobbi had written to her almost every week up until the last month of her life, but she'd always intimated that things were not better between her husband and son.

"That surprises you, huh? Woulda me, too, except

things changed between them after Mom died. I overheard a conversation between them the night of the funeral. . . ." She stopped, her eyes widening. "I guess you
don't want to hear all about my family life, huh? Not
like you don't have enough to think about yourself. I
mean, coming back—"

"No, I want to hear. They were good to me, your
folks. I'd like to hear what happened between Bert and
Bo."

"Well, Dad was real torn up when Mom died. I was
surprised. Me, I missed her, but I was glad to see her go.
She suffered something awful those last two months. I
thought Dad would be relieved, but he was a mess.
Couldn't accept that she was gone. Couldn't even sit
through the funeral. He left. Bo went looking for him
later. Found him sitting on the floor in their bedroom
holding her favorite dress. I got there right after that.
Dad was bawlin', talking about how much he loved her.
Then he looked up at Bo and said, 'I loved her from the
time we was tadpoles in the bayou but she only had eyes
for your daddy. When he died, I moved in, asked her
right then and there to marry me. She did, but only because she knew you needed a daddy. She even told me
that was why. Bobbi was the most honest person I ever
knew. I built this whole goddamned resort just so she'd
be proud I was her husband. Named it after the three
of us like we really was a family. But I always knew we
wasn't. I was just the man who couldn't fill my brother's
shoes. That's why I was always so angry with you and
her. To me you was my boy and she was my woman,
just like there never had been anyone before me. I did
it all wrong. For both of you.' "

Petite shrugged. "That's not exact, but it's pretty
close. I remember it pretty good 'cause Bo was crying
too by this time and then they were holding each
other." She shrugged. "Dad didn't get better. He just
moped around the hotel, not paying much attention to

business. Bo didn't want to go back to school. He wanted to stay and help, but Dad got mad. They had a real knock down drag out just like they used to have before. I thought that was a good sign that Dad was getting back to his old self, but as soon as Bo left he got worse. Bo came home at Christmas and more or less took over. They went shopping together, out drinking at night. Carousing, Dad called it. They went out New Year's Eve. Didn't come back in 'til after four. They were bumping into everything, laughing, talking loud. Woke me up." Petite hunched her shoulders. "How did we get on this morbid subject anyway?"

Rikki ignored the question. "What happened? I read about it in the paper, but it just said he'd died in his sleep. Was it alcohol poisoning?"

"No, would have been better for Bo if had been." Petite looked out the window for a long time. "Have you seen him yet?"

"Bo? Yes, we've run into each other a couple of times."

"He looks like shit, doesn't he?" She grinned then. "Don't get me wrong. He's still the handsomest man west of the Mississippi, but he's doing his best to destroy that. I worry about him." She gave her head a quick shake as if she could shake off her fears as well. "Maybe now that you're here that'll change. That's why I was glad when Sally Jane called and told me you'd leased the place."

"You mean because he's my landlord now? You think he'll take an interest in the place just because I'm living here?"

"Fuck—oops, sorry. I mean, heck no. He couldn't give a fig if we razed the place tomorrow. That's just it, Ericka, he doesn't care about much of anything anymore."

"At least he still has his work. That must keep him occupied."

"I don't think he's tried a case in months. Mary Beth Reynolds, the assistant P.A., does most of the work."

Rikki chewed on her knuckles for a long moment. "I'm thoroughly confused," she admitted finally.

"He blames himself for everything, Ericka. For not being here for you, for Dad's death, even for his marriage not working out. Some people don't feel guilt for anything. Not my brother. He feels it and doesn't let it go. He's real brown right now."

"Brown?" Ericka shook her head. "Sorry, you've lost me again."

Petite laughed. "Brown, the color of guilt. It's heavy. I'm an artist. I see everything in colors. My old man gets crazy when I tell him he's a certain color. But I'm always right."

"That's different. I hadn't heard anyone described by color. What color am I today?"

"You really want to know?"

"Sure. It's interesting."

Petite stared at her hostess for a long moment before announcing, "You're purple mostly. Sure of yourself. Determined. Confident. But there's some red and blue in there too. Red is the color of anger. Blue is melancholy or lonely."

Rikki gave her head a little shake. "That's pretty amazing. But how come Bo's all brown?"

"Like I said, he blames himself for all the ills of the world, and it's real heavy. Brown."

"I'll talk to him about . . . well, about what happened between us. We were just kids. Both of us. He couldn't have changed what happened that night." She got up from the chair she'd been sitting in. Walked over to the window as she shrugged off memories of that night. "You didn't say what happened to your father."

"He killed himself. Left a note that we could hardly read. Guess he'd written it after they got home. He was so drunk I don't know how he wrote anything, but he did."

"Oh, my God, I didn't know."

Petite shrugged. "Hey, it's over and done with. I'm not like Bo. I don't dwell on the past."

"That's good. It can be very debilitating."

Their eyes locked. After a moment, Petite said, "Yeah, I guess you would know a lot about that. That's why you've come back, isn't it?"

Rikki didn't answer. She was staring out the window. She saw movement in the fishing cottage below. She was sure of it this time. "Petite, I just remembered, I was going to call the realtor tomorrow. Is there anyone living in that house by the lake?" She turned to glance at the tiny woman seated behind her. Petite's eyes were as big as saucers. "Why are you looking at me that way?" Rikki asked.

"Are you serious? No one told you?"

"Told me what?"

"Bo. Bo lives there. That's what I meant when I said I was glad you'd leased the house. Maybe with you to keep his mind busy, he'll forget about killing himself with the bottle."

She didn't wait for an invitation, just pulled the screen door open and went in shooting . . . verbally. "Just who in the hell do you—" The house was empty.

She heard the toilet flush, felt herself flush with the sound. She almost retreated. Probably would have if the bathroom door hadn't opened just then.

He wore a towel. Around his neck. Otherwise he was stark naked.

"Thought I heard someone come in," he said, pausing casually in the doorway. He folded his arms over his chest. "So, what's up?"

Rikki turned her back to him as she answered. "I . . .

I want to know why you didn't tell me you were living here in this. . . ." Her voice trailed off as she noticed the shabbiness of the room for the first time. "Good God, Bo," she said, forgetting her embarrassment at his nudity and spinning back around. "You're probably the richest man in St. Joan. Why do you live here?"

"Why not?" he countered, crossing the room to pick up the jeans he'd discarded before his nap.

"You could live anywhere. Up in the house I've leased, for example. Anywhere would be better than this."

"I like living on the water. I like my privacy. This place affords both. Besides, the money's not important to me. It provides bread and. . . ." His gaze rested on the empty glass and beer bottles he'd left in the window. "Whatever else I need and I don't need a lot."

It was her turn to fold her arms over her chest. "Oh, I get it. You're into the martyr thing."

He frowned as he zipped his jeans, keeping his gaze on her. "Nope. I just don't need fancy digs."

"The money wasn't what made it all wrong, Bo," she said softly.

"Nope, but it didn't make it right either."

"So, you've just given up."

An insolent smile came into place as his gaze made a slow, seductive pass over her from head to toe, stopping at purposeful intervals. "No, baby, there are some things I've definitely not given up on."

She felt her face catch fire. He was still the sexiest man she'd ever met, but she'd be damned if she'd let his handsome puss and incredible biceps distract her. "I just came to tell you that I don't need a keeper. I would never have leased the house if I'd known you were living here. But it's too late to do anything about it now. Frankly, I don't have the time nor the interest, to look for another place. So just keep your nose out of my business."

"My nose isn't what's interested, Blue," he said softly, meaningfully.

She almost cursed, but she sensed rightly that he would have loved that, seeing her flustered and annoyed. She stood her ground, reversing their roles as she let her eyes make a slow inspection of their own. Then she took a step forward. Reaching out, she placed the flat of her hand on the bulge in his trousers. "Down boy. No one's taking you for a ride today."

He laughed. "You've changed, Blue."

She hadn't expected that. She lifted her chin a bit. "You've got that right. I'm not a little girl anymore."

"Hey, that's good by me. I liked you as a little girl. But I got a feeling I'm gonna like you even better all grown up."

"Don't bet on it," she said, finally retreating. She was at the door before she looked back. "My friends tell me I do bitch better than anyone they know."

He grinned again, looked down at his crotch. "Hear that, boy? She's a bitch."

"Oh, God, give it up, Bo. I'm not here to play games."

That sobered him. She saw the change in his black eyes. Heard it in the timbre of his voice when he spoke.

"That's exactly what you're doing, Blue. Only thing is I think you've forgotten that the loser in this game always ends up dead."

"I'm changing the rules."

He didn't answer, and she could see the control it took him to check a response in the rippling muscles in his jaws.

For the first time, she wished they had gotten off to a better start. She might have outgrown the crush she'd had on him once upon a time, but she still wanted to be his friend. She let the screen door bang shut. "Look, Bo, we both know why I'm here. I'm staying." She offered a smile. "Since we're neighbors, I hope we can be friends."

He answered with a sardonic grin. "Funny, the way I heard it around the lake, I'm one of your suspects. Isn't that why you sent me an invitation to your fancy dinner Tuesday night?"

She sighed. He wasn't going to make it easy. "I don't know who killed my parents and the others. I just know that it was someone who was with us the night I graduated. It had to be." She turned away to look out the window and ran a shaking hand over her hair. When she looked back, he was watching her, waiting for her to finish. "I went to the storage shed where my parents' things have been stored. I picked up some boxes. I hope the tapes my mother made with Dr. Grant are in there. If they are, maybe I'll know more after I listen to them."

Bo exploded. "Goddamn it, Blue! What if I was the killer? You just gave me the perfect excuse to kill you, too."

Their gazes met, locked.

"But you're not," she said in a tight whisper.

"Thank you," he said.

Suddenly, all the fight seemed to drain out of her. She thought of Petite, laughed faintly. What would she color empty? she wondered. "I never blamed you, Bo. Never. I loved you."

He didn't miss the tense. Past. He felt the knife slice into his heart ever so easily. "Go back to Boston, Blue. Don't push this any further."

"I have to," she said. She pushed the door open again, hesitated, but didn't look back as she said, "You should understand more than anyone."

He did understand, he thought, as he watched her climb the hill. He understood that he should have done this for her. If he had she would still be safe . . . and not here reminding him of what he'd thrown away. Now it was too late. All he could do was try to watch out for her, hope he could keep her alive . . . hope he could survive watching her, loving her, not having her.

Chapter Thirteen

"This is Rikki Blue coming to you live from KSTJ in gorgeous, springtime St. Joan, Missouri. Some of you may have listened to my show in the past. I've been broadcasting from Boston for the past five years. The show I'll be bringing you each day, Monday through Friday, will follow much the same format. So let me line it out for you.

"Each day I'll introduce a topic. It might be that we'll follow important issues for an entire week. I'll give you my point of view, discuss the views of others in the world, and then you and I will talk about it.

"For example, today we're going to discuss St. Joan. We're going to talk about events that took place here ten years ago. Some of you may remember what I'm talking about. The murder spree of 1985. Six people were brutally slain by a person who I believe lived right here in St. Joan."

For the next fifteen minutes, the radio celebrity detailed the murder of each of the victims, quoting from newspaper articles, statements made by Sheriff A. R. Witcomb, and Warren Hatch, the then prosecuting attorney. By the time Rikki went to a commercial break, perspiration had dampened her brow and her throat was dry. She left the booth to get herself a drink of wa-

ter and ran into the sheriff just as he rounded the corner.

"You're making a mistake," he told her without preamble.

"I'm doing what I have to do, Sheriff," she said stiffly.
Then capitulating, she offered a smile. "Look, you were
kind to me when my parents were killed. I haven't forgotten that. In fact, it's the only reason I'm not going to
come down on you hard for failing to find the killer. But
Sheriff, I made a promise. I said if you didn't find him,
I would. I have access to the killer through this medium,
and I'm going to use it."

"All you're going to do, missy, is stir up the folks in
St. Joan County and put yourself in real serious danger.
I can't sit by and let you do that."

Rikki stared at him for a long moment, turned to her
assistant, signalling her to give the weather update, then
looked back at Scooter. "I'm afraid there's not a damn
thing you can do about it. I own the radio station and
as long as I don't do anything to jeopardize my license,
I can talk about anything I like. I'm guaranteed that
right under the first amendment." Her voice had been
as cold as the steely glint in her blue eyes, but she was
a pro who knew how to work people. She backed off, offered another easy smile, and gentled her tone. "I'll tell
you what. Instead of working against one another, why
don't we work together?"

The sheriff sighed in exasperation as he swept off his
hat and smoothed his gray hair back. "Gawdamn it,
girl, there's nothing to work on. I did my best to discover the identity of the bastard who killed your mama
and daddy. I didn't get so much as a clue. It's been ten
years."

"Come on the show with me right now, Sheriff,"
Rikki said with determination and a fair amount of cajoling in her tone. "Let me interview you, then we'll

open the phones. Someone out there saw something. Let's help them remember. You and me together."

"All you're gonna do is make someone come after you."

"If that happens, Sheriff, I promise you, I'll be ready."

"You talk tough, but I know you, girl. Knew you when you wasn't—"

"I'm not the same person. Trust me on that."

No, he thought, I don't reckon you are. Problem is, the killer more'n likely is exactly the same. Thirty seconds later, though, he was sitting in the radio booth with his town's newest celebrity.

"We're back, St. Joan, and when I say we, I'm talking literally. In the studio with me right now is Sheriff Witcomb, St. Joan's finest. He's agreed to join me for the next forty-five minutes or so, tell you what he knows about the crimes committed against six of St. Joan's citizens, then help me take your calls." Her laughter was deep and sultry. "The lines are already lighting up, but I'm going to ask you to wait a few minutes until I've talked with Sheriff Witcomb here. Then we'll get to you.

"Sheriff, is it true that the person who committed the violent murders in the spring of '85 took a souvenir from each of his victims?"

"Gawd—"

Again the laughter. "Careful, Sheriff, we're on the air."

He reddened. "Sorry. I was just going to say that that was privileged information. We never released that to the public. I don't rightly think you should have brought it up."

"What about you, St. Joan? It's been ten years. The sheriff admitted to me before we came on the air that he has no idea who the killer is. Don't you think he should share everything he knows with you?"

"All right. Yes, ma'am, that much is true. But we

don't know why, and I don't know what good it does to talk about it."

"It might not do any good, but the point is, what can it hurt? Now, Sheriff, I had planned to tell my audience about the murders, one by one. But you were there after each one. Why don't you tell them. Starting with Bunny Apperson."

"What do you want me to tell them?" he asked uncomfortably.

"Everything you remember. Start with the date and the time. Tell us how each person was killed. Take us through the immediate investigative work that you and your department performed."

The sheriff swallowed hard. Lawd Gawd, how had he gotten himself into this?

Rikki made notes for the next ten minutes, calmly detached until he came to the murders of Linda and Lawrence Cassidy. But she forced herself to keep writing. Only her shaking hand betrayed how difficult it was for her to listen. When he finished, she took her turn at the mike. "Thank you, Sheriff. Now I have some questions for you. For example, you told us that the m.o. wasn't the same in all of the murders. Isn't that unusual?"

"Sure it is! That's why we wasn't certain we was dealing with the same fella."

"But the fact that he took a shoe from each of the victims tied them together. Isn't that correct?"

"Yes," he admitted reluctantly.

Rikki's smile held a hint of satisfaction over her victory. "So, now you'll admit that it was important to share the secret of our killer's souvenirs with the public. Most of them probably didn't even know that the same person had committed them all. Isn't that right?"

"I guess so," he said.

"We'll take a break for news headlines, then come back to you, St. Joan." She sat back, turning her attention to her guest. "Thanks, Sheriff."

"Don't think you're gonna be thanking me when this creep comes after you, missy."

"Oh, you don't understand, Sheriff. I'm forcing him to do just that because I'm going after him."

"Well, don't think you're going to get a lot of support. Folks around here like everything kept simple. You stir everybody up, you're gonna affect the tourist trade, turn neighbors into suspects, get folks real mad. And, missy, it ain't gonna be me they're mad at."

"I'm not here to win a popularity contest and quite frankly, I don't feel particularly friendly to the good citizens of St. Joan."

Sheriff Witcomb opened his mouth to comment on that, but Rikki held up a finger, silencing him as she hit a couple switches and went back on the air.

"We're back, folks. I've been sitting here talking with Sheriff A. R. Witcomb if you're just tuning in. We're discussing the murders that took place here in St. Joan ten years ago." She paused a beat. "Why don't we take some calls, Sheriff.

"Hello, you're on the air."

"My name's Martha Felder. I remember the murders real well. But I think the sheriff's right. Why are you stirring all this up again, young lady? You want more good people to get killed? Ain't it bad enough six people was murdered?"

Rikki was unaffected by the charge that she might well be starting another spree of killings. She'd expected it. "Let me ask you a question, Martha. Doesn't it bother you to know that someone you might well know killed those people and continues to live here in St. Joan? I don't know how you sleep at night with that knowledge."

"We don't know it's anyone from St. Joan," Martha countered. "There hasn't been another killing here in ten years . . . not by the same guy anyway. More'n likely it was some crazy tourist."

Rikki smiled. Thank you, Martha. You just gave me my cue to impart the most important information.

"As a matter of fact, I know for a certainty that it was someone from St. Joan," Rikki said. "And let me tell you how I know that. I lived in St. Joan at the time of the murders. I was personally involved in the murder investigation. My parents were Linda and Lawrence Cassidy." She heard Martha's gasp which coincided with Scooter Witcomb's groan. She disconnected the call, shot the sheriff a look which instructed him clearly not to interrupt. "Yes, folks, this was my playground. I was only eighteen years old. Too young and naive to know better than to trust everyone simply because they called themselves my friends. I had a lot of so-called friends, but that spring, I fell in with a group of playmates that I trusted more than I should have. Just like the rest of you, we discussed the murders. Some of you may remember that my parents were authors. Well, my mother was researching a book at the time that required research which Dr. Jason Grant assisted her with. He made some comments about the murders that I mentioned to my cronies. That same night Dr. Grant was killed. Shot down in his own kitchen by someone who hoped to make it look like a burglary gone awry. But the killer made a mistake. He took a souvenir. One of the doctor's shoes. Isn't that right, Sheriff?"

"Yes," Scooter said quietly, then at her disapproving look, louder. "Yes."

"Now, I didn't even think about what I'd said that night. Not until much later. But the following week, I overheard my parents discussing Dr. Grant's murder. They were convinced that he'd been killed by the same person. They mentioned that Dr. Grant had even put together a profile of the killer. He'd discussed it with my mother and gone so far as to mention a list of possible suspects. I promised that I wouldn't say anything, but I told my playmates that night. Four hours later my parents were dead. Coincidence? No way." Rikki's hands were shaking so hard now she had to grab the edge of the control panel to still them. "The fact is, I know that one of those seven people, my friends, my playmates, killed my parents and the others. There wasn't time for them to tell anyone else. Who would they have talked to that night between nine o'clock and one a.m.? I'm not at liberty to share their names with you on the air. After all, only one of them is guilty. But I'm asking you, my listeners, to think about those murders, all six of them. Sheriff Witcomb has given you the dates and probable times of the murders. Any one of you could have seen something that you didn't notice at the time. Call me if you remember anything at all that can help."

The telephone panel went wild after that. No one called because they'd remembered anything, but everyone seemed to have an opinion on the sagacity of bringing it all out in the open now so many years after the fact. The vote seemed about equally divided.

When they took a break for network news, Scooter left the studio, but not without a word of caution. "You've stirred it up now, missy. You just cover that pretty little backside of yours."

"Don't worry, Sheriff, I won't be depending on you to do it for me."

He flushed, turned a dull crimson from his neck to the brim of his Stetson.

She laughed softly. "That wasn't an insult. At least it wasn't intended to be. I just meant that I've learned to depend only on myself."

"Must get awful lonesome," he observed, not unkindly.

"Life is full of drawbacks, but the upside of that is I don't get hurt very easily anymore."

"Now, that's exactly what it looks like you're trying to do. Get hurt, that is."

After he left, Rikki returned to the studio, closed the

door, and put the headset back on. She was suddenly tired. Confrontation, she was learning all too quickly, was debilitating. But the satisfaction of bringing the killer to justice—and she didn't doubt a minute that she would do exactly that—would make it all worthwhile. With firm resolve, she hit a switch and went back on the air. But the first phone call almost took the wind out of her.

"Why you talking about your folks and them others and nobody's said a word about my little girl who was stolen just three years ago from her own backyard?" a woman asked. "Ain't she important, too, Sheriff?"

"Uh, the sheriff's gone, but I'm still here. Why don't you tell me about it?"

Rikki listened to the pitiful woman's tale about her daughter who had been eight years old when she was apparently kidnapped while playing alone in her backyard. She could feel the woman's grief, her misery, and her anger, and empathize, but she didn't know what she could do to help. It had nothing to do with the murders she'd come back to solve. She sighed heavily when the teary woman ended her account.

"You're doing exactly what you should, Mrs. Murphy. Talk about it. Don't let people forget. Make them think about it. Maybe someone will remember something that they hadn't even thought about before." She disconnected the call.

Her assistant held up a note. *Got a strange one on line four. A whisperer.* Rikki depressed the button. "Hello, this is Rikki Blue. You're on the air."

The voice that greeted her was raspy and quiet. A whisper just as she'd been warned. "We don't want you here, Ericka."

Rikki shivered. This was obviously someone who knew her from before. But who?

"I'm sorry you feel that way," she said.

"Go back to Boston. We don't want strangers here."

"Do I know you?" Rikki asked.

"I know you. That's all that matters. You and your kind."

Rikki laughed. "And what kind is that?"

"Brazen. Nasty. Flaunting yourself in those nudie magazines. We're good, decent people," the rasping whisper continued.

Rikki felt her skin knot in goose bumps, but she forced calm into her voice. "So you've seen the photo layout. Good. Let me explain to our other listeners.

"What our caller is all hush hush about, folks, is a photo layout I posed for in *Playmates Magazine*. It's in the January issue in case any of you missed it. I sent a copy to some of my playmates here in St. Joan. I thought it was a clever way to announce my return to my old playground. The pictures are tastefully done, but I *am* nude in them. There was a reason for my agreeing to do the shoot. It symbolized my coming out as it were. The shedding of my fear, my inability to face the horrors of my last week in St. Joan. I wanted to make a statement about my newfound freedom from the past which has haunted me while announcing my return in a way that was just as symbolic." Rikki turned her attention back to her caller. "Are you one of my playmates who received a complimentary issue?"

The receiver was quietly hung up on the other end.

Rikki sighed as she wiped her sweating palms on her jeans.

"Well, that was interesting. Let's take the next call. Hello, you're on the air."

The next ten phone calls were mostly more of the early variety, people expressing opinions. Rikki listened, countered, or thanked the caller for his or her support. By the time the clock indicated that she had arrived at the end of the last hour, she almost sagged with relief.

"Well, folks, I'm afraid it's time to turn you back over to the pros around here for more music. It's been fun, and it's been interesting, but most of all, it's been stimulating. That's what I'm going to try to give you every day. Food for thought. The mind's our most important asset. Let's use it. This is Rikki Blue. I'm back in my old playground, and I'm here to play hard ball. Talk to you tomorrow."

Rikki spent the next four hours in her office at KSTJ. She paid bills, sat in on a meeting the radio's news director had called, met with her chief executives, but she was drained. She hadn't done anything so different in her debut on radio in her hometown than she'd done in Boston . . . except put it on a personal level. But that was enough to exhaust her. At just a little before five, she grabbed her purse and told her assistant, "I'm outta here."

Lucy Fisher shook her head adding a few tsk tsks. "You look beat." She got up from behind her desk and approached her new boss. "For what it's worth though, I thought you were great today. A lot of us were worried when we got word that you'd bought the radio station, but I think you got a unanimous thumbs up today."

"Thanks," Rikki said, slinging her purse over her shoulder. "See ya in the morning."

The setting sun was brighter than normal, and Rikki blinked rapidly a few times as she exited the building. In spite of her weariness, she'd been bolstered by Lucy's parting praise. She was still thinking about it when she felt a hand on her arm. She jumped, almost shrieked with surprise. "Oh, Lord, Junior, you probably took ten years off my life."

"Not so tough now, huh?" he said, but the words were teasing rather than challenging.

Rikki laughed. "Actually I almost treated you to a demonstration of my karate skills."

"Yeah? What belt are you?"

"Black, but I'm glad I recognized you. I'm pretty beat. I don't doubt it would have taken more outta me than I feel like giving right now." She offered a smile. "So how are you?"

"Pretty ticked off right this minute."

"At me," Rikki said rather than asked as she continued toward her Cherokee.

"Damn straight! I was part of that group you were calling your playmates on the air. I don't exactly like being considered a suspect."

Rikki's sigh was impatient. "You get my invitation to the dinner party tomorrow night?"

"Yeah, even went out and rented me one of those tuxedos, but I'm not sure I'm coming now that I know how you think of us. Doubt anyone shows up knowing you're gonna be trying to decide which one of us killed your mama and daddy."

They'd reached her vehicle by then. She inserted the key, opened the door, and slung her purse across the front seat before answering. "That's up to you. But the way I figure it, Junior, if you were my friend back then, you'll want to come help me celebrate my return." She slid in behind the wheel. She gripped the steering wheel as she looked up at him again. " 'Course if you've got something to hide, I guess that would put a different slant on it, wouldn't it?"

Rikki's thoughts were consumed with her brief conversation with Junior Witcomb as she drove home. Of the group of eight young adults, Junior had been the one they all could count on for laughs. He was their comic. He hadn't changed all that much in ten years, except that Rikki suspected that he didn't go for many laughs anymore. She couldn't quite put her finger on what it was that made her think that. Then it hit her. It was in his eyes. A look that hinted of secrets.

Oddly, the realization that the young boy who had always been so open, so ready with a joke, and so quick to laugh at himself had disappeared inside adulthood. His looks had suffered as well. Not that he'd ever been exceptional in any way. Average height. Five eight, maybe nine. A complexion that had suffered through adolescent acne which had left its mark. Light brown hair that was thinning prematurely. But it wasn't so much the physical changes that she had noticed as the metaphysical ones. The sullen twist of his mouth, the slumped shoulders and shuffling gate, and the gaze that never quite met hers directly. She hated to consider him a suspect. Probably more than most ... all except Bo and Carrie. Even as a child she'd found it hard to accept the fact that clowns weren't always what they seemed. Happy, innocent, the bearers of joy.

It was approaching six o'clock by the time she turned the car into her driveway. Time to whip up a light meal for dinner, then review the notes she'd made of today's program in preparation for tomorrow's show. But she felt restless.

Dropping her purse and keys on the kitchen table, she exited the house again only moments after entering it. She had decided on a walk along the shoreline. She paused on the deck to study the fishing cottage below her to the south. It didn't appear that anyone was home. Still, she thought she'd play it safe and head in the opposite direction.

She walked briskly for the first twenty minutes or so, but with the setting sun and the accompanying onset of night sounds—croaking frogs, the songs of cicadas, and the distant call of a hoot owl, she slowed her pace, letting the countryside which she'd almost forgotten in her decade-long absence, soothe away the day's tension.

She was just rounding a curve when she saw lovers kissing in apparent farewell in the not too far distance in front of a lake side cabin. Rikki paused, not wanting to intrude on the private moment, yet unable to tear her gaze away either.

It was a moment that could have been captured in a commercial or on one of those greeting cards that were becoming more and more popular. The scene was perfect. Him dark, muscular, barefoot, and clad in jeans and T-shirt. Her fair, dressed in a pastel blue sundress with a full skirt that the breeze stirred and ruffled, her arms wound around his neck, one hand resting on the small of his back, the other buried in his shoulder-length, near-black hair. The cedar wood house, the dogwood and wild flowers, the glistening blue lake, all a fairyland backdrop. Rikki felt envy stir inside her for it was obvious from the way the pair touched each other that this was merely the afterplay of an afternoon of lovemaking.

Rikki was mostly hidden by an accommodating giant oak and whimsically, she patted the tree's massive trunk. "Bet you've witnessed a lot of this over the years, huh?" She sighed and laughed softly at herself. She was talking to trees. Probably not as serious as talking to herself or her parents, but close. With that thought she remembered her promise to call Kit as soon as she could, and it occurred to her that she hadn't even checked to see if the phone company had kept their promise to have the telephone connected today. Dusk was fast settling over the valley and she decided that she ought to be making her way back home, but ahead the lovers came apart then and as the woman stepped away from the man, Rikki could see her fully for the first time. She inhaled sharply with surprise. Carrie? But it couldn't be. Carrie was married to Brett and this man definitely was not the fair-haired preacher.

Rikki watched as the woman climbed into a small black car, backed out of the driveway, and disappeared around a sharp curve in the road.

Her brow was still furrowed. Had Brett and Carrie divorced? No, that wasn't possible. She would have read about it. And who was the dark-haired man she'd been kissing so passionately, touching so intimately?

Curiosity might well kill the cat, but Rikki decided it was worth the risk.

As she approached the cabin, she stepped carefully, stealthily, not intending to sneak really, but not wanting to announce her snooping either. For the second time that day, she jumped and nearly shrieked when the man she'd seen before stepped out of the shadows directly in her path.

His eyes widened with hers. "Ericka?"

"Danny? Danny Lightner?"

He laughed. "I heard someone coming, but I would have never expected it to be you in a million years. Of course I heard you were back—"

"But not in your own backyard, right?"

"Something like that, yeah."

"Sorry, didn't mean to surprise you." She hadn't meant to be seen at all. She felt her face heat with her guilty secret and Danny must have noticed, too, for he was suddenly looking at her oddly.

"Kinda late to be starting out on a walk, isn't it? How far do you live from here? I'll give you a ride back."

"Oh, no, that isn't necessary. I'm only a couple of miles up the lake." Rikki was already turning, starting for home.

"Ericka, wait! Let me drive you. It'll give us a chance to catch up. It's been what? Ten years."

"Almost." She shrugged. "Okay, you can drive me, but only if you'll come in for a beer."

In the cab of his pickup truck, Rikki could no longer contain her curiosity. "Danny, when I left St. Joan you were away, studying to be a priest . . ."

He glanced her way, then directed his gaze back to the road. "You saw Carrie, didn't you?" he asked.

"Yes," she said.

"Well, I'm not a priest, so I guess it's only half as bad as it seems."

Rikki waited.

"I didn't take my final vows, Ericka—"

"It's Rikki now, Danny." She grinned, hunched her shoulders in apology. "Sorry, I didn't mean to interrupt. Go on."

"I thought I could do it, but it was my mom's dream for me to become a priest, not mine. I've always wanted to write. I even thought I could do both, but I couldn't give my heart to the Church like I should have. I came home the summer after your . . . after you left." He cast her a sidelong glance again. "I was real sorry about your parents, Rikki." He shook his head, whipping his long hair with the action. "Doesn't sound right, Rikki. Never thought of you like that. You were always so pretty, so feminine."

She laughed and even blushed. "Didn't think you ever noticed," she teased.

"Who wouldn't have noticed? I used to watch you and Carrie everywhere you went."

"I'm flattered," she said honestly. Then she remembered how Carrie used to talk about him. 'Probably a faggot. He never even looks at girls.'

"My mom was real disappointed when I came home. She made my life hell, actually. I moved out. Got a job at the filling station in Jeff City and put myself through school. I sold my first book the year I graduated."

"But that's great," she said, pointing at her drive at the same time. "What do you write? Do you use a pseudonym? I've never seen any books by Danny Lightner." And then she remembered some newspaper articles about a local author. "Wait! D. A. Light. Right?"

"Right. How did you know?"

She told him about keeping up with local news through the paper. "But I never made the connection.

Of course, I don't suppose I would have since I thought you had long ago gone into the priesthood."

"Carrie works part-time at the *Banner*. She interviewed me after my second book hit the shelves. Then again about a year ago when I celebrated my first time on the *New York Times*. We started off as friends, Rikki. Neither of us intended for it to go any further. One day I just told her the truth. That I was in love with her. It probably wasn't the best timing. She began to cry. We were at the library, pretending to be working though we'd already started meeting a couple of times a week just to talk." He pulled the truck to a stop behind her Cherokee and shut off the engine. "The offer of a beer still good?"

"Sure, come on up. But be warned," she said as she opened the passenger door, "I haven't had time to get settled yet. You're liable to have to clear a place to sit."

Inside the house a few minutes later, she handed him a frothy can of Bud Light, then motioned for him to join her in the living room. She sat on the sofa. He took a chair opposite her. "So, go on. You told her you were in love with her and she started to cry. What did you do?"

"I got her out of there. You remember Wanda Lou who has been with the library practically since the first brick was laid on the building? Biggest gossip in these parts. I figured she'd be on the phone to Carrie's mother in seconds if she saw Carrie in that condition.

"Anyway, I brought her to my house. I didn't expect anything from her, I swear to God. I just wanted her to know how I felt. Besides, I knew she was married, and I was aware of her prejudice against Catholics. But she told me she'd fallen in love with me, too."

"Then why doesn't she get a divorce?"

"Come on, Rikki, you know Carrie. You have to remember how important it is to her what people think of her. I know that's not necessarily a good quality, but it's part of who she is, so I accept it."

"She's obviously not happy in her marriage to Brett or she wouldn't have fallen in love with you."

"Brett's not an easy person to live with. He's rigid and demanding. And sometimes I think she's afraid of him."

"So you're content just to sneak around?"

"Whoa, I didn't say anything about being content. We argue about it sometimes, but it makes her cry, and I can't stand to see her miserable."

"But you've got to realize that Carrie's never going to have the courage to leave him. You just said it yourself. She cares too much what others think."

"You don't think very highly of her anymore, do you? I'm sorry to hear that. I remember how close the two of you were." He set his beer on the end table, leaned forward and clasped his hands between his knees. "She still talks about you, you know? Once she even said that she wished you were here. That you'd know how to help her get away from Brett. She said you had courage."

Rikki looked away into the darkness that had finally fallen. "Did she tell you why I've come back?" she asked, her eyes still averted.

"She said you're on a witch hunt. But I don't think she meant it unkindly. She scares easily, and I think she's frightened of what you'll find out although she's never said as much."

Rikki didn't answer at once. "Does she think it might have been Brett who killed my parents?" she asked at last.

"Good God, no! She doesn't love him anymore, Rikki. And it's true that she's afraid of him in some ways, but not in the way you mean. She's afraid that he'll bring the wrath of God down on her, not to mention her mother if he finds out about us." He laughed with the last, but Rikki knew that he was serious.

"Sounds like a no win situation, and I'm sorry for that. I really did love her, too, Danny."

"Past tense."

She laughed. A quick "ha" filled with regret. "I don't have present or future tenses in my life. I won't have until I get the past behind me and that won't happen until I've discovered who killed my parents and the others." She offered a weary smile. "Pretty sad, huh? Both the girls who tied for most likely to succeed so messed up?"

He stood up, crossed the room and pulled her to her feet. He took her into his arms and held her. "I may not be a priest, Ericka Cassidy, but I'm a good listener, and I think I make an even better friend. You need anything, you come running. I'll be there for you."

She swiped surreptitiously at a tear, then stepped out of his arms. "It's probably not the safest thing to be right now. My friend, that is."

His grin was wide and warm. "But that's where Carrie and I differ, sweetheart. I don't give a damn about playing it safe."

"I think Carrie's a lucky woman to have you, Danny."

"I think she'd be even luckier if she had her best friend back."

"Maybe when this is all over."

He draped an arm around her shoulder and started for the door. They walked outside onto the deck before either of them spoke again. He gave her another long hug then kissed her brow. "I hope it's over for you real soon."

She watched as he went down the steps and drove away. But as she turned back toward the house, she saw Bo standing outside the cottage below. He was just standing there, leaning against a window sill. He raised a hand in a mocking salute.

She raised her chin slightly and smiled before going back inside. She knew what it had probably looked like to him. Well, too damn bad about that. In fact she was glad that he'd more than likely gotten the wrong impression from the embrace he'd witnessed. Maybe now he'd leave her alone. He didn't have to know that Danny belonged to Carrie. That Rikki Blue had no one.

Chapter Fourteen

The show on Tuesday was much the same as the first, and Rikki was just as drained when she left the station a few minutes after six. But there wasn't time for a relaxing walk as she'd taken the day before. Her guests would be arriving for the private dinner party at Bar-Ber-Keen at eight. She had barely enough time to get ready.

She arrived at the resort hotel at seven-thirty a little breathless and more nervous than she had thought she would be. She'd seen Aaron, Junior, and Bo. Now she would be reunited with the rest. For the first time since her parents' funeral, she would come face to face with people she'd once called friends, and who were now little more than strangers and suspects for murder. The thought chilled her, and she shivered as she inspected the table that had been set for eight.

The private dining room was richly appointed and elegantly decorated for her party. Perfect for the mood of formality she had been determined to set. This was not a cozy get-together between friends, a reunion of long lost chums. It was a set-up, pure and simple. A stage play that she would direct. After all, she was the only one who knew the scenario. That thought brought about a modicum of calm. She was in control tonight. After the party . . .

She went to the mirror that ran the length of the wall and gave herself one last inspection.

Her dark auburn hair was piled high on her head, one long tendril allowed to hang free, to follow the contours of her face and the graceful line of her throat. Her makeup was not heavy yet slightly exaggerated in deference to the occasion and hour. The full-length, fitted, black crepe gown was elegant in its simplicity. Diamonds glittered from her ears and wrist. She looked regal and elegant. Exactly as she'd wanted. Ericka Cassidy, a beautiful yet unfinished girl, was no more. In her stead, Rikki Blue, a worldly sophisticate, had returned to St. Joan.

The hotel manager stepped into the room. "Your guests are arriving, Ms. Blue. Would you like us to show them in?"

"Give me five more minutes," she said.

The room was not overly large, but it suited her needs to perfection. A staircase led to a second floor loft, and Rikki climbed it now. She would watch them come in. Study their expressions. Listen to what they had to say. All without being seen. Then she would join them. All of them? She didn't know. Everyone had called the hotel manager to accept the invitation except Bo. She'd been disappointed that he hadn't acknowledged the invitation, but perhaps it was best. She had never seriously considered him a suspect. At least, now, she wouldn't be distracted by him.

Aaron and Pamela Sue were the first two to enter the room. Amazing how different they looked in their formal attire. Especially Aaron. No country bumpkin doctor here. His wife, on the other hand, had not been as successful in her transformation. She wore a red and white taffeta gown that showed off shapely legs yet failed to disguise the twenty or thirty pounds she'd gained since her marriage. In spite of her resolve not to form opinions, Rikki realized she was already discounting Pam as a possible suspect. But then she probably had

never really considered her anyway. Pam was a nurturer. A giver.

Rikki's attention was drawn to the door again and to
Junior who entered alone. She almost giggled at his look
of complete bemusement and discomfort. Some men
just weren't cut out to wear tuxedos. Allan Witcomb was
one of them.

He joined Aaron and Pam at the bar. "We supposed
to wait on ourselves?" he grumbled.

"Probably not," Aaron told him, handing his wife a
Coke, "but I decided to help myself. You want something, Junior? I used to be pretty good at this bartending
stuff when I worked part-time during college."

"Got any beer?"

Aaron clapped the man on the shoulder. "Brother,
they've got everything. Our hostess is putting on the
dog."

"Yeah, looks like she went all out to impress us. Me,
I feel like a fucking idiot dressed up in this monkey suit."

"I think you look great," Pam said sweetly.

The door opened again. This time Sally Jane Matthers
entered. Rikki was taken aback by the change in the
woman. She would never have recognized her. Like herself, Sally Jane wore black. Still slender, the pants suit
complemented her narrow proportions, and it was obvious
that in spite of her rural upbringing, she knew fashion.
Her carrot red hair had been streaked and was cut in a
very contemporary style that was handsome and flattering.
Her freckled skin was successfully covered with makeup,
and her overlong teeth had been capped. All in all, the
ugly duckling, while not quite metamorphosing into a
swan had nonetheless become quite attractive.

"Hi, guys," the real estate magnate greeted the others
off-handedly. "You doing the honors, Doctor?" And at
his nod, "Fix me a gin and tonic. How's the newest
baby, Pam?"

"Not tonight, please. This is the first time we've been

out for more than a quick movie in two years. I don't want to talk kids, think kids, or even remember kids."

Sally Jane's laughter was rich and alluring. Rikki had forgotten the woman's magnetism. Or had she ever even noticed it? She thought not. She wondered if the changes in Sally Jane had been merely physical.

Bo entered the room next. Rikki was surprised by how pleased she was that he'd come. The warmth that spread through her at his handsome appearance surprised her less. He'd always inspired heat.

"Hey, Bohannon, long time no see," Junior said. "Step on up to the bar. Doc here's doing the honors."

Before Bo could answer the last of the party arrived. Rikki watched them carefully. She remembered how in love they had been as young adults, and wondered what had happened between them, *to* them to drive Carrie into the arms of Danny Lightner. She had not forgotten Danny's hints about Brett's cruelty and realized that this coupled with her own dislike of the man years earlier had probably put him at the top of her list of suspects. She had to be careful. She was jumping to conclusions.

She sighed. It was time.

All eyes turned in her direction as she stepped out of the shadows and started down the steps. She almost felt foolish for the theatrics of her entrance. Almost. Not quite. This was her show. She'd intended to have the advantage. The dramatic descent down the staircase definitely set the tone.

No one spoke. Only Bo was smiling. Grinning, really, like a parent tolerating a child's moment of self-indulgence. Rikki felt like slapping the insolence off his face. Instead, she smiled radiantly in return, then included each of her guests in the silent greeting. "I'm so glad you could come. All of you. It's been a long time."

No one spoke.

"Have you each had a drink? If not, please help yourselves. I asked the management not to come in until it's time to serve dinner. I wanted us to have time to ourselves."

"When's dinner?" Junior asked. "I'm starved."

"We'll eat at eight-thirty, but there are hor d'oeuvres on the side table." She turned her attention to the others. "You look fantastic, Sally Jane."

The woman laughed. "I'm not sure I like the amazement in your tone, but thanks."

"How are you, Pam?"

"Overworked and underpaid. Motherhood has its moments, but mostly it's just a pain in the ass."

"She loves every minute of it," Aaron said. "Don't let her kid you."

"I agree. She's a regular earth mother," Sally Jane said.

Rikki wasn't so sure. The Pamela Sue she remembered had been bright eyed and sassy. This woman merely looked tired and defeated. She turned her attention to Carrie and Brett. "And how are the Reverend and Mrs. Pearson?"

"Honestly?" Brett asked.

Rikki saw Carrie put a hand on her husband's arm. A gesture that was a warning. Rikki's smile widened. "Of course, honestly. That's why we're all together again."

"Then by all means," Brett said, his handsome face so cold and remote, Rikki barely suppressed a shiver. "I came tonight to try to talk you out of this absurd mission you've set upon. You're stirring up the good people of St. Joan. And to what end?"

"Brett," Carrie breathed.

"No, Carrie, I'm glad Brett's speaking his mind. I want an open exchange tonight."

Six of the seven guests had formed a half-circle around their hostess now. All of them except Bo, who was leaning against the wall, one brow raised in amusement. Rikki ignored him.

Junior looked at the others, picked up where Brett had left off. "Any of you listen to her radio show yesterday and today? She announced to the whole world that one of us is a murderer. I don't know about the rest of you, but I almost changed my mind about coming tonight."

"Then why didn't you?" Sally Jane asked.

" 'Cause I didn't want the rest of you thinking I was the one she was talking about." He chuckled then. " 'Course I guess if she's right, not *all* of you would have thought that, 'cause one of you *is* the killer, right?"

"I think the theory is ridiculous. We were all hardly more than children," Pam said. "We weren't raised in street gangs like kids in the city today. We didn't go around killing people. We were just simple country kids whose biggest problems were getting through school or getting that phone call from our boyfriend we had waited all day for." She laughed nervously. "And for heaven's sake, you couldn't possibly consider Aaron or me as suspects. His own father was one of the victims."

"Why don't we sit down?" Rikki suggested.

A few minutes later they were all seated around the elaborately appointed table. It wasn't lost on Rikki that the seating arrangement ended up much as it had ten years before with the Pearsons seated side by side, then the Grays, then herself and Bo seated together, and Sally Jane to Junior's right.

"Kind of like the old days," Aaron offered apparently noticing the pairing of couples as Rikki had.

"Not quite," Rikki reminded them. "We were friends then."

"Most of us still are," Junior pointed out meanly.

No one spoke for a long moment until Carrie raised her gaze to Rikki's. "You look beautiful, Ericka."

"Thank you. So do you, but if you don't mind, I don't go by Ericka anymore. That girl died a long time ago. She was killed as surely as her parents."

"Oh, for God's sake, don't you think that's a little melodramatic?" Sally Jane asked.

"It's the way it is," Rikki said simply.

The double door opened before anyone else had a chance to comment. Three uniformed waiters entered the room pushing carts heavily ladened with food, champagne, and wine.

For the next ten minutes conversation was all but stopped except for a quiet exchange between Aaron and Pam. Then Aaron excused himself.

"He's going to call home, check on the kids," Pam told the others. "That's why we hardly ever go out anymore. Either we're checking on them or Aaron's getting paged by his service. It's hardly worth the effort."

When one of the waiters began pouring champagne, Brett put his hand over the top of his glass. Rikki motioned to one of the others to bring over the bottle of sparkling grape juice she'd requested in deference to the teetotaling minister. "For you Brett ... and Carrie, of course."

"Thank you," he said grudgingly, removing his hand from the glass and accepting the grape juice.

Rikki raised a brow when Carrie refused the nonalcoholic beverage and asked for the "real stuff," noticed the angry scowl her husband directed her way but didn't comment. Instead, she raised her glass. "I'd like to propose a toast."

The others exchanged uncomfortable glances, then dutifully raised their fluted glasses and waited.

"To us, and to our memories as playmates."

A moment later, Carrie surprised everyone by raising her glass again. "I'd like to make a toast, too." She looked at her former girlhood friend and smiled. "May you find peace, Rikki. You deserve it."

Tears that she hadn't expected, didn't want, flooded Rikki's eyes. She'd missed her best friend though she hadn't realized how much until that moment. Maybe she was wrong, she thought. Maybe she was looking in the wrong place. "Thank you," she said quietly.

"She won't find peace until she gives up this ludicrous witch hunt, Carrie Ann," Brett told his wife. Then to their hostess. "Vengeance is mine, sayeth the Lord. You're going against His word, Rikki, and thereby alienating Him. Without His help, you'll never find happiness or contentment."

"I believe the scriptures also talk about an eye for an eye," Rikki told him with just the beginning of anger in her voice.

"Touché," Bo said, the first word he'd spoken since they'd sat down.

The party quieted for the next several minutes, no one seeming to know what was appropriate to say after that. The first course of the meal was served and Rikki watched as she ate and sipped her wine.

Pam and Aaron were tense, glancing at one another every few minutes throughout the meal.

Junior continued to wear a belligerent expression.

Sally Jane was relaxed, though strangely aloof and distant.

Bo was as watchful as Rikki but she thought he was laughing at them, at her as well. She was irritated. This wasn't a game she was playing.

Brett was cold and hostile. Rikki noticed that his once flawless good looks had been marred by the fanatical gleam that shined in his eyes and the sullen set of his full lips.

Rikki hadn't believed Carrie could become any lovelier, but in fact she had. Only the sadness which shined from her gold-flecked, brown eyes dimmed the glow. Rikki felt a sudden urge to reach across the table and take her hand in hers, give it a squeeze, and encourage her to dump the self-righteous hypocrite her youthful ignorance had saddled her with. She felt the love she'd known as a young girl stir in her breast. But that wasn't what tonight was about, was it? She'd arranged this party not to revive friendships but to take the first step in ferreting out a killer. Perhaps it wasn't possible. It might be that the killer who had escaped detection all these years was too clever to dance to the tune she was playing, and thereby give himself or herself up.

For the first time in more than five years, since she'd first conceived the idea of returning to St. Joan to find the person who had butchered her parents, Rikki felt discouraged.

"How is your grandmother?" Carrie asked her, drawing her away from her reverie.

"She's dead."

"Oh, I'm sorry."

But Rikki wasn't sorry that she'd brought her grandmother up. It reminded her how different Julia Hanover's death had been from her parents. She smiled. "That's all right, Carrie. She died in her sleep. She was old and tired. It was the way she would have wanted it."

"So how come you bought the radio station here in St. Joan?" Junior Witcomb asked abruptly. He wiped at his mouth with his napkin, then followed up the question with another one. "I mean, we know why you're here. But why not just come back, give this detective thing a go, then hightail it on back East?"

"I like being in charge. As owner of KSTJ, I don't have to answer to anyone."

"So you're rolling in clover now, huh?"

"I'm very comfortable, yes," she answered candidly. "But of course, we all are, aren't we? That's rather why we became friends in the first place, wasn't it?" She paused to look at each one of her guests, passing quickly over Bo. "You know, in all the years that I've been away, and in all the traveling I've done, I've never seen separatism as effective as it is here."

"I resent that, Rikki. I am the shepherd of a flock of

good, God-fearing people that come from all walks of life," Brett said.

"But, darling, we're not all as fucking good and pious as you," Sally Jane said.

Pam giggled.

"I wasn't saying that," Brett said, his face as red as the taffeta of Pam Grant's dress. "I was merely defending a charge that is unfair."

"Naw," Junior said leaning his chair back so that it rested on only two legs. "Much as I hate to, I have to agree with Rikki, here. I probably don't have as much as most of you, but on the other hand I wouldn't starve if I quit the sheriff's department tomorrow. My grand-daddy set me up a nice trust, not to mention the land he left me. But I see prejudice every day at work. Why, even you were treated better than most would have been, Rikki. You gotta admit it. If Waylin had brought anyone else's dress in all covered in blood like yours was, that person would have gone to the top of the list of suspects."

Rikki barely stifled a groan as the painful, humiliating experience slammed back into the forefront of her consciousness.

"What is he talking about?" Brett asked his wife.

"Nothing," Carrie said softly. Then with full-blown anger. "Nothing, damn it." She sent Rikki a look of apology then aimed a glare Junior's way.

No one else spoke, but Rikki could feel Bo's eyes on her and for the first time, she regretted ever having returned to St. Joan.

"Mind an impertinent question, Rikki?" Junior chipped in.

Rikki granted him a smile, then replied in a teasing tone, "Do you know any other kind, Junior?"

"Your folks leave you filthy rich or did you make all this dough at that fancy job of yours in Boston?"

"That's not only impertinent, Junior," Sally Jane said. "That's downright rude."

"I don't mind," Rikki said. "After all, I'm probing into all of your lives. I guess turnabout's fair play." Then to Junior. "My parents left me very well off, but I earned a good living working for WBOS in Boston, too. And I invested wisely."

"How did you go into radio in the first place?" Carrie asked.

"Ah, dull story, that."

"But you became as big a celebrity as Oprah and Donahue, except in radio, of course," Sally Jane said.

Rikki could feel Bo's eyes on her and was careful to keep her gaze directed away from him. The question about her unexpected segue into radio reminded her of Ripley Van Welder, and he had always reminded her of Bo. Perhaps that was why she had allowed Rip to persuade her away from newspaper journalism and onto the air waves. Like Bo, Rip was tall and dark, handsome and charismatic. He'd been her first boss as the owner of WBOS as well as her first lover. But though he'd been right about her natural instincts that would serve her well and take her far in the medium of radio, he'd been all wrong for her as a lover and mate.

Like Bo, Rip had been born with the proverbial silver spoon dangling from his mouth. Unlike Bo, Rip had assumed all the negative accouterments of wealth. He was a snob. He was arrogant. He was a boor.

He'd been crushed when she'd abruptly ended their affair. So devastated, in fact, it had taken him all of three months to announce his engagement to socialite Penelope Princeton. The pineapple.

Rikki smiled with memory of her nickname for Rip's fiancee. Her golden, perfect looks and prickly disposition had earned her the comparison.

"What are you smiling about?" Sally Jane asked. "Is the story that funny?"

"No," Rikki said with a small shake of her head. "I was just remembering something that had nothing to do with what you want to know. But back to the subject.

"I majored in journalism and communications intending to go to work for a newspaper. One day I was involved in a debate and Rip Van Welder, the owner of WBOS was in the audience. He approached once the debate was concluded and asked me if I would be interested in doing a talk show. He said radio journalism was the wave of tomorrow. He wanted a liberal who would employ the same format as Rush Limbaugh, countering his conservative views. I turned him down no less than a half dozen times. Then Fate, as she has a way of doing, stuck her nose in. The host of one of his shows was hurt in a car accident. Rip called me and begged me to just pinch hit for him. I argued that I'd never even been inside a radio studio, but he said I wouldn't have to worry about the mechanics. Just get up there and talk about anything that was on my mind." She shrugged. "The rest is history. I told you it was a boring story."

"Too bad you didn't do television instead," Carrie put in. "As beautiful as you are, it seems a waste to hide it on radio."

Rikki was touched by the compliment. "Thanks, but you'd be surprised how many benefits and dinners radio celebrities are required to attend. My face became pretty familiar around Boston."

"Not to mention your body," Junior said with a leer that traveled to her cleavage and stopped there. "After that layout in *Playmate*, I don't guess there's an inch of you folks aren't familiar with."

"Junior!" Pam said, using the tone she reserved for scolding her children.

"It's all right," Rikki said, though with a weary sigh. "I think Junior misses the point on purpose."

"Well, I certainly missed the point for that lude exhibition," Brett said. "Why don't you explain why you did it while you're offering the reasons for what you're doing here in St. Joan."

"I wasn't aware that's what I was doing. But the answer to why I posed for *Playmate* is simple. The magazine was doing twelve months of celebrity centerfolds. They asked me and I turned them down. But two days later I called them back and asked if the offer was still good."

"Why?" Pam asked, her expression rapt.

Rikki glanced her way then directed her gaze to a picture of the lake on the far wall as she answered. "For five years I'd dreamed of coming back here and forcing the person who murdered my parents out of hiding. At first it was only that, a dream. There was still too much of the girl who had fled our fair town inside me. That girl didn't like confrontation. She was afraid and weak and still hurting. But the woman who went on the radio everyday, who attacked major issues, who dared take on heads of state, supreme court justices, inmates on death row, etc., etc., eventually replaced the scared little girl who ran away with her tail between her knees. And I realized that all trace of little Ericka Cassidy was gone. In a symbolic rite, if you will, I shucked the last of my inhibitions with that layout."

No one spoke for a long moment, and then Aaron surprised them all by pointing out that not all of Ericka Cassidy had been eradicated with the creation of the new persona.

"How's that?" Rikki asked.

"Ericka promised to return to St. Joan and find her parents' killer," he reminded her.

"Yes, but it's Rikki Blue who's going to do that for her," their hostess said, turning her head slowly to include each of them in that declaration.

After the last of the dishes were cleared from the table, and coffee and aperitifs were served, Rikki folded her hands in her lap, grateful that the terrible moment had passed, that her composure had returned. She still couldn't look Bo's way, but she'd deal with that later . . . or not. She hoped she wouldn't have to see him again after tonight. But that was probably an absurd wish.

"I want to thank you all for coming. I'm not sure I would have if the shoe had been on the other foot." She smiled at each of them. All except Bo, who had not taken his eyes off her since Junior's revelation. She'd felt his gaze on her since then, but she couldn't look at him. She just couldn't.

"Well, like my old man said, you got gumption," Junior said.

Rikki laughed. "Thank him for me."

"I think so, too," Pam said, "although I believe you're wrong. I mean I understand *why* you got the idea in your head about it being one of us, but it could be nothing more than coincidence. I can tell you this much, Ericka . . . I mean, Rikki, it couldn't have been Aaron or me. We were together when your parents were killed."

"How do you know? I didn't think the papers published the time of death and Scooter didn't tell anyone, did he? My grandmother phoned him a few months after we left. He wouldn't even pinpoint it for her. Said there were some facts they were keeping to themselves."

"Well, of course, I don't know exactly what time they were killed, but Aaron didn't take me home until after one. I don't know why, but I got the impression from someone that they were killed earlier."

Before Rikki could answer, Aaron corrected his wife. "No, hon, I dropped you off just after midnight, remember? I was worried about leaving my mom alone too late. She was real nervous after my dad was killed."

"Oh. Then I guess we're not off the hook either," Pam said weakly.

"I reported for duty at midnight," Junior said. "And

I know what time your parents were killed. Right around one o'clock according to Dr. Ohtau."

"You reported for duty, Junior, but *where* were you at one a.m.?" Sally Jane asked.

"I was on patrol," he said, then realizing that that left him without an alibi as well, he reddened. "I was over by the strip," he offered lamely.

"I was all alone at home. Junior dropped me off at eleven forty-five. I read a book, then went to sleep," Sally Jane volunteered. "My dad was out of town, so guess I'm still suspect too."

"What about you and Brett, Carrie?" Junior asked.

"I was at home," Carrie said quietly. But then to Rikki, "But I couldn't have killed your parents. I loved them. They were like second parents to me, too."

"Seems to me you—" Junior started before Rikki cut him off. She thought she knew what he'd been about to say, but she didn't need to be reminded that Carrie hadn't been there for her in the last few days before she left for Boston.

"Did you go straight home, too, Brett?" she asked.

"No. I drove around a while. Went over to the church and sat there for an hour or so." His face flushed slightly as he added. "I was dreaming about graduating from the seminary, marrying Carrie Ann, and getting my own church. I knew Reverend Paulson was getting ready to retire. I was hoping he'd recommend me as his replacement pastor."

Rikki saw Carrie cast her husband an odd look, wondered about it, but then Aaron was asking Bo for his alibi. "I guess you and Rikki were still out together, huh?"

"No," he said quietly, for the first time not looking at Rikki. His gaze was directed to the centerpiece in the middle of the table. "As a matter of fact, I was back at the hotel throwing some things into a duffle bag. I left for St. Louis around one-thirty to catch a plane for Jamaica."

"So, looks like we're all still on the list of possibles," Sally Jane said, and Rikki detected amusement in the other woman's eyes.

"Yeah, but so what? Just like my dad said today while you was on the air, Rikki. It's all a bunch of poppycock. None of us killed your mom and dad or Aaron's dad or any of the others. You're whistling against the wind. You haven't got a prayer of discovering who the jerk is. If we couldn't do it, how can you?"

She smiled. "I have the tapes my mother made with Dr. Grant."

"He named one of us?" Aaron asked incredulously.

"I don't know. I haven't listened to them yet."

"Why not?" Sally Jane demanded. "It seems to me that would have been the first thing I would have done."

"For two reasons," she said calmly. "For one, I don't think he named anyone specifically. From what I remember, my mother said they discussed profiles rather than names."

"What's the other reason?" Carrie asked.

"I haven't been able to go through their things yet. I'm going to, but I just haven't been able to make myself. If I can learn something another way, I'd rather do it."

Aaron shook his head. "But why even tell us about the tapes if you think one of us is the killer? Isn't that like waving a red flag?"

"No, this isn't a come on, an invitation to kill me. It's more of a warning as well as insurance."

"You lost me," Junior said.

Rikki smiled patiently. "It's simple, really. I believe that one of you is a killer. By telling you all about the tapes, I am also alerting the rest of you who are innocent that if something should happen to me *before* I learn who the guilty party is, you'll all be able to help Sheriff Witcomb. And if someone should go after the tapes now, he'd be mighty foolish, I think. After all, we'll all be watching now."

Junior scratched his head. "Yeah, but you told us about the tapes back then, didn't you?" At her nod, he said, "If it was one of us, how come he . . . or she didn't look for the tapes at the time of the murder?"

"I don't know. I don't have all the answers. That's why I'm back. To get them."

Silence settled over the room again as each of them considered the conversation that had just been exchanged.

Brett shattered the quiet suddenly, unexpectedly. His voice was raised for the first time, and both Carrie and Pam jumped at the unexpected intrusion. "You have no right to sit in judgment of us! To point your finger!"

Rikki's chair crashed to the floor as she sprang to her feet. "I have *every* right. One of you took my youth. You took my future. You took two of the most loving, decent people who ever lived. You have the gall to tell me I don't have the *right*, Brett? One of you . . . ," she looked around the table slowly including every one of her guests as she inhaled deeply and struggled with her anger. ". . . One of you destroyed my life. Oh, yes, I have *every* right. It's called entitlement," she finished more quietly before turning away and leaving the room.

"I think the party's over," Junior said sardonically.

Bo stood up. "I think you're wrong there, pal. I think the party's just getting started."

Chapter Fifteen

Brett wasn't inclined to conversation on the drive home from the dinner party and Carrie was grateful. She wanted to think, reflect on the changes in her childhood friend. And Ericka had changed . . . more than just her name.

Rikki. How odd that sounded. And yet it suited her. It had a strong ring to it. Almost brazen. Definitely bold. Gutsy and indomitable. Like the woman herself. The antithesis of Carrie.

Carrie almost moaned aloud with the last thought. But it was true. She was everything that Rikki Blue was not. Weak, malleable, soft. A puppet controlled by everyone else. Except when she was with Dan. She pushed the thought of her lover away. She had a fast rule about thinking of him when she was with Brett. She didn't trust herself not to give her secret away. Back to Rikki.

Carrie'd missed her. She hadn't realized how much until she'd seen her tonight. And she believed that Rikki had missed her as well. She'd seen it, Rikki's own longing reflected in those magnificent blue eyes. She'd seen other things. Amusement, approval—when Carrie had accepted the champagne rather than the nonalcoholic grape juice—anger, and loneliness. Carrie frowned. She didn't like to think how hard the past ten years must have been for Rikki. But she knew it must have been hell, for Rikki Blue was as a woman of steel that had been tempered by the fires of Hades.

She, on the other hand, had not grown, not matured. She was still the wimp she'd always been. She allowed her husband, whom she'd grown almost to detest, and her mother, who was little better than Brett, to control her . . . abuse her. Her mother's mistreatment was subtle, mental pressure applied with the artful hand of a genteel Southern woman's manipulations. Brett's was more overt, worse. She shuddered with the thought of the ways he degraded her, hurt her, used her. If she had Rikki's courage . . . but she didn't. Danny was her one act of defiance, and even that she couldn't do right.

As they turned into the driveway that separated their house from the St. Joan First Baptist Church, Brett reached for her hand. "I'm glad we went tonight, Carrie Ann. It was good to be reminded how blessed I am."

"Because I'm nothing like Rikki Blue," she finished for him.

He smiled at her, the preacher's benevolent grin of approval that she'd watched him give his parishioners a thousand times. She hated him then even more than usual. He was a hypocrite. He was vile, disgusting. A wolf in sheep's clothing.

"I'm glad we went, too," she said, meeting his gaze with defiance. "I think she could be very good for me. I'd forgotten how much I loved her." She opened her car door, started to step out, but Brett grabbed her arm with her last statement: "I think I'll call her and ask her to meet me for lunch Saturday when she's not taping—Ow, you're hurting me!"

"I don't want you to have anything to do with her after tonight," he said in a soft, menacing voice.

Carrie fought to ignore the pain his grip was causing. "Why, Brett? Are you afraid of her?"

He let go of her then, but the threat in his gaze didn't diminish. "Why would I be afraid of her? Don't be ridiculous. I simply don't want her to influence you with her worldly ways." He reached out to stroke her hair, but she dodged his touch. "I like you just the way you are, Carrie Ann. I've taught you the importance of heeding the Lord's counsel on being like the little children. I saw her influence on you tonight when you accepted the liquor."

Carrie didn't answer. She couldn't. She scampered from the car and hurried toward the house. If she could just get to the bathroom and lock the door before he caught up with her . . .

Brett laughed as he climbed from behind the steering wheel and sauntered after her at a leisurely pace.

It was a game with him. She knew that. She unlocked the front door with trembling fingers and almost ran to the bathroom where she slammed the door and jammed the lock into place. She sat down on the toilet, buried her face in her hands, and rocked back and forth. It wouldn't matter how long she stayed in there. The past had taught her that. He would wait. *Oh, Danny.*

She'd go to him tomorrow. She'd suffer Brett's humiliating treatment of her tonight, but tomorrow . . . she'd see Rikki, too.

She stood up then, washed the tears from her face and opened the door.

He was waiting for her.

She didn't go to him. She forced him to come to her. Then she stood there, a wooden doll, as he undressed her, led her to the bed, and forced her down on her stomach. She almost retched when his hands began their trek over her body, stopping as they always did on her buttocks. She felt him part her cheeks and braced against the pain that experience had taught her was almost upon her.

He ran his hand over her sex. "You didn't shave," he said in the complaining whine that was all too familiar.

"How can you be like a child if you are covered with hair like a whoring woman?"

Carrie bit her lower lip harder and harder. *You're sick,* her mind screamed. And then she wondered. Had someone else known about his fetish? His unnatural lust for prepubescent innocence? Had he killed those people to keep his secret safe?

He rammed into her anus then as was his preference, driving the questions from her conscious mind while she fought the waves of nausea that always accompanied the act. She bit harder into her lip, then clamped down on the bedspread with her teeth when she thought she might scream.

When it was over, she lay there hurting, her rectum throbbing, her heart breaking. And then she remembered the question. She knew she was married to a madman. Was she also married to a murderer?

Sally Jane crawled into bed with her lover.

"How was it?" her partner asked.

"Amusing. Boring. Predictable. All of the above."

"And your old friend, Rikki Blue? How was she?"

Sally Jane snuggled into the crook of her lover's arm, "Beautiful, but then she always was."

"It still bothers you?" her bedmate asked.

"No, of course not. I've outgrown my childish jealousies, and in fact, I admire her. She's not letting this town cower her. It can't be easy returning to face the devil."

Her lover laughed. "You sound almost awestruck. Perhaps *I* should be jealous."

It was Sally Jane's turn to laugh. "Now that would be different. But I don't believe it's possible. You're the most secure person I know."

"Besides yourself, you mean?"

Sally Jane didn't answer for a long moment, and when she did, she heard the weariness in her own voice.

"I wasn't always. Once I was frightened. I was sure everyone would find out."

"About what? Your proclivities or him?'"

"Both, I suppose."

"But no one ever did. And Rikki Blue won't either. I promise. If she proves too nosy, I'll make sure she doesn't dare jay walk without being picked up. Now come here. Don't think about it anymore. You're a respected woman in St. Joan. Everyone looks up to you. You've turned your father's dream into reality and amassed a fortune. And most importantly, your secret's safe."

"I don't know. I'm not so sure. Rikki Blue isn't everyone else."

Junior went directly home, but he didn't go inside the house. Instead he went to the garage. He opened all the locks. Flipped the switch on. His thumbs hooked in his trouser pockets, he looked around. Everything was just as he'd left it. But he hadn't expected anything else. No one would dare to snoop around his territory. He was a Witcomb after all. His daddy was sheriff and he a sworn deputy. But more important, the Witcomb name went way back in St. Joan history. People respected it. They feared it, too. All except the outsiders who didn't *know*. Outsiders like Rikki Blue.

The woman worried him. She was too tenacious for *his* own good. He'd have to watch her. He'd worked too damn hard, done too many things he hadn't enjoyed, to have her ruin it all for him now. He scratched the back of his shaggy head. He had to give it to her. The woman had guts. Coming back to St. Joan after all these years. And if he was any judge of people, she wasn't a quitter. She wouldn't back off unless someone scared the beejees out of her.

He locked the doors, stuck his hands fully in his pockets, and started whistling. No particular tune. Just one that accompanied the refrain that was going through his mind: "You're a helluva woman, Rikki Blue. But I'm just the man who can handle you."

"Is she asleep?" Pamela Sue asked her husband as they dressed for bed.

"Mom? Yeah, sawing logs."

She sat down on the side of the bed as she buttoned the bodice of her flannel nightgown. "Good, 'cause I want to talk to you, and I didn't want her listening."

"Why would she listen?" Aaron asked as he stepped out of his boxer shorts and into pajama bottoms.

Pam rolled her eyes. "For the same reason she listens to everything we do. She's nosy."

Aaron sighed. "Not tonight, babe. I'm tired. I don't want to argue about Mom or anyone else."

"I don't want to argue, either," his wife said as she pulled back the covers and climbed between the sheets. "But there's something I want to ask you."

He circled the foot of the bed and climbed in beside her. "This has to be a first. The kids all asleep and not one phone call from my service." He groped for her hand beneath the covers, found it, and drew it to his belly. "Let's not jinx it by talking about anything heavy. We had a nice time tonight, another first for a long time, I might add. Let's just savor the hour." He flipped off the switch on the lamp.

"You're not worried about what Rikki is doing?"

"What—? Oh, you mean trying to find Dad's killer? Sure, I guess. I mean, I worry about her. I hope she doesn't get herself in trouble."

"Do you worry about us? About yourself?" Pam pressed, holding her breath at the same time.

Aaron turned on his side, raised up on his elbow to

look at her. He was frowning. "What are you asking, Pammy?"

"Your mother believes you killed them. Your dad, Rikki's parents, all of them."

He laughed shortly and flopped over onto his back once again. "That's pure silliness. Mom knows I loved my dad. Why would I have killed him or any of them?"

Pam didn't answer.

Silence filled the room as oppressively as the darkness.

With the keenness of a mother's ear, Pam heard Kevin, their oldest, rustling beneath his covers in the room across the hall. Tears filled her eyes. Oh, God, let Rhonda be wrong. Let me be wrong. "She called the radio station, Aaron." She heard her husband's exasperated sigh, ignored it, and went on. "I was coming upstairs to put away some clothes I'd folded. I heard her talking to Rikki on the air. She was whispering. Telling her to go away. Telling her that no one wants her kind here."

"So, she's eccentric. You know that. We both know that. That doesn't mean she thinks I killed Dad or the others."

"She's scared, Aaron, and so am I. You can tell yourself all you want that you loved your dad, but we both know that's not true. You hated him for leaving your mother, for being so dictatorial to you." She took a deep breath before adding, "And I know you dated Cindy."

"So what! That doesn't mean I killed either of them. My God, Pam, I'm a doctor! I work at the other side of the killing fields."

She heard the plea in his voice. But was there also a note of panic? It didn't matter. She was a nurturer. She turned onto her side and took him into her arms. She wanted to believe that he was innocent of those vile crimes that were almost as vivid in her mind today as they had been ten years before. She loved him. Somehow she *would* believe in him . . . and she would protect him.

Bo blinked as the lights of the Cherokee Jeep passed over his living room window. He'd been worried about her. She'd walked out of the party more than two hours before. Where had she been? What did it matter? She was obviously safe now.

He lifted the bourbon bottle from the floor beside his sentry post, refilled his water glass. Drinking alone and not just one unless one meant one bottle. He was sure the teleshrinks would have something to say about that. He raised his glass in salute to them before emptying almost half the glass in one long swallow. He saw her on the terrace, and watched as she disappeared inside the house. He drank again.

Odd that the liquor was doing its trick on his legs and arms, making them numb, while failing to numb his mind as he'd hoped.

He couldn't forget what he'd heard at the dinner nor dull the guilt he'd felt in that moment when Junior had reminded her of the dress. He didn't know exactly what had gone down in the sheriff's office when the dress had been produced, but he could imagine, and the guilt had rubbed his conscience raw in the past couple of hours. He'd been coaching himself in his best subject ever since: denial. But tonight he wasn't learning.

He set the glass on the window sill before burying his face in his hands. Life was a bitch and he was a bastard. She hadn't deserved what he'd left her to face all alone. He hadn't known her parents would be killed. That the police would find the dress. That she'd be subjected to humiliation on top of grief he couldn't even fathom. As much as he'd hurt over his parents' deaths, it wasn't the same. Didn't even come close.

He groaned as the guilt gnawed at him painfully.

"Oh, God, Blue, no wonder you never answered any of my letters or took my calls."

He hadn't cried since Bert's funeral. But he cried now. It occurred to him that these might be tears that were alcohol induced. He hoped not. He hoped he cried for her, for himself, for them. For what had almost been.

Rikki didn't turn on the lights when she entered the house. She liked the darkness. Its heaviness was warming like a blanket one wrapped himself in. But when the telephone shrilled suddenly behind her, she almost shrieked. *Damn it!*

It had to be close to midnight. Who would be calling her at this hour? She stumbled over a box she'd forgotten she'd left near the book shelf. Cursed again, then bumped her shin painfully on the edge of the end table. The phone pealed three more times before she grabbed it from its hook. "Hello!"

"Where the hell have you been? And why haven't you called?" the voice on the other end demanded without preamble.

Rikki laughed, though she cut it off quickly to apologize. "Oh, Kit, I'm sorry. I tried once, I swear. I've been so busy, but I am sorry. It was rude and selfish of me not to get in touch with you."

"Ah, well, at least now I know you're safe, I can sleep tonight. You are safe, aren't you?"

"Yes, I'm here, I'm safe, I'm fine."

"So tell me," Kit prodded, then added, "and say hello to Sadie. She's just picked up in the bedroom."

Rikki laughed. She loved Kit Hollins and though she didn't know his new bride, Sadie, as well as she would have liked, she approved of the marriage. Kit was a reknowned actor who had landed a starring role in a daytime soap three years before. A handsome man with an air of sophistication that was uncommon in men as young as he, he'd nevertheless vowed to remain a bachelor until he was at least forty. Many young actresses had done their best to disabuse him of that promise, but Sadie Martin, his tax attorney, had accomplished what none of the others had been even remotely close to doing. Sadie was not conventionally pretty. In fact, Rikki remembered how surprised she'd been when she'd first met the woman. Like everyone, she'd assumed that the good-looking thespian would fall in love with one of the beautiful people in the "biz," but if anyone thought that Sadie had hooked the best fish in the ocean, Kit thought differently. As far as he was concerned, he was the lucky one, and he was positively ga-ga over his new bride. "Now I finally believe it's true. You're an old married man who shares everything with the little woman."

"Careful, Rikki, the last person who referred to Sadie as the little woman is still trying to get the fresh produce out of his shorts."

"The fresh—what is he talking about, Sadie?"

"He's exaggerating. Wally at the corner market—you know him—did make a smartass comment and I *did* make a suggestion about where he could put his lettuce, but I *didn't* put it there. But enough of that. How are you, girl? And why the fuck haven't we heard from you?"

"I'm sorry, Sadie, really. They didn't get my phone on until late yesterday and today I haven't stopped. I just came in the door when the phone started ringing. But I was going to call you in the morning, I swear."

"So tell us what's been happening . . . in detail," Kit cut in.

Her eyes now accustomed to the darkness, Rikki wended her way to a chair by the window and sat down as she took them through her four days in St. Joan. At the end of the telling, she settled back to endure the lecture from Kit that was inevitable. She listened with only half an ear as she gazed out the window.

She saw him at once, sitting in the house below, though if she hadn't known who the occupant of the tiny bungalow was, she would never have recognized the man she saw now. His shoulders bowed, Bo held his face in his hands, and even from the distance she thought he shook as if with sobs. But that was impossible. Keen Bohannon cry?

Still, she stood up and leaned closer to the window, but in that instant, Bo stood as well and disappeared out of sight. Rikki sighed.

"Rikki, are you still there?" Kit demanded, his voice rising a notch with concern.

"Oh, I'm sorry, Kit, I was distracted. What did you say?"

"I *said* perhaps Sadie and I should come down there. I'm on hiatus for the next six weeks and now that tax time is up, Sadie can get a couple of weeks off."

"Don't be ridiculous. You didn't even have a honeymoon, for God's sake. If you're going to take some time to get away, go somewhere exotic and romantic like newlyweds do."

"St. Joan sounds pretty exotic and romantic to me," Sadie put in. "It certainly doesn't lack for a mysterious ambience. Besides, who knows, with Kit's flair for the dramatic and my talent in logical deduction, maybe we could help you find the answers you're after."

Rikki opened her mouth, but Kit preempted her. "And we might be able to keep you alive."

"Oh, come on, Kit, I'm fine. In fact, the only serious threat I've received since arriving is from my end table when you called. I banged my shin pretty soundly. Probably have a hell of a bruise in the morning."

"Don't make light. If the killer still lives in St. Joan, you are going to be in very grave danger, honey," Kit said. "Especially if you're right and it's one of your old playmates. You're taunting a madman, Rikki."

Rikki sighed. "I know what I'm doing."

"And you don't even have the good sense to be scared," Kit accused.

"Of course I'm scared. But I can't do anything else. I owe it to my parents." She turned her gaze back out the window, but Bo was nowhere to be seen. "If it had been me who was killed, they wouldn't have rested until the bastard was brought to justice. I can't either."

"We just worry because we love you," Kit said.

Rikki smiled into the receiver as she twisted the cord around one of her fingers. "I love you, too. But trust me. This won't take long. I've tossed the gauntlet into the middle of the arena. The person I'm after will pick it up."

"Be careful," Sadie admonished.

"I will, and I'll do better about calling, I promise." But she heard the extension click even as she was replying and knew that Sadie had hung up.

Kit picked up the conversation. "You'd better if you don't want us showing up on your doorstep in a couple of days. Check in every night, Rikki. It doesn't matter how late. We'll be waiting."

Rikki felt tears burn behind her eyes. "I really do love you, Kit," she said, then added a choked, "bye."

"That was touching," a voice said just beyond the screen door.

"You scared the crap out of me," Rikki said as she crossed the room and replaced the receiver. Her heart was beating a mile a minute even though she'd recognized Bo's voice at once. "What are you doing sneaking up on my terrace in the middle of the night?"

"Showing you how vulnerable you are, maybe. Or maybe I was just lonesome. Or maybe I was just listening in on your conversation with your lover. He calling from Boston?"

Rikki went to the door but didn't open it to go out. Instead she turned her back to him as she leaned against the mesh. "He's my friend, Bo. But he's none of your business."

"Guess that's right," he admitted with a drunken slur.

Rikki closed her eyes as she shook her head and laughed. She wasn't laughing at him. She was laughing at herself. She'd been worried about him, thought he was crying. Instead, he'd only been reeling from drink. "Go home and go to bed, Bo. Sleep it off."

"Can't sleep," he mumbled.

"Why not?"

"Can't stop thinking about you," he answered with the candor that came with inebriation.

Rikki sighed, then started to tell him to go home and take a shower, but her words were stopped by a sudden racket on the other side of the door. She spun around, placing her hands against the screen now as she tried to find him in the darkness. "Bo? Where are you? Are you all right?"

He answered with a pain-wracked groan.

With reluctance, Rikki stepped out to the terrace to investigate.

The swaying flower pot that hung from the eaves explained what had happened. Bo was seated on the wood flooring, holding his head. He still wore the tuxedo trousers and the shirt, though it was unbuttoned, revealing his powerful chest and lean midsection. "Here I was worried that you couldn't take care of yourself. Pretty good defense, those flower pots. They could be deadly. Like walking a mine field."

Rikki chuckled softly under her breath as she crouched down in front of him. "There's only one."

Bo peered from beneath his hand, his gaze focusing on the velvety swell of her breasts above the deep cut of her gown. "You're falling out of your dress," he mumbled.

"Are you complaining?" she asked with just a hint of amusement in her tone.

He could feel her breath against his face, like a whispered invitation. Pushing himself to his feet, he turned his back to her to look out at the night. "Where'd you go?" he asked.

"When?"

"After your dinner party. I've been watching for you, worrying."

She went to stand at his side, placing her hands on the railing and followed his gaze into the darkness. "You don't·have to worry about me, Bo. I'm a big girl. I've been taking care of myself for a long time."

That admission cut through him cleanly. He ignored the pain. "But you haven't been trying to ferret out a killer."

Rikki glanced his way. He sounded much more sober now. Had his run in with the heavy clay pot had that effect on him or was it something else? "Why don't you go home? Get some sleep."

"I can't. Not until you tell me what happened at the sheriff's office the night your parents were killed."

Of course she knew what he was talking about. The dress. She'd felt the tension in him even though she hadn't looked his way as soon as Junior mentioned it at the dinner. But it wasn't something she wanted to talk about. Hell, she didn't allow herself to even think about that time. Not in detail. It still hurt too much. "I don't blame you, Bo."

"Why not? It's my fault you were humiliated."

"I wasn't humiliated," she said with a long, ragged sigh.

"I know better. I know *you*, Blue. I know that something that personal had to be devastating. If I'd stayed around, been there for you, no one would have dared question you about it." He slammed the palms of his hands against the railing. "Damn it, Blue, I'm sorry. That's what I've been waiting to tell you."

The pain in his voice pricked her heart. But she couldn't let him know that. She had never admitted to anyone, even herself, how badly his defection had hurt her. She wasn't going to start now. She turned, rested her backside on the railing and folded her arms over her chest as she looked at him straight on. "Give me a break, Bohannon. My parents were not just killed, they were butchered. My mother's throat was slit and my father was stabbed over twenty times. Do you think having to tell them about the blood, about my first experience with sex mattered to me? Do you think I cared because you weren't there? I wanted my parents back, alive and safe. Nothing else. So stop beating yourself up. We were just two kids who got carried away. It was fun while it lasted, but no big deal."

He dropped his arms to his sides, straightening and looking at her for a long moment, and she almost closed her eyes against the hurt she saw in his. "Guess I'm making a big deal out of nothing, huh?"

No! She did look away then. She couldn't voice the lie while staring into his eyes. "Yes, you are."

He didn't move and after a few seconds, she was forced to look at him again. The expression in his eyes was different suddenly. Defiant, negating. His jaw was rigid, and a muscle flexed there. He grabbed her, his hand going to the nape of her neck, surprising her, confusing her. But before she could react he lowered his mouth to hers. His lips were bruising, demanding, his tongue seeking and taking.

The kiss didn't last long, but she got the message even before he spoke. He laughed deep in his throat. Then stuck his hands in his pockets. "Damn, you had me going for a minute. I didn't know if it was the booze that was muddying my brain or if my memory had just created something that never was." He winked as he stepped past her. He got as far as the first step down before he added over his shoulder. "Deny it to me, babe, if that's what you've gotta do, but don't lie to yourself. I didn't make it up. It's still there, and it ain't gonna go away."

Chapter Sixteen

Rikki awakened early on Wednesday morning. She hadn't slept well the night before, yet she was alert and energetic. She showered hastily, slipped into biker shorts, a cropped top, and running shoes before pulling on a cap and looping her hair through the back. She was on the road, jogging at a good pace thirty minutes after climbing from bed. She had a lot of pent-up emotion to work off, and it had nothing to do with the investigation she was making into her parents' murders. She chanced a glance at the little fishing cottage in the distance before diverting her gaze back to the road with firm resolve. Bo had been right when he'd said "it was still there." She'd experienced the same thrill, the same desire she'd known ten years before. But there was a difference now. Now she didn't want to want him. Now she had other things to attend to.

Later? her betraying mind demanded, but she pushed the question away, and clinching her fists, ran with even more determination.

She forced her thoughts back to the dinner party the night before. It had gone well, she thought, in spite of the note she'd departed on. Anger, just like love, was an emotion she couldn't afford right now. She had to stay calm and collected . . . focused.

Hearing a car horn, she swerved closer to the curb.

The car didn't pass but kept its speed as slow as hers, and then the driver signalled to her again. This time Rikki glanced over her shoulder. The morning sun created a glare over the windshield of the Lincoln Towncar, preventing her from identifying the driver. But she altered her pace, eventually jogging in place until the vehicle pulled up beside her. "Oh, hi," she said with a slight wave. "Sorry, I thought you were telling me to get out of the way."

Sally Jane's smile was wide and friendly. "I'm the one who should apologize. Did I frighten you?"

"Not at all. Like I said, I just thought it was some irate driver telling me to get off the road. Were you coming to see me?"

"Actually, no. I was headed down the road to the lake. There's some property that's come up for sale. I was going to check it out. Then I saw you, and decided to use the opportunity to invite you to lunch. You go off the air at one?"

Rikki nodded. "Lunch sounds good. Want me to meet you at your office when I finish up?"

"No, I won't be in today. Why don't we just agree on say two o'clock?"

"Okay. Where?"

"You remember the Spotted Heron?"

"Of course," Rikki said with a smile though she was wondering why Sally Jane seemed so much more tense this morning than she had the night before. She shrugged the question away as Sally Jane waved and pulled away, disappearing shortly around the curve in the road. Maybe, like herself, the realtor had not slept well. Then Rikki remembered the data she'd collected on the real estate mogul over the past ten years.

Her father, Clemens Matthers, had died in a tragic, fiery car crash just months after Bo's dad. Sally Jane had only been twenty-three at the time, but she'd taken over the responsibilities of his company with the competence and foresight of a woman many years older. Clemens had been a born salesman who had managed the difficult task of balancing his daughter's upbringing with a demanding career, while amassing millions at the same time. No one had ever learned why he'd divorced his young wife when Sally Jane was little more than a baby, but no one had ever argued with the court's decision to award him sole custody. Everything he did, he did well, including raising his daughter. Now it seemed Sally Jane was even better at business than Clemens. She'd multiplied his millions several times over putting CMA Realtors on the list of most successful privately owned companies in America and without giving into pressure to move her headquarters to a big city such as St. Louis or Chicago.

Yet, it didn't appear that the young woman had been any more successful than Clemens in the love department. There had been a few brief mentions about the heiress attending benefit dinners and the like, but the men who escorted her were always different from the time before.

Rikki chuckled as she jogged along the same bend Sally Jane had disappeared around a moment earlier. Maybe the tension wasn't anything a good romp between the sheets wouldn't cure.

The smile on her face fell apart as a picture of Bo came to mind. "Go away," she ordered aloud, but he stayed with her for the next three miles until she returned home.

Bo had slept soundly. Booze was the best cure in the world for insomnia. But the moment his eyes opened that morning, he thought about Rikki, about the kiss they'd shared. No, scratch that. They hadn't shared anything. He'd taken it. Well, he didn't regret it. He'd do more than kiss her if she gave him half a chance.

Sitting up and throwing his legs over the side of the

bed, he ran his hands through his hair. He remembered the last few minutes of the telephone conversation he'd overheard. Who the hell was Kit? Was she really in love with the guy? He'd heard her say she loved him, but she'd lived in Boston for the past ten years. People up there talked like that all the time, didn't they? It didn't necessarily mean they were *in* love.

He didn't convince himself, but he didn't forget the way she'd felt in his arms either. Or the way her lips had parted beneath his. He'd told her it was still there between them, and he knew he was right.

Standing up, he went to the mirror. That was a mistake. The face that stared back at him looked like hell. He needed a haircut, his eyes were bloodshot, and the stubble on his chin was dark and heavy. He grimaced at his reflection. "What you need is a good stiff shot of whiskey." That probably was the quickest route to recovery, but he knew he wasn't going to indulge himself. Not this morning.

He'd done some tall thinking—amazing considering how much he'd drunk—after he'd returned from her place. He wanted her more than ever. He'd fallen in love with her when they were both little more than kids, but it hadn't gone away. He'd tried. Shit, he'd even married someone else in his efforts to escape the memory of her. He'd given up hope for a time. But that was before she'd come back. She was here now and he was going to prove to her that they belonged together.

He filled a glass with water from the tap, then raised it. "Sorry, bucko," he said to the man Blue had been talking to on the phone the night before. "You shoulda never let her come back, 'cause I'm not letting her get away."

Which brought him back to the realization he'd come to just before sleep had claimed him in the early morning hours.

She was intent on finding her parents' killer. Stupid

and dangerous. He wasn't sure he shared her conviction that the murderer was one of her former friends. In fact, he hoped she was wrong. Not because he felt any loyalty to any of them. Except for Aaron and Pam Gray, he didn't even like most of them. But if she was right, she was in greater danger than she would be from a stranger. She was inviting one of them to come after her. He couldn't just sit by and let that happen. He'd made up his mind to help her.

He grinned as he imagined the temper tantrum she'd throw if she knew he was about to jump into the middle of her game, but that was just too damned bad.

His gaze fell on the copy of *Playmates* she'd sent him a few months before. He bent down to retrieve it from the floor where he'd dropped it the night before. He met her cool blue gaze. He touched the spot on the glossy paper where her deep dimples enclosed her smile. "Like it or not, Blue, I'm taking this ride with you." He tossed the magazine onto the bed.

As he stepped beneath the hot spray of the shower five minutes later, he was thinking about where to start. He decided on Aaron and Pam. He'd already dismissed them from contention, but he might as well prove their innocence and narrow the field of competitors.

He was whistling as he left the house. He actually felt good for the first time since he could remember. He slid behind the wheel of his car just as Rikki left the house above him on the hill. "I always knew you were good for me, Blue," he said as he watched her climb into the Jeep and drive away. "You should never have come back if you didn't want me 'cause I'm gonna be stuck to you better than gum on pavement."

Rikki was ten minutes late for her luncheon with Sally Jane. The other woman was gracious about her tardiness, waving Rikki's apologies away. "Forget it. We're both busy career women. I understand."

As Rikki took a sip of water, Sally Jane told her, "I listened to your show again this morning. You're really getting the townsfolk involved, aren't you?"

"It's so easy. People get apathetic, accepting. Then you remind them that they don't have to be mindless victims, and they wake up. That's all I do. Wake them up. Shake them up."

"And you do it well. I just hope you don't wake up a killer in the process."

Rikki met the censor in Sally Jane's tone with a long silence that was lengthened by the waiter's appearance to take their orders. Rikki scanned the menu quickly, then ordered a hamburger. "Load the goodies on it. The works. And pile the fries on the side," she told him.

Sally Jane ordered a cobb salad, then said to Rikki, "You always could eat the rest of us under the table." The statement was given with a smile, but Rikki sensed resentment in the tone.

"Which reminds me, I wanted to tell you how fabulous you look, Sally Jane. There must be a special man in your life."

"I have a lover, yes. What about you?"

"As a matter of fact, no."

"That surprises me. I thought a hot shot celebrity like yourself would have men trampling down her door."

"I don't have time. Right now my career is my lover." Rikki smiled with a new thought. "You know I always thought you and Junior would end up together. But now I realize that would never have lasted."

Sally Jane had been edgy, her comments each containing a note of tension, but at this she laughed. "You're right there. Junior is—how do I put it? Not evolved enough for me."

Rikki laughed with her. "That's very good. I think

you just hit the nail on the head. So tell me about your current guy."

"It's not a relationship I can talk about," Sally Jane said without hesitation.

"Oh," Rikki said, the interviewer in her disappointed, but understanding. "I can't talk about it" almost always meant married. She changed the subject. "Well, then let's get back to the subject of my show and uncovering a killer. I'm not worried that he . . . or she will go after anyone else. Why should he when he hasn't in years? He might come after me, but it's a risk I have to take."

"Why did you wait ten years?"

"That one's easy. My grandmother made me promise not to come while she was still alive. She died last year and it took me this long to get my affairs in order in Boston and to negotiate the purchase of KSTJ."

"Which brings up another question. People are wondering how long you're going to stay. They wonder if you're going to get things stirred up, then bail out on them."

Rikki didn't answer the question. She couldn't. She didn't have an answer. Instead, she said, "Sally Jane, are you angry with me about something?"

Sally Jane blinked, her cool demeanor crumbling for just a second. "Of course not. Why would you even think that?"

Rikki shrugged. "Maybe I'm wrong, but in my line of work, you learn quickly to pick up voice tone, and I hear anger in yours."

Sally Jane had recovered. She laughed, gave her head a small shake and said, "My lover accused me of being jealous of you. I denied it, of course, but it's really true. I've always been envious of you. I think that's what you're hearing."

"But you look wonderful. You're rich, successful. Why would you be jealous of me?"

Their food was delivered before the realtor could answer and as Rikki left the restaurant an hour later, it occurred to her that Sally Jane had successfully avoided the topic after that. As Rikki turned the jeep back toward her office, she went over their meeting in her mind.

Sally Jane had changed, not just physically, and the other changes weren't as complementary. She was poised, confident, but brittle now as well. Her laughter was forced, and in spite of her denial, Rikki still felt the underlying anger that she was certain was directed at her. So what did it mean? Probably nothing more than a successful business woman protecting her territory.

As Rikki pulled into the KSTJ parking lot, a new thought struck. What if it was more than that?

She sat in the jeep for several minutes toying with the question. She'd never really considered the women in her group of friends as suspects in the grisly murders. A chauvinistic attitude she'd never have admitted to. But why not the women? Why not Sally Jane?

Aaron was seated behind his desk when his receptionist showed Bo in. "This has got to be a first. I don't think you've ever been here before. Let me guess, you look like hell, but you're not sick, so you must have something on your mind."

Bo took a seat, crossing his legs so that one of his shoes rested on his knee. "I don't want to take you from your patients, but yeah, I wanted to talk."

"About a certain beautiful woman who is wreaking havoc in the lives of all those who once loved her."

"Yeah, something like that. She wreaking havoc in yours, Aaron?"

Aaron scratched the bald spot in his thinning hair as he answered. "That's probably overstating it a bit, but she's definitely complicating things."

"How so?"

"Well, for starters, some of my patients are scared. They're sure the guy who killed Dad and the others is going to come out of hibernation now that she's poking around. You remember old Mrs. Hawkins from over near Maggie's Crossing? She cancelled her appointment this morning. Said she's not stepping out of her house until this fella's caught. I had to go out there this morning. Fifty miles round trip. But she's got a bad heart."

"You said for starters. What else?" Bo pressed.

Aaron rubbed his jaw. "This you're not going to believe. Last night after we got home from the dinner party, Pam told me my mom had called the radio station. Pam says she overheard her whispering, making threats. And you know why? Because my own mother thinks I'm the killer. I didn't sleep too well after hearing that, let me tell you."

"Why would she think that?"

"Because Dad and I didn't get along. Because I resented him trying to direct my life and for leaving Mom. You ever meet Bunny Apperson, Bo?"

"Who?"

"Bunny. She was one of the murderer's victims. A real little looker. Came up here from Arkansas or some place. She was three or four years older than me, but I took her out a couple of times the summer of '84. Then one night I decided to just drop in on her, you know? Guess who I ran into as I was heading up her steps?"

"Your dad," Bo guessed though it wasn't difficult to figure out.

"Yep, you've got it. I don't know why I got so mad, but I saw red, let me tell you. It wasn't like I was real hot for the girl. I mean she was pretty and sexy and all that, but I knew she was a real swinger, too. So, it wasn't like I felt any proprietary claims on her. But my own dad." He paused, shook his head as if even now, eleven years later, he couldn't believe it. "A few weeks later he came by the house to see Mom." He laughed with a memory that he shared with Bo. "She was never happy with Dad. Bitched at him almost nonstop, but she couldn't stand him being free to see other women either. So, she'd call him up complaining about something hurting and he'd give in and come by to check her out. Anyway, this day, he tried to make peace with me over the Bunny incident. Told me he'd backed away from her. He didn't want someone like her coming between us. Mom was upstairs but she must have overheard, because they had a hell of a knock-down-drag-out over it. After that, Dad refused to come over to the house anymore. I didn't even see him much."

"Must have been rough," Bo said just because the gap that fell between them needed filling.

"You know the ironic part? We were just starting to get close again when he was killed. That hurt, man. I loved the old guy for all his faults. I could never have killed him."

"I believe you," Bo said sincerely.

"Anyway, much as I like Rikki Blue, she's causing me some problems, and to tell you the truth, Bo, I'm worried about her. I don't think it's real smart going after this guy the way she is. I can't help but wish she'd give it up. Go back to Boston."

"I don't think that's going to happen."

Aaron smiled. "And you don't want it to happen, right?"

Bo laughed. "I want her safe. But, no, I guess I don't want her to leave."

"What about her theory that it's one of us? You think she's right?"

"I don't know. I mean, I can see where she's coming from. She did confide in us, not once but twice. And the funny thing is, I *hope* she's right."

"Good God, man, why? We've all been friends for a helluva long time. I'd sure hate to think that my judgment is that impaired."

"Yeah, but if she's not, then she's shooting in the dark and in the meantime, someone we don't even suspect can sneak up on her."

"I see your point. Well, for what it's worth, you can assure her it wasn't me." He laughed again, this time without amusement. "Even if my own mother doubts me, I'm not a killer although there have been times when I could cheerfully strangle her."

"Like I said, *I* believe you. Thing is, Aaron, if not you and not me, who? Which one of us is clever enough to have fooled the rest of us all these years?"

"Now that's the sixty-four thousand dollar question."

Rikki left the radio station later than usual. It was almost seven by the time she turned into her driveway. She was bone tired but relaxed as she hadn't been in a long time. It had to be the spring air and the burst of color in the trees and flowers that had taken place almost overnight. She slowed the Jeep on the drive, taking in the red bud, forsythia, and dogwood. Wild daisies dotted the hillside to her right, while below her and to the left, the lake water glistened like an ice blue satin sheet sprinkled liberally with sapphires and diamonds. She'd forgotten how much she loved the wilderness that was the Ozarks. Humans had conquered it but never tamed it.

She thought back to Sally Jane's question about her intentions to stay or leave once her mission was resolved. Her heart urged her to stay while her mind intellectualized all the reasons why she shouldn't even consider it. Not that it was a question that had to be resolved today. She'd been there for five days and she wasn't any closer to answers. In fact, it had gotten more complex after her lunch with Sally Jane.

Taking her foot from the brake and depressing the accelerator, she sighed as the Jeep made the slow climb up the hillside. She had hoped to be ticking names off her list, not adding them.

As she stepped from the vehicle, she thought about the tapes her mother had made with Dr. Grant. She shuddered. She hadn't wanted to go to the storage garage where most of her family's possessions had been stored all these years. Now, she supposed she didn't have any other choice. But, God, she dreaded that painful task.

She was lost in thoughts of the dismal task that had to be faced tomorrow or the next day when movement on her terrace caught her eye. Stopping on the bottom step, she called out. "Who's there?"

Petite appeared in view at once. "It's me, Rikki. I've been waiting for you. Hope you don't mind."

Rikki noticed the motor bike parked near the garage then and silently rebuked herself. She was going to have to be more alert than that if she were going to be effective at sleuthing. She turned her attention to Petite. "In fact, I'm glad to see you. You just surprised me. For a minute I thought it was—"

"Bo?"

Rikki felt her cheeks heat with the question. That's exactly what she'd thought, but she opted for a small lie. "No, actually I was afraid the killer might be waiting for me."

"In broad daylight? I don't think so," Petite said.

Rikki took her keys from her purse and unlocked the door. "So what brings you around? I know the rent's not due."

Petite rewarded her with a chuckle, then shook her head. "I've been listening to your show. It's really wild, ya know? I keep thinking: that's Ericka, my brother's old girlfriend. Now she's a major celebrity."

Rikki held the door open and waited for the smaller woman to enter first. "Funny, I didn't think you'd be impressed with celebrity."

"You mean because of my avant garde attitudes? Well, you're right, except with you it's different. I still remember you when you were just a kid."

"It's no big deal. Just what I do for a living."

"Used to be just what you did for a living. Now you're using the medium to get a message out to a killer. Which is why I'm here. I was listening today when you reminded us again like you have every day that someone out there knows something he's forgotten. And then it hit me. *I* know something. Maybe it's nothing, but on the other hand it might just be important."

"Sit down," Rikki said, tossing her purse and keys onto the table. She was excited but careful not to show it. As Petite had just said, it might not be anything. She knew better than to get her hopes up. Her training as a broadcast journalist had taught her that. This was different. This was personal. But that made it all the more important that she not let her emotions get in the way of her objectivity. "Would you like a soda?"

"Nope, my old man's watching the brats for me. I can only stay a few minutes."

In spite of her eagerness to learn what Petite had remembered, Rikki couldn't ignore her surprise. "You have children? I can't believe it, Petite. I didn't even know you were married."

"Yes and no. I have two kids. Both boys. Jesse's two. An adorable monster. The baby—Luke—is five months. But I'm not married. Billy, that's my old man, didn't want to do it legal. He said if we did, I'd always wonder if he's after my money. This way, he has no rights, so I know he's with me just because he loves me."

"He sounds like a great guy," Rikki said sincerely.

"Billy? He's a bum. Doesn't do anything except tinker with cars, his first love, but he's right for me, you know?"

"Yeah, I know," Rikki said as she thought unwillingly

of Bo. She changed the subject. "You were going to tell me something you remembered?"

"About Junior Witcomb," Petite said.

Rikki waited.

"Like I said, it might not be anything important."

Rikki's patience failed her. "Just tell me."

"Well, a few years back, he and I went out a few times. Nothing serious. God, you know Junior. He's dated every woman at the lake at one time or other. Anyway, one night we went to his place. We were just sitting around drinking with a couple of other guys. Friends of Junior's. I wasn't feeling any pain after a while, but I wasn't bombed. Junior was. One of his pals sat down on the floor next to me and put his arm around my shoulder. No big deal. At least it didn't feel that way to me. But Junior went ape shit over it. Pulled a knife on the guy. He was waving it in front of him and screaming. Sounded real crazy. I wasn't paying much attention to what he was saying. Guess I was floating too high from the booze and grass we were smoking. But I remember one thing he said. He told Donny— that's the guy's name, I think—that he was just like that whore, Bunny Apperson. He said she couldn't keep her hands off what didn't belong to her either. Donny was pretty scared but he was mad, too. He said he didn't know what Junior was talking about."

"Did Junior explain?" Rikki asked, hoping her excitement didn't come through in her voice.

"He shouted a few more things. I don't remember exactly what, but I do remember that in the middle somewhere he said that his old man had been boffing Bunny Apperson just before someone killed her. Then he said, and I think I'm quoting, 'You want to end up like her?' "

"Oh, Petite, you may have just given me the answer I've been looking for."

"I think so, too, but I want you to be careful, Rikki.

Junior's not quite right upstairs, you know? He's twisted and he can get real mean."

"I will be. I promise." Rikki couldn't contain her exhilaration any longer. She crossed the room to hug the other woman. "Oh, thank you, Petite."

"Yeah, it's okay, but I'll never forgive myself if you get yourself in trouble." She stepped out of Rikki's embrace and smiled. "Besides, Junior's not the only one who's got a temper. I don't want my brother coming after me if something happens to you."

Rikki ignored that. She was excited. This might be just the break she'd been hoping for, and the last thing she wanted was to be distracted by thoughts of the handsome prosecuting attorney. She thanked Petite again, then showed her to the door with a promise to come see her art once she had the murder business all wrapped up.

Petite touched Rikki's arm. "Be careful," she said. "I'm going to have some real heavy duty guilt if you get hurt."

"Please don't worry about me. We don't *know* that Junior is the killer. He might have been blowing smoke. I get the feeling he's real good at intimidation, so he may have just been trying to frighten the guy."

"Just be careful."

Rikki offered a wide smile that she hoped would reassure the other woman. "Look, the truth of the matter is that life isn't as simple as this. I'll probably find out he has alibis out the kazoo for when these murders were committed."

"One part of me hopes that's the case. But either way, let me know." She wriggled her fingers in farewell, got as far as the steps, then stopped to add, "And about Bo. He wouldn't be a bad person to confide in. He's smart. He might just be able to help you."

Rikki stood in the doorway long after Petite was out of sight. She thought about what Petite had said about her brother. She suspected that Petite was right. He might very well be able to help her. The only problem was, Rikki doubted she'd be able to keep her thoughts focused with him around. As much as she'd fought to forget him over the years, now that she'd seen him again, it was impossible. And when she was near him, catching a killer wasn't what she thought about.

Chapter Seventeen

Bo was frustrated. He'd spent most of the evening with a chart headed with six names. Junior Witcomb. Carrie Pearson. Brett Pearson. Sally Jane Matthers. Aaron Grant. Pam Grant. Beneath each one, he'd intended to list possible motives. Aaron had been easy. Hell, the man had spelled it out for him in his office that day. Beneath the other names, the paper was blank.

He was on a slow boat headed nowhere. Tossing his pen onto the table he leaned back in his chair, crossing his arms behind his head. It was obvious he needed more information. As a lawyer, he knew you didn't build a case without all the facts. The few he had were memories and they'd been tarnished by more than a decade. Well, there was a way to rectify that. He'd been on the right track that morning when he'd gone to visit Aaron, but hell it could take forever talking to each of his old friends. Besides, he doubted most of the others would be as receptive to his questions as the doctor had been. He stood up, grabbed a light weight jacket, and headed for the door. He was going straight to the man with the answers. Scooter Witcomb might not like his interference—word had it he was pretty riled about Blue's investigation—but hell, if the prosecutor didn't have a right to look into the crime, who did?

* * *

Rikki was way ahead of him. After Petite had left, Rikki had found her appetite, which had been ravenous before the visit, had abandoned her. She'd paced the house, mulling over Petite's tale about Junior until she'd worked up a good head of steam that was directed not only at the deputy but towards his sheriff father as well. She'd decided to confront the senior lawman and find out what he knew about his son's whereabouts the night Bunny Apperson had met with her brutal end. And that wasn't all she was going to ask Sheriff Witcomb about.

She'd phoned the sheriff's office before leaving home, but the dispatcher had told her the man was off duty. Rikki headed toward his house. She was relieved when she spotted his cruiser parked in his driveway.

Althea Witcomb answered the door, her eyes widening with surprise. "Ericka Cassidy! My land, for a moment there I felt like I was seeing a ghost. Come in, come in. How are you, girl?"

Rikki managed a smile though she was uncomfortable with the effusive greeting. "It's good to see you again, Mrs. Witcomb," she said, not stepping into the house as she'd been invited. "I would love to visit with you, but I'm afraid I'm here on business. Is the sheriff home?"

"Scooter? Yes, of course. But do come in the house. You can talk to him in his den. Then if you have time afterward, I'll make us some fresh lemonade and you can tell me everything that's happened to you since you left."

Rikki followed dutifully behind, listening to Althea's nonstop prattle with half an ear until the woman finally left to find her husband.

Then Rikki sank into a chair. Her dread of the approaching confrontation had mounted in the few minutes that she'd been in the sheriff's home, and she almost hoped that Junior was innocent of any wrongdoing. She didn't enjoy destroying people's lives as proving Junior guilty of her parents' murders would do. She'd been on the other side of destruction and she knew how severe the ramifications could be.

But as soon as Scooter stepped into the room, Rikki felt most of her anger return.

"Rikki, this is a surprise. Does this mean you've uncovered some detail I overlooked in my investigation?" the sheriff asked without the usual exchange of greetings.

"That's exactly what it means, Sheriff."

He took a seat at her side, crossing his slippered feet at the ankles and half-turning in the chair so that he faced her. "Well, spit it out, missy. What have you learned?"

"That you once had an affair with one of the murder victims, for starters."

His expression of pleasant curiosity didn't slip, but Rikki noticed that he paled significantly.

"Go on," he said mildly.

"I was also told about an incident in which Junior threatened to kill someone the same way Bunny Apperson was." She paused a beat, giving the lawman a chance to comment. When he didn't, she pressed harder. "I have two questions for you, Sheriff, and I'd like answers to both."

"I'm listening."

"First, did all those tragic murders go unsolved because you were covering your butt? Were you so goddamned afraid of your constituents voting you out of office if they found out you'd had an affair with an acclaimed party girl that you let my parents' murderer go free? Or were you covering for your son? Did he murder Bunny and the others? That's the second question."

She was trembling by the time she'd finished. She folded her hands in her lap, her fingernails digging into her skin in an effort to calm herself.

"Lawd Gawd," Scooter mumbled as he ran a hand over his face. He pursed his lips for a long moment as he stared silently at the young celebrity seated beside him. "I'm going to answer your questions, missy. But not because I'm obliged to just because you got yourself a radio show and think you're hot stuff all of a sudden. I'm going to answer them as honestly as I know how because, as you remind the good folk of St. Joan every day, your mama and daddy were fine people who deserved better than they got.

"I met Bunny when she first came to St. Joan. She might have been a party girl as you said, but to me she was a warm, good-hearted girl who made an old fart feel pretty special. I wasn't proud of what happened between us, but if it had come out, I wouldn't have run from it either. She was there for me in a time in my life when I needed someone. Right or wrong, that's the way it was. I took it real hard when she was killed, and I give you my solemn oath I did everything I knew of to find the person who did it to her. She wasn't a saint, but she was a sweet little gal who liked almost everyone she met."

"Obviously Junior found out about your affair—"

Scooter held up a finger, silently asking her to hold on.

"I was getting to my boy."

Rikki nodded her willingness to let him tell her in his own way. "Yes, Junior found out and he was real burned up at me over it. I tried to talk to him about it, but he didn't seem to want to listen. We had a lot of fights over it, but by the time Bunny was killed, we'd patched things up. He'd already gone into training for the deputy sheriff's program."

"But do you know where he was the night Bunny was killed? Or Cindy? Or any of them?"

"No, I can't truthfully say I know with absolute certainty what he was up to, but I know my boy, and I know he ain't no killer. He's not a saint anymore than his daddy is, but he's not cold blooded enough to inflict the kind of fear and agony that killer did on his victims. That's not to say he isn't hotheaded. He is. I've seen him lose his temper more times than I can count, but he's not violent."

Rikki heard the plea in his voice, looked down at her hands for a moment, then back up at the man's weary face. "You love your son, Sheriff. I understand that. No parent would ever want to admit that their child is capable of the violence we're talking about, but the fact is I have a witness who says Junior threatened to kill someone the same way Bunny was killed. That sounds pretty violent to me."

"He talks big, always has. That don't prove nothing."

"No it doesn't, but you can't prove he didn't commit the murders either," Rikki said, aware that her voice had risen. She lowered it. "I'm sorry, Sheriff, but I'm going to continue to pursue this until we prove his innocence or guilt one way or the other."

"And someone's going to get hurt."

"Not if he's not guilty," Rikki countered.

"What you gonna do?"

"I'm going to talk to Junior first. Just ask him some questions. Feel him out. If I can't find anything out that way, I'll start checking out his alibis for the nights each of the victims were killed." She glanced at her watch. It was just a little after eight. Not too late to pay Junior a visit tonight if she got going. "Can you tell me where Junior lives now? Or if he's on duty tonight, I'll go to the station and wait on him."

"He's not on duty," Scooter said. "He lives out at his granddaddy's old place. But why don't you wait? I'm not trying to protect my boy, I swear it. It's just that I think you'd be better off talking to others first. That way if you find out you was barking up the wrong tree, you won't end up with sap all over your face, and you and my boy can remain friends."

"I can't, Sheriff. I wish I could wait, take my time, but I can't. I've waited ten years already as it is." She reached out, touched his arm, and offered a smile. "But I hope you're right and I'm wrong, okay?"

"I am right," the sheriff said in a gruff voice as he pushed his hefty form to his feet. "Like I said, my boy ain't no goody two shoes. He ain't lily white either. He's got a wild side same as most young bucks, but he ain't a killer. You have my solemn word on that."

"Then I'll find that out, and by the process of elimination I'll be closer to the real criminal, won't I?"

"Let me go with you while you talk to him," Scooter suggested.

"Thanks, Sheriff, but I think Junior and I will have a more open exchange if it's just the two of us."

"You'll get back to me?" he asked, and Rikki felt her heart twist at the meek request.

"Of course."

"Well, then, I don't suppose we have anything else to discuss. I'll walk you to the front door."

Althea joined them as they stepped out into the hall. "You're not leaving already, are you, dear? I've just squeezed some fresh lemons."

Scooter answered for their guest. "Rikki's going to go out to my dad's place to visit with Junior. I reckon she wants to get going before it gets too late."

"Oh, how nice. Have you seen Junior since you got back?" Althea asked.

"Yes, ma'am. We had dinner just last night."

As Rikki drove away, she thought about her last words with Althea Witcomb. She felt a twinge of guilt for deceiving her. She'd made it sound like they'd dined together in friendship when in fact even then she'd been looking for a killer. But she hadn't thought it would be Junior.

* * *

Scooter Witcomb exited the front door of his house just as Bo raised his hand to press the doorbell. Both men stepped back in surprise.

"Damn, boy, you could take ten years off a man's life that way."

Bo grinned. "Sorry about that, Sheriff. You got a few minutes before you go rushing off?"

"You wanting to discuss business, Mr. Prosecutor?"

"As a matter of fact, I am, and you don't need to look so incredulous. I am still the prosecuting attorney."

"Yeah, well, been so long since I've seen you at the courthouse, I'd almost forgotten." He fitted his hat onto his head, adjusting the brim just so, then motioned for Bo to follow him. "You got about two minutes. I've got my own business to see to. What's on your mind?"

"It's not actually official business . . . yet. I want to talk to you about Rikki Blue's list of suspects. She won't appreciate my interference, but I've decided to run it for her anyway. I don't want her getting hurt and I can't help but think that she's headed for trouble."

"Even as we speak," the sheriff grumbled. "And as for her list of suspects, she's narrowed it to one."

Bo stopped in his tracks to question the man, "What are you talking about, Scooter?"

"I'm talking about your gal and my boy. She's got it in her head that he's the one who killed her folks and the others. She came by here about twenty minutes ago, and far as I know, she's headed for Junior's place now. Like I told her, I'd bet my life Junior didn't kill any of them people, but I don't know as how he's going to be too happy to answer charges from her. Thought I'd better go on out there myself and make sure everything stays nice and peaceful." He walked around to the driver's side of the car and motioned toward the passenger side at the same time. "Get in. You can come along and we can talk as we go."

Bo didn't hesitate. He wasn't forming any opinions on Junior Witcomb's guilt or innocence in the murder spree of '85, but he knew the man was a hothead. Several "guests" of the county, who'd spent time in the St. Joan jail had filed brutality charges against the over-eager deputy over the past ten years. None of them had come to anything, and Junior had claimed that the prisoners were all just ready to hang a lawman. Possibly. Over the past three years, since the Rodney King beating and subsequent riots in L.A., cries of law enforcement brutality had spread countrywide. Still, Bo wasn't so sure Junior was the saint he liked to claim he was, and he sure wasn't willing to bet Rikki's safety on it. He glanced at his watch before shutting his door and dousing the overhead light. "Hope you know a shortcut Blue's not familiar with, Sheriff."

"I'll get us there, don't you worry. But while you're hopin', why not hope my boy's not home?"

"You sound a might worried yourself," Bo observed.

The sheriff didn't answer as he backed out of the drive and headed north. Only when he evened his speed off to sixty did he reply. "You got one determined female who's got a powerful ugly notion in her head and a fella who's not too keen on taking criticism of any kind plus having a short fuse. Sounds like the right combination to start some sparks flyin' at the least."

"And at the worst?"

"My boy's no killer," the sheriff insisted, but the odometer crept up to eighty.

Rikki made only one wrong turn, veering left instead of right at the Y in Hawknest Road. She recognized the mistake after half a mile and turned the Jeep around. She arrived at the property line of the Witcomb land just thirty minutes after leaving the sheriff's house. The house was still a good two miles ahead, but even from that distance, it looked like it was dark. She felt her hopes plummet. Still, she slowed the car as she approached. There might be lights burning in the back. She turned off the lights on the car about a hundred feet from the house and almost missed the driveway. She decided to leave the car on the road and walk up the drive. She was probably over-dramatizing the situation with the exaggerated caution, but on the other hand, a little added discretion couldn't hurt.

The house was indeed dark and though Junior's cruiser was parked behind it, his truck wasn't around. Then she saw it parked about a hundred feet down the drive near a massive metal barn. Focused on the building now, she was certain she could hear some kind of buzzing noise coming from there. She quickened her step only marginally. It was a moonless, starless night and the blackness was intimidating.

As she reached the building, she could hear the sound clearly now though she couldn't identify it. She hesitated at the door. Should she just burst in on him? Start making accusations? The door was slightly ajar, she noticed, and opted to peer in first, see what he was doing before barging in.

She gasped with involuntary surprise at the inside of the building. There were at least a dozen cars, all apparently late models, though clearly in the process of being disassembled. A couple of the vehicles were expensive foreign makes. The license plates had been removed from all of the bumpers. A man whose face was hidden by a welder's mask but whom she assumed was Junior Witcomb, was wreaking destruction on one of the vehicles with a blow torch. She'd never seen a chop shop before, but she knew what she was looking at now.

Her heart pounding in her chest, she stepped through

the doorway and called out to him. He didn't look up from his work until she was within twenty feet of him.

He pushed the mask up off his face and turned off the torch. "Well, if it ain't our resident celebrity come to pay me a social call," he said. "Or is it snooping you're doing?"

"It's neither," Rikki said calmly though she'd noticed the way his eyes had flashed with anger when he'd removed the mask. She adjusted the shoulder strap of her purse, putting her hand over the small leather bag for reassurance. She could get to her gun if she had to. "I'm here because I want to ask you some questions."

"About my little side business?"

"I don't have any interest in what you're doing here. I want to ask you about the six people who were killed ten years ago."

"I don't know nothing about those murders," he said.

"That's not what a little bird told me today."

"Yeah, well, birds never was my favorite creatures. I used to shoot them out of the trees just for the hell of it."

His arrogance annoyed Rikki. "Damn it, Junior, this isn't a game I'm playing. Someone told me that you threatened to kill a guy the same way Bunny Apperson was killed."

"Yeah? So what? I talk big. That don't mean I slit anyone's throat or bashed their heads in with a baseball bat."

"You just steal cars, is that it?"

He set the torch on the work table behind him and pulled off the welder's mask, but Rikki noticed he didn't move away from the table that was loaded with all kinds of tools that could be used as weapons. She put her fingers on the purse flap.

"Thought you wasn't interested in what I'm doing here," he said, his tone hostile now.

"I'm not, but I can't help remembering that my father once said, 'A man without morals doesn't much care what crime it is he's committing.' I'd say a deputy sheriff who profits from stolen cars might not hesitate to murder someone who found out. Is that what happened, Junior? Were you already into your 'side job' back then? Bunny or Cindy or that pawnshop owner find out and tell the others? Is that why you killed them? What about Doc Grant and my parents? Were they onto you, too?"

He grinned then, but it wasn't the pleasant smile of an amused man. "That's pretty clever. Guess that would be motive for murder, wouldn't it? Oh, but then you probably don't know how profitable my business is, do you?"

"I don't care how much money you make. I want an answer to my question. Did you kill those six people? You can tell me or you can talk to your dad when I send him out here to arrest you." She'd taken a couple of unconscious steps nearer as she spoke, but stopped suddenly with the realization that only about ten feet separated them now.

"I ain't killed anyone yet. Haven't had to. No one's ever come nosing around here before you." He grabbed the blow torch from the work table and lunged for her.

Rikki was surprised by the squeak of fright which escaped her throat as she dodged his hand. She struggled with her purse, giving him time to almost catch her. He managed to grab hold of the purse strap but she twisted free of it, eluding him once again. She'd sacrificed the gun in the process, but at least he hadn't caught her. She could still make a break for the door.

Junior anticipated every move, cutting her off no matter which way she turned. She managed to put a car between them, but there was no escaping him from there. She couldn't run left. There were auto parts, tires, and tools strewn everywhere. She'd only fall. If she ran right, she'd run straight into his arms. Behind her there was only the wall . . . and the tool bench. She grabbed a long, heavy crowbar, brandishing it like a sword in front of her. If she could just knock the blow torch from his hands, she could put him down with a couple of well-executed chops and kicks. But the best option was to talk him out of violence.

"Look, Junior, I don't want you to hurt me, and I don't want to hurt you. I meant it when I said I didn't care about your business. I shouldn't have threatened to tell the sheriff. I don't care about anything except finding the person who murdered my parents and the others. If you'll prove to me that you didn't do it, I'll walk out of here and not tell a soul what you've got going."

"Yeah, right. You think I'm a country yokel who'll fall for any line you dish? Sorry to disappoint you." He laughed then. "And I ain't afraid of your martial art skills." He flicked the switch that ignited the flame on the torch. "This baby is a mighty humbler." He was advancing as he spoke, pushing Rikki back until she was against the wall with nowhere else to run.

"Please, Junior—"

"Drop the torch, boy!" Scooter Witcomb yelled from the doorway.

Rikki heard him, glanced his way. She saw Bo as well, but Junior was within six feet of her now. She focused her attention on him, wielding the tire iron. "Did you hear him, Junior? Your dad's here."

Junior kept coming.

She jabbed at him with the weapon she carried, but the heat from the torch forced her back.

"Drop it, Junior, *now!*"

Junior laughed but Rikki was almost certain he was laughing at the sport he was having with her. She knew he hadn't even heard his father's voice. Her hands trembled with terror even as she struck out at him again.

He dodged the blow deftly then raised the torch, aiming it at her face. The hot flames licked her cheeks and she screamed and crouched down.

She heard the shot ring out, but she was huddled now, her arms over her head. She didn't see Junior spin around as the bullet struck him in the shoulder. She heard him cry out with surprise. She didn't look up. Not until Bo was holding her in his arms.

"Feeling any better?" Bo asked two hours later.

Rikki leaned against the railing of the Witcomb farm house front porch and hugged herself. "No, Bo, I don't know when I'll feel better. Did you see the sheriff's face as he held his son? He shot him, Bo, because of me. Because I thought I was such a hotshot. Thought I could take care of myself. I had a gun, Bo. I'm a black belt in martial arts, but the sheriff had to shoot his own son because I fell apart."

"That's not true, Blue. He shot his son because the man was trying to kill you. Hell, I doubt Chuck Norris could have defended himself against a blow torch." He put his hands on her forearms as he examined the injury on her cheek. "Speaking of the blow torch, how's your face feel?"

Rikki shrugged the question away. "You heard the paramedic. It's not serious."

"That doesn't mean it doesn't hurt."

Rikki turned her back to him. She didn't want to discuss the burn. It throbbed painfully, but it wasn't significant. She couldn't get the picture of Scooter and Junior out of her mind. The deputy had looked so amazed as his father had rushed to pick him up, cradle him in his arms. "You shot me, Dad," he'd whispered.

"You didn't stop when I called out to you, boy. I didn't have much choice."

"I didn't murder those people. You have to believe that," Junior had said. "I know you're disappointed in me now that you know about the cars, but I never killed no one."

"I believe you," Sheriff Witcomb had said in a voice so choked with pain, Rikki had not been able to listen to more.

As the paramedics had loaded their patient into the ambulance, Scooter had started to follow after them, but had stopped to tell Bo, "Call Waylin and Tom, Bo. Tell them to come out here and search the place. Tell 'em not to miss a thing. They find those shoes the killer took after the murders, you have 'em call me at the hospital right away."

"Yes, sir."

Scooter had looked at Bo, then at Rikki. "How and the hell am I going to tell his mother I shot her boy?" he asked.

Now Rikki stared up at the sky which was as dark as her mood. "They didn't find one shred of evidence linking him to the murders. He didn't kill them, Bo. I destroyed their lives for nothing."

"Not for nothing, Blue. He was running a chop shop. You heard what Waylin said about the paperwork they found hidden behind the tool cabinet. Junior has run thousands of cars through here in the past ten years. Some of them were stolen as far away as California. This wasn't any nickel and dime operation."

"I don't care if he imported them from Europe, Bo. Junior is in critical condition because I jumped to conclusions and made assumptions based on hearsay. Damn it!"

"Come on, Blue. Let's go home."

She allowed him to lead her to his car but hesitated before getting in to look around. "Do you know what my grandmother told me on her deathbed? She said I had to learn to forgive and forget. She said that if I didn't, I'd end up destroying myself. I didn't listen because I thought she didn't understand that the killer had already done that for me. I didn't think about what I would do to others."

"Get in," Bo said, opening the car door for her. He hated the devastation that shone in her eyes, but he knew nothing he said then would brighten the blue that was clouded now with her pain.

They drove in silence, hers so complete he thought for a moment that she'd dropped off to sleep until he turned in to the driveway that veered to the left toward the house on the hill, to the right down to the lake cottage. He started left when she stopped him. "I don't want to be alone tonight."

His breath caught and he reached for her hand. "I won't leave you alone, baby. But you don't want to come to the cottage. It's not a place for you."

She leaned her head back, sighed. She wanted to argue, point out it was him she wanted to be with no matter where it was. She was just too tired. "Then stay with me on the hill."

He continued left.

Inside the house, Bo turned on a light, then leaned against the wall waiting for her to tell him what she wanted next. His heart told him what he wanted, but this was her show. She was too vulnerable tonight for him to risk hurting her by making demands she wasn't prepared to agree to.

She dropped her purse on the floor without stopping on her way to the bedroom.

Bo didn't move.

When she re-entered the room five minutes later, she wore a short silk wrap and her hair spilled around her shoulders. But it was the expression in her eyes and on her mouth that answered his questions. He pushed himself from the wall and approached her without hesitation.

He put his hands on her waist as his eyes probed her face. "You sure?"

She didn't answer but pulled the sash, freeing it and

allowing the robe to fall open, revealing her exquisite nudity beneath.

"Oh, baby," he groaned as he picked her up in his arms and carried her to the bedroom. He placed her on the bed before stripping hastily from his clothes. Then he was beside her.

"You sure this isn't just because you're scared and hurting?" he asked, silently cursing himself for giving her the chance to change her mind, send him away.

"Does it matter?" she asked, her eyes closed.

"No," he lied and covered her mouth with his.

She sucked greedily on his bottom lip and explored his chest with her fingertips.

He pulled back from her to look at her, not just her face, but all of her, every perfect inch. "I thought you were the most beautiful woman in the world ten years ago, Blue. I was wrong. That was just a promise of what you are today."

She pressed two fingers to his lips. "Don't talk anymore. Just make love with me. Come inside me and make the world go away."

Her need hurt, for it wasn't need of him but need of forgetfulness she was after. In spite of his love for her, he was suddenly, unexpectedly angry with her for using him while not loving him at the same time. "You want to fuck, babe, I can treat you to a ride you won't forget."

Her smile fueled his frustration as he raised up above her, pushed her legs apart with his knees and knelt between them. When she moved her hands to wrap them around his neck, he captured them in his, penning them on either side of her face. At her wide-eyed query, he ordered in a husky whisper, "Don't move. This one's on me. You just lay back and enjoy."

He cupped her breasts in each palm, then began to massage the nipples with his thumbs. He didn't hurry, and even when he took one of them in his lips, his pace was leisurely, punishing.

By the time his fingers left her belly that they'd kneaded and teased, her skin was red with fire and slick with dewy perspiration. He parted her sex, felt the contrast of her hot center as the curtains billowed behind him at the open window to kiss his back with the cool evening breeze. He shivered as he plunged deeper inside her, then shuddered when he felt her stiffen with her first orgasm. He moved down, kissing her belly, then rested his chin there as he looked up at her face. "The world disappeared yet, Blue?"

She didn't answer with words, but responded with her hands which grabbed at his shoulders, urging him up, between her legs, inside her.

He laughed deep in his throat. "Not yet, babe. Not yet."

"I want you, Bo . . . *now.*"

"Uhn-uh, Blue, you don't want me yet. Not like you're going to in a few minutes."

"Please, Bo . . ."

He didn't argue further. Nor did he give in. He slipped lower until his face rested between her legs which he spread farther.

She bucked when his tongue touched her for the first time, but he gripped her buttocks, ignoring her cries and fighting his own need which was so intense now he almost gave in . . . almost. Not yet. Not until he'd done what she'd asked. Not until the world disappeared into oblivion for her.

She put her feet on his shoulders, pushing him away, twisting out of his reach.

He raised up above her once again, stared into her face which glistened with perspiration. He let his gaze travel to her throat where her pulse throbbed, and to her breasts which heaved with her passion. Then with his lips pulled back from his teeth, he plunged into her.

Only then did his control almost fail him. He paused, steadying himself as her pubic muscles tightened around him. He fought the groan which rose to his throat and lifted his hips, pulling out of her a couple of inches, forcing her to come up to him, meet him, and pull him back all the way inside.

It was a wild ride that drained him, and less than ten minutes later, he slid off of her and rolled onto his back. With his need sated, and his passion ebbed, her words returned to slam into him. He crossed his arms beneath his head, careful not to touch her now that he'd given her the release from the pain she'd sought.

Rikki felt the change in him almost at once and though it puzzled her, she came to him, laying her head on his chest and covering his thighs with one of her long legs. "Don't pull away, Bo. Talk to me. Tell me what you're thinking."

He was thinking how much he still loved her, how much it hurt him to know that sex was all she'd wanted, needed, but he'd be damned if he'd tell her that. He pulled one arm from beneath his head to swat her bottom, then scooted away from her to sit up on the edge of the bed.

"I'm thinking how much I need a drink. You got anything here?"

"Some beer, and I think there's a bottle of vodka," she said, hurt in her tone. "Help yourself."

"Thanks," he muttered as he left the room. He felt like a shit. She didn't deserve this. Hell, it wasn't her fault she'd forgotten him, fallen in love with some dude named Kit. And it wasn't like she hadn't just done what he had a thousand times before, used someone to forget the only person in the world he wanted to be with. Only difference was he'd used others to forget her.

In the kitchen, he found the bottle of vodka, unopened underneath the sink. He didn't bother with a glass but took the bottle out onto the terrace where he started to work on his own pain.

When he went back into the bedroom a couple of hours later, she was sprawled out on her stomach sound asleep. The booze may have fogged his brain, but it hadn't touched his heart. The pain which knifed through it at the sight of her was as sharp as ever.

Chapter Eighteen

When Rikki awakened, the space in her bed that Bo had occupied the night before was empty. She glanced at the clock, surprised to find that it was almost nine a.m. She rarely slept past seven and though she'd not drifted off until just before three, she felt guilty. And something else. Loneliness for Bo.

It was then that she realized someone was knocking on the back door. Her heart did a miniature flip flop as she hoped it was Bo who had returned and found himself locked out.

She grabbed the silk wrapper and padded barefoot to the door.

Surprise must have registered in her eyes when she discovered her early morning caller to be Carrie, for the other woman apologized quickly for bothering her. "I know it's early, and I'm not expected, but I'd hoped we could talk for a few minutes."

Rikki smiled her welcome as she pushed the screen door open. "Come on in. Excuse the way I look. I overslept."

"It's no wonder after the night you had."

Rikki hadn't wanted to think about the tragic turn of events that had led her to near death and Junior's subsequent shooting. "It's already on the news?"

Before Carrie could answer, Rikki spied the bouquet

of freshly cut daisies and pulled a sheet of paper from beneath the water glass which he'd used for a vase.

I remembered that you love wildflowers. Thought these might put the sparkle back in your eyes.

"Bo?" Carrie asked, apparently having read the note along with her.

Rikki didn't answer. It wasn't that she was embarrassed that they'd spent the night together. It was just that it was still too new, too wonderful, too *hers* to share yet. "How did you learn where I live?" she asked instead.

Carrie averted her gaze as she answered. "Danny told me. He said he told you about us, too. I want to explain."

"Not necessary," Rikki said, walking away from the note and memories of her shared lovemaking with Bo to sit on the sofa. She pulled the fabric of her robe together modestly in front as she tucked her legs beneath her. "Have a seat."

Carrie complied, taking a seat on the sofa beside her former girlhood friend. "Look, Rikki, I don't blame you for being angry with me. I know I let you down when your parents were killed. I know I should have been there for you. But please, can you give me another chance? You were my best friend, and I've missed you."

"I'm not angry with you, Carrie. I *was*, and so hurt, but not anymore. I'm angry with myself this morning."

"Why? You don't mean because of what happened out at the Witcomb ranch?" At Rikki's nod, Carrie took her hand in hers. "But what you did was wonderful. Junior was the head of a major car theft ring. By noon, folks will be calling you a heroine."

"I didn't go out there to bust him for car theft. I don't care that he was profiteering on the side. I went out there on a rumor that almost got me killed and resulted in destroying a family and possibly even in getting Junior killed. It was rash and foolish."

"I think you're being too hard on yourself."

Rikki changed the subject. "About you and Danny, Carrie. You don't have to explain it to me. It's your business."

"You weren't shocked?" Carrie pressed.

"Of course I was shocked. My God, you were so in love with Brett when I left here ten years ago, not to mention devout in your religion and adamant in your conviction that all Catholics were practically the devil's disciples."

"In other words a royal pain in the ass," Carrie said with a smile that quickly disappeared with her next words. "I let everyone else do my thinking for me, Rikki. Would it surprise you to know that the day I made my marriage vows I already knew I was making a mistake? I *knew* it, but I didn't have the gumption to back out."

"Why not get a divorce?"

Carrie stared at her hands as she answered. "Because I'm afraid of Brett."

"Does he abuse you?"

Carrie's dark eyes shone with tears when she looked up. "Not in the way you mean. He doesn't hit me, toss me around."

"Then what?"

"He's not right, Rikki. He's . . . he's a sexual deviant. And I think he might be worse. I think he might be the one who killed your parents and Doc Grant. All of them."

Rikki unfolded her legs as she sat forward. "You have proof? Have you seen the shoes?"

"No, no. Nothing like that. But the other night when he said he was parked out in front of the church the night your parents were murdered, he lied, Rikki. I know. I was there that night. I was thinking about him, about marrying him. I already knew it was a mistake."

"So maybe he just confused the nights. The murderer killed five different times. It's been a long time."

Carrie shook her head. "It's not just that, Rikki, he's . . . he's not normal. Remember years ago you kept asking me about sex. I kept telling you we hadn't done anything yet. We had, but not the way other people do. Brett doesn't like sex the normal way. I didn't know how sick he was until . . . well, until Danny and I . . ."

"You don't have to tell me this, Carrie," Rikki said gently.

"Yes, I do. You have to understand. When I say I didn't know, that's not exactly true. I knew that anal sex wasn't the right way to have intercourse, of course, but I didn't know that lovemaking could be exciting and wonderful and the sweetest experience in the world."

Rikki's thoughts skittered over her moments in Bo's arms the night before, but she forced the memory away as she fastened onto what Carrie had just said. "Brett prefers anal intercourse to normal sex?"

"Not just that. I have to shave myself." She paused to dash away tears and cope with her embarrassment at what she was admitting, then rushed on as if she were afraid she wouldn't be able to tell it all. "Do you know what I'm telling you, Rikki? He wants me to be like a little girl. Sometimes I have to dress in panties and a undershirt instead of a bra and fix my hair in pigtails. He makes me call him "Daddy," and while he's touching me, doing it, um, in my rectum, he quotes scriptures about being like children. Coming to God through meekness and innocence. Last night he told me he wished he'd left me a virgin so I'd still be pure in the eyes of God."

Rikki didn't speak for a long moment. She was digesting the horror story her friend was describing to her. "You're right, Carrie, he's a sick person, but that doesn't explain why you're afraid of him or why you think he might be the man the media was calling the lake stalker."

"He's threatened me, for one thing. He hasn't said in so many words that he would ever kill me, but he's repeatedly used the scriptures again to tell me how God deals with sinners. And he used to talk about Doctor Grant and your mother—oh, not in the same breath. I don't mean to infer that he thought there was anything going on between them, but he was always railing about the doctor's adulterous ways."

"What did he say about my mother?" Rikki asked, feeling nausea well up within her.

"That she was a temptress, that God would mete out justice to her for putting temptation before the men. He was talking about the clothes she wore when she jogged every morning."

Rikki ran her hands through her hair, thinking for a long time about what Carrie had told her, but finally she shook her head. "No. It's not enough, Carrie. I can't take the chance of being wrong again like I was with Junior unless I have proof." She squeezed her friend's hand. "You might get hurt, and I won't take that chance."

"What if I can find you the proof you need? If he's guilty, there will be something, won't there?"

"The sheriff said he's almost positive that whoever killed them would have kept the shoes he took. There has to be some significance to that, some obsessive thing the killer has that he wouldn't quickly let go of."

"So what if I can find something? What should I do?"

"Don't confront him, whatever you do!" Rikki said pressing Carrie's hand even tighter. "Call me or Scooter, but don't say anything to Brett. I couldn't stand it if he hurt you."

"I'll look. Today." Carrie stood up, determination shining in her tawny eyes. "He's gone to Springfield for a conference. He won't be home until tonight."

"But where would he keep something like that, Carrie? You're his wife. It isn't like he could keep a secret like that hidden."

"Yes, he could. In his office in the church. He has a closet he keeps locked all the time. No one else has a key except him."

"But if you don't have a key, how will you open it?"

"I'll call a locksmith out. I'll just tell him and Amanda Rhodes who works for Brett that he lost his keys and asked me to have someone come out. Then I'll send Amanda on an errand while I look." Her eyes were gleaming now with anticipation and excitement. Impulsively, she pulled Rikki into a tight embrace. "Oh, Rikki, I'm so glad you came back. I don't think I would ever have had the nerve to do this if you hadn't inspired me with your determination. I love Danny." She giggled as she stepped away from the other woman. "That's probably the grandest understatement of my life, but I've been too afraid to move, to do anything."

"Speaking of Danny, Carrie, have you told him anything of your suspicions? Does he even know what your sex life with Brett has been?"

"No! I can't tell him. Not ever. He's gentle, Rikki, but I don't know if he could sit back and let me go through what Brett . . . well, I'm afraid someone would get hurt if he knew."

Rikki didn't answer, but questions must have been written in her expression, for Carrie blushed as she answered what she knew her friend was wondering.

"He thinks I shave myself for him. I told him once that I'd never known sex could be like it is between us, and he thinks I'm just being kinky."

"I'm sorry you and Danny found each other too late," Rikki said softly.

"Oh, no, it wasn't too late, Rikki. It was just in time. I think I would have killed myself eventually if I hadn't found Danny. He's been my lifesaver." She turned away

then and hurried to the door, pausing there as her gaze
went to the bouquet of wildflowers on Rikki's table. "It's
not too late for you and Bo either, Rikki. The man's
been in love with you for a long time."

"Thanks."

"I'll call you by tonight."

"Be careful," Rikki said. "I couldn't stand it if you got
hurt, too."

"Don't worry about me," Carrie said, sounding more
confident by the minute. "I'm going to find the answers
that will set us both free."

Rikki hoped she was right. She wanted to believe, but
she couldn't, not yet, not after last night.

Rikki arrived at the radio station just minutes before
it was time to go on the air. She arrived to a hero's welcome, her entire staff except Mike Peters, the DJ who
was on the air, converging on her to congratulate her
for uncovering the auto theft ring.

Rikki tried for graciousness, but their approval wasn't
what she wanted. She didn't want to even think about
it, for the memory of Scooter Witcomb's pain-ravaged
face was too quick to surface. She managed a smile,
thanked them, then shooed them all back to work. "I
appreciate your support, gang, but you're giving me too
much credit. It was an accidental discovery that resulted
in a tragic shooting." One of the men who worked in
advertisement shouted something about it being too bad
the bastard hadn't died yet, but Rikki ignored him. "All
right, everyone back to work. It's still another day in the
salt mines."

She ducked into the ladies' room and didn't come out
until it was time to sign on.

The phones lit up within the first two minutes of her
broadcast. Rikki groaned inwardly as she punched in

the first call. "Hello, this is KSTJ, and you're on the air. Go ahead."

"My name's Fred Stockingbird, Ms. Blue, and I just want to tell you that I'm damn proud of you, girlie. About time someone came down here and cleaned things up. Damned disgrace the way the law has let things slide around here. I've been saying it for years, but you think anyone would listen to me? No, siree. I'm just an old country fart—whoops, can I say that on the air?"

In spite of her dismay at the tone of her first phone call, Rikki chuckled. "Well, it seems to me you just did, Fred. Thanks for your call. I—"

"Wait a minute, girlie, don't be so quick to cut me off. I want to say to all the folks out there listening to ya that maybe now they'll wake up and put an honest man in the sheriff's seat."

"I appreciate your call, Fred, but I'm afraid I couldn't disagree with you more. I've known Sheriff Scooter Witcomb for a long time. He is one of the most upstanding men I know. I don't want you confusing him with his son's crime."

"Didn't solve your parents' murders, did he? Might be he knows who the killer is and just looked the other way like he did with his boy."

Rikki didn't argue with him further. She thanked him quickly for his call once again then addressed her audience at large. "I hope that caller doesn't speak for the way the rest of you feel. Sheriff Witcomb had nothing to do with his son's alleged auto theft ring. We can't forget that Allan Witcomb is innocent until proven guilty. But no matter what a jury decides, should the deputy survive his gunshot wound—which I might add, I pray he will—Sheriff Witcomb is completely innocent of any wrongdoing. Now let's go to our next caller.

"Hello, you're on with Rikki Blue."

"Yes, Ms. Blue, this is Feona Franklin calling. I'm

afraid I agree with what that man just said. It's not just this car thing that you found last night. Crime is out of hand in St. Joan. Why, do you know, over a dozen of my friends have been put out of their homes by the United St. Joan Bank in the past ten years? And they're not the only ones. Why, a person just has to read the paper each week to find the names of more victims."

Rikki almost sighed with relief. At least this woman didn't want to discuss Junior's shooting the night before. Rikki pounced on the subject. "When you say they've been put out, what do you mean? Are you saying the bank has wrongly foreclosed on them?"

"That's precisely what I'm saying. Would have happened to my husband and me as well if my son hadn't come to the rescue and paid off the mortgage."

"Why don't you just tell us exactly what happened, Feona."

"Be glad to, Rikki, be glad to. Now I don't know how familiar you are with the financial cycle that most of us live by here in the lake area."

"Not very. Please explain it."

"Well, most of us are business owners, and our business is seasonal. Always been that way, always will be. In the fall and winter business falls off to almost nothing. No tourists, no business. Simple as that. In the spring and summer we do real good."

"All right, I understand."

"Well, then, let me tell you this," Feona continued, encouraged by the radio celebrity's interest in the plight of her friends. "Fact is, most of us let our house payments slide when business is off. Then in the spring when business starts up again, we catch up with what we were in arrears. The bank has always worked with us, trusted us, and they haven't been let down too often, let me tell you. Then suddenly, they started calling in the notes when the payments got five or six months late, not listening when folks tried to explain that they'd always caught them up and would again. The homes went into foreclosure, and Judge Lilah Montana sided with the bank each and every time. A couple of times, the folks who lost their homes raised the money from friends and family but when they went to the courthouse steps to buy it back when it came up for auction, they couldn't do it. Someone was always there to get it for just a mite more money than what they had."

"Have your friends talked with the bank officers or Judge Montana to see if they could find a way around this before the property is foreclosed on?" Rikki asked.

"Not the bank officers. Not unless you're talking about Jimmy Burns, and he's just a mouthpiece for the higher ups. They've tried to talk to someone with clout, you know? But they're always given the runaround. As for Judge Montana, she just tells them all that they have to do something before it gets to her court. She says it might not seem fair, but the bank has the law on their side. A person signs a legal document agreeing to make monthly payments, they gotta pay even if the bank won't go along. But I'm thinking there's something dead up the creek. The bank always went along before."

"I'm afraid I agree with the judge, Feona, but I can't disagree with you either. Why don't you call the prosecuting attorney's office? His name, if some of you aren't familiar with the man you've put in office for the past six years, is Keen Bohannon. I'm sure he'd be willing to talk to the bank officers, look into it for any wrongdoing on their part."

"I'll sure do that. It's just not right."

"Call me back and let me know what progress you make, Feona. I'm sure all my listeners will be interested as well." Rikki disconnected her caller, then instructed her audience that she was going to a commercial break but would be back with them in just a few minutes to take some more calls.

As she slipped off her stool and went into the next

room to get a soda from the refrigerator, she was grinning, wondering what Bo would think about the business she'd just thrown his way.

She didn't have long to wait. Her assistant brought a note into the broadcasting booth just moments later. He'd already called and had left a number for her to get back to him. In spite of her rocky start that morning with memories of the shooting and Carrie's unsettling revelations about the Reverend Brett Pearson, Rikki enjoyed the remaining hour and a half on the air more than she would have expected.

Carrie wasn't able to get a locksmith to come out to the church until one o'clock. More than two hours away. To fill the time and calm her nerves, she turned on the radio and listened to Rikki as she cleaned her already spotless house.

She was so lost in her friend's smooth, effortless handling of her callers, she almost jumped when the doorbell pealed. She glanced at the clock, hardly believing that it was already ten minutes to one.

Rushing to the sink, she rinsed her hands, then toweldried them quickly before opening the door to the locksmith she'd almost forgotten about calling.

"It's a door over at the church, Mr. Loomis. If you'll follow me, I'll have to explain to my husband's secretary what we're doing." As she led the way across the yard, she cursed herself for losing track of the time. She'd intended to come over thirty minutes before time for him to arrive with an errand of copies to be made in town for Amanda. Now, she'd just have to hope the woman didn't become suspicious enough to call Brett at the church meeting in Springfield to alert him.

Her hands shook as she opened the door at the rear end of the building. She stuck them in her pockets before entering her husband's office, then almost sagged with relief when she found the cubicle usually occupied by the diligent, faithful secretary empty and the phone recorder on.

She glanced over her shoulder at Mr. Loomis. "Apparently the reverend's secretary is at lunch," she said, then mentally kicked herself. Why had she told him that? She had to calm down. If she didn't, no telling what she might say. She thought of Rikki, wishing she possessed some of her cool reserve. "Well, here it is. Just a supply closet, but my husband stores things in there that he needs."

"Have her open in a jiffy," the man said matter-of-factly as he knelt before the door and examined the lock. "Pretty standard lock. Surprised your husband didn't try to open it with a bobby pin or a little screw driver.

It was that easy?

Carrie paced the floor for the next five minutes until the grizzle-haired man stood up and announced, "That got her! Tell the reverend he really should get some extra keys. Seems a shame to spend sixty dollars when a spare fifty-cent key coulda done the trick."

"I will. Thank you. We'll send you a check. That be all right?" she asked, already going to the door and doing her best to hurry the locksmith without appearing to anxious.

"That'll be just dandy," the man said, taking his time about putting his tools back into his box. "Can't trust the church, who can a man trust, I always say."

"Isn't that the truth?" Carrie agreed with a small laugh that sounded phony and nervous to her ears. "Can you find your way out or should I come with you?"

"Think I can handle it, Mrs. Pearson," Jake Loomis said, handing her a bill. "You have a good day now, ya hear, and give my regards to the reverend."

Carrie locked her husband's office door behind her as

soon as the man disappeared down the hall. If Amanda returned before she was finished searching the closet, she'd just make up something about pushing the lock inadvertently when she closed it.

The contents of the small closet held few surprises and Carrie began to fear she was going to come up empty until her hand brushed a loose board in the back that fell away without any resistance. Her entire body trembled as she kneeled down and tried to see into the dark recess. The secret, hollowed out compartment was small, not more than four inches high and eight inches wide. Big enough to hold six shoes taken as souvenirs from murder victims? Not unless it was deeper than she suspected. Carrie felt her heart plummet into her stomach as she reached inside the dark space. She pulled out a manila envelope that was almost an inch thick, apparently stuffed with papers.

Carrie sat back on her bottom on the floor as she slipped the rubber band from around the envelope and peered inside. Photos.

Her brows knitted, she pulled one out. She flinched, shutting her eyes tightly as soon as she saw the picture. "Oh, my God," she murmured, pressing the back of her hand to her mouth.

It was a picture of a little girl. Carrie recognized the face. It was the same one that had been on the news for weeks the year before. The little girl had been missing for more than three months before her decomposed body was found in a shallow grave. The only difference between the photograph on the news and the one she held in her hand was that the child had been smiling in the former, a school picture. She was dead in this one.

Swallowing convulsively to force down the bile that had risen to her throat, Carrie opened her eyes and pulled out another picture. It was of the same child, only in this one, the little girl—Sarah Morton—was alive. She was nude and crying while sitting on a man's lap. The Reverend Brett Pearson's lap.

Carrie began to weep as she went through the agonizing process of examining each of the photos. There were several more of Sarah as well as pictures of six more children. Two she didn't recognize. But the others . . .

With trembling fingers, she stuffed them back into the envelope, then scrambled to her feet. She didn't bother locking the closet door. Nor did she stop when she ran almost headlong into Brett's startled secretary. She dashed past her, not even hesitating when Amanda called after her.

At the house, she locked all the doors and pulled the shades. Then she sat on the edge of her bed and phoned the radio station.

The girl who answered told her that she'd just missed Rikki by two minutes. "She'll be back, though. May I give her a message?"

"No. Yes, tell her Carrie called. Tell her it's urgent that I speak with her." She slammed down the phone, then dialed the sheriff's station. This time she groaned aloud when the dispatcher told her that Sheriff Witcomb was on the way to the hospital to visit his son. She hung up without listening to more.

"Oh, God, what do I do?" she asked as tears spilled over her lashes.

But she didn't do anything. There was nothing else to do. There was no one else to call. She couldn't involve Danny. Not in this. Once, years ago, she would have called her mother. But not anymore. She knew what her mother would say. "This is your fault, Carrie Ann. Brett wouldn't have this aberration if you'd been the kind of wife I raised you to be."

So Carrie sat there, holding the incriminating envelope in her hand, rocking back and forth, hating Brett, hating her mother, and hating herself as her mother had taught her to do.

* * *

"Ericka!"

Rikki turned at the sound of her name from another lifetime. She'd fled the radio station as soon as she could after going off the air. She'd needed time alone, space, and had decided to walk. She usually loved the time she spent with her listeners, exchanging viewpoints, debating issues, challenging principles. Not so today. Today she'd merely gotten depressed. Probably still the residue from last night's traumatic events as well as Carrie's revealing visit. She promised herself to call the minister's wife as soon as she recovered her equilibrium. But now as she paused outside a quaint antique shop to admire some lace work, she wished she'd stayed at the station and made that call before leaving, for headed directly for her was Carrie's mother, Marylou Roberts.

The smile that came automatically to the celebrity, faltered, but she regained it quickly. "Mrs. Roberts, how are you?"

"*I'm* just fine, Ericka, but I'm afraid the judge, here, is a little upset with you."

Rikki looked at the woman who had approached with Marylou and now stood at her side. She was a stranger, Rikki decided, or at least someone she didn't remember from that other life. "I'm sorry," she said, extending her hand at the same time, "I don't believe I know you. I'm Rikki Blue."

"That's her stage name, Lilah. Her *real* name is Ericka Cassidy. This is Judge Lilah Montana, Ericka. I believe you'll recognize her now. You *were* talking about her on the radio this morning, suggesting that one of your listeners call the prosecutor about her?"

"Judge Montana, I'm glad to know you. I'm afraid Mrs. Roberts was misinformed. I—"

"I wasn't misanything, Ericka. I heard you myself."

"Then you didn't listen well, Mrs. Roberts. I told my

caller to speak with Mr. Bohannon if she had questions regarding the bank's practices. I didn't say anything about talking to him about the judge." She turned her attention back to the pretty woman whom she would have guessed to be about her own age if not for the silver in her short, cropped hair and the sharp eyes which she imagined could well intimidate a defendant brought before her court. In as few words as possible, Rikki recapped the telephone conversation, even giving the judge her caller's name. "I certainly wouldn't say anything to impugn your name or even that of the bank without knowing there was an irrefutable reason to do so, Judge Montana."

The judge smiled and Rikki thought she looked even younger.

"I'm sure Marylou was merely concerned," she said gently.

"Yes, I agree. I knew Mrs. Roberts several years ago. She always was prone to exaggeration born of excitement."

Marylou Roberts inhaled sharply, clearly offended. "You always were a rude young woman. Your upbringing, no doubt."

Rikki wanted to slap her, but true to her upbringing, she merely widened her smile. "Well, it was a pleasure meeting you, Judge Montana. If you ladies will excuse me, I decided on a walk to get some fresh air. It's feeling a little stale right here, so I think I'll move on."

She didn't wait for either woman to speak as she stepped past them and hurried down the sidewalk in the direction from which she'd come. When she reached the KSTJ station parking lot, she decided against going inside. She was even more uptight and in need of space than ever. She climbed behind the wheel of her Jeep. At least, if she were driving she wouldn't run the risk of being verbally assaulted, and if anyone did try to intercept her, she'd be able to run them over. She laughed with the satisfying thought but it was short-lived as she remembered that Carrie was supposed to call her if she found anything. Just as quickly as she thought of it, she dismissed it. Carrie had married a creep. No doubt about it, but creep and murderer were not necessarily synonymous. The chances of Carrie finding evidence that would incriminate her husband in the murders of six people a decade before ranged from grossly improbable to impossible. In fact, Carrie had more than likely gone to spend the afternoon with her lover after coming up empty-handed in her search. Rikki sighed. She wished she knew where Bo was right now. The thought of spending the rest of the day with her lover instead of thinking about murder was delicious.

Chapter Nineteen

Carrie could think of nothing but the children whose lives her husband had destroyed ... after terrorizing and brutalizing them. Nausea welled up in her mouth.

She lost track of the time. She heard the clock chime distantly. One ring. Did it signal two-thirty, three-thirty, what? The phone rang, and she snatched the receiver off the hook. The pungent odor of burning food reminded her that she'd forgotten the pot of kidney beans she'd put on to cook that morning.

"Hello?" she asked as she thought absurdly that Brett would be angry about the waste.

"Carrie, it's Rikki. Sorry it took me so long to get back to you. The receptionist said you called just after I left for lunch. She said it was urgent. Does that mean you found what you were looking for?"

"No," Carrie said, intending to explain about *what* she had found, the horrifying evidence of her husband's depravity, but the sound of the front door opening froze the words on her tongue.

"Then you must be relieved," Rikki said. "But Carrie, just because he isn't the one who—"

"I can't talk anymore," Carrie said, cutting the other woman off. "Can you come over here?" She lowered her voice to a whisper. "I need you, Rikki."

She didn't wait for Rikki's answer as she hung up the

phone. She turned to the door to find Brett already standing there. As her eyes locked with his, she knew he'd already been to the church, discovered the closet door open and the envelope missing. And strangely, she felt sorry for him as he staggered over to the bed to drop down beside her.

Neither of them spoke for a long moment, and when Brett finally broke the silence, Carrie was surprised by how loud his voice sounded though he spoke with more softness than she'd ever heard.

"I loved them all, Carrie Ann. I didn't mean to hurt them. I just wanted to love them, cherish them. My father used to love me that way. I never cried. But they did. All of them. I didn't try to hurt them. I just had to make them stop crying. They had to listen, to understand that I wasn't being mean to them. I was *loving* them."

Carrie tried to answer him, but the bile she'd pushed back earlier, filled her mouth and she could only drop the envelope to the floor while she fled to the bathroom.

When she returned to their bedroom, the room where she'd spent so many nights hurting, feeling repulsed and sick, and frightened as each one of those children must have felt, Brett stood up and turned to meet her.

"I know you have to call the authorities, but would you give me an hour? I want to go to the church, spend a few minutes with my Heavenly Father, then write out some instructions for Reverend Parker. I imagine they'll send him right up to take over. I'd like to make it as easy for him as possible."

When he neared her, Carrie shrank back, pressing herself against the wall.

Hurt shone in his eyes. "I wouldn't harm you, Carrie Ann. You're the wife God gave me to honor and cherish." He reached out then to brush away a tear that had trickled from the corner of her eye. "Just one hour, please."

She didn't answer him. She looked away as she struggled for the breath that the intense pain in her chest was preventing. But as soon as she heard the front door close behind him, she dashed across the room to call Rikki.

"I'm sorry, Mrs. Pearson. Rikki didn't come back to the station after her lunch break. She called in for her messages. I told her you'd called earlier."

Carrie didn't answer, just replaced the receiver in its cradle. What did she do now? Would Rikki come as she'd asked?

Rikki took the time to call Bo at the prosecutor's office. He came on the phone at once.

"Hey, Blue, thanks a lot for putting that Feona Franklin woman on me. She talked my ear off. I think she might be onto something, though. I'm just headed over to the courthouse. I thought I'd check out the plats. See who's buying up all the property the bank's foreclosing on. Might have a case of consumer fraud. I think—"

"Bo, I just talked to Carrie. I don't have time to explain, but I think she's in trouble."

"What kind of trouble, Blue?" he asked, his tone all seriousness now.

"I don't know exactly. Look, this morning she came to see me. She thought Brett might be the killer. The lake stalker. Now she says he's not, but she sounded real scared. She was whispering and then she hung up the phone before I could find out anything. Would you try to reach Scooter? Then meet me over at the Pearson place?"

"Sure, but Rikki, don't go rushing over there. Wait for me. I'll come by and pick you up. If there's trouble over there, I don't want you walking into the middle of it."

"I called the hospital to check on Junior about thirty minutes ago. Scooter had just left. I don't know if he was headed back to the station or home. I don't have time to track him down."

"Rikki—"

"I have to go, Bo. She needs me."

Bo cursed as the phone clicked in his ear. He jumped to his feet, pausing only long enough to grab his keys from his desk, then sprinted out the door. He paused only long enough to tell his secretary to find Sheriff Witcomb. "Tell him to get over to the Pearsons pronto."

It had started to rain by the time Carrie stepped outside and crossed the yard which separated the house and church. The tulips looked particularly vibrant, she thought and then wondered why she'd noticed. But it struck her then that it was the contrast of their beauty with the ugliness she'd just uncovered that had drawn her attention. A sob escaped her throat and she doubled over, hugging herself as the rain continued to pelt the earth, soaking her. She crouched down in the grass unable to go on.

After talking with Rikki, the pain had lessened, replaced by a rush of anger. How dare Brett appeal to her for time, try to explain away the vileness of his deeds? He'd murdered those children, the innocents he'd vowed to God to lead His way.

She'd left the house intending to go to the church to tell him how vile and disgusting he was. To spit in his face. But she hadn't realized anger could be so debilitating. It crippled her now. She couldn't move. She could scarcely breathe.

Rikki pulled to a screeching stop in the driveway. The rain was coming down in torrents now and she could barely make out the outlines of the two buildings through the gray mist. She grabbed a jacket from the passenger seat and threw it over her head as she stepped from the jeep.

She heard another vehicle pull in behind her and ran in its direction as she recognized it as Bo's.

"What's going on?" he demanded as soon as he stepped out.

Rikki shook her head and shouted above the storm. "I don't know. Only that Carrie's in trouble."

He grabbed her hand and pulled her after him. "Come on, we'll check out the house first."

They almost stumbled over Carrie who was still doubled over in a tight ball in the middle of the lawn.

"Carrie!" Rikki yelled. "What are you doing out here? Is Brett here? Did he hurt you?"

Sirens approached from the road, but Bo and Rikki focused their attention on the woman who appeared to be in a state of shock.

"Are you hurt, Carrie?" Bo shouted. "Did Brett do something to you?"

Carrie mumbled an answer that was lost in the wind and rain which had intensified in the past several minutes. Over her head, Rikki signalled Bo to help her get Carrie on her feet.

"We need to get her in the house."

They pulled her up, but when they tried to steer her toward the house, she hung back, then turned in the direction of the church. "He's in there," she said loud enough to be heard.

The sirens which they'd heard in the distance, screamed at them from the drive now before whining to a stop as Scooter Witcomb turned them off and stepped from the cruiser. Bo motioned for him to follow them to the church, then continued on after Rikki and Carrie.

The foursome reached the church door just as a gun blast reverberated through the building. "Wait here," Bo shouted to Rikki as he and Scooter bolted through the door.

"He's killed himself," Carrie said with quiet certitude.

"Brett?" Rikki asked though she knew that of course Carrie was talking about her husband. "Why, Carrie? What happened?"

Carrie didn't answer as she stared into the empty hallway toward her husband's office. After a moment, she said, "Because he was a coward."

Rikki didn't understand, but she didn't ask any more questions. There wasn't any point. Carrie was shaking almost uncontrollably now, her teeth clicking together loudly enough to be heard over the pounding of the rain against the walls around them.

"Let's go to the house," she said, putting an arm around the smaller woman's shoulders. "Bo will come tell us what's happened as soon as he can."

Both Bo and Scooter appeared in the kitchen less than fifteen minutes later. Both were pale and shaken.

"Brett?" Rikki asked over Carrie's head as the minister's wife sat at the kitchen table, her face lowered.

"He shot himself," Bo answered.

Scooter pulled out a chair, placed it in front of Carrie, and sat down. "You wanna tell me what happened, honey?" he asked in a voice that Rikki had heard before, a long time ago. Rikki shuddered at the oppressive feeling of déjà vu.

"All those babies . . . those little children. He killed them." Carrie spoke in a voice so faint Rikki and Bo had to lean closer to hear. "I found pictures. He didn't deny it." She laughed shortly, bitterly. "How could he with me holding the evidence in my hands?"

"Where are the pictures, honey?" Sheriff Witcomb asked.

"In the bedroom. I dropped them on the floor by the bed. I think they're still there."

The sheriff patted her hand. "Some of my men will be here in a few minutes, Carrie Ann. One of them, Waylin or Tom, will come in here to get a statement. Think you can answer some more questions for him?"

Carrie looked up at Rikki, her eyes so filled with pain, Rikki felt tears prickle behind her lids. "Will you stay with me?" Carrie asked.

"We'll both stay," Bo told her.

"Do you want me to call Danny, hon?" the sheriff asked, surprising Rikki.

"No! Please don't call him! I'm too ashamed."

The sheriff had been half out of his chair, but he sat back down and took both of Carrie's hands in his. "Now, you listen to me, missy. You ain't got one single thing to be ashamed of. Brett's sin isn't yours. He's the one who did wrong. You were his wife, but that don't make you responsible for the terrible things he did. You understand that?"

"Yes, but I feel responsible. I should have *known*."

"Sometimes, missy, we can know something's wrong without knowing what it is, without wanting to know what it is, because if we know what's wrong, we might get hurt. It's human nature to protect ourselves from that."

Carrie managed a slight smile of gratitude, and Rikki knew that she and the sheriff had just formed a bond of understanding. He'd been talking about Junior and himself as much as Carrie and Brett.

Rikki turned away. She knew what neither of them realized yet. *She* was the one who had started the landslide that was demolishing so many lives.

Many hours later, she followed Bo home in her Jeep. It didn't surprise her when he turned left instead of right in the driveway.

He reached for her hand as they walked slowly up the stairs to the house. The storm which had beaten the lake area with unmerciful fury, had worn itself out after only a couple of hours. The setting sun was bright behind them in the west now.

"Why don't we sit out here for awhile?" Bo suggested.

"The chairs are wet," Rikki pointed out, surprised by

how wonderful such normal, banal conversation could be.

"So you grab a towel, while I get us both a beer."

When they sat down five minutes later, Bo sitting across from her, his legs raised so that his feet rested on her chair on either side of her legs, he chuckled. "Your hair is lopsided."

Rikki stuck her tongue out, but raised a hand to fluff out the mass that had been mangled by the storm. "You have a real flair for making a lady feel beautiful, Keen Bohannon."

"Hey, it comes natural. What can I say?"

"Well, you don't look so hot yourself. As a matter of fact, your shirt and pants look like you slept in them."

"Might have. Don't remember. Today's the first day I've put a suit on in weeks. Seems to me, though, it looked a little better than this when I went into the office this morning."

Rikki laughed but quickly sobered. "She's going to be okay, isn't she?"

"Carrie? Sure. She's from good Southern stock. Besides, she's got Danny. You saw how he was fussing over her when he got there. She'll have it rough for a few weeks—Marylou will see to that—but Danny's not going anywhere and I've got a feeling he'll only put up with so much of Marylou's crap before he sets her straight."

Rikki smiled. "She is a piece of work, isn't she? I couldn't believe it when she started making sandwiches for everyone. She acted like nothing had happened."

"Probably denial."

"Must be. She was even cordial to me."

"Why wouldn't she be? You didn't have anything to do with what her son-in-law did."

"Trust me when I tell you that before this is all over, I'll be the villainess. Marylou stopped me in town earlier today. She had Judge Montana with her. Apparently she'd been filling the Judge's head with a bunch of crap about me inciting the natives against her."

"Because of the foreclosures Feona Franklin called me about?"

Rikki nodded, then sipped on her beer thoughtfully. "You think there's anything to Feona's theory that something dead up the creek?"

"Who knows? Could be. On the other hand it could be that the bank is simply not going to risk losing money like they did before. The economy's stressed. Banks have gone under. But I'll do some more checking tomorrow."

"I'm beginning to think I opened a nasty can of worms by coming back here. First Junior, now Brett, and this bank thing. And I'm still no closer to finding out who killed my parents. Maybe I should give it up before someone else gets hurt."

"I would have agreed with you a week ago because I don't want you to be the one who ends up hurt, but look at it this way. You've broken a major car theft ring and solved the murders of those kids." He paused, shook his head as if he still couldn't believe that someone he'd known could be responsible for anything that horrible, then continued, "Besides, Blue, you've cut down your list of suspects. We know it wasn't Brett or Junior. At least we're reasonably sure. I talked to Aaron and I'd bet everything I've got he and Pam are innocent. I don't think Carrie could hurt a fly. So that leaves me and Sally Jane."

"You're a smartass, you know it?"

"*Moi?* Why would you say that?"

"Because you know as well as I do that you've just proven I was wrong to begin with. I know you didn't kill them, and I'm pretty sure it wasn't Sally Jane. So that leaves me worse off than when I started. At least then I had a list of suspects."

"Looks like it, but I don't like the disappointment I see in those incredible blue eyes of yours. You should be glad it wasn't one of your friends. I know I for one am relieved."

"I am, Bo, but naturally I'm disappointed, too. Without even a shred of evidence to go on, I don't have a chance of finding out who killed them."

"Hey, you could always go on the radio and ask all your listeners to search their closets, see if they have six unmatched shoes lying around."

"Oh! You—"

The phone rang in the house, cutting off what she'd been about to say.

"Saved by the bell," he muttered as she went inside to answer it. He heard her pick up, heard her excited tone when she greeted her caller.

"Kit, hi! No, I haven't been neglecting you. It's been crazy around here."

Bo listened to her recap the events of the past two days. He swilled his beer as his insides roiled with the liquor. In the past several minutes of sitting there with her, he'd almost forgotten that she was in love with someone else. He'd almost believed that she was with the one person in the world she wanted to be with. Reality was bitter. Jealousy was worse. He tipped the bottle up to his lips and drained the contents. Setting the bottle on the railing, he stood up. He was almost to the steps when he heard her ending the conversation.

"I'll call you tomorrow night, I promise." A pause, then the part he'd wanted to miss. "I love you, too, Kit and I miss you like crazy."

Bo almost ran down the steps. He might be a fool, but even fools had limits.

Rikki heard Bo's car roar down the hillside, and she was pretty sure she knew why he'd left. He obviously hadn't stuck around long enough to hear the part of her telephone conversation that had included Sadie.

Rikki went out onto the terrace again, reclaimed her beer and chair. As her finger traced a drizzle of condensation on the bottle, she grinned. She'd told herself she was well past her childhood crush on Keen Bohannon, but in fact, that crush had matured into full-blown love. And as soon as he returned to the fishing cottage, she was going to set him straight on that.

She heard tires crunching on the gravel drive and jumped to her feet to run to the edge of the terrace and lean over the railing. It wasn't Bo.

In spite of her disappointment, Rikki's eyes widened with surprise when she spied the sheriff's cruiser. And her heart clutched painfully in her chest. Had he come to tell her that Junior had died? He'd promised to let her know of any change in his son's condition. Oh, God, don't let it be.

Scooter paused as he stepped out of the car to pull on his Stetson, taking his time, arranging it just so in an obvious stall tactic. Rikki's heart twisted tighter in her chest.

"You asked me to let you know if there was—" Scooter began as soon as he neared the top of the stairs.

"What's happened?" Rikki interrupted, too anxious to wait.

"He's out of the woods, sugar. I called Althea just before leaving the Pearsons. She said the doctors had just upgraded his condition. They're moving him to a private room and they tell us the prognosis for a complete recovery is good."

A little squeak of joy escaped Rikki's lips as she sprang forward to hug the sheriff tightly. "Oh, Sheriff, I'm so glad!"

Flustered by the display of emotion, Scooter patted the girl's back, then stepped away and asked if he could sit down.

"Of course," she said, her brow furrowed. "Is something else wrong?"

Instead of answering her, he motioned with his chin toward her bottle of beer. "You got another one of those, Missy?"

Rikki's answering smile was wide with relief. "Sure. Sit down, Sheriff. I'll get it and be right back." At the door she hesitated. "Unless you'd rather talk inside."

"No, I like the outdoors. Tonight particularly. The earth always feels so clean after a good storm."

Rikki joined him again a moment later, handed him the icy bottle and sat down across from him. "How was Carrie when you left, Sheriff?"

"She was all right. Down in the mouth, but that can't be helped. That mother of hers, though." He shook his head to emphasize his amazement, then changed the subject. "You know, missy, you always were the politest youngun' in these parts. Never once heard you call an adult by his given name. Your parents raised you real good, but you're all grown up now. Think you could call me Scooter?"

"I suppose so," she said slowly, wondering where the question had come from.

Scooter explained in a long, round about way, "You don't remember my dad, do you?"

"No, I don't think so," she said, curious about the unexpected segue in conversation.

"He was a good man, but pompous. Proud of his wealth, you know? Never could understand it, myself. His daddy was the one who made the money, but you would have thought Jared Witcomb, my pa, had done it all single-handed like.

"He hated it when I didn't go to college. Couldn't understand me wanting to be a lawman. Said if I was so fired up to be working on the side of the law, I should go get my license to be a lawyer. Anyway, he never forgave me for going into the sheriff's office. Said it was beneath a Witcomb to put on a common uniform like a common nobody. Sorta turned his back on me after that

. . . or maybe I turned my back on him. Ya see, I was just as ashamed of his arrogance as he was my lack of ambition."

"I'm sorry," Rikki said for lack of knowing what he wanted from her.

"No need to be sorry," Scooter told her. "I was happy with my life and he was happy with his."

"But it must have been tough not having your father to turn to when you wanted to talk." She looked down at her hands. "I know it's been rough for me."

"Not the same thing at all, missy. I got a feelin' your mama and daddy would have been okay about anything you did."

"I imagine you're right. They were special."

He nodded his agreement, took a long pull on the beer, then continued with his narrative. "Anyways, my dad was real excited when Junior came along. Guess he saw it as another chance to raise up an heir he could be proud of. Junior spent most of his summers out on his granddaddy's land. By the time he was ten, he talked just like him. Althea and I laughed about it for a time until it got out of hand." The sheriff paused unexpectedly, looking embarrassed. "Listen to me going on and on, talking your ears off about things that aren't of any interest to you. I'm sorry, missy, I didn't intend to do that."

"Oh, no, I'm enjoying it. Please, go on."

"You sure?"

"Positive."

"Well, by the time Junior was about fourteen, Althea and I realized we'd let my father create a monster. He was rude to his mother, contemptuous of me, my work, our house. Said he didn't understand people living like peasants when they had money." He shook his head. "That was the first and only time I ever hit that boy. I don't regret it. He deserved it.

"I drove out to see my dad, told him Junior wasn't

going to be spending as much time out there in the future, that he was ruining the boy."

"What did he say?"

"Oh, 'bout what you might expect. Said I was the one teaching the boy wrong values. Said there wasn't anything wrong with ambition and pride.

"Well, to make a long story short, it became a tug of war between my dad and me."

"But you won. Junior went into the sheriff's office just like you did." The sentence trailed to a near whisper as Rikki realized what she was saying. Junior had gone into the sheriff's office, but it was obvious now that his reasons weren't the same as his father's.

Apparently following her thoughts, the sheriff nodded. "You see where I'm going now, don't you? Junior figured he could walk the line between his grandfather's world and mine. He went into the department because he knew I'd be appeased, but he knew he'd have access to cars. He was already stealing them by then, you see. His deputy's uniform was the perfect cover for his real business as a thief."

"But why? I remember him bragging once about the trust fund he was going to come into the day he turned twenty-one. It was a lot of money, a fortune!"

"Because his grandfather had taught him greed, and Junior was too lazy to work like most greedy men are. He found a shortcut that was lucrative."

"I'm sorry, Sher—, Scooter. I know how hurt you are by this. What will happen to Junior now?"

"He'll go to prison. No doubt about it. But that's not why I'm telling you this."

Rikki waited.

"Before I left the Pearson place tonight, Carrie Ann said something I want to share with you. I know you been blaming yourself for what happened with Junior, me shootin' him and all. And fact is, I was looking to blame you myself. But Carrie Ann walked me to the door tonight and she said, 'You know, Sheriff, I knew there was something wrong with Brett even before I married him. But I just closed my eyes. I wonder if I would have ever opened them if Rikki hadn't come back and forced me to.'

"Well, the truth is, Missy, I knew Junior was up to something, too. I didn't suspect he was breaking the law, but I knew something wasn't right. He'd disappear when he was supposed to be on duty. I chastized him, of course, but I never looked into it. It's my fault it went on as long as it did. And I want to thank you for making me find out."

"That's very gracious of you, Scooter. Thank you for saying that."

"Gawddamn, girl, I'm not trying to be gracious. I'm telling you the way it is. You've shaken folks up. No telling what we'll discover about ourselves now that you've forced us to take a good look. We all owe you."

Tears needled at Rikki's eyelids, but she blinked them away.

"I'm sorry I never found the person who killed your folks, hon. But you tell me how I can help you do that now and I'll do it."

"Thank you, Sheriff, but I don't know what there is left to do. I thought I had it all figured out. Now I realize I was probably barking up the wrong tree. There are still the tapes that my mom and Dr. Grant made." She shrugged. "I haven't bothered with them, because I'm pretty sure the discussions they had are going to prove too broad to help . . . and because frankly, hearing Mom's voice would tear me up and, well, I don't think I could stand it. But I'm sure Dr. Grant didn't actually *know* who the killer was, and even if he listed names of people who fit the profile, I pretty much imagine he was shooting in the dark. Just wild guesses." This time, she shook her head. "Truthfully, I don't know if we'll ever find out who killed them."

"And how do you feel about that? Can you live with it?"

She grinned. "Probably not. I can't say I'll give up, but I won't be shoving it down people's throats like I have been." She looked past the sheriff toward the tiny lake house below. "I've decided to stay in St. Joan, Scooter . . . for good."

The sheriff grinned knowingly. "Well that's real fine, missy. A lot of folks will be real glad to know that. Especially a certain young fella who's been pining for you for a good long time."

Rikki chuckled. "Seems to me I read he got married in the interim."

"Oh, shoot, that wasn't nothing. A mistake from the get-go. I remember well the day he brought his bride home. Wasn't a person who knew the two of you didn't realize he'd gone out and found himself an Ericka Cassidy look alike. But that was as far as it went. She was tall, pretty, redheaded, but on the inside there wasn't an ounce of likeness to the girl he was really in love with. No one was surprised when they got a divorce a few months later."

The sheriff glanced over his shoulder toward the house where she'd been looking just a moment before. "Speaking of the esteemed prosecutor, where is he? I thought I'd probably find him here with you."

"He was, but he misunderstood something he heard me saying on the phone. I'm going to wait until he gets home and straighten it out. I love him, Sheriff. I didn't want to. I told myself I wouldn't let myself fall in love with him all over again, but . . ." She shrugged.

The sheriff's rumbling laughter made her smile.

"What?" she asked.

"I was just thinking that you might have your hands full with that one. He's got a bull head if I ever saw one."

"What do you mean?"

"Well, just like him marrying that gal because she reminded him of you. Everyone tried to warn him, but he didn't listen. Had to find out the hard way. After their divorce, I told him he should go up to Boston and see you. Think he would listen? Hell, no! Stubborn as a mule. Yep, you're going to have your hands full." He handed her the empty beer bottle and stood up. " 'Course, I know you're up to it. Hell, no one's seen him in the office or the courthouse until you came back. I almost fell over on my way to the hospital this morning when I saw him step out of that fancy car of his in a suit. And don't think I didn't know who was responsible for that."

Rikki set both bottles on the railing beside the one Bo had left. "Thanks for coming by, Sheriff. You've made me feel a lot better about things."

"No, missy, thank you. Junior has a rough road ahead of him, but Althea and I will be able to help him get through it now that you forced us to take our blinders off." He walked to the stairs, stopped, and looked back. "Don't let him keep you up all night waiting. You gotta be on the air tomorrow. Folks look forward to your program."

"He probably won't be out long."

The sheriff was halfway down the stairs. He stopped once again. "Now I wouldn't count on that if I were you. If he's upset about something he thinks he heard, I gotta feeling he won't be home 'til he's forgotten what it was. It wouldn't be hard for me to find him. I'm kind of familiar with the watering holes he frequents. You want me to go roust him out? Give him his marching papers?"

"No, thanks, Scooter. Let him get it out of his system. I'll do the rest when he gets here."

Rikki was more relaxed after Scooter Witcomb's visit than she'd been in years though it took her several minutes to understand why. It wasn't his praise that had made the difference. People had praised her all her life. And then it hit her. It was the acceptance. His and the townsfolks' but her own as well. Her acceptance of the things she might not be able to resolve, finish. She thought of her parents and for just an instant she imagined that they were there with her, smiling their happiness and their approval.

It seemed impossible that she could feel so content, so at ease on top of the events of the day and the evening before. Why, it was less than twenty-four hours ago that she'd fought for her life, and less than seven hours before that she'd practically witnessed a man's suicide. Was she that quick to recover from such terrible tragedies? No, it wasn't that. It was an ability to accept the horrors of life while enjoying the few and far between good moments. Like falling in love with Bo again. Like rediscovering her bond with Carrie. Like realizing that her move back to St. Joan was a homecoming rather than only a painful task she hadn't been able to ignore any longer.

She dozed off sometime around midnight in spite of her vow to wait for Bo. She was awakened nearly two hours later when the lights of his car splashed up the hillside bathing her in their brightness.

Sitting up, she blinked several times as she rubbed at a stiff muscle in her neck. It took her several seconds more to realize that Bo had returned. She leaned forward in her chair, but he doused the lights drawing darkness back around her and the hillside. She couldn't even see him get out of his car though she heard his car door open and close and then the bang of the screen door as he entered the house.

Stretching, she worked the kinks out of her legs and back, then went in the house for a flashlight. She thought better of walking down the hill as she remem-

bered that she'd once heard that snakes liked the dark
and grabbed her keys instead.

Three minutes later, she was following Bo inside his
house.

The lights burned in all three rooms. Bo was already
sprawled out on the bed, his arms thrown above his
head, his legs spread wide.

She called out his name, got no response, and leaning
against the doorjamb, she smiled and shook her head.
"Beat yourself up pretty badly tonight, didn't you?" she
asked him, though in a voice so low, she was sure she
wouldn't disturb his sleep.

He'd dropped on top of the covers fully dressed. With
a sigh, Rikki crossed the room. She pulled off his shoes
and unfastened his belt. He didn't move except to flex
one of his feet when the shoe tickled it as it was removed. Rikki went to the closets in search of a blanket
with which to cover him. She finally found a quilt in a
cedar chest. As she lifted it out, she discovered a picture
of her taken years ago on the picnic with Bo at Stone
Fall. He'd fashioned her a wreath of wild daisies for her
hair and she wore them in the photograph. It touched
her that he'd kept the picture. As she dropped it back
into the chest, she discovered others as well. More of her
as well as the two of them together. There were pictures
of her parents and Petite, too. Rikki grinned. For all his
tough guy, Joe Cool attitude, Bo was a sentimental slob.

She covered him with the quilt, then brushed a lock
of black hair from his forehead with her fingertips. She
stepped back to look at him. In sleep, his face looked
much as it had the first time she'd seen him almost
twenty years before. Without the slashes edged by time
and heartache and disappointment, he looked like a
peaceful little boy. She bent down and kissed his lips
tenderly. "I love you, Bo. I've always loved you."

She locked the door on her way out as he hadn't
bothered to do. Now that she'd found him again, she in-

tended to keep him safe . . . in spite of his determination to do everything in his power to make that impossible. Like driving home drunk.

There were going to be some changes now that she'd rediscovered where she'd left most of her heart so many years ago. She grinned as she stared back at the house, her mind's eye going through the walls to where he slept. Correct that. There were *already* changes, and they felt damned good.

Chapter Twenty

It was three minutes until air time when Lucy peeked her head into the booth. "Uh, sorry to bother you, Rikki, but I've got a minor problem here."

"I like that word, minor. Okay, shoot. What is it?"

"Every Friday for the past five years—maybe longer—Mrs. Hurskies has brought in a list of adoptable pets. She's not with the shelter. At least not officially. But she loves animals, so she goes by there every Friday morning bright and early. Sort of visits with the dogs and cats, then brings us a list to put on the air. It's pretty detailed. Tells all about the pets, their characteristics, everything. Anyway, I guess we forgot to call her and tell her about the program change. I could ask her to come back for Daryl's segment at one. What do you think?"

"No, have her stay. Tell her we'll put her on the air in about thirty minutes. I've decided to lighten up the show today anyway. Talk about something besides murder."

Lucy shook her blond frizzy head. "I don't know, boss. I think the phones are probably going to go wild after the Reverend Pearson's confession to those kids' murders was discovered beside his body yesterday. That's probably all anyone's going to want to talk about."

"You may be right, but I'm going to do my best to steer them away from it." She glanced at the clock. "Well, it's time. Offer Mrs. Hurskies a cup of coffee and I'll get to her as soon as I can."

Rikki put on her head phones, listened to the last of the national news broadcast, then leaned into her mike. "Good morning, St. Joan. This is Rikki Blue coming to you live from the paradise capital of the world as I do every day, Monday through Friday.

"Most of you have probably heard all about the tragic events that took place yesterday evening at the United Baptist church. I know some of you are going to want to discuss it, but I've been thinking about it. We've been talking about murder and crime all week. Now, I'm not discounting the severity of what the reverend did, but why don't we save talk about it until Monday? Give the families of his victims a chance to recover from the shock of last night's news, and talk about life today instead of death. What do you think?

"Driving in here today I saw a family of deer. They were just standing near the edge of the road, kind of watching traffic. Then a family of squirrels caught my attention as they ran between the trees, jabbering and playing. So I thought we might talk about family life here in St. Joan. What do you think St. Joan has to offer us as families? Are there drawbacks? Is the resort atmosphere a good place to raise kids?

"When I was a kid, I remember my parents talking about the way life perpetuates itself here as it doesn't seem to do anywhere else in the world. Think about it. Every spring and summer when the trees take bud, people from everywhere flock to our community to bask in its beauty, play in all the natural settings that God gave us and intended for our enjoyment, and just relax and be renewed. Then with the coming of autumn and winter, they return home and our little town gives a grateful sigh that it's time to rest and rejuvenate. I think it's grand!

"So let's take some calls, see what you think." She depressed a button. "Hello, this is Rikki Blue. Who is this and what do you think about living in St. Joan?"

"This is Jackie Waters. I think it's probably great if you're one of the lucky ones who's got money. My husband and I barely make a living here. We get paid minimum wage, but the cost of housing is high."

"So why do you stay? Why not go somewhere else where the wages are more in sync with the cost of living?" Rikki asked, not unsympathetically. "And answer me this, Jackie. Do you think there is a distinctive line between the haves and have nots in St. Joan? And if so, what can we do about it?"

Jackie Waters was the kind of caller talk show hosts love. She was articulate in the simple way that people relate to. She made sense and proposed valid solutions. Rikki encouraged her with congenial comments and questions, but after five minutes, she knew it was time to move on. The phone lines were blinking impatiently.

She pushed in another call. "You're on the air. Tell St. Joan what you think about life in our fair town."

"I know who killed Doc Grant," the caller said in a soft voice.

"I beg your pardon?" Rikki said. "Did you just say you know who killed Dr. Grant and the others?"

"I know who killed the doc. *You* say the same person done 'em all. I don't know nothin' about the others."

Rikki's hand shook as she gripped the edge of the control board and she felt droplets of perspiration bead on her forehead and upper lip. "How do you know? Did you witness the murder?"

"Yeah, I was there," the man said. "Saw the whole thing."

"But that was ten years ago and you've never come forward with this information before. Why now?"

"The doc had me arrested for trespassin'. I wasn't hurting nobody. Just living out in the middle of his land in a tent. I didn't poach, I didn't take nothin' that was his. But he had me arrested anyhow. Why should I tell anyone what I saw? I didn't want the sheriff accusin' me."

Rikki noticed the small knot of radio employees who had gathered outside the booth, their expressions anxious, excited, worried. She gave them a thumbs up sign, then crossed her fingers in a silent plea for them to hope this was the real McCoy and not some hoax. She turned her attention back to her caller. "Why now?"

"You mean why am I telling you what I saw after all these years?" the man asked, though he didn't wait for an answer. "Wasn't ever gonna tell. Why should I risk my own life for people who never done nothin' for me or my kind. You heard what that last caller said. Either you've got it or you ain't, and lady, if you ain't, then you're nothin' as far as most folks is concerned. Well, I ain't got a pot to pee in. But then I heard what you was doin', comin' on the radio every day asking for information that would help you find the person who killed your mama and daddy. You said it was the same one that killed the doc. I figure you know what you're talkin' about so I accept that. Then I heard you brought down that deputy who was stealin' from folks even though he's stinkin' rich, and then you was there when that preacher confessed. That's why I decided to call you and tell you what I know. I knew that preacher was no good. I went to him for help once—he claimed to be a man of God, didn't he? But he said there wasn't nothin' he could do. The way I see it, you're one of 'em. That's to say you got money and all, but you're still helpin' the rest of us by exposing them all for the rotten, no-goods they are. So, I decided to help you."

Rikki swallowed hard. This was it. She was about to get the answer she'd prayed to find for ten long years.

The man hadn't told her who he was, but she knew. She remembered her parents talking about the man Jason Grant had had arrested. Rubin Cruthers. She remembered more as well. Like the fact that he wasn't just some poor slob down on his luck. He'd told the doctor he'd taken a fancy to his land and was going to live there whether the doctor liked it or not. When Doctor Grant had threatened to have him arrested, he'd countered with threats of his own, promising to make the physician sorry if he caused him trouble. Rikki swallowed again. "May I ask you how you happened to witness the murder?" she asked.

Rubin laughed. "You're a smart girl, aren't ya? Yeah, I'll tell you. It ain't like I got anything to hide. I went to see the doc real late that Friday night. He wasn't home. I figured he was making one of his house calls, so I decided to come back later. I went back to the campsite where I'd been before he had me kicked off his land. I couldn't see anything from there, but I could hear if his truck came back, ya know? Anyway, I must have dozed off, 'cause I didn't hear him come back. 'Course he might of come back by boat. Anyways, about three-thirty in the morning I hear a car go by. I went up to the house thinkin' it was the doc. It wasn't."

"It was the murderer?" Rikki asked, hoping her voice didn't sound as nervous to him as it did to her.

"Yeah, but that's all I'm saying about it on the radio, lady. I know who the killer is, but I'm not going to get myself killed, too, by giving out a name. You wanna meet me somewhere? You can bring the sheriff if you want. I'm not afraid of him. 'Sides, I can prove I saw what I did. I know something no one could know if they wasn't there."

Rikki was shaking almost uncontrollably now. She swiped at her brow with the back of her hand as she leaned even closer to the mike. "Let me take us to a station break, folks, while I talk to my caller off the line.

He's a very brave person for coming forward as he has. I don't want to do anything that would put his life in jeopardy." She moved a couple of levers, then went back on line with her caller in a conversation that only she could hear. "I'm back with you. Give me an address. I'll meet you as soon as I go off the air. How about one-thirty?"

"Make it three o'clock, lady. I've got a job. Don't get off 'til two. Fact is I scheduled my break so I could call you, but I gotta get back to work now."

"All right, three it is. Just tell me where?"

"You gonna bring the sheriff?"

"I can or I can meet you alone. Just tell me which you prefer."

"Don't make me no never mind, like I said. Thing is, if you're coming alone, I'll meet you right outside my work. But if the sheriff's gonna come along, I'd rather do it somewhere else more private like. I don't need my boss gettin' spooked thinkin' I'm in some kind of trouble."

"I'll come alone," she said quickly.

"Okay. I'll be waiting for you out back of Hank Pal's Tire and Muffler. It's out on—"

"I know where it is. I'll see you at three."

"Name's Rubin Cruthers, Miz Blue. No sense telling you what I look like. I know you. Seen your picture in the paper when you came back to town last week. I'll be waiting for you."

Rikki heard the line disconnect, but she didn't move for a long moment. Her eyes filled with tears. Was it possible that she really was going to know the name of her parents' killer in less than four hours? After ten long years, that wasn't such a very long wait.

She slipped off her stool, opened the door, and signalled victory to the small crowd gathered outside. "I'm meeting him at three. After everything's wrapped up, which should be sometime tonight provided the killer still lives here, I'll come back and tape a short segment for tonight's news. Lucy, have Scott hang around and wait to hear from me." She dashed away a tear. "Oh, and Lucy, why don't you do the interview with your animal activist while I take five minutes to calm down."

"Will do, but Rikki, are you all right?"

Rikki smiled so widely her face hurt, but it was a good hurt. The best damned hurt in the world.

Bo's head hurt like a son of a bitch. *Everything* hurt. Even his heart.

Especially his heart. But the ache in his chest had nothing to do with the physical hurt in the rest of his body. He'd caused that by drowning it in a bottle of Remy Martin. The sharp insistent pain in his chest was something else all together.

He'd dreamed about Blue during the night, dreamed she'd been in the cabin with him. He'd felt her lips on his, heard her whisper to him, tell him she loved him. That's what had inspired the heartache.

He opened his eyes again for the second time in as many minutes, squinting, forcing them to stay open in spite of the piercing pain that shot through his skull, induced by the bright afternoon sunshine. He brought the fluorescent numbers on the clock into focus, muttered a curse, and sat up . . . too quickly.

He groaned. Twelve o'clock. Son of a bitch. He'd intended to be at the courthouse by nine to look at the plats, then get upstairs to Judge Montana's office to talk to her before she left for the day. Well, he'd certainly screwed that up. He and the Judge had worked together for almost five years. He was as familiar with the schedule she kept as his own. They were both easy. She worked full days Monday through Thursday, nine to five, religiously. On Friday she was outta there by noon sharp. No exceptions. His schedule had been more flexible until the past couple of years. After that anyone knew his hours. They were nonexistent. Until Blue had returned to give him a metaphorical kick in the pants.

He reached for the phone. Maybe he could still catch the assistant P.A., ask her to pull the list of properties he'd gotten from Feona Franklin off his desk, check them against the plats in the surveyor's office. That would save him a couple of hours. He'd promised Mrs. Franklin to try and have some answers by this evening.

Mary Beth Reynolds was at lunch, her secretary told him. Bo thanked her and hung up. Well, so much for saving time. He'd just have to hurry it up, which meant ignoring his body's insistent complaints.

As he swung his feet over the side of the bed, he noticed the quilt which covered him for the first time. His brow furrowed with perplexity, but not for long. It smoothed out with the smile that spread slowly across his face. Son of a gun, maybe he hadn't dreamed Blue after all.

Rikki could hardly contain her excitement for the rest of her stint on the air. She managed to keep things on track, her attention on her callers, but just barcly.

She phoned Bo during one of her breaks, but his secretary told her he'd phoned from home to say he was going by the courthouse. He probably wouldn't be in until late afternoon. She tried Scooter Witcomb next. No luck there either. He was out on the highway lending the state boys a hand with a major six car pile-up. Rikki accepted the news in stride. She hadn't intended for either man to come along, after all, but she had hoped to fill them both in. Or maybe she'd merely wanted to share her thrill.

A voice in her head warned against too much optimism. This could be nothing more than Rubin Cruther's idea of a cruel joke. The man had sounded bitter. No, she told herself, she knew better. This was it. The break she'd hoped for, waited for, prayed for.

Rikki arrived at the tire and muffler repair shop five minutes early. She decided to park on the street, then walk around back. She thought it a friendlier approach. She checked her reflection in the rear view mirror, laughing at her vanity as she stepped out of the Jeep. What difference did it make how she looked? Rubin Cruthers certainly wasn't here to appraise her physical attributes.

As she stepped onto the curb, a man came rushing from the shop, waving his arms frantically. "You don't wanna come in here, lady."

"I'm not," she said. "I'm meeting an, um, acquaintance out back."

"You can't go back there, lady. Trust me, that's not a place you want to be right now."

It was then that Rikki noticed how pale the man was, ashen really. An intuitive suspicion of what might have happened sent adrenaline coursing through her limbs. "What's happened?" she asked in a choked whisper.

"Man's been murdered, miss. Like I told you, you don't want to go back there. The police is on the way."

Rikki bolted into action, running toward the parking lot in the rear of the shop. She had to push her way through a throng of onlookers, but she saw him there. She'd never met him. Had never even seen a picture of him, but she knew it was Rubin Cruthers who was lying in the pile of cardboard boxes that had been stacked beside the dumpster. "Oh, my God, did anyone see who did this?" she asked, scanning the faces of the people around her.

"Yeah," a man replied from behind her.

"Who are you?" she asked as she spun around to face the stranger. "Did you see it?"

He shook his head. "Nope, not me, but one of my customers did. She's inside right now."

"Where?" Rikki asked though she didn't wait for an answer but dashed toward the rear door of the square, gray cinder block building.

The man caught up with her, grabbed her arm, stopping her. "You can't talk to her now. *Nobody* can talk to her. She's bad off. Having some kind of panic attack. We called Doc Grant. He's on his way. She can't get her breath. Her husband says her throat closes up when she's real excited or scared." He looked back to the place where Rubin was lying dead, his throat slashed from ear to ear. "Jesus, it's enough to make—"

"What about her husband? Did he see the killer, too?" Rikki asked, grabbing his arm this time and forcing him to look at her.

"Nope, he was inside with me, settling his bill. She came on out here to wait for him in the car. Next thing I know, she's running back in screaming that some guy's just been murdered in my parking lot. I came out here to investigate. Me and some of my boys all ran out here. Next thing I know, I go back in to call the sheriff and I find the woman on the floor, holding her throat and gasping for breath. "Jesus, it was awful. Her husband said she needed space. I called the doc, then the sheriff, then cleared the rest of my customers and workers outta there."

Rikki didn't wait to hear more. She ran for the back entrance, this time making it inside before the man who was obviously Hank Pal caught up with her.

"I told you, lady, you gotta wait—"

"It's all right, Hank," a voice said behind them. "Let her stay."

Rikki sagged with relief. "Aaron, thank God you're here."

He lifted his chin in greeting but didn't hesitate as he

rushed to the front of the store where a middle-aged woman was lying on the floor, her head in her husband's lap as she struggled for breath. "Anaphylactic shock," Aaron said in way of explanation as he knelt by the woman's side, Rikki right beside him.

"Can you give her something?" Rikki asked.

Aaron didn't answer for a moment as he opened his bag, pulled out a syringe, then a small labeled bottle. He uncapped the syringe with his teeth, then inserted the needle into the small bottle. "I'm going to give you a shot of epinephrine, Mrs. Pack. You'll be able to breathe in just a few seconds." He pinched the flesh on her upper arm, then jabbed the needle in. Once the syringe was empty, Aaron laid it aside, and patted the woman's arm. He looked into her husband's worried eyes. "You okay there, Barney?"

"This one was bad, Doc. The worst ever. I didn't think you were going to get here in time."

Rikki stood on the sidelines feeling useless and impotent, but grateful Aaron had arrived as quickly as he had. She opened her mouth to tell him when he suddenly put his head to his patient's chest.

"Get back, Barney!" Aaron barked, his no-nonsense tone surprising everyone. "Let her head drop to the floor, man, she's stopped breathing completely!"

Rikki could only watch the events of the next five minutes with ever mounting disbelief and horror as Aaron fought to save the woman's life. He fought frantically for her. But all of his effort was in vain. The trach, the CPR, the slammed fists to her chest—none of it did any good. The woman died there on the floor. Rikki let loose a cry of pure anguish and felt arms encircle her from behind.

"You hang in there, missy," Scooter said softly. "Doc's got his hands full dealing with Barney over there."

Rikki turned, went into the sheriff's strong arms. "Oh, Sheriff, why? Why did she die? He gave her a shot, said she would recover in a few minutes and suddenly she was gone. What happened?"

"I don't know, hon. The doc will tell us what happened as soon as he can."

Rikki stepped back, dashed at the tears which poured from her eyes. "How . . . how long have you been here?" she asked.

"Not long. My men are cordoning off the area outside. I came in here to try and talk with the witness. Saw what was going on, noticed that you weren't looking too steady."

"I'm okay," she promised.

"Wanna tell me how you happen to be here?" he asked gently.

In as few words as possible, Rikki related the phone call and the subsequently scheduled meeting with Rubin Cruthers. The tears had started again and unable to finish, she fished in her purse for a tissue. After a time, she swallowed hard, squared her shoulders and faced the sheriff again. "It isn't hard to figure how the killer knew where to find Cruthers. Obviously he was listening to the show and knew who and where Rubin would be. What I can't figure is how he could have gotten the jump on him. Rubin would have recognized him at once."

"I thought about that while I was outside. Looks like to me he must have lured him behind the dumpster and those boxes."

"But how? Rubin was bound to be wary."

"Money, more'n likely. Probably told him he'd pay him well to keep his mouth shut, suddenly forget who he'd seen."

Rikki considered this, then slowly nodded her agreement. "Yes, I think you might be right. Cruthers sounded bitter. Money would have been a powerful inducement to forget his fear."

The sheriff put his arm around her shoulders, guiding

her toward the front door. "Why don't you go on home? Have a drink. I'll let you know if we come up with anything."

She stopped as he pushed the door open and turned to meet his gaze. "You know what's funny, Scooter? Last night I'd accepted that I'd probably never find my parents' murderer. Today I can't accept it at all."

"Hey, you were this close," he said, holding his finger and thumb about a half inch apart. "You're bound to be disappointed, but don't you give up. The way I see it, Cruthers was a bitter man just as you said. Men who feel sorry for themselves often talk about it over and over again. My guess is, he probably told someone about what he saw. I'm going to reopen the investigation. Talk to everyone Cruthers even passed on the street."

"Oh, Scooter, you're right! I'm sure of it!" Impulsively, she hugged the man, but as she did so, she caught sight of Aaron still huddled on the floor beside the dead woman's husband. He was obviously offering comfort, but he looked like he could use a good healthy dose of it himself. "Tell Aaron how sorry I am," she said as she stepped away from the lawman again.

"I'll do it. This one is sure to be rough on him. He's a damn good doctor, Missy. He doesn't lose many."

Rikki's shoulders sagged. "Life is damned hard, Scooter."

"That it is, so you remember that and drive carefully. I don't want it getting any harder today."

As Rikki pulled away from the curb, she couldn't get the gruesome picture of Rubin Cruther's body out of her mind. Nor could she forget that if she hadn't started her campaign to catch a killer, the man would still be alive. Not to mention the poor woman who had witnessed the murder.

Tears started again.

It was only ten miles to the house she'd rented in the countryside, but at the rate she was crying, the drive along the winding mountain road would take forever. She turned her thoughts to Bo and glanced at the clock on the dash at the same time. Four o'clock. Maybe he'd be home by now. She hoped so. She needed him, needed his strong arms around her.

She swiped at another tear just as she started into one of the sharp mountain curves.

Rikki hadn't even noticed that she was being followed so when the car rammed into her rear bumper, the jolt was a complete shock. Her head snapped back then forward with the hard hit. She slammed on the brakes as the Jeep careened wildly toward the other side of the road and the sharp drop-off below.

"Stupid idiot!" she raged at the driver behind her, though the sun spilling against the windshield of the other car prevented her from seeing who the driver was.

Only a few seconds could have passed, but the fight to straighten her course had already shaken her, made her weak. She looked for a place to pull over just as the car hit her again. "Damn it!" she cursed as she tasted blood on her bottom lip where she must have bitten it with the second impact. Then she realized that the other car was still with her, still pushing her. She was headed directly for the low railing on the opposite side of the road as she approached a hairpin curve.

Instinct prompted her to step on the gas, pull away from the other vehicle. The Jeep shot forward and Rikki gripped the steering wheel tightly as she barely maneuvered the curve.

She was shaking now as the car zoomed up behind her once again obviously with the intent of slamming into her again. Rikki held her breath as she depressed the accelerator farther. The road snaked left and she hugged the right shoulder as the speedometer needle climbed to eighty-five. *Too fast, too fast.* She'd never be able to make the next turn at that speed. She darted a glance in the rear view mirror and whimpered when she saw the car drawing closer. "Leave me alone!" she cried uselessly.

As they rounded the next curve, a small car passed on the left and Rikki blared her horn hoping the driver behind her would back off now that a witness had been signalled. The compact passed on by and the car behind her drew closer. Rikki whimpered again with frustration and fear. But as they passed a sign that warned of another sharp bend ahead, she urged the Jeep even faster. The needle climbed to ninety.

"Oh, God," she whispered.

Then she saw it, a narrow strip of flat ground to the right. She wasn't certain she could stop the Jeep quickly enough. More than likely, she'd end up slamming into the mountain wall at the end of the small patch of shoulder, but the alternative was to careen off the mountain side to the left. She slammed on the brakes and pulled the steering wheel sharply to the right at the same time. The other car seemed to fly past her.

She saw the car sail off the mountain, but hardly registered it as she fought to stop her own vehicle. She almost did it. Almost but not quite. The Cherokee came to a hard stop against the ungiving mountain wall.

Her head slammed into the windshield hard with the impact, but she didn't pass out. She'd heard once that victims of automobile crashes didn't feel the impact, never remembered it, but she'd felt it all. She'd heard the windshield shatter as her head smashed into it, felt her chest slam against the steering wheel, even the shoulder strap of her seat belt burning into her neck.

It took her several minutes to realize that other than being slightly cut, bruised, and shaken, she was all right.

Then she remembered the other car . . . the one that had been trying to drive her over the edge.

She freed the seatbelt, then opened the door and climbed out. For just a second, she wasn't sure her wobbly legs would support her. She leaned heavily on the door for a long moment, taking in great steadying breaths of air.

She was halfway across the road when a car approached from behind. She turned, waving her arms and stepping back toward the edge of the mountain in case the driver failed to stop.

The man behind the wheel of the station wagon pulled in behind her damaged vehicle and hurriedly stepped out of the car. "You okay, lady?" he shouted.

She opened her mouth to answer, but she was still too weak to shout back. She shook her head and pointed below her where she could barely make out the top of the car that had gone off in the foliage a hundred feet below.

"Holy shit," the man muttered as he came to stand beside her and saw the wreckage below. "You stay here. Stop anyone you can and have them go call for an ambulance. I'll go down there and see if anyone's alive." He shook his head before starting down. "Not likely," he said as he slid down the incline.

Rikki watched the man's progress which was painstakingly slow until the sound of another approaching vehicle drew her attention away.

In a matter of minutes, three more cars had stopped. One had gone on to phone in the accident. Rikki knew it wasn't an accident but she didn't correct the misconception.

One of the women who'd stopped to see if she could help, led Rikki to her car where she had a first aid kit. "I'll just get that bleeding on your forehead stopped, honey. It doesn't look bad." She patted Rikki's hand which she held in hers. "You'll be okay."

Five minutes later, Rikki still sat in the woman's car. Sirens approached from both the west and the east. She reasoned that the ambulance would be coming from the west where the hospital was, Scooter or his deputies from the east where they'd been investigating Rubin Cruther's murder. Laughter bubbled from her lips. Why was she playing a guessing game of which vehicle would come from where? What difference did it make? Someone had tried to kill her.

The man who had gone down the mountainside to check on the driver of the other car appeared on the road again. Rikki heard him talking to the small crowd that had gathered on the road. "Dead," he said.

"Tourist?" another man asked.

The first man shrugged. "Don't know. It's a woman, but she's so banged up I didn't look real hard. Felt for a pulse. That's about it." He looked toward the Cherokee, not seeing Rikki. "How's the other one?"

All faces turned in her direction.

"Lucky to be alive," one man answered. "Man, you see those skid marks. Looks to me like the one that went over the edge was trying to run that Jeep over."

Rikki shuddered.

Chapter Twenty-One

"Look, I'm okay," Rikki told the doctor who was making notes on her chart. "I just want to go home. *Please.*"

The doctor lowered the chart and smiled. "I think that's exactly what you should do, Ms. Blue, now that we've checked you out. But I'm going to give you a sedative, something to calm you down."

"I know what a sedative is, and I don't want one," she said as she slid off the hospital bed. "I don't want anything except to go home." *And be with Bo.*

The doctor restrained her when she would have slipped by him with a hand that was gentle yet firm. "Whoa. Come back up here and sit down for a few minutes. I want to talk to you."

Rikki rolled her eyes but complied. Once she was again seated on the bed, the hospital gown tucked modestly beneath her hips and thighs, she sighed. "All right, Doctor. Deliver your lecture."

"No lecture. More of an either or. You sustained a nasty blow to your head. But that's not what concerns me at the moment. You went through a very frightening ordeal according to the deputy who escorted you here, and you suffered some shock. Now, I want to give you a sedative—so mild you'll hardly be aware I've given you anything—or I can insist you stay the night."

Before Rikki could answer, the door opened and Aaron Grant stuck his head in. He smiled when he caught Rikki's attention. "How's she doing, Dr. Pond?"

"I'm giving her an ultimatum. A sedative or a night in our fair establishment for observation."

"Take the medication, Rikki. I wouldn't wish my worst enemy to have to spend a night in this dump."

Rikki wrinkled her nose. "You take it. You look worse off than I do."

Aaron stepped into the room. "Yeah, I guess you could say we've both had better days." He sat down on the bed beside her and took her hand in his. "Let Dr. Pond give you the medication, Rikki. You'll relax." He motioned for her chart, looked it over, then handed it back to his colleague. "Shoot, it's a baby dose. Won't even put you out. But it will mellow you out." He winked at her as he asked Dr. Pond, "Think you could get me one of those, too?"

"Okay! I'll take the shot. Then will you let me get dressed and go home?"

"Yep, but you'll have to let Deputy Parker drive you," Dr. Pond said. "Then it's twenty-four hours of rest and relaxation. No driving, no alcohol, no exercise."

"I think I have a better suggestion for a chauffeur than Deputy Parker."

"Oh, no, Aaron. You should get home to Pam and your kids. No doubt you could use a little R and R yourself."

"I'd be more than happy to make a detour to your place, but I wasn't talking about me. A friend came over as soon as the radio picked up the story of your accident."

"Bo?"

The door opened and Sally Jane stuck her head in. "May I come in yet, Aaron?"

Rikki's disappointment was acute but she managed a smile for her friend. "Run while you've got the chance," she told the other woman. "Otherwise you're going to be roped into driving me out to my place."

"Hey, no problem," Sally Jane said as she stepped into the room. She approached the bed and put a hand out to run it over Rikki's hair. "I'm sorry about what happened. Pretty bad, huh?"

"Scary, yes. But I've got to tell you I think I look better than you or Aaron."

Sally Jane's face was puffy and red from weeping. Her lips were pale and her hand shook when she let it rest on Rikki's shoulder. "You hear who was in the other car?" she asked softly.

"Yes. Waylin said it was Lilah Montana, the judge. Was she a friend of yours?"

Sally Jane nodded. "You can't imagine how upset I was to hear that you'd been injured and that she was killed in an automobile accident. I was just leaving my office when it came over the radio. They said you'd been brought here, but I had to sit down for a long time before I could come. Otherwise I would have been here sooner."

Rikki reached up to squeeze the other woman's hand.

"You still look a little shaky, S.J.," Aaron observed. "Maybe I should drive you both home."

"Nonsense, I'm fine. You know me, Aaron. I'm as stable as a rock." She chuckled softly then looked at the other doctor. "So, can we get out of here?"

"I'm going to give Ms. Blue an injection. Then one of my nurses will help her dress and you can take her home. But make sure she stays off her feet. I've already explained about the sedative I'm giving her. It's mild, but she may still feel some slight dizziness. I wouldn't want her to have to come back here because she took a fall."

Twenty minutes later, Sally Jane pulled up to the curb in front of the hospital doors. A nurse wheeled Rikki out to the car. "Slowly, now," she said as she helped Rikki maneuver from the wheelchair into the front passenger seat of the roomy Lincoln Towncar. "There you go. Now you take it easy."

Rikki thanked her, then let her head drop against the back rest as Sally Jane started down the drive. "Close your eyes and rest," she told her passenger.

"I couldn't hold them open if I wanted to," Rikki said, hearing the slight slur in her speech. "If this drug is mild, I'd hate to know what a strong one feels like."

It seemed no time at all that the car stopped and Sally Jane announced they were home.

Rikki managed to open her eyes to slits, but even then her head swam. "This isn't—"

"No, we're at my place. You were so out of it, I thought we'd better cut the trip short. You can rest here, Rikki. Then when you're feeling better, I'll drive you back up the mountain."

Rikki was too light-headed to argue. All she wanted was to lie down. Then she thought of Bo. She wanted him with her. Even in her sedated condition, she knew she needed him. "Call Bo," she muttered.

"Just as soon as we get you settled indoors," Sally Jane said, getting out of the car and hurrying around to the other side. "You just lean on me now."

"Call Bo," Rikki repeated.

"Any calls?" Bo asked his secretary as he raced into the reception area of his law practice, his briefcase bulging under his arm.

"No, but Mary Beth is in your office."

"Super," he said with a wide smile.

His secretary merely stared after him, wondering at the sudden change in her boss.

"So what have you found?" Bo asked without preamble as he dropped the briefcase on the round table he often used for small, informal conferences.

Mary Beth took the pen she'd been playing with from between her teeth. "I think you already know. But how?"

"How did I know what you'd find? I didn't, not for sure. I was just hoping this would be one of those rare instances were X and Y really do equal Z. So give it to me."

"Well, as you suspected, Judge Lilah Montana and Sally Jane Matthers are in fact both on the bank board. In addition, they are partners in a company called M & M Investments. So now I have to ask, so what?"

Bo had been pulling papers out of his briefcase as she spoke. Now he spread out copies of the plats he'd made in the assessor's office at the courthouse in front of the assistant P.A. "These plats cover fifty square miles in and around St. Joan. See anything odd?"

Mary Beth studied them for several minutes before emitting a long, soft whistle. "Wow. You mean to tell me M & M Investments owns two-thirds of the land in a fifty mile area?"

"Yep. They've been buying it up on the auction steps for the past ten years. From what I could find out, they've sold approximately twenty properties in that time, and all to major conglomerates who are buying the land for prospective theme parks and tourist attractions."

"And M & M has turned a hefty profit. But how did they do it?"

"Think, Reynolds. M & M are Judge Lilah Montana and Sally Jane Matthers."

"Yeah, I got that, and they're both on the bank board. So what?"

"So, they knew when people got in arrears with their bank mortgages. They foreclosed, and then showed up on the courtroom steps to pick up the property for a fraction of its worth."

"Isn't that a violation of the Consumer Fraud Act or the Deceptive Trade Practices Act?"

Bo rubbed his jaw which was scratchy with a day-old beard. "That's what I thought, but so far it doesn't look like it. Oh, there's no doubt there's lender liability involved, but I don't know if we can find any criminal codes to prosecute under. Might have to recommend civil action. Mind a little overtime?"

"Overtime? What's that?" Mary Beth asked tongue in cheek. Since the prosecutor had been shirking his duties, which was for more weeks than she cared to count, she hadn't put in less than a sixty-hour week.

Bo laughed and chucked her underneath the chin. "You're much too pretty to be a smartass."

"While I try to figure out whether or not I've just been complimented, why don't you tell me how you got on to this scam."

"You've heard of Rikki Blue, the gal who just bought the radio station?" It was a rhetorical question. Everyone within two hundred miles of St. Joan had heard of the radio celebrity. He didn't wait for an answer. "One of her listeners called in complaining about the bank's sudden reluctance to work with their borrowers. When I say sudden, I'm talking about over the past ten or eleven years. Anyway, Rikki suggested she call me. Her name's Feona Franklin, by the way. You may have occasion to talk with her, though she was one of those who was able to avoid losing her property."

"Then that might explain why the judge tried to run Rikki Blue off the road today."

"*What?*"

"This afternoon. About two hours ago, I guess. It's been on the news. Haven't you listened to the radio?"

"Mary Beth, if I'd heard I wouldn't be asking, would I? Just tell me what happened? Was Rikki hurt?"

"The judge was killed. I think the other woman was taken to the hospital."

"When?" he asked in a tight whisper, his voice choked by fear.

"Like I said, a couple of hours ago. Why? Is she a friend of yours?"

Bo didn't answer as he shot out of his chair and crossed the room in three quick strides to grab the phone and dial the hospital. "Emergency," he barked as soon as the operator answered.

A few endless seconds later, a man's voice came on the line, "Emergency, Dr. Pond speaking."

"I'm calling to check on the condition of Rikki Blue, Doctor."

"Who's speaking?" the doctor asked.

"Jesus," Bo muttered with an angry shake of his head. "Look, fella, this is her, uh, husband. Now how in the hell is she?"

"Just a moment," the doctor said, putting the line on hold. Another voice picked up almost immediately.

"Bo?"

"Aaron?"

"Yeah, as soon as Dr. Pond told me it was someone claiming to be Rikki's husband, I figured it was you."

"So, tell me how she is, Aaron."

"Suffered a few cuts and bruises. Dr. Pond gave her a sedative and released her about an hour ago."

"You let her just walk out of there?" Bo shouted.

"Hey, calm down, buddy. Of course we didn't just let her walk out of here. She was pretty shook up. Judge Montana tried to run her off the road, did you hear?"

"Yeah, I heard, but where's Rikki?"

"I was going to drive her home, but Sally Jane heard about it on the radio and came right over. She offered to drive her out to the house."

Bo frowned in the direction of his assistant prosecutor though he didn't even see her. He was seeing Sally Jane's Lincoln Towncar pull into her garage as he had when he'd left the courthouse less than an hour before.

He hadn't even registered it then. Sally Jane owned the antebellum home that faced the courthouse. He'd seen her pulling in and out of there so often, he hardly noticed it anymore.

"Hey, Bo, you still there?" Aaron asked.

"Yeah, Aaron. Listen, you say you checked her out an hour ago?"

"Yeah, approximately. You want me to get her chart and tell you the exact time?"

"No, but Aaron, get on the horn and reach Sheriff Witcomb. Send him to Sally Jane's. He may be in his office in which case he can be there in five minutes. But if he's out, find him and get him over there."

"What's up?"

"I don't know for sure, but I know Sally Jane didn't drive Rikki home. I just saw her pull into her garage about a half hour ago."

"So, she probably thought the ride out to the house on the hill would be too hard on Rikki. She was pretty out of it by the time she left here."

"Just get the sheriff, Aaron, now!"

"You got it—" Aaron began as Bo hung the phone up.

"What are you thinking, Bo?" Mary Beth asked as soon as he hung up the phone.

"Not now, Mary Beth," Bo said, running his hands through his hair. He opened his bottom desk drawer.

Mary Beth's eyes widened when she saw the gun, watched him slip the clip in. "Bo, she's guilty of cheating some people, *maybe*. I don't think she'd . . ."

"You said yourself that the judge tried to run Blue off the road today, Reynolds, and I've got a bad feeling in my gut that my friend Sally Jane has done a lot worse."

"Next you'll be telling me she's the one who slit that poor man's throat this afternoon."

Bo was almost out the door. He stopped. "What man?"

"Rubin something or other. He called your friend's show this morning. Don't you ever listen to the radio, Bo?"

He crossed the room to grab her shoulders. "He called the show, and what?"

"He said he knew who killed Dr. Grant. Your friend was going to meet him this afternoon, but according to the radio, someone got to him before she did."

"Oh, God," Bo muttered as he dashed from the office. "Don't let me be too late."

"Well, you're finally waking up, huh?" Sally Jane asked Rikki. "It's about time. You've been out for almost an hour. It's getting late."

Rikki blinked against the bright light which Sally Jane had turned on beside the bed. "I'm sorry. I didn't mean to fall asleep." She rubbed her eyes, then ran her tongue over her lips. "Have you got anything to drink, Sally Jane? My mouth feels like someone stuffed it with cotton."

"I brought you a glass of water. Thought you might be dry."

Rikki managed a lopsided grin of appreciation before greedily gulping the water.

Sally Jane pulled up a chair, positioning it near the head of the bed. "You awake enough to talk?"

"Sure," Rikki said uncertainly. What could Sally Jane want to talk about?

"Good. I've had a bad day."

Rikki remembered the man she'd seen lying behind the dumpster, his throat laid wide open, then the car crashing into her. She groaned. She knew all about bad days.

"Lilah and I were lovers," Sally Jane said bluntly. "Lilah Montana, the judge? The woman who was killed today? You remember? Good." She laughed then. "Oh, not that I blame you. She shouldn't have tried to run you off the road. Stupid. I would have taken care of everything. I always have . . . except for Daddy."

Rikki still didn't understand. She shook her head slightly, indicating her confusion.

"I was seventeen when I realized I didn't like boys the same way other girls did. Daddy had a great deal to do with that, but you know who helped me *realize* it? Your mother." She smiled. "Surprised? I was, too, believe me. You probably don't remember when I used to come to your house after school. You were only thirteen or fourteen, after all, and not too interested in a homely girl your mother was tutoring." Sally Jane smiled, but her eyes were raised toward the ceiling as she thought about that long ago happy memory. "I was so intimidated at first. She was so damned beautiful. And not just on the outside. Even when I realized that I was in love with her, and I told her, she was so kind to me. She told me that she understood, but that she loved her husband." Sally Jane wrinkled her nose with distaste. "How could she have been in love with someone so *old?* I couldn't understand it then. I still can't."

A frisson of fear snaked up Rikki's back as understanding dawned at last. She shivered.

"Cold?" Sally Jane asked in a solicitous tone as she reached for a crocheted blanket on the bottom of the bed and tossed it over her, taking the empty water glass from her and setting it on the nightstand. "Better? Good. I don't want you distracted. I want you to listen to my story. Now that Lilah's gone I don't have anyone else to talk to."

"Sally Jane, wait. You don't have to tell me this. It's too personal. I mean, I'm glad my mother wasn't offended, but——"

"Shut up!" Sally Jane screamed, slamming her hands down on the edge of the nightstand. It seemed to take her several seconds to recover her equilibrium, but when she spoke again, her voice was calm, her eyes curiously flat. "You'll remember Bunny Apperson and Cindy Richvalski. They were fun girls. Liked to party and they didn't care if it was with guys or girls. We had a good time for awhile. Got real close. Then I met Lilah. She'd known she was a lesbian for years. I don't know how she knew about me, but she always said she could just see it. We became lovers right off. Then of course we went into business together." Sally Jane stood up and began to walk around the room as she spoke.

"We were so clever. No one guessed a thing." She stopped, turned to Rikki and smiled again, then reclaimed her seat. "Of course I made a mistake by telling Bunny and Cindy what we were up to. Cindy told her friend, Lonny Roper, and then they tried to shake me down. Stupid, stupid, stupid!"

Fear was coursing through Rikki in rivers, now. The drug the doctor had injected her with was wearing off, but even though she was still too addle-brained to think as clearly as she should, she knew she had to get out of the room. Out of the house. The question was, she thought as she looked at the door, even if she could get the upper hand, find a way to slow Sally Jane down, was she steady enough to make it down the stairs without falling? Maybe hurting herself seriously and making escape an impossibility? Probably not. Definitely not, she thought as a bout of dizziness assailed her.

"It would have ended there if Dr. Grant hadn't started playing shrink, trying to figure out the wheres and wherefores that make people tick."

"And that's why you killed my parents?" Rikki asked. "A moment ago you said you loved my mother. That doesn't make sense."

"Oh, don't think I wanted to kill her. I *hated* that part of it." Sally Jane wrapped her arms around her shoulders as if chilled by the memory. "I killed her quick, though, Rikki, so she wouldn't suffer." Then she laughed. "But I had fun with your dad."

"You're sick," Rikki whispered. She backed into the corner of the bed until her back was pressed between the headboard and wall.

"Why is that the first thing people always assume? Just because some of us aren't afraid to do what we have to do, doesn't mean we're sick. Oh, Rikki, how disappointing. You of all people. You're so intelligent, so superior to most people in so many ways. I thought you would be different." She slapped her palms against her knees as she stood up. "Well, too bad. Lilah was right." She laughed. "She usually was."

Sally Jane walked to the French doors that led to a terrace overlooking the back yard. She began talking again without turning back. "She was the one who insisted Daddy had to go, you know?"

Rikki didn't answer. Terror had frozen her tongue.

"He just couldn't accept my relationship with Lilah. No matter how I explained, he couldn't seem to get it. So Lilah forced him off the road. They said on the news that his car blew up. 'Course I already knew that. Lilah made sure he was dead." She glanced back over her shoulder. "I hated it that we had to kill him. It was such a disappointment that he couldn't accept us. Why, I understood everything about him. Even why he killed Mama. She was bad. She was going to take me away from him and never let me see him again. Did I tell you about that? No?" Sally Jane pointed to the bed. "I was right there where you are when he did it. And she was standing here, looking out at the garden just as I am. I was only five years old when he came in here and stabbed her, but I remember it. I was scared, until he explained everything to me. Then I knew he was right." She opened the doors. "Oh, don't you love spring? Everything is so fresh and new."

Rikki thought she had her chance to escape, but as

she started to move over the bed, Sally Jane spun around and came towards her.

"That's why I was so fucking mad when he turned on me. *I* understood what he did. I hated it, but I understood."

"What did he do that you hated so much?" Rikki asked, hoping the tremor in her voice wasn't detectable.

"Oh, you know," Sally Jane said with a giggle. "That thing that men think is the be all of end alls."

"Your father had intercourse with you?" Rikki asked with a gasp she couldn't manage to check.

Sally Jane leaned her head against one of the French doors. "You know, I think that's why Mama got so mad at him." She stepped away suddenly to cross the room and reach across the bed for her captive. When Rikki hung back, she whisked a knife from a pocket in the folds of her skirt. "Come look at my garden, pet," she said in a soft voice as she pulled Rikki off the bed, then locked her arm around her throat.

Panic threatened, but Rikki reached inside for calm. She allowed herself to be led across the room, and even managed to find a question that she hoped would buy her time. "You want me to look at your garden before you kill me?" Her voice was strained by the hold Sally Jane had around her throat, but otherwise she was surprised by how composed she sounded.

"Why, yes," Sally Jane said brightly before she gave Rikki's hair a hard tug.

"Aren't you worried I might scream?" Rikki asked as she was taken out onto the terrace.

"Of course not. You're too intelligent for that. You know I'd slit your throat." Still holding her in a head lock, she forced Rikki to lean over the low wall. "See those lilacs? Those were Mama's favorites. I planted them over her grave so she could smell them every spring. Don't you think she'd like that?"

"Sally Jane!" A man shouted from the doorway.

Both women jumped with surprise, and Rikki felt the blade of the knife bite into her skin. Blood trickled to her shoulder blade. She breathed Bo's name, though as a whisper only she heard.

He stood in the murky dimness of the hallway, visible only as a dark silhouette.

Sally Jane tilted her head to the side slightly, her expression confused for a moment until she smiled. "Daddy?" Her cheek was pressed against her captive's shoulder. Rikki felt Sally Jane's face split in a wide smile of excitement. "I was showing my friend Mama's flowers. Don't be mad. She won't tell."

"I'm not mad, Sally Jane," Bo said in a calm, even tone that Rikki could only wonder how he managed. "Why don't you let your friend go, so we can talk?"

"No! I know what you want to do. You want to spank me."

"Now, why would I want to do that, Sally Jane?" Bo asked, fighting his terror and the urge to ball his hands into fists.

"I don't know," Sally Jane said with a little girl whine. "You always do. That's why I lined the shoes up on the floor by the bed, so you could pick the shoe you want to use." Her voice trailed away with the last, but suddenly she spun around toward the bed, bringing Rikki with her, and when she spoke again it was in an outraged protest. "But you can't! You're dead! Lilah told me! You're dead!"

Rikki could hear the panic and confusion in her captor's voice, but at that same instant, she saw the shoes. Six of them. All unpaired. She recognized two of them. A small blue satin slipper that had belonged to her mother and a tattered moccasin that her father had refused to throw out even when Linda bought him another pair.

Rikki cried out, raw fury unleashing her strength which the sedative and her fear had zapped. She twisted with all her might against the madwoman's hold. The knife bit deeper into her flesh, but she didn't care. She wasn't going to die like this. Not now that she'd found the lunatic who had butchered her parents.

The struggle carried the two women further out on the terrace, both of them twisting and fighting . . . Bo forgotten behind them.

Rikki was taller than her assailant by several inches, muscled and trained, but Sally Jane's strength was greater because it was strength derived of madness.

Bo ran toward the balcony shouting at Sally Jane, but sirens suddenly screaming below them, obscured his voice. He stopped, raised the gun and prayed for a clear shot that would arrest Sally Jane without harming Rikki.

Rikki grabbed Sally Jane's wrist and moved the knife a couple inches away from her neck. With the threat of having her throat sliced open temporarily removed, she jabbed the other woman fiercely in the ribs, then stomped hard on her foot. Sally Jane's hold loosened, and Rikki spun free.

The growl from Sally Jane's throat in that instant wasn't a human sound but the crazed sound of a rabid animal. Bo fired the gun just as Rikki crouched out of his line and Sally Jane raised the knife over her victim's back.

There was no scream as the bullet's momentum drove Sally Jane over the terrace wall. Only a dull thud as her body hit the cobbled patio floor below.

"It's all over, Blue," Bo told her as he gathered her into his arms. She didn't look up. Only pressed her face against his shirt and let him hold her as she wept.

Scooter Witcomb burst into the room, followed closely by two deputies. "Bo? Rikki? You two all right?"

"Not all right, Sheriff, but alive. Rikki's been cut but I don't think it's too serious."

"You gonna be okay, missy?"

Rikki managed a small smile. "I think so, Scooter."

"That's good, missy. That's real good." The sheriff patted her arm then turned his attention to Bo. "What the hell happened in here?"

"Sally Jane tried to kill Rikki. I shot her. She's down there." Bo explained with a jerk of his head in the direction of the terrace.

"Gawddamnit, boy, I know *that* much. But *why?*"

"I think those will answer your questions for now," Bo said, indicating the neat row of unmatched shoes on the floor by the bed. "You got any other questions, we'll answer them tomorrow."

The sheriff swept his Stetson from his head and ran a hand over his grizzled head. "Yeah, well, I guess that sorta says it all, don't it?"

Chapter Twenty-Two

Rikki hadn't wanted to go back to the hospital. Bo had insisted, and the sheriff had backed him up. When Dr. Pond refused to treat and release Rikki, insisting that she spend the night, she glared at Bo, who merely shrugged. She turned her attention back to the doctor. "But you said yourself that the cuts were superficial."

"And they are," Dr. Pond said, giving her shoulder a reassuring squeeze, "but you've had two nasty go-rounds with shock in less than six hours. Hard on the body. I don't expect there to be any serious consequences, but I think it important that we keep an eye on you tonight."

Rikki capitulated without further argument. She was simply too tired. She turned a weak smile on Bo. "Well, I guess that's it. You might as well go on home."

"Not a chance. I'm staying right here with you."

Dr. Pond stood up from the stool he'd been occupying. "Okey dokey, then you just lie back and relax. An attendant will be in shortly to take you to your room." At the door he paused. "Incidentally, Miss Blue, I for one am glad you've taken up residency in our fair town. You're single-handedly giving me more job security than I've had in the three years since I came here."

"Ha ha ha," Rikki granted him.

Bo didn't hear the rest of their exchange. He was

thinking about the doctor's comment that Rikki had taken up residency in St. Joan. Had she? Or would she close up shop and head back to Boston now that her goal had been accomplished.

The question stayed in the forefront of his mind throughout the night as he sat by her bedside and into the morning as he drove her home. He made up his mind to talk to her about it as soon as they were alone.

"You're quiet," Rikki said as they drove out of the hospital parking lot.

"Tired," he muttered.

She reached out to touch his arm. "You should have gone home last night instead of sitting by my bed."

He cast her the smile that had always made her heart skip a beat. "Couldn't do that."

She let go a long satisfied breath. It was all over. Now, she could look forward to life with the man she'd loved for more than ten years. She started to tell him that, then changed her mind. Not yet. She'd wait until they reached the house. She wanted to hold him, feel his arms around her when she told him exactly how she felt.

Bo turned on the radio.

"And on the local front, Rikki Blue, radio celebrity who recently returned to St. Joan, narrowly escaped death yesterday, not once but twice. However, two other local women were not so lucky. Judge Lilah Montana died when she allegedly attempted to run Ms. Blue off Butter Forest Highway yesterday afternoon. The second casualty was that of Sally Jane Matthers, who according to Sheriff A. R. Witcomb, was shot in her home as she tried to murder Ms. Blue. All the facts aren't in yet, but this reporter has learned that Ms. Matthers and Judge Montana were partners in an alleged real estate scam which was uncovered by Prosecuting Attorney, Keen Bohannon. We'll—"

"Turn it off, Bo," Rikki said wearily. As soon as he complied, she turned her head in his direction. "Did I thank you for saving my life last night?"

"Not in so many words."

She smiled. "How did you know I was at Sally Jane's?"

"Pure luck, babe. Mary Beth Reynolds and I were working on the foreclosures when she happened to tell me about your run-in with the judge. I hadn't heard. Then she told me about Cruthers. I called the hospital and Aaron said that Sally Jane had taken you home. But I knew better because I'd seen her car pulling into her garage. I got lucky. If I'd left the courthouse a minute earlier or later, I wouldn't have seen her at all."

"But did you know she would try to kill me?"

"Not for sure, but coupled with the fact that Lilah and Sally Jane were partners in the real estate thing, and that the judge tried to run you off the road just minutes after someone killed your witness . . . ," he shook his head. "Too much of a coincidence to suit me."

Rikki shuddered when she realized how lucky she was that Bo had uncovered the two women's relationship in time to save her.

He brushed a stray tendril of hair from her cheek. "Don't think about it, Blue."

But she couldn't *not* think about it.

For even though the resolution to her parents' murder had been achieved, it hadn't been without cost. Several lives had been turned upside down in the process of uncovering the killer. And in some ways, she even felt sorry for Sally Jane.

The woman had apparently been the victim of horrendous violence as a young child, not to mention the incestuous relationship her father had subjected her to. Rikki couldn't even comprehend what such an upbringing could do to a child's mind, and compassion fought for prominence with the satisfaction that the woman was dead.

She thought of the tapes made by her mother and Dr. Grant that were still sealed in boxes that had never been opened. Had the doctor known about Sally Jane's abuse as a child? Had her name been one of those he'd come up with in his profiles? Rikki sighed. She'd never know. Not now. It didn't matter anymore. As soon as she could, the boxes would be taken back to the storage shed where they'd stayed for ten years undisturbed. She was going to put the past behind her where it belonged. She glanced at Bo. Well, maybe not *everything* from the past. With a slight quirk of her lips that bore the slightest resemblance to a smile, she sighed again contentedly. It was going to be good to get home, have time with Bo alone.

But as they turned into the drive, she straightened in her seat. There must have been two dozen cars lined up in the drive that led to the house on the hill.

Bo reached for her hand, taking it into his lap. "Looks like the press wants a word or two with you."

Oh, God, how did they know where she was? She squeezed his hand.

"Want me to go down to the cottage instead? I can sneak you in there, then come up here and deal with them."

Rikki bit her lip, then shook her head. "No, I might as well get it over with. You don't know them like I do. They're as tenacious as pit bulls. They won't go away until I give them a good chunk of myself."

They got no further than the bottom steps leading to the terrace before mikes were shoved into her face and Bo was amazed at the finesse with which she handled the plethora of questions. She leaned on his arm, seeming to draw strength from him, which made him proud, but he knew she would have done as well on her own, which scared him.

Thirty minutes after arriving at the house, Rikki held up a hand. "That's all, guys. I'm really done in. Thanks for being so easy on me. Now, if you have any more questions, I suggest you talk to Sheriff Witcomb."

A couple of the more persistent pushed for more, but Rikki shook her head. "That's it."

Bo took his cue and put his arm around her shoulder as he led her up the stairs. But the crowd now visible to Rikki on the terrace was even more dense than the pack of journalists below.

"Jesus," he muttered.

Rikki recognized a few faces—Petite, Carrie, Danny, and Marylou—but for the most part, the horde of faces was composed of strangers. "Who are they?" she asked Bo.

Before he could answer, a woman pushed past several others and rushed forward to take Rikki's hand. "I hope you don't mind. The doctor at the hospital told us you were coming home. We wanted to be here to welcome you, tell you how grateful we are to you for all you've done."

Rikki managed a thin smile.

"You don't know me, Miss Blue," the woman continued. "I'm Amanda Durant. My little girl, Molly, was one of the children Reverend Pearson ... well, you know. My husband and I owe you so much. We didn't think we'd ever know who had killed her, but because of you, we can let her go now. Let her rest in peace. That's what you've given us, Miss Blue. Peace of mind."

Rikki smiled, started to thank her, but a man stepped forward with a similar speech. His daughter had been one of the minister's victims as well.

A woman approached from the sidelines, holding out a large bouquet of flowers. "This is from several of us who lost our homes to the bank, Ms. Blue. An officer called from the bank early this morning. Seems they're going to work to help us regain our homes. We owe you more than we can ever repay."

Rikki cast Bo a questioning glance.

"While you were sleeping last night, I talked to Scooter. Told him about the scam Sally Jane and the judge were running to buy up land. He in turn gave a statement to the press. It was on the news, so I suppose the bank jumped into action."

"That they did, little lady," an elderly man said from the rear of the crowd. "And all because of you."

Rikki shook her head. "All I did was bring out the problems on the air. You people helped yourselves by not taking it lying down. As for the reverend, you should be thanking Carrie Pearson back there. She's the one who found the proof of his guilt." She smiled, which took more effort than she would have imagined. She was getting tired. "I do appreciate you all coming, but I think I need to lie down for awhile."

There was a murmur of disappointment, but the well-wishers who'd gathered to thank her for her help gave up with relative ease, though they were insistent about presenting her with the bevy of gifts they'd brought.

Petite and Carrie stepped forward to help her as she accepted the presents which ranged from gigantic flower arrangements to hand-crocheted pillows and home-cooked dishes.

It was another fifteen minutes before the last of the presents were dispensed, and Rikki was left alone with only the people she knew.

"Sorry, about that," Petite said. "Carrie and I came by because we were worried about you. We had no idea half the population of St. Joan would converge on you."

Rikki smiled. "It's all right. They're good people." She was as surprised as the others by the tears which suddenly stood in her eyes.

"Are you all right?" Carrie asked.

Rikki nodded as she swiped the tears from her eyes with a fingertip. "Just a little overwhelmed, I think."

Before anyone else could speak a voice boomed from behind her on the stairs.

"Kit!" Rikki said, turning and running into his arms. She hugged him tightly.

Bo felt his heart sink to his feet. The man was inordinately handsome, and Rikki's squeal of delight spoke volumes. He could only stand there and hurt as he watched their embrace.

"What are you doing here?" Rikki asked at last.

"What the hell do you think? The last time we spoke you had almost been killed by a man who was running a chop shop, you'd uncovered a murderer, and on the way in they're talking on the radio about how someone tried to drive you off a cliff just before one of your friends almost succeeded in slicing your throat." He stepped back to examine the bandages which covered her wounds. "I told Sadie I hoped we got here before someone successfully did you in."

"I'm fine, really."

Who the hell was Sadie? Bo wondered.

"Where is she?" Rikki asked as she looked past the man she still held onto.

"Sadie? She's coming. Wanted to fix her makeup. Women!"

Rikki laughed. "You adore us, and you know it."

"I'd adore one a lot more if she didn't keep scaring me to death," he said with a grin Bo couldn't help but notice only made the man better looking.

Kit caught Bo's eye and offered a hand. "You must be Keen Bohannon. I'd recognize you anywhere from the description Rikki gave me. I'm Kit—"

Bo accepted the man's hand, interrupting him ungraciously. "I know. You're Rikki's *friend* from Boston. Nice to meet you." Bo turned his attention on Rikki. "Well, Blue, looks like you've got enough people to watch over you for awhile. I think I'll go on down to the cottage. Catch a few winks."

Rikki understood his sudden pique and smiled. "You'll do no such thing. Not until you've met Kit's bride, Sadie. They've made the trip all the way from Boston, and you're going to stick around."

Kit's bride? Bo grinned. "Sure. Can't wait."

The woman in question arrived on the stairs in that moment, starting up a new volley of excited squeals as the two women embraced. Rikki was subjected to another round of questions and answers until Kit interfered.

"She'll fill us in, sweetheart. Give her a chance to catch her breath."

Carrie stepped forward. "Mother and I have to go, Rikki, but we wanted to make sure you were all right."

"Brett's funeral is in two hours," Marylou said.

Rikki didn't miss the accusation in the older woman's tone. She chose to ignore it as she took Carrie into her arms. "I'll be there, hon."

"Nonsense," Carrie said. "You go to bed and stay there."

"I think she should be there," Marylou said. "The least she can do is offer her condolences to Phoebe. Poor woman is absolutely destroyed by this." She glanced at Danny who still hung back on the fringes. "Of course, *some* people should stay away."

Carrie blushed at her mother's rudeness, but for the first time that Rikki knew of, she didn't take it meekly. "Mother, shut up. Rikki does not need to say anything to Brett's mother." She smiled at Danny. "As for who shouldn't attend the funeral. That's for me to decide. I've been a hypocrite for too long as it is. I'm not going to pretend I don't need Danny at my side. If people have trouble with that, they can go to hell with my husband."

"Carrie Ann!" Marylou said with a hand to her throat in a gesture of genuine shock.

Carrie ignored her, turning to her friend once again. "I hope once everything settles down, we can find a way back to the friendship we had ten years ago, Rikki. Only this time, I won't be letting others dictate how and what I feel, I promise."

Rikki smiled. "I'd like that."

She and Kit moved out of the way as Carrie and Danny followed Marylou down the stairs.

Petite returned to the terrace from inside the house where she'd taken the gifts Rikki's well-wishers had brought. "Well, I think that's it. Got the food in the fridge, and the flowers in water. Everything else, you'll have to decide where it goes. I've got to get home to my old man and the brats." She slipped an arm around her brother's waist and stepped onto tippy toes to kiss his cheek. "Jesse'd love to see his Uncle Keen sometime."

"Tell him I'll be by this week. Want to see the baby, too."

Petite shook her head. "Wow, you've been good for him, Rikki. He hasn't been out to our place in over a year. Hasn't ever seen the little one." She stepped forward and added in a whisper. "Incidentally, I'd color him yellow, now."

"Yellow?" Rikki asked, her brows raised.

"Um-hmm. That's the color of love, kiddo." Petite laughed. "Matter of fact, you're looking pretty yellow yourself."

Rikki laughed while the others looked on with perplexed frowns.

"What was that all about?" Bo asked once his sister had gone.

"Not now. I'll fill you in later when we're alone."

"Is that a hint, love?" Kit asked. "Because if it is, Sadie and I can certainly go to a motel."

"You'll do no such thing. I'm delighted that you're

here, but I do need a few minutes with Bo. Why don't you and Sadie go on in and freshen up. Bo and I will go down to the cottage."

"We can talk later, Blue," Bo said, feeling very magnanimous now that Kit had been removed as a threat.

"Huh!" Sadie said. "You obviously don't know Rikki as well as you think you do. She says she wants to talk, that usually means right that instant. Maybe you can take some of that bull-headed determination out of her."

"Not a chance," Rikki said with a giggle. Then to Bo, "But she's right, I am pretty hard headed. Shall we go?"

Suddenly Bo wasn't as confident. What did she want to tell him that couldn't wait? He prayed to God it wasn't what he was afraid it was.

But as they made their way down the hillside, he didn't push. He wasn't in any hurry.

In the cabin, he stalled. "Why don't you lie down for awhile. I know you're beat." As he spoke, he crossed the room to the bed to tidy it up. He'd left in such a hurry the day before, he hadn't even folded the quilt.

"I'm sorry about the welcoming committee, Blue," he said, not looking at her. "I should have expected the media and asked Scooter to send a couple of deputies over to get rid of them."

Rikki sat at the table, her hands folded in her lap. She smiled as she watched him. He was nervous and his uncertainty touched her. Such a beautiful, complex man. So strong and sure of himself in so many ways, so vulnerable and unconfident in others. "Bo, I want to talk to you."

"Oh, right. So you said." He sat down on the bed, keeping distance between them as if then the blow wouldn't hurt as much when she delivered it. "So talk, Blue. I'm listening."

She chuckled as she moved from the table to the bed beside him.

His heart constricted in his chest. "So?"

"Hold me," she said.

"Just spit it out, Blue. Or do you want me to say it for you?" He stood up and jammed his hands into his pockets as he looked down at her. "Okay, here goes. It's been great. You're real glad we shared the time we did, but now that the bad guys have all been rounded up, you're heading back East."

Rikki shook her head. With a small laugh, she stood as well. She put her hands on his chest, maneuvering them so that the back of his legs were against the bed. Then she shoved him down, coming with him. She wrapped her arms around his neck. "How can such a smart guy make such stupid assumptions?"

He didn't answer. He couldn't. She felt too damned good lying atop him like she was.

"First of all, why would I want to leave now that all the bad guys have been rounded up, as you put it?"

"You're staying?" he asked.

"Second of all, how in the hell could I go anywhere when my heart's committed here?"

"Okay, in answer to your 'first of all,' why would you need to stay now that all the bad guys are out of the picture?"

"You just like being contrary, Bohannon?"

"I'm being reasonable," he countered, enjoying the game he hadn't even realized he was starting.

"Reasonable, huh? Okay, then let's reason this out. There are always going to be bad guys. The way I see it, I can keep ferreting them out with my radio program, then you can put them away. We'll make a hell of a team."

The laughter faded from his eyes. "Will we, Blue?"

She kissed him, then grinned, her lips still pressed against his. "You got any doubts?"

"I can't joke about this, Blue. I'm too damned in love with you."

"That works," she told him, "because I love you,

too." The smile disappeared and she raised her head to look into his dark eyes. "With all my heart, Bo. I always have. I told you the other night, but you were asleep. You didn't hear."

"I heard," he admitted, "but I was afraid to believe."

"Believe."

He grabbed her then around the waist and rolled them over so that he was on top of her. "You sure about staying, Blue? 'Cause I'll leave. I'll go anywhere you want to go."

She shook her head. "I don't want to go anywhere. I love it here, Bo. I always did. Besides, that corny old saw about home being where the heart is, is true. My parents are buried here. You're here. I want my kids . . . our kids to be born here." She looked around her at the dismal rooms. "Well, maybe not right *here.*"

He chuckled. "I'll build you the biggest damned house in St. Joan. People will drive by and point and say, 'Wow, look at that place.' It'll be grander than Stone Hill."

"I don't need grand, Bo. I just need bright and happy like you make me."

He frowned. "What about all the painful memories, Blue? I can't chase them away no matter where we are."

"They aren't all sad. We have happy ones. We'll make more." She buried her face against his chest for a moment then looked into his eyes again as she expanded on the memories she was referring to. "Like the first time we made love. Or like the second time a couple of nights ago."

"Oh, God, I love you," he said in a husky voice.

"Then show me," she whispered.

"Right now? You sure?"

"I've never been more sure of anything in my life. I love you, Keen Bohannon. I want to make love with you."

"Trust me, Blue, there's nothing I want more than to

make love right here, right now. But what about those two damned Yankees up on the hill? You told them you'd be back in a few minutes."

Her blue eyes twinkled with lust and laughter. "But darling I'm a Southern woman now. And there are two things we Southerners do better than anyone."

"Oh, yeah? What?"

"We make the hottest love," she purred as she traced his jaw to the vee of his shirt with a fingernail.

"Uh huh," he said as he kissed the hollow of her throat. "And the other one?"

Her voice was as sweet and silky as homespun taffy when she answered. "Why, we lie, sugar."

"In other words, we aren't going right back."

She giggled. "And that's what I particularly like about you Southern men. You're so damn smart."

CATCH A RISING STAR!

ROBIN ST. THOMAS

FORTUNE'S SISTERS   (2616, $3.95)
It was Pia's destiny to be a Hollywood star. She had complete
self-confidence, breathtaking beauty, and the help of her domi-
neering mother. But her younger sister Jeanne began to steal the
spotlight meant for Pia, diverting attention away from the ruth-
lessly ambitious star. When her mother Mathilde started to return
the advances of dashing director Wes Guest, Pia's jealousy sur-
faced. Her passion for Guest and desire to be the brightest star in
Hollywood pitted Pia against her own family — sister against sister, mother against daughter. Pia was determined to be the only
survivor in the arenas of love and fame. But neither Mathilde nor
Jeanne would surrender without a fight. . . .

LOVER'S MASQUERADE   (2886, $4.50)
New Orleans. A city of secrets, shrouded in mystery and magic.
A city where dreams become obsessions and memories once again
become reality. A city where even one trip, like a stop on Claudia
Gage's book promotion tour, can lead to a perilous fall. For New
Orleans is also the home of Armand Dantine, who knows the secrets that Claudia would conceal and the past she cannot remember. And he will stop at nothing to make her love him, and will
not let her go again . . .

SENSATION   (3228, $4.95)
They'd dreamed of stardom, and their dreams came true. Now
they had fame and the power that comes with it. In Hollywood,
in New York, and around the world, the names of Aurora Styles,
Rachel Allenby, and Pia Decameron commanded immediate attention — and lust and envy as well. They were stars, idols on ped-
estals. And there was always someone waiting in the wings to
bring them crashing down . . .

---

*Available wherever paperbacks are sold, or order direct from the
Publisher. Send cover price plus 50¢ per copy for mailing and
handling to Penguin USA, P.O. Box 999, c/o Dept. 17109,
Bergenfield, NJ 07621. Residents of New York and Tennessee
must include sales tax. DO NOT SEND CASH.*